Evelyn Abbott, Lewis Campbell

The Life and Letters of Benjamin Jowett

Vol. I

Evelyn Abbott, Lewis Campbell

The Life and Letters of Benjamin Jowett
Vol. I

ISBN/EAN: 9783744720779

Printed in Europe, USA, Canada, Australia, Japan

Cover: Foto ©Raphael Reischuk / pixelio.de

More available books at **www.hansebooks.com**

LIFE AND LETTERS

OF

BENJAMIN JOWETT, M.A.

B Jnett

from a drawing by George Richmond, R. A.

THE

LIFE AND LETTERS

OF

BENJAMIN JOWETT, M.A.

MASTER OF BALLIOL COLLEGE, OXFORD

BY

EVELYN ABBOTT, M.A., LL.D.

AND

LEWIS CAMPBELL, M.A., LL.D.

WITH PORTRAITS AND OTHER ILLUSTRATIONS

IN TWO VOLUMES: VOL. I

E. P. DUTTON AND CO.
No. 31 WEST TWENTY THIRD STREET
NEW YORK
1897

PROFESSOR JOWETT'S life naturally falls into two sections—the period before the Mastership, and the Mastership. The first of these volumes contains the first period, and is the work of Professor Campbell; in the second, I have written the story of the Mastership; and I am responsible for the whole. The plan followed in both volumes is of course the same. A few letters have been worked into the narrative; others, far too numerous to be used in such a manner, but of a personal character, have been appended to the chapters according to their dates, and thus form as it were illustrations of the text, giving in Jowett's own words his thoughts and feelings at the time[1]. In the second period the material was to some extent different from that in the first, for Jowett's personal memoranda became far more numerous as he grew older, and from these, as in some respects the truest record of his life, it was necessary to draw largely. The second volume is also somewhat more annalistic than

---

[1] A number of very valuable letters on more general topics, to Sir R. B. D. Morier, the Marquis of Lansdowne, and others, could not be included in the Life, and are reserved for a separate volume.

CONTENTS

—◆—

LIST OF ILLUSTRATIONS

LIFE OF BENJAMIN JOWETT

CHAPTER I

BIRTH AND PARENTAGE

JOWETTS of Manningham in Yorkshire—The Master's great-grandfather, Henry Jowett, and his four sons—The Evangelical movement—Musical cultivation—The Master's father and mother—The Langhorne family—The Jowetts at Camberwell—Changes of position and circumstances—The Master's sister Emily—His brothers, Alfred and William Jowett.

BENJAMIN JOWETT was born in the parish of Camberwell, Surrey, on April 15, 1817, and died on October 1, 1893. The following entry, headed 'On rising in life,' was found in one of the note-books in which it was for many years his practice to write down thoughts and observations :—

'My ancestors lived at Manningham near Bradford, where they had land, part of which they sold in 1740. They were probably in the condition of yeomen. The Reverend Dr. Joseph Jowett, Regius Professor of Civil Law in the University of Cambridge, who died in 1813, was my great-uncle. He had a brother, Henry Jowett, Rector of Little Dunham in Norfolk, and another brother, John Jowett, a wool-stapler I believe, who had three sons, clergymen, the Reverend William Jowett, a Missionary among the Copts, the Reverend Joseph Jowett, Rector of Silk Willoughby, Lincolnshire, and the Reverend John Jowett, Rector of Hartfield.'

At the beginning of the eighteenth century, two Jowetts of Manningham[1] were doing business in London and York. Henry Jowett, of London, is described as a man of character and probity and a strict Churchman, who attended the week-day prayers at his parish church. His brother Benjamin, of York, counts likewise amongst the Master's ancestry, through an intermarriage of cousins to be mentioned by-and-by.

This Henry Jowett, of Manningham and London, had a son Henry, the Master's great-grandfather.

Henry Jowett, of Leeds and Camberwell, 1719–1801.

He was born in London in 1719, and passed some of his childhood at Whitby, where he conceived a passion for the sea. After one voyage, however, he was apprenticed by his father to a hat-manufacturer in London. While thus employed, he heard the preaching of Whitefield, and the impression was deep and permanent. When his apprenticeship came to an end, he set up for himself as a skinner or furrier. In 1757 he removed with his young family to Leeds, where he remained till 1773. Here he formed two intimacies which had an important influence upon the life of his sons. William Hey, the well-known surgeon and Fellow of the Royal Society, not only shared the same religious impressions, which were then still comparatively rare, but was also an accomplished musician, and a student of great writers whom he loved to introduce to younger men; and Henry Venn, who came to Huddersfield in 1789, helped to confirm the spiritual work which Whitefield had begun.

[1] The Jowitts (formerly Jowetts), an old Quaker family in the neighbourhood of Leeds, if traced far enough back, might prove to have a common origin with the Jowetts of Manningham; but in the period now under review there was no connexion between the branches.

About two years after the death of his wife in 1771,
Henry Jowett removed his place of business to London,
and his home to Camberwell Green. He resided there
until he died in 1801, having survived his eldest son,
John, by one year. He is a dignified, patriarchal figure,
of a strong, determined nature, profoundly imbued with
genuine piety, ruling his house with authority, and
bringing up his children and his grandchildren with
vigilant care 'in the nurture and admonition of the
Lord.' His sons in middle life still deferred to his
authority, and prized his counsel, addressing him in
their letters as 'Dear and honoured Sir.' His correspondence is marked by simple gravity of style, and while
often expressed in the peculiar dialect of Methodism, has
the ring of true affection, sagacity, consistent purpose,
and resignation to the Divine Will. In early life he
had owed much to Mr. Hill, a Nonconformist minister,
and in his old age was inclined to Wesleyanism, react-
ing not against the formalism, but the too pronounced
Calvinism, of the parish clergyman[1]. There still remains

[1] The following excerpt from the manuscript record of his granddaughter, Mrs. Elizabeth Pratt, is characteristic both of the times and of the man :—

'In the government of his family my grandfather was thought to be strict. His children greatly reverenced him ; yet it must be confessed that they often felt a degree of awe in his presence which made them in their boyish days rather shrink from his company. His family worship, too, was perhaps somewhat calculated to exhibit religion in an austere light, and, to young minds, make it appear wearisome and gloomy. He usually in the evenings read a whole chapter of the Bible with Matthew Henry's commentary ; which occupied so much time that the children and servants got sleepy and tired. If the boys showed symptoms of drowsiness, they were required to stand up, and their father would occasionally ask them their opinion of a sentiment or put some question which required them to have attended to the reading in order to answer it, ... I shall never forget the patriarchal benediction which he in his handwriting a solemn form of self-dedication, signed, sealed, and doubtless executed, October 27, 1770, identical with that recommended in Doddridge's *Rise and Progress of Religion in the Soul*, chap. xviii. § 7.

To the last he followed with keen interest the course of public affairs; disliking the war with America, but rejoicing in Admiral Duncan's successes; although he feared that they might unduly minister to national pride.

Henry Jowett, of Camberwell, had four sons, John, Joseph, Benjamin (the Master's grandfather), and Henry; and two daughters, Elizabeth, who died young, and Sarah, who lived to old age. The sons, except John, the eldest, who had been at St. Paul's School for a time before they left London[1], attended the Leeds Grammar School, in company with John Venn, who lived with the Jowetts as one of the family. Joseph and Henry Jowett, as well as John Venn, proceeded to the University of Cambridge; while Benjamin, like his eldest brother, John, was apprenticed to his father's business.

As three of these men, his great-uncles, are mentioned by the Master himself, and as more is known of them than of his grandfather, it may be allowable to give a short account of each of them before proceeding in the main line.

pronounced upon me and Mr. Pratt, when we went to take leave of him. He was sitting by the fireside in his dressing-gown with his night-cap and a large cocked hat on his head; and before we left him he raised himself on his feet, feeble and tottering as he was, and with a most graceful air took his hat off his head, and prayed that the blessing of God the Father, God the Son, and God the Holy Ghost might rest upon us. He did this with much emotion, and I could have imagined that it was the patriarch Jacob blessing his posterity.'

[1] According to the belief of his daughter, Mrs. E. Pratt; but his name is not on the Register of St. Paul's scholars.

John Jowett, of Leeds and Newington Butts,
1743–1800.

John had been at work in his father's office from the time of going to Leeds, 1757, being then in his fourteenth year. But he continued his education through intercourse with William Hey, who read with him such works as Locke, Butler, Jonathan Edwards, &c., and conversed with him on theological subjects. The two friends often walked to Huddersfield together to listen to the preaching of Henry Venn. Mr. Hey, who was a student of thorough-bass and a lover of Corelli and other early composers, also encouraged his companion's love for music, and John learned to play the organ.

John was already in partnership with his father, when in 1771, shortly after his marriage to Elizabeth Bankes, younger sister of Mrs. Hey, he removed to London, and opened a warehouse in Red Lion Court, Bermondsey. Here he was joined by his father and by his brother Benjamin. The business prospered after a while, and in 1790 John Jowett purchased the lease of a house and grounds at Newington, Surrey[1], where he was often visited by his brothers from Cambridge and their friends; and also by the 'worthy Mr. John Newton[2],' who is said to have designated John Jowett's household as *par excellence* 'the Christian family.' He was in fact a pillar of the Evangelical party in the Church, and his home was also a centre of musical culture. He died at the age of fifty-six in 1800, having shortly before assisted at the foundation of the Church Missionary Society. His profoundly religious

[1] The proceeds of the Manningham estate had before this been divided amongst the cousins, by the will of Eleanor, the last heiress.

[2] This was in the later period of Mr. Newton's career, when he was Rector of St. Mary Woolnoth.

character, combined as it was with persistent practical
energy, gives him a just claim to prominent consideration in these preliminary pages. His 'enthusiasm,' as
it would then have been termed, was tempered, in
a remarkable degree, with candour and moderation.
On his death-bed, he told his relatives who surrounded
him that he felt 'not rapture, but peace.'—' The Scriptures speak of the Spirit bearing witness with our
spirits, &c. I should like to feel that, but I am not
anxious about it; I leave the matter to God[1].'

---

[1] John had five sons, Henry, John, Joshua, Joseph, and William, and two daughters, Elizabeth, who married the Rev. Josiah Pratt, and Hannah, who married Mr. Hudson. Three of the sons became beneficed clergymen, as appears in the Master's note-book above quoted: the most remarkable of these was William. He was twelfth wrangler at Cambridge in 1810, a Fellow of St. John's, and the first Cambridge graduate who volunteered for the foreign service of the Church Missionary Society. He ended his days in the rectory at Clapham Rise, where he succeeded John Venn. He had some peculiar expedients for rousing the interest of a sleepy congregation. 'And now I will read you a dispatch from a great commander at the seat of war:' this prelude was followed by a quotation from the Book of Joshua. The reader will find more about him in the *Dictionary of National Biography*.—Joseph, the Rector of Silk Willoughby, applied the musical skill which he inherited to the composition of hymn-tunes, which have been much appreciated by persons of religious feeling and fine taste. His *Musae Solitariae*, 'A Collection of Original Melodies, adapted to various measures of Psalms and Hymns' (fourth edition, 1826), was much valued by James Martineau and used in his family and congregation in connexion with his own selected hymns.—John, the Rector of Hartfield, held for a time an evening lectureship at Clapham. It is quite possible that the Master of Balliol, when a boy, may have heard the preaching of more than one of these men, his cousins, during some of his visits to the Courthopes at Blackheath or the Langhornes at Clapham.

Joshua appears to have opened a business in Liverpool before 1823; but he afterwards returned to London, where he set up as an ironmonger, and his home was again the centre of musical reunions, similar to those at his father's house at Newing-

Joseph Jowett, of Trinity Hall, Cambridge, 1752-1813.

Joseph Jowett was a prominent figure in the Cambridge of his day, where he was Professor of Civil Law, and the main particulars of his life are clearly recorded in the *Dictionary of National Biography* [1].

The biographer of his grand-nephew may be permitted, however, to dwell, before passing from him, on some characteristic traits: (1) his persistence in companionship

PEN AND INK SKETCH OF THE CONCERT GIVEN AT TRINITY HALL, CAMBRIDGE, JUNE 4, 1789.

with his early friend, Isaac Milner, with whom he spent two hours twice every week in Term-time, until his death; (2) the freshness of his interest in young men; (3) the fearless promptitude (called by his friends 'precipitancy') with which he promoted the foundation of

ton Butts.—Henry was for a time a partner in the furrier trade.

[1] For some interesting details concerning him the reader may be referred to the *Life of Isaac Milner, Dean of Carlisle.* It appears that the elegance of his Latinity was much admired.

the Cambridge Auxiliary Bible Society, supporting the efforts of the serious undergraduates, when even Isaac Milner recoiled before the fulminations of Doctor—afterwards Bishop—Marsh; (4) as a minor feature, his keen interest in the progress of music. He sang 'alto[1]' in concerts which he had organized, and which took place in the Combination Room, and on one occasion certainly (June 4, 1789) in the Hall, of Trinity Hall.

Henry Jowett, of Little Dunham, 1756–1830.

Henry Jowett, after passing several years as Lecturer and Tutor at Magdalene College, Cambridge, succeeded his friend John Venn as Rector of Little Dunham, Norfolk, in 1792. He married Charlotte Iveson, of Leeds, and had eight children. His daughter Charlotte became Mrs. Whiting. A good many of his letters have been preserved. They exhibit him in a very interesting light, as a faithful pastor, a tutor of young men[2], a keen lover of music, and an active and observant traveller. He assisted in starting the Norfolk branch of the Bible Society, and is known to have been the founder of the first of many Clerical Societies.

He was a genial parish priest, who upon occasion, as at the Peace of 1814, knew how to organize a village festival, with dancing, &c. There is a touch of playfulness in his letters to his sister Sarah, who kept house for him after he became a widower in 1809. He showed paternal interest not only in his own, but in his brothers' families. His life-long friendship with the Venns proves his warmth and constancy.

---

[1] See below, p. 11.

[2] See the *Life of Henry Venn Elliot* (who was one of his pupils), chap. i. Another pupil was James Stephen, afterwards Sir James, who, when old enough for Cambridge, went to Trinity Hall because of Joseph Jowett. See the *Life of Fitzjames Stephen* by his brother, chap. i.

Benjamin Jowett, of Camberwell, 1754–1837.

Benjamin, the third son of Henry of Leeds, was grandfather to the Master of Balliol. After leaving the Grammar School, he commenced business with his father in Leeds; and when the family was settled in London, he became John's partner in the warehouse in Bermondsey. In 1785 he married his cousin, Anne Jowett, of York, whose father is mentioned several times in letters of this period with a sort of respect, as 'Cousin Jowett[1].' In right of this lady, who was his grandmother, the Master (then Professor Jowett) inherited, some eighty years after this, a property in Yorkshire[2]. She died in 1799. leaving five children, Elizabeth Maria, Benjamin, Josiah, and Henry. In a letter dated February 20, 1799, Henry Jowett the elder, now of Camberwell, and in his eightieth year, speaks feelingly of his son Benjamin's loss. Soon after his father's death, Benjamin married again, and had a daughter, Irene. He appears as a witness to the marriage of his son, the Master's father, in 1814. Nothing more is known of him until the year 1823, when the success of Joshua (John's third son), who had opened a business in Liverpool, seems to have induced Benjamin senior and his two youngest sons to migrate thither. They were accompanied by the elder daughters, Elizabeth and Maria. Benjamin senior remained in Liverpool until the spring of 1837. In March of that year he writes an affecting letter to his sister Sarah. It is the year of influenza, and the prevalence of illness has interfered with the progress of music. 'Nothing new has been produced of late.' At this time he must have been about eighty-two years old. He died very shortly afterwards, in April, 1837.

[1] Henry Jowett, of York (son of Benjamin, see p. 2), flax-dresser, was Sheriff of York in 1784–5.
[2] See p. 375.

The preceding narrative has carried the reader into the heart of English Methodism in its earlier stage. The names of Whitefield and Wesley, of Henry Venn, John Newton, Isaac Milner, Farish, Simeon, Robinson of Leicester, are as household words to all this family. The impression which the documents produce is irresistible—that in the immediate followers of Wesley and Whitefield, personal religion was a very real thing. It was the mainspring of conduct, affecting all relationships, not in word only, but with power. Their theological attitude had its limitations, certainly: 'conversion' meant separation from 'the world[1]';—but it contained a principle of expansion too. John Newton was not far from the kingdom of universal brotherhood when he wrote as follows in 1800: 'I pray the Lord to bless you and all who love His Name in Scotland, whether Kirk, Relief, Burghers, Antiburghers, Independents, Methodists, or by whatever name they choose to be called. Yea, if you know a Papist, who sincerely loves Jesus, and trusts in Him for salvation, give my love to him.' 'Christianity,' he says elsewhere, 'is not a system of doctrine, but a new creature[2].' If the religion of the 'Clapham sect' appeared to cast a sombre colouring over social intercourse, this apparent sadness was lightened and relieved in the case of many of them by the warmth of home affections and by their devotion to music. The scene at Newington Butts, where Mr. Latrobe of the Moravian brotherhood introduces Haydn and Mozart to the lovers of Handel, is suggestive of anything but gloom :—

---

[1] 'Come out from among them, and be ye separate,' is a text of which young converts thought with zeal and awe.

[2] See *Letters and Conversa-tional Remarks,* by the late Rev. John Newton, Rector of St. Mary Woolnoth, Lombard Street, London, 1809.

'They had discovered,' he says, 'the secret of making *Home*
the most pleasant place on earth. The young people were
not restrained from following the so-called pleasures and
amusements of the world by any coercive means, but rather
encouraged to be attentive to whatever was innocently and
profitably amusing. It was at home, however, that they
found the greatest happiness, and love and peace and cheerfulness reigned in their dwelling.

'What was my astonishment and delight, to find here
a choir of vocal performers, the most perfect of its kind.
The two daughters sang the treble; Dr. Jowett[1], the alto;
Reverend H. Jowett[2] and the father, the tenor; the eldest
son, Henry, the bass. They sang all Handel's Oratorios, or
rather select portions of them, with great precision, and, by
employing me at the harpsichord, as I was more accustomed
to read scores than any other of the party, I became acquainted
with the exquisite beauties of that inimitable and gigantic
composer. All their voices were good, but Eliza's treble and
Dr. Jowett's alto were, I may truly say, the sweetest and
richest of their kind *I* have ever heard, either in public or
private. When the doctor was not in town, we tried as well
as we could to supply the alto in choruses, and could always
perform in four parts[3].'

In the matter of education also, they were before
their age. When we find Mr. Hey, the surgeon at Leeds,
sparing time from a laborious profession to read Locke
and study thorough-bass with young John Jowett; or
when old Henry, the patriarch, wishes that his grandson
could have gone to school with Cousin Marriott, 'who has
profited so greatly by Mr. Penticross's tuition' at Walling-
ford; or when Mr. Robinson, of Leicester, is carefully
selected as an instructor for young Benjamin (the Master's
father), these incidents are to be noted as instances, not of
obscurantism, but of an expanding culture.

---

[1] Joseph, the Professor of Civil Law.

[2] Henry of Little Dunham.

[3] Latrobe, *Letters to his Children*.

Is it wonderful, considering such antecedents, that
the Master should have delighted always in religious
biographies—that when most suspected of heresy, he
should have heartily joined with private friends in
singing simple hymns—that to the sentimentalities of
more recent hymnody he greatly preferred Dr. Watts'
version of the ninetieth Psalm—or that in his latest years
he should have delighted in commemorating Richard
Baxter and John Wesley from the pulpit of Westminster
Abbey? When most convinced of the poverty and
narrowness of the Evangelical school, and the inadequacy
of its scientific and literary culture, he never failed to
distinguish between its earlier and later phases.   It
seemed to him that its earlier spirituality had faded,
and that an overgrowth of mingled cant and worldliness
was stifling its vitality.

There is considerable force in the following observations of the Rev. W. H. Langhorne: 'In estimating
the religious views of the late Master, those which he
inherited should be taken into account; and which had
descended to him through four generations. By the
time they reached him, much of what had been lively,
vigorous, and real had become conventional and spirit-
less. The salt had lost its savour—and the religious
"movement," as it has been called, was nearly spent[1].'

Benjamin Jowett, 1788–1859.

Benjamin Jowett, son of Benjamin, and father of the
Master of Balliol, was born at Camberwell in 1788.
Beyond the fact already referred to, that after his
mother's death, when he was about eleven years old, he

[1] The Warden of Merton (the Hon. G. C. Brodrick) says: 'While I often heard him comment harshly and even bitterly on High Churchmen, I never heard him speak unkindly or disrespectfully of the Evangelical School.'

was sent to school with Mr. Robinson, of Leicester, nothing is known concerning the course of his education. His father's second marriage may have in some way interfered with it. That while retaining the impress of Evangelical pietism, his mind had been impelled towards some kind of literary ambition, is evident from the sequel. He joined his father's business, and at the time of his marriage in 1814 is designated as 'a furrier.' In the *Directory* for 1817, the firm at Red Lion Court, Bermondsey, is described as 'Benjamin Jowett and Son[1],' so that by this time he was in partnership with his father. When the latter removed his family to Liverpool in 1823, Benjamin junior seems to have remained in charge of the Bermondsey business, his cousin Henry, son of John, being in some way associated with him for a time.

In 1825 the firm 'Benjamin Jowett and Sons, Furriers, Red Lion Court, Bermondsey,' occurs for the last time in the *London Directory*, and in the same year there appears the name of 'Benjamin Jowett Junior, Furrier, 10 George Yard, Lombard Street.' This entry is continued during the years 1826-1836. It would seem therefore that the furrier business lasted all this while, no doubt with 'fluctuations,' and it is probable that the removal from Bermondsey was caused by some depression[2]; for 10 George Yard was the place of business of his brother-in-law, Mr. John Bryan Courthope, stationer, &c., with whom it is natural to suppose that Mr. Jowett took refuge, when no longer able to maintain the warehouse in Bermondsey. But he seems also to have ventured

[1] In the same year, in his son Benjamin's Baptismal Register in the church of St. Giles, Camberwell, the father is described as 'Benjamin Jowett, Peckham, Furrier.'

[2] It is right to bear in mind that 1826 was a time of great commercial depression.

upon a wholly different line of business. In the *Directory* for 1826 there appears for the first time the firm of 'Mills, Jowett, and Mills, Printers, Bolt Court, Fleet Street,' and this entry is continued until 1835 [1]. That the Jowett of this firm was the Master's father is proved by the form of his son Benjamin's nomination to St. Paul's School, dated June 4, 1829. Here the boy is described as 'son of Benjamin Jowitt (*sic*) of Bolt Court, Fleet Street, Printer.'

The marriage of the Master's parents took place in 1814.

He himself wrote as follows on February 24, 1893 [2], with reference to his mother's ancestry : 'My mother told me that her father, who died young, lived at or near Kirkby Lonsdale (*Kirkby Stephen?*), and that Langhorne the poet was her great-uncle; she had no doubt of this. Also I remember her brother joking her about the member of their family who was executed for treason.'

Isabella Jowett, née Langhorne, born December 25, 1790; *died October* 16, 1869.

Isabella was the daughter of Joseph Langhorne, who appears from the above statement to have been a nephew of John Langhorne, the Rector of Blagdon, the poet, and translator of Plutarch. Joseph is said to have been a Lancashire cotton merchant, who, after retiring from business, lived first at Walworth and then at Stockwell, in the neighbourhood of Camberwell. 'The member of their family who was executed for treason' is Richard Langhorne, the lawyer of King Charles II's reign, who fell a victim to the accusations of Titus Oates, for the

[1] The volume of the *Lancet* issued in 1826 bears the imprint of Mills, Jowett, and Mills.

[2] To the Rev. W. H. Langhorne, acknowledging the latter's book of *Reminiscences*.

alleged Popish Plot in 1679[1]. Burnet[2] speaks of him as 'in all respects a very extraordinary man.' But the supposed connexion of Richard Langhorne with the Kirkby Stephen Langhornes is not clearly proved, unless a constant family tradition may be taken for proof.

If the Jowetts of Leeds exemplify an important phase of English pietism, the Langhornes of Kirkby Stephen are fairly representative of the mental refinement, classical taste, and liberal culture, which has always characterized some portion of the clergy of the Church of England.

Joseph Langhorne's son Henry was a banker in Bucklersbury[3], and about 1820 retired to Mitcham. He moved his family again to Clapham in 1829. Besides Isabella, there were two elder daughters, twins, both of whom have a place in this biography: Jane, married to John Bryan Courthope, above-mentioned, and Frances, married to the Rev. William Smith. There was frequent intercourse between the Jowetts and the Courthopes. In earlier days, while Mr. Courthope was successful in business, he dwelt in a handsome residence at Blackheath Hill. He afterwards removed his family to a smaller house in the same neighbourhood. He died in 1844. His wife had died in 1840, and they had lost many children. Mrs. Courthope retained her charm and youthful looks until very shortly before her death. She left behind her the impression of an active practical nature, which had a great influence on those surrounding her.

[1] Further particulars about him may be found in the *Dictionary of National Biography* and Granger's *Biographical History of England*.

[2] Burnet's *History of my own Time*, vol. ii. p. 259 of the Edinburgh edition (1753).

[3] The bankers were Brown, Langhorne, and Brailsford. 'The firm suffered in the financial panic which followed the second American War. H. L. then started as an Insurance Broker.' (So writes Mr. C. Langhorne, of Corncliffe, Sydney, N.S.W.)

The Rev. William Smith was Rector of Brandsby, in Yorkshire. He died in 1823. His widow, who was considerably younger than he was, survived him many years, during which she lived at Bath. She died in 1835, leaving some house property in Bath to the Jowett family.

Mr. and Mrs. Jowett appear to have spent the earlier years of their married life at Peckham, in the parish of Camberwell, where they formed a lasting friendship with the Channells[1]. There were nine children of the marriage, two of whom, Isabella and Francis, died in infancy. The others were Emily, Benjamin, Agnes, Alfred, Ellen, William, and Frederick. Emily and Benjamin were the only two who survived their parents, and passed the meridian of life.

A change in the family history occurs in 1829, about the same time as young Benjamin's admission to St. Paul's School. Mrs. Smith, who was now alone at Bath, knowing that the Jowetts were in straitened circumstances, offered a home to her sister and the children. This was accepted on behalf of all but Benjamin, whose education was already provided for. 'The little fold at Bath[2]' remained there after Mrs. Smith's death until 1841. The father went to and fro between Bath and London, while young Benjamin stayed in lodgings in the City. A journey to the West of England was in those days a matter of no small trouble and expense. Meanwhile Mr. Jowett's employments, if not very profitable, were strangely varied. He aspired to be a publisher's reader, and sought opportunities for

[1] See below, p. 27. The late Baron Channell was then a boy of ten years old.

[2] Letter of Mr. Jowett to Mrs. Irwin in December, 1838.

dabbling in journalism, especially on questions of philanthropy. Mr. Wood, of Bradford (brother-in-law to
Mr. Gathorne-Hardy, now Lord Cranbrook), the first
person who seriously took up the question of Factory
Legislation[1], employed him as a writer, and it was
probably through Mr. Wood's recommendation that
he became known to Lord Ashley, afterwards Lord
Shaftesbury. For several years he laboured at collecting
statistics and in other ways promoting the great work
which Lord Ashley had so much at heart. At this
time he must have been a familiar figure in the lobby
of the House of Commons. The following entry occurs
in Lord Shaftesbury's Diary for August 24, 1840 :—' Let
no one ever *despair* of a good cause for want of coad-
jutors ; let him persevere, persevere, persevere, and God
will raise him up friends and assistants ! I have had,
and still have, Jowett and Low ; they are matchless[2].'

In 1835 Mr. Jowett was consulted by Captain F. C. Irwin
with regard to the publication of a work on Western
Australia[3]. Captain, afterwards Colonel, Irwin always
retained a high regard for Mr. Jowett, whom he used
emphatically to describe as ' a Christian, a scholar, and
a gentleman.' The acquaintance ripened into friendship,
and before his return to his post of Commandant of the
troops at the Swan River settlement, Major Irwin had
married Mrs. Jowett's niece, Elizabeth Courthope.

Mrs. Jowett, meanwhile, had been anxious about her
son Benjamin's future, and appealed to several friends
for counsel about his proceeding to the University.
He was at the head of St. Paul's School, and in his
nineteenth year, and himself desired to go to Trinity

---

[1] *Life of Lord Shaftesbury*, vol. i.
p. 143.
[2] Ibid. p. 301.

[3] Major Irwin's book was
published by Simpkin, Marshall
& Co.

College, Cambridge: but a Scholarship or some extraneous help was absolutely necessary [1].

Mr. J. Walker, now Rector of Great Billing, North-ampton, but in 1835 still resident Fellow and Tutor of Brasenose College, Oxford, replied to Mrs. Wood, Mr. Gathorne-Hardy's sister, who inquired of him on Mrs. Jowett's behalf without mentioning the name, that it was near the time of examination for open Scholarships at Balliol, and that 'the said youth, if he was thought clever enough, might try for one of them.'

This hint may have encouraged him to try at Balliol, but it can hardly have been necessary, as the Turners, intimate friends at Bath, had already their son John entered there, who would naturally be eager to second such a proposal. However this may have been, the Scholarship was gained.

Cadetships for William and Alfred Jowett, 1842 and 1846.

Benjamin's younger brothers, Alfred and William, were educated at the Bath Grammar School; where the most active teacher was Mr. James Pears [2]. The boys seem to have profited at school, and their after history may be briefly told. Both obtained Indian cadetships at the recommendation of Lord Ashley. William went out as Ensign in September, 1842, to Madras, and after doing excellent service as Quartermaster and interpreter to his regiment, died at Saugor, September 11, 1850.

---

[1] See p. 44.

[2] His father, the Head Master of the Grammar School, had by this time practically retired to the living of Melcombe which he held with the Head Mastership.

Alfred, having qualified as surgeon, went out in September, 1846, and after various services which became more than ever exacting in the year of the Mutiny, died at Banda, October 4, 1858. His brothers were probably in the Master's mind when he wrote afterwards to a cousin in India: 'I hope you know how to live and not die in India, which I believe to be greatly an art.'

But for the great and solid happiness of Benjamin's election to the Balliol Fellowship in 1838, the later years at Bath must have passed heavily with Mrs. Jowett. Her husband's constant absence on business of uncertain profit; the delicacy of her two younger daughters, of whom Agnes died in 1837; the weakness of Frederick, consequent on an accident in infancy, which arrested his education, and the anxiety about ways and means —made more trying by her husband's absorption in that unproductive labour, the metrical version of the Psalms, which occupied him during the remainder of his life—must have weighed upon her spirits, and induced a certain tone of depression which is noticeable in her letters.

The younger daughter, Ellen, was already drooping, and died shortly afterwards (1839) at Tenby, whither they had removed for a time on her account. She was deeply mourned, especially by John Turner, who was attached to her, and afterwards called his eldest child by her name.

If we except the promise of the cadetships which were due to the connexion with Lord Ashley, the father's prospect of improving the fortunes of his household was not encouraging. His philanthropic employments, his leader-writing, his advice to authors, and other 'incidental

work,' such as the Secretaryship of the Church Extension Society, had all given way before the fascination of
the metrical Psalter.

In 1841 Mrs. Jowett and Emily returned from Bath
to Blackheath with Alfred and William [1], whose Indian
careers were now in prospect, and towards the end of
1842 removed to Teignmouth. By this time William
was in India, and Alfred must have been ' walking the
Hospitals' in London. In 1846 (Alfred also being now
in India) the home trio, father, mother, and surviving
daughter, took up their abode in a neatly furnished
apartment on the fifth floor of a house in the Rue
Madeleine in Paris, spending the summer months
mostly at St. Germains or Fontainebleau. In 1848 they
were driven by fear of the Revolution to sojourn for
a while at Bonn and Aix-la-Chapelle. But they soon
returned to their old quarters, and in 1850 were visited
there by Mr. F. T. Palgrave, who has thus recorded his
impressions :—

'Mr. Jowett had some theories upon Milton's rules of
versification, in which he took great interest, and tried to
set them forth for me. He looked like a man rather past
middle age, and had the manner, more easily recognized
than defined, of one who had not been successful in his
profession. . . . The mother (venerated as much by Jowett
as the father) was a pale, white, graciously dignified lady
of about her husband's age ; her voice, her features, her
bearing, wore the air of a long, perfect, uncomplaining resignation [2]. The sister, apparently rather younger than the Master,
was also of a thoughtful cast of mind. She had a true feeling
for music, and used to play for me, when I called, several

---

[1] During this brief sojourn
at Blackheath, Lord Lingen's
mother, in visiting her sister,
Mrs. Rea, met Mrs. Jowett, 'and
the two, after the manner of
Mammas, fell to talking about
their sons at Oxford.'

[2] This was the year in which
William and Frederick died.

little pieces, which she kindly copied in a writing fine and clear, much akin to her brother's.'

In removing to Paris they appear to have been guided by the advice of Benjamin, who had already begun to contribute largely towards the support of his mother and sister. In this action, after a few years, he was nobly seconded by the sons in India, who before 1850 had arranged to remit considerable sums out of their pay, to lighten the burden which 'their brother had so long borne.'

After the death of William Jowett in 1850, quickly followed by that of poor Frederick, who had been left in England under proper care, Mrs. Jowett's letters to Alfred in India have a somewhat plaintive tone. but they also evince a noble calmness of resignation and a loving spirit of conciliation. The conditions of the little household were made more difficult by the step which Emily took about this time, in being received into the Roman Catholic Communion. This was due to the influence of their most intimate acquaintances in Paris, the Cruick-shanks, who were friends of long standing and neighbours in the same house. Helen Cruickshank and Emily were fast friends, and Helen's brother was a priest, having joined the Roman Catholic Church while still a youth. Mrs. Jowett partly sympathized with Emily; she had found comfort for herself in Bossuet and Fénelon [1]; and her letters to her son Alfred show some indication of what was passing in her mind. The father no doubt

---

[1] Jowett wrote to A. P. Stanley in 1856: 'If you go over to St. Germains, my mother would, I think, like to see you. . . . She is much worn with care and years, and I cannot expect that she should live much longer. At one time I told Mrs. Stanley I had reason to think she would become a Roman Catholic, but that phase has passed away with her, ending in universal charity to all the world.'

remonstrated, but, absorbed in his unprofitable task, seems to have left his wife and daughter very much to themselves. He would shut himself up in his study, even in the evenings, which had heretofore been enlivened with Emily's exquisite playing on the piano. In early days she had been used to accompany her father, who had a fine bass voice.—So things continued for some years; but prices rose under the Empire, and living in Paris became more difficult. The metrical Psalter, too, was approaching completion. At last, in 1856, the 'trio' are found at Dover for a while. Here Mrs. Jowett's letters reveal fresh uncertainties, and speculations about trying Germany again. But before the spring, all shadows had cleared away, and the wish of the mother's heart was gratified by their returning to their former lodgings at Tenby. Emily shrank from the scene of old sorrows, but Mrs. Jowett found comfort in being there, in the house of Mrs. Lewis, who had known and been kind to her daughter Ellen. She was again much alone, through the temporary absence of Emily, in attendance on her friend, Miss Cruickshank. Mr. Jowett meanwhile renewed his friendship with the Laws of Kennington [1], the Channells, and Dr. Blundell (who gave him an annuity of £40), and at last he published anonymously, with Samuel Bagster and Sons, *A New Metrical Translation of the Book of Psalms* [2].

In 1857, the year of the Indian Mutiny, deep anxiety was naturally felt on Alfred's account. He sent his usual remittance in that year, but died in October of the year following. His father survived him by only six

[1] See Mr. F. Law's account on p. 27.

[2] The work is by no means contemptible, although doomed to failure by the impracticable notion of *chanting* common English metres. Mr. Jowett had learned enough Hebrew to make elaborate use of English Commentaries on the original Text.

months, and was buried at Tenby in March, 1859. The inscription on his tombstone is probably from the hand of his son:—

> 'He was greatly beloved for his simple
> and disinterested character.'

In one sense it may be said of him that he was *too* disinterested. He cared nearly as much for the things of others as for his own. When Sir W. Channell was made a judge, he was hardly less rejoiced, and certainly much less surprised, than he would have been if Benjamin had been made a bishop. He seems to have worked most effectively when he was labouring on behalf of some one else. While he inherited, even to overflowing, the traditions of Methodism, he managed to combine them with a kindly and intelligent outlook upon the world at large. But his mind was like an eye which cannot be focussed upon nearer objects. His letters to Australia are pamphlets on the treatment of Aborigines. Those to India during the Mutiny are full of just reflections on the situation—the views are excellent, if they were not aimed from so far off—and they are not without a family likeness to many passages in his son's private letters in which he expatiates on home and foreign politics from a speculative point of view.

Emily speaks of her father with real affection, but complains that he has so little power of understanding others or of being understood. Too pliable where firmness was required, he was persistent even to obstinacy in unpractical ways: a precisian in unimportant matters, but without much real power of command. He seems always to have been too little demonstrative at home. His children hardly saw the best side of his nature: and the effect of this reserve upon his son Benjamin is not to be ignored. An unchecked flow of love and confidence, and the frank expression of a just pride in the achievements of his son, might have given a different turn to some aspects of that son's after-life. Though he was passionately fond of music, his daughter's playing drew from him no praise. While affectionately solicitous for his children's highest welfare, as he conceived it, he was superstitiously afraid of exciting their vanity by open encouragement. The Master, in later life, spoke of his father as having been 'one of the most innocent of men.' Mr. F. Law, who remembers him well, says, 'He was a lovable old man. I never heard him say a harsh word of any one.'

After her husband's death, Mrs. Jowett with her daughter Emily resided at Torquay, where she was soothed and consoled for her past trials by the devotion of her two surviving children. She died there October 16, 1869, only a few months before it became a certainty that her son was to be the Master of Balliol. Those who knew her during these years describe her as a dignified and gracious lady of the old school[1]. Her alabaster complexion, touched with shell-pink, was often suffused with a girlish blush at some casual surprise. Her simple black dress, with a white shawl, and a white drawn satin bonnet, setting off her slim upright figure, made a beautiful picture of refined old age. Her manner retained much of its early charm, for young as well as for old, and she was a favourite with children. She would not be photographed, and never sat for her picture although her son desired it. Her niece, Henry Langhorne's daughter, has spoken of her as she was in early days, describing her as 'gentle, sweet, highly educated in every way, and so devotedly attached to her children that she sacrificed everything for their sakes, being so

---

[1] This is the impression of Lady Lingen, who saw her at Torquay.

constantly with them that it was not easy to see her.'
Another hint of the impression which she made on those
nearest to her is afforded by a letter of Mr. Courthope's,
after his wife's death, to his daughter Elizabeth Irwin
in Australia, May 10, 1840:—

'I feel much the absence of your dear Aunt Bella, so cheerful
and affectionate, with sweet feminine person and mind. I fear
that while supporting and consoling others, she had tired
herself too much. I never felt more the distance between
us. Dear Ben is an excellent fellow, so fond of her and so
kind to his beloved mother, it is gratifying to see it.'

With all this softness and amiability she was not
without a touch of womanly pride. On the whole she
well deserves Queen Katharine's praise of 'a great
patience'; having borne the vicissitudes of a chequered
lot with meekness and dignity.

Emily survived her mother thirteen years. She lived
quietly, kept up her accomplishment in music, and saw
her brother from time to time, visiting him more than
once at Balliol. She suffered from a stroke of paralysis
in 1880, and spent her remaining time with her cousins
the Irwins at Clifton, in whose house she died in 1882 [1].
She was devoted to her family, above all to her mother,
from whom she was never separated for long together,
and when her brothers went to India she parted with her
share of Mrs. Smith's bequest, in order to furnish them
forth. She was exquisitely refined, but shy and diffident,
above all in the presence of her brother, under whom her
'genius was subdued.' It is said that she could not do
herself justice even in playing the piano before him; and
when her cousins were inclined to mock at the pomposity
of some Oxford personage, she mustered courage to reply,
'My brother has a high opinion of him.'

[1] Mrs. Irwin had died in April of the same year.

In hours of gloom and misunderstanding she loved to dwell on the earlier days of free and joyous intercourse, which could never be recalled.

An impression long prevailed at Oxford that Jowett had no family ties. It used to be jestingly said that he was like Melchizedec, 'without father, without mother, without descent.' When one of the Irwin cousins who was in business at Madras declared his relationship, the Governor, an old Balliol man, professed to regard him as a prodigy: 'I thought he had no relatives[1].' Mr. F. T. Palgrave was almost equally surprised when, on Jowett's invitation, he was introduced (as above mentioned) to the little family party in the Rue Madeleine in the summer of 1850.

The mistake was due to the profound silence in which Jowett habitually buried what was personal to himself. Only at rare moments of intimate converse, under some exceptional stress of feeling, the veil was lifted, and disclosed the treasures within. Still less could it be divined that in later years his thoughts were occupied with his own family. And yet to more than

[1] This impression appears to have been shared even by Arthur Stanley until, at Jowett's own request, he paid a visit to the little *ménage* at St. Germains in March, 1856. He wrote to (Canon) Hugh Pearson: 'On Saturday last I went to St. Germains, and saw—the parents of Melchizedec ! a truly antique and venerable pair, each bearing a slight resemblance to the son, each with some of the qualities in him concentrated; very kind and rapt in interest concerning him, relating singular stories of his childhood—how deeply historical he then was, studying Rollin's *Ancient History*, well versed in Assyrian dynasties, standing long in silent contemplation of a "Stream of Time" suspended in his little bedroom. . . . Deeply musical also, he listens with pleasure to Beethoven played by his sister, while at work, and even proposes corrections.'—*Letters of Dean Stanley*, p. 248. This visit of Stanley's took place a short time before the parents' return to England.

one friend who suffered from bereavement—after speaking
of those of his kindred whom he had lost—he wrote:
'I do not expect to see them again, but I am always
thinking about them.'

Mr. F. Law, whose father and the Master's father were
friends, as mentioned above, has favoured us with the
following reminiscences :—

'My mother's family had been on very intimate terms with
the family of the late Master, from the early part of the
century[1]. There was not much difference in the ages of
the children, and the two daughters Ellen and Emily Jowett
were amongst my mother's greatest friends; the friendship
continued after my mother's marriage, and until death put
an end to it.

'My earliest distinct recollections of the Jowetts date back
to 1841, when we were living at Blackheath. Mr. and Mrs.
Jowett, with their surviving daughter Emily and their younger
sons, came to live near us. Mrs. Jowett was not a strong
woman; in fact, during the rest of her life she was always
delicate, requiring constant care, and she did not go out
much; but Mr. Jowett or some of his children came to
our house several times a week, and in the course of our
daily walks we were frequently taken to see Mr. and
Mrs. Jowett. Mr. Jowett was not then in business. Ben
was settled at Oxford, and Alfred and William were working
for their future careers in life.

'Mr. Jowett was tall and carried himself well, and as he
had a large face and head, with a quantity of white hair,
which was worn longer than is usual at the present day,
he was conspicuous in a room. His face was entirely shaven.
When I first remember him, he invariably dressed in black,
and usually wore a dress coat, and, until his latter days,

[1] This must have been during the Jowetts' early married life at Peckham, where the Channells also lived, at the corner of Peckham Lane. Mrs. Law was a younger sister of the late Baron Channell.

he very rarely put on a great-coat, whatever the weather
might be. He was still active and fond of walking, and
took his constitutional with great regularity till age interfered
with his doing so. Though not a teetotaler, he was most
temperate as regards stimulants. On general subjects he was
a well-informed man, and had an extensive knowledge of
the English Poets. I do not remember his showing any
acquaintance with foreign authors. Still he certainly knew
the French language, in which he could converse fluently,
although his accent, I imagine, was very English. From
time to time he would write a few hymns, and paraphrases
of portions of Scripture, and sometimes set them to music ;
but, so far as I can recall, his translation of the Psalms
was the only thing he published. His handwriting was somewhat cramped, and the formation of his letters small and not
regular, though he gave much time to his pen.

'He was very fond of sacred music, caring little about
secular—I do not remember his voice until it was failing
him ; it must have been a powerful and deep bass in its
prime—and he was never happier than when he could get
some one to accompany him in the songs from Handel's and
Mendelssohn's Oratorios, to which he would sing by the hour,
without seeming to tire. He himself only touched the piano
when none of the ladies were at hand to accompany him.

'Though not devoid of imagination and sentiment, Mr. Jowett
had not much originality of thought, and was by no means
inclined to develope any new theories, whether in reference
to religious or secular matters.

'Upon political matters, his views were strongly Conservative.
He was a very regular attendant at Divine Service, and a good
Churchman according to his own belief as one of the old
Orthodox School of thinkers. He did not obtrude his opinions
upon others ; but, proud as he was, and he was very proud
of his son's success at Balliol, his most intimate friends understood that he entirely dissented from and deeply regretted his
son's convictions upon these points.'

CHAPTER II

EARLY training and companionships—Camberwell—Blackheath—
Mitcham—Entrance at St. Paul's School at the age of twelve—
Dr. Sleath and his methods—School-fellows and school successes
—The Balliol Scholarship—'Apposition Day.'

FROM the preceding survey of two hundred years
we return to the second decade of this century,
and to the child Benjamin. He, who all his life was
the friend of children, must have had a happy childhood ; but few traces of it can be recovered now. There
is a family rumour or tradition that he was brought up
by two maiden aunts, but if there is any foundation for
this, it must be extremely slight. Mrs. Jowett was
never very strong, and in the years from 1820–1823 her
maternal cares may have been largely engrossed by little
Frank, who died at four years old. Benjamin was then
a child of five or six, and would be often at his grandfather's, much petted by his father's sisters, Elizabeth
and Maria, after the grave and solemn manner of that
household. Their cousin, Mrs. Whiting (Henry of Little
Dunham's daughter), was often heard to remark on the
docility and gentleness of the child.

But this state of things ceased, as we know, in 1823,
when the old home at Camberwell Green was broken

up for the removal to Liverpool[1]. In the years which followed it is unlikely that the boy owed much to any one except his mother. No doubt there were visits to his uncle Henry Langhorne at Mitcham, whose good looks he was supposed to inherit, and to the Courthopes' house at Blackheath Hill. There he was seen by some who long remembered it, 'a bright and merry child, running about on Blackheath Common.' An early recollection, which came back to him in his last years, although of trivial import, may be touched in passing. He remembered that when a child, he had been made to stand upon the table after dinner and to repeat poetry for the entertainment of the guests. At Mitcham, as the years went on, he also received some of his earlier lessons in Latin and Greek from the tutor who was employed in teaching his cousins. Miss Langhorne (H. Langhorne's daughter) writes: 'He was a pale, delicate-looking boy, of unusual mental precocity, and he learned for a while with my brothers' tutor, Mr. Richardson. I have heard them say that they had no chance against him in their Greek lessons.' At other times it is said that his father used to instruct him[2]. The visits to Blackheath Hill were of a more holiday kind; but sometimes, while the other children were at play, young Benjamin would be stretched upon the hearth-rug with Pope's *Homer* or a volume of Rollin's *Ancient History*.

If there were bright memories associated with those early playmates, there were also sad ones. Four of the Courthope cousins, Jane, Fanny, Emma, and Harriet, died before reaching the age of twenty-five. Emma

---

[1] p. 9.

[2] The authority for this is Mrs. Thomas Courthope, of Rother-hithe, who told it to her grandson, the Rev. R. B. Gardiner, now a master at St. Paul's School.

and Harriet were of an age to be companions of Emily and Benjamin. They were accomplished young women, with a great natural gift for drawing. Sidney Courthope, nearly of the same age with Benjamin, early became an invalid. He died shortly after his father. in 1845. His cousin Benjamin was very attentive to him during his illness.

Speaking of the years after 1826, when Henry Langhorne had removed to Clapham, Miss Langhorne says : 'It was customary for Benjamin to shut himself up with his sister Emily in a room with their books, where they spent hours in close study together.' Emily was a good Latin scholar.

It is obvious, from the previous chapter, that the family life, though attended with some degree of religious severity, was cheered with graceful music, with the companionship of books, and an atmosphere of liberal culture. The force of home impressions appears in the delicate and characteristic handwriting which Jowett long retained in spite of school exercises, University essays, and other causes usually destructive of such an accomplishment. This was evidently learned from his mother, who wrote the finest of 'Italian' hands, and as late as 1844 his writing closely resembled that of his sister [1].

The poet most in favour with that household, as with others of a similar type, was naturally William Cowper. When a lady who met Jowett at C. Bowen's [2] house in Chester Square (at some time in the seventies) happened to quote Cowper, he said, 'I was brought up on Cowper'; and they continued for good part of an hour repeating familiar lines without exhausting either's repertory.

[1] It appears, however, that Mr. Bean, his master during his first year at St. Paul's, was very particular about the neatness of exercises.

[2] Lord Bowen.

St. Paul's School, 1829-1836.

Jowett was admitted into St. Paul's School June 16, 1829, on the nomination of Thomas Osborne of the Mercers' Company, Surveyor-Accountant of St. Paul's School, who is said to have been an engraver and printer at 72 Lombard Street. Benjamin was now twelve years old, and in consequence missed some advantages which would have been secured by entering two years earlier. His previous education, whatever it was, must have been fairly efficient, for he was placed high on entrance, and rose rapidly in the school. There were eight forms then as now, and he was entered in the sixth, where he remained only for one year. The High Master at this time was Dr. John Sleath, of Wadham College, Oxford. He held the post from 1814-1837, and during that time gained much credit for the school, which was not then regarded at the Universities as on a level with the great public schools. He used to say, 'I do not profess to be a good scholar, but I make my scholars polish one another[1].' The 'Sur-master' was a Mr. W. A. C. Durham (commonly called 'Whack Durham'), but Jowett never came under him, as the sixth were taught by Dr. Sleath's assistant, Mr. John Phillips Bean. The hours of school-work in those days were from seven or eight to eleven or twelve in the morning, and from two to four in the afternoon three days a week. In the interval Benjamin, who had his own separate lodging (it was a lonely boyhood), used to be taken by his father to dine at some literary chop-house, such as 'The Cheshire Cheese.' The *habitués* of the place were embarrassed by the presence

---

[1] In this boast he was more than justified, having amongst his former pupils such men as Prince Lee, Canon Blakesley, and many others. Sleath had been private tutor to Walter Savage Landor when a boy at Rugby.

of the boy, the more so as the father would 'put him through his facings' in their hearing.

There is a tradition that at first coming to school young Jowett was more distinguished in Mathematics than in Classics (there was little mathematical teaching then in St. Paul's), but he must have made marked progress in Greek studies before 1833, in which year several of his Greek exercises were copied into the school album or 'playbook,' entitled *Musae Paulinae*, where they are still preserved[1]. They are not without school-boy errors (which to the credit of the authorities remain uncorrected), but they already show a fine sense of literary form, and a true feeling for Greek tragedy; and as they are not translations, but original compositions on set themes, they evince no little resource and dexterity in a boy of sixteen. The following epigram in elegiacs— the other exercises are all in iambics—may be quoted as a sample of his youthful invention:—

In Mercurii Imaginem.

Ὦ φίλος, εἰ κακὸς εἶ, λαβέ μ' ἐς χέρας, εἰ δ' ἀμελεῖς μου,
μὴ σύ, κλοπεύς περ ἐών, κλέψον ὃ μὴ νοέεις·
σοὶ δὲ φίλος τοῖς σοῖσί τ' ἔφυν· ἐμὲ δ' εὔχομαι εἶναι
τοῖσι καλοῖσι κακόν, τοῖσι κακοῖσι καλόν[2].

[1] Cf. G. R. Kingdon, S.J., in *The Pauline*, 1884: 'Now and then the High Master would say to the captain just before the end of morning school-time, "Fetch the playbook." Then we knew that we were in for a half-holiday; and at the sight of the big, morocco-bound, gilt-edged book brought in from the library, there would be a deal of finger-snapping among the smaller boys. Taking the book on his arm at prayer-time, the captain standing aside, Sleath would say in his most solemn tone, "There will be a play to-day for the good compositions of ...," whatever the names of the favoured ones happened to be.... The particular compositions which gained the half-holiday had to be written out in the playbook, for the admiration of future generations, or, perhaps, more often for their amusement.'

[2] I have thrown in the accents,

(*Inscription for a statue of Mercury.*

'Are you a rogue? Then take me in your hand.
But steal me not before you understand.
I am your friend! a god of varying mood,
Kind to bad men, but evil to the good.'—L. C.)

Puerile as the verses are, and not quite accurate, they
have something in them of the sly simplicity which
marked many of Jowett's sayings in after life.

In these years he formed the habits of industry, of
neatness, and of methodical study, which never left him.
The teachableness, which he always regarded as the best
sign of promise in boyhood, must have been strongly
characteristic of him; and the rarity of outdoor amusements, of which the educational value was then little
recognized, also left its impress on his after career. In
compensation for this want he early became a voracious
reader. He would 'fly upon a new book,' as he once
told me, and in the holidays passed with his sister at
Blackheath or Clapham this taste must have been indulged to the full. The habit of learning poetry by

which had been omitted according to a fashion of the day. It
is worth observing that in a
truly mercurial spirit the form
of the epigram is 'conveyed' from
one on Thucydides, quoted by
Bothe in the preface to his

edition :—

'Epigramma, fortasse sepul-
crale, ex persona Thucydidis, ad
calcem codicis Augustani adiec-
tum' (v. Jacobsii *Anthol.* gr. t. 4,
p. 231).

Ὦ φίλος, εἰ σοφὸς εἶ, λαβέ μ' ἐς χέρας· εἰ δὲ πέφυκας
νῆϊς Μουσάων, ῥῖψον ἃ μὴ νοέεις.
εἰμὶ γὰρ οὐ πάντεσσι βατός, παῦροι δ' ἀγάσαντο
Θουκυδίδην Ὀλόρου, Κεκροπίδην τὸ γένος.

(Friend, art thou learn'd? Then take me in your hand :
But if unlearn'd, stay till you understand :
Few find their way in me; the many scorn
The son of Olorus, Athenian born.—L. C.)

heart was at that time far more cultivated than it is now, both at school and in enlightened homes. One of his latest recollections was that he and Emily had once tried who could first commit to memory a thousand lines of Virgil. Before he left St. Paul's he could repeat the greater part of Virgil and Sophocles, probably also the Trilogy and *Prometheus* of Aeschylus. He never regretted this, although he sometimes wished that the same attention had been given to English literature. But he had more of English verse at his command than is at all common nowadays, and could recite long passages from his favourite authors. His intimate familiarity with Shakespeare came later.

The teaching at St. Paul's appears to have been well adapted, if not to produce the extreme accuracy of verbal scholarship for which (some years after this) other great schools were famous, at least to imbue the minds of boys with a genuine love of literature. And one method was in use, that of retranslating from English into the original Latin or Greek, in which Jowett himself always firmly believed.

A characteristic anecdote is told of his early school life. A statute of the foundation, by which a boy who had been absent more than a certain number of days forfeited his place in the school, was about to be revived. A comrade of Benjamin's was running dangerously near the limit, and was supposed to be unaware of the declared intention to put the rule in force. At this boy's home in some far-lying suburb, the bell was rung late at night, and a small figure was found on the doorstep. It was little Benjamin, who had walked for many miles to warn his friend of the danger he was incurring.

The following reminiscences contributed by persons

who were at St. Paul's with Jowett will be read with
interest :—

1. The Right Rev. C. R. Alford, late Bishop of Victoria,
who was a class-fellow of Jowett's, writes (July 4,
1894):—

'His image as a youth is still before me, a slim weakly
figure, gentle and polished in manner, keen eyes, very intelligent countenance. In reading and construing he had a clear
expressive voice, and in class he spoke out as one who knew
what he meant to say. I only remember Jowett in the eighth,
i. e. in the first class of the school under Dr. Sleath. I think
he stood second boy, and was much associated with Arthur
Shelly Eddis, the captain of our year. Eddis and Jowett had
the charge of, and chiefly occupied together the School Library,
located in the old buildings, between the High Master's house
and the great schoolroom. They seldom appeared in school
except at prayer-time and when we assembled around and
before the table of the High Master in class. Eddis was
Chancellor's Medallist of his year (1839), Fellow of Trinity
College, Cambridge, Professor in Lincoln's Inn, and Judge at
Clerkenwell County Court. As captain, Eddis always took the
lead, daily reading the Latin school prayers from the step of
the days on which the High Master's chair was placed—
Dr. Sleath, in cap and gown, standing behind him—a figure
of great presence and commanding appearance.

'. . . I can call to mind Jowett's return to school after his
successful competition for the Balliol Scholarship. We boys
held up our heads an inch or two higher than we did before,
and it was a sight worth beholding to gaze on the beaming
countenance of our dear old High Master, Dr. Sleath, whose
frown was dreaded, but whose smile of approval and encouragement, never grudgingly bestowed, was a joy and coveted
reward.

'I remember one personal circumstance with pleasure. On
my wedding-day (1841) I alighted at the Great Western Railway
Station, Paddington, with my wife, and as chance would have
it, as I got out of the carriage at the station Jowett was there!

He greeted me warmly, was introduced to my wife, and as he shook hands with us both wished us all happiness. We travelled by the same train to Oxford. This was the last occasion on which we spoke to one another. Some forty years after, I saw him and heard him say a few words at an "Apposition" at St. Paul's School, West Kensington. Then he was an elderly, venerable man in figure and feature and speech, the Master of Balliol; but still he reminded me much of old St. Paul's School and the youthful scholar of 1836.'

2. From the Rev. John B. Brodrick, Rector of Sneaton, near Whitby, April 9, 1894 :—

'There was so much difference between my standing and Jowett's as to prevent our having any very intimate intercourse, and the higher we got in the school the fewer those intimacies became. My recollection of him at Paul's is of a pretty-looking boy-youth who wore a perpetual sort of green sateen which never got, in my time, to the dignity of a coat-tail, but stuck to the less dignified one of a jacket. He never associated much with anybody, and on the strength of his looks we used to call him, though perhaps not to his knowledge, "Miss Jowett." We used to put him up to say curious things to old Sleath, which would certainly not lead that scholastic divine to predicate anything like what was the real future of his simple-minded pupil. . . . The only thing in the least memorable that I bear in mind is that on one occasion I, along with another class companion, went either with or for Jowett to that historical spot, Bolt Court, where Jowett Senior was then living, and the door was opened by William Cobbett, who sported a tricolour ribbon in his button-hole, which then meant a little more than it would do now. . . .'

3. From Baron C. E. Pollock, May 18, 1894 :—

'I joined the school September 30, 1833, at the age of nine. Jowett was then in the highest class, the eighth, and consequently a monitor. . . . My brother, George Pollock (now Queen's Remembrancer), remembers going with Jowett to see his father's printing-press in Bolt Court. . . . I can myself

remember Jowett when in the eighth class, a very young-
looking boy with round face and bright eyes, retiring in
manner, but holding his own, and much respected. Barham
and my brother Robert used to speak of him as "the boy
Jowett," and made fun of his journeys to Oxford outside the
coach and his supposed conversation with the guard.

'On one occasion, when Jowett was in the seventh, he was
struck by a boy bigger than himself but of inferior capacity.
This was immediately resented by his other school-fellows, who
treated it as an offence and thrashed the bigger boy.'

4. From the Rev. John Couchman, of Thornby Rectory,
near Rugby, who was Jowett's class-fellow:—

'Concerning Jowett's school-days, I have not much to say.
He was of a very taciturn and gentle disposition, more devoted
to books than to play: but as far as I remember his quiet
disposition gained him many friends amongst his school-fellows
and no enemies: he was what we all called "a very nice
fellow," and got on very well and amicably with us all. . . .
Dr. Sleath told me that he thought Jowett to be the best Latin
scholar he had ever sent to College. . . . Personally I had
always a great regard for him.'

Amongst his contemporaries at school, in the eighth
form, were the late Lord Hannen; Charles C. Roberts,
of Trinity College, Cambridge, Assistant Master at
St. Paul's; Arthur Shelly Eddis, Trinity College, Cambridge, Judge of the Clerkenwell County Court; Robert
John Pollock, Trinity College, Cambridge, of the Madras
Light Cavalry, and afterwards of the Inner Temple (who
died in 1853); R. H. D. Barham, Rector of Lulworth,
and author of the biography of his father, R. H. Barham
('Thomas Ingoldsby'); C. J. Clay, Printer to the University of Cambridge. This list makes it readily understood
why Benjamin Jowett, when head of the school, began
to turn his thoughts to Trinity College, Cambridge.
But the suggestion that he should try at Balliol,

which had come to Mrs. Jowett in the way already
described[1], had the approval of Dr. Sleath, and it was
no doubt the more readily acted on from the fact that
John Turner, of Bath, who had been at Winchester
School, was already at Oxford. At all events it was
expected that Turner should take some charge of his
young friend; and as the latter had not been recently
at Bath, and might have grown out of knowledge, it
was arranged that when he met the coach, John should
recognize Benjamin by the colour of his tie[2].

The following anecdote connected with Jowett's election to the Scholarship is given in the words of the
Rev. Hay S. Escott[3], who was a witness of the incident,
having gained an Exhibition the same year :—

'On the morning after our election we met by appointment
in the Master's dining-room to pay him a formal visit.
Dr. Jenkyns had not yet appeared, and Jowett had seated
himself on a chair in the bay-window overlooking the chapel
quadrangle, arrayed in academicals, then first put on for the
purpose of Matriculation. But, alas! he had forgotten that the
college cap was only intended for protection out of doors, and
it was still on his head when the door suddenly opened,
and the Master with his usual quick, jerking step swung
himself into the room. Then apparently startled, and inflamed
with real or simulated passion, he attacked without mercy the
innocent young Scholar for so flagrant a breach of the primary
laws of good breeding. "Do my eyes deceive me, or do I see
a gentleman in my dining-room with his cap on?" The whole
scene was most painful, and the impression it made on me is
indelible. It was one of those occasions on which Dr. Jenkyns
showed his want of sympathy, of the power of appreciating
other minds, and of allowing for circumstances. But his good
feelings quickly came to his aid, and he commenced a more

[1] p. 18.

[2] John Turner became a parish
clergyman, Vicar of Hennock,
Devon, and died in 1858. Jowett

had visited him not long before.

[3] Rector of Kilve, Somerset;
late Head Master of Somerset
College, Bath.

friendly and complimentary address, by the half-jesting, half-sarcastic remark—"I suppose it was the novelty of the bauble." These were the *ipsissima verba*[1].'

A welcome glimpse of him in the Christmas vacation following his election to the Scholarship, and his entrance at Balliol, is afforded by the Rev. Henry Holden, Rector of South Luffenham, who was then a Balliol Scholar of three years' standing. Dr. Holden begins his recollections from the time of the election. He says:—

'My first acquaintance with him was when he was elected Scholar at the usual examination in November, 1835, from St. Paul's School—a school at that time not of very high classical repute, but which has since gradually risen to distinction inferior to none amongst our greatest schools. I well remember introducing myself, on the evening of his election, to the slightly built, curly-headed lad, who seemed the last candidate likely to gain what was then considered the blue ribbon of scholarship, nearly all other colleges at that time confining their privileges to Counties and Founders' kin. The acquaintance thus commenced was increased during the subsequent winter vacation, when, being in London, I frequently visited him at his lodgings in the City Road. He had attended St. Paul's School as a day-scholar, being one of the 153 Foundationers, and remained even during vacations in London, to avoid the expense of long journeys to a distant home. Dr. Sleath was then Head Master, and it was by his advice that he was sent to try for the Scholarship. All that I then saw of him bore testimony to his industry, frugality, and simplicity of character. We worked together frequently during that winter vacation. When I returned to Oxford he continued

---

[1] This tale is confirmed, with some slight variations, in a letter from the Rev. H. C. Adams, Vicar of Shoreham, and late Fellow of Magdalen College, Oxford. Cf. Jowett's own remark on Jenkyns in *W. G. Ward and the Oxford Movement*, p. 441 : 'He was a considerable actor, and would put on severe looks to terrify freshmen, but was really kind-hearted and indulgent to them.'

at St. Paul's School, and I saw nothing more of him till he came into residence at Balliol.'

When in December, 1835, he returned to London, bringing with him the 'blue ribbon' of Oxford, an honour which no Pauline had at that time won, young Jowett at St. Paul's was a distinguished figure. There are contemporaries who still remember how, after his return, he used to be assailed from all sides whenever he passed among the younger boys in school, with cries of 'Give us a construe,' a request with which he complied as far as he could[1]. Now also he must have taken a leading place in the little debating society to which he belonged, and which met somewhere about St. Paul's Churchyard[2].

The school was under the shadow of the great cathedral, and one lasting impression, which may be with confidence referred to this early period, was his love of classical architecture, and in particular his reverence for Sir Christopher Wren[3]. Nothing delighted him more in after years than to take his guests to the Library of All Souls, Oxford, and to go over with them the various

[1] G. R. Kingdon, S.J., in *The Pauline*, 1884: 'The eighth were supposed to have so many books in use that their own lockers were not enough for them. Consequently they were allowed the use of the unoccupied ones on the bottom bench of some of the lower forms. I remember when I was in the second, the boys on the bench just above the bottom used to take advantage of a monitor's coming down to his locker, and coax him to translate a lesson for them. I can almost hear myself now, when stooping under the desk I would urge my petition: " I say Jowett, give us a con., there's a good fellow!" Jowett was captain at the time. He was always too good-natured to refuse, and with his locker open would translate Valpy's *Delectus* for me "straight off," to my great satisfaction.'

[2] The Rev. W. Guillemard, late Rector of St. Mary the Less, Cambridge, told me of this in 1880. —L. C.

[3] He once heard Sydney Smith preach in St. Paul's. See *Benjamin Jowett*, by L. A. Tollemache, p. 14.

plans for the rebuilding of St. Paul's Cathedral, copies of which are there preserved.

He very rarely made any reference to his school days, but eagerly embraced opportunities of renewing acquaintance with old Paulines, and, when occasion served, he spoke affectionately of those that were gone. In the light of after years his boyhood does not seem to have been regarded by him as, on the whole, a time of brightness or of enjoyment. The pleasures which it had for him lay chiefly in the region of his studies.

The spirit of self-culture, of loyalty and devotion, of generous and manly ambition, mingled with a pious aspiration to be doing good, already lay warmly at his heart. But his hold upon life and upon the outer world was weakest at the first, and grew steadily with the increase of his years and the widening of his opportunities.

In a familiar letter of 1861, he writes, with a humorous turn which hides a serious meaning: ' No day passes in which I don't feel the defects of early education. I was never taught how to play at cards, or even at billiards, and it seems too late to repair the error now. Do you think I could learn to waltz ? '

Partly no doubt from the circumstance that his school-fellows mostly went to Cambridge, no life-long friendship seems to have been made by him at school.

In one respect, however, the system at St. Paul's was well suited to prepare the cleverer boys for making their mark in after life. The 'speeches' on 'Apposition Day' were so managed as to give something like a real training in elocution. School lessons were suspended for the rehearsals, which were serious things. 'On one occasion,' says an old Pauline [1], 'during the delivery of

---

[1] G. R. Kingdon, S.J., in *The Pauline* for March, 1884.

a dialogue from Milton's *Samson Agonistes*, the boy who
personated Harapha, in the line

"I am of Gath, men call me Harapha,"

put rather too much emphasis on *men*. Sleath instantly
thundered out, "And what do *women* call you ?" I need
not say that the criticism was appreciated.'

Young Jowett's appearance at his last 'Apposition' (i. e
Founder's) 'Day' is thus recorded in the *Times* of May 6,
1836 :—

'The Apposition of the Scholars of St. Paul's School took
place yesterday. We had the misfortune not to be present
at the early part of the proceedings, which commenced with
speeches in Greek, Latin, and English, in commemoration
of the founder, by Messrs. Jowett, Wright, and Jephson, the
three senior scholars. Then followed the prize compositions,
Iter ad Emmaum in Latin Hexameters, and *Fatale Jephthae
Votum* in Greek Trimeter Iambics, both by Mr. Jowett, the
senior scholar. . . . We may here remark that gesticulation
appears to be very properly more encouraged at this than at
other public schools, and under the guidance of excellent taste,
rarely, if ever, is ridiculous or degenerates into acting. . . .
The closing piece was highly entertaining ; it was a scene from
the *Ranae* of Aristophanes, where Bacchus (Mr. Jowett) is
alarmed by his man Xanthias (Mr. Harriott), while in the
Infernal regions, with a supposed spectre. . . . The comic
distress of the former excited much laughter even amongst that
portion of the audience customarily presumed to be ignorant
of the learned languages.'

All these distinctions did not smooth away the financial
difficulties of his entrance at Balliol. It was usual for
the head boy of St. Paul's to take with him the Campden
Exhibition of £100 a year for five years to Trinity
College, Cambridge ; but Jowett was debarred from this,
and also from other Exhibitions which were tenable
at any College in either University, by the fact that he

had passed his twelfth birthday before entering the
school [1].   Under these circumstances his old patrons of
the Mercers' Company stepped in, and on July 14, 1836,
Jowett was elected to one of Lady North's Exhibitions,
and at the same date a small sum was given to him
by the Company as senior scholar of St. Paul's School,
on his going to College.   His friends at St. Paul's be-
thought themselves of a further expedient for rewarding
him.   The school library had grown to considerable
magnitude, and had not been catalogued.   To this congenial task Jowett was appointed, and gained for it an
honorarium of 100 guineas from the Mercers' Company,
which was paid to him in 1837.   Even with these
additions to the Balliol Scholarship, his means for living
at Oxford were narrow enough, and must have required
the strictest economy [2].

[1] G. R. Kingdon, S.J., in *The
Pauline*, 1884 : 'There were then
two Campden Exhibitions of £100
and £75, the holders of which must
go to Trinity College, Cambridge,
and besides these as many others
of £50 per annum as there might
be deserving candidates.   These
last might be held at any College
of either University.   These Exhibitions, in my time, lasted for
five years. . . . In order, however,
to be eligible for them, you must
have been on the foundation, i.e.
you must have been admitted
before you were ten years old.'

[2] 'On February 10, 1837, the
then Surveyor-Accountant laid
before the Court of the Mercers'
Company copies of a newly printed
Catalogue of the Library of the
School, prepared by Mr. Benjamin
Jowett, late Senior Scholar, and
shortly afterwards a present of
100 guineas was made to him for
the care and attention he had
bestowed in forming an entirely
new Catalogue of the Library of
that Establishment' (Letter from
Mr. John Watney, Secretary of
the Mercers' Company, April 18,
1894).

CHAPTER III

EARLY friendships at Oxford—The Hertford Latin Scholarship
—A Balliol undergraduate sixty years since—Reminiscences of
surviving contemporaries—The Master, Richard Jenkyns, and the
Tutors, Tait and Scott—The Balliol Fellowship won by the under-
graduate Scholar—Work in private tuition—Death of Ellen Jowett—
Graduation—Letters to W. A. Greenhill.

IT was the common practice then as now at Oxford
to interpose two or more 'Grace Terms' between
the election to a Scholarship and coming into residence.
Accordingly the new Scholar of Balliol entered as a freshman in October, 1836, being then nineteen years of age.
How or where the Summer Vacation had been spent does
not appear, except that it seems probable that part of it
had been occupied in the task of cataloguing the St. Paul's
School library. He seems to have remained at St. Paul's
until July, although his attendance there should strictly
have ended with his nineteenth birthday, April 15, or at
latest with Apposition Day.

In old age he spoke of his election to the Scholarship
as the happiest event of his life; and his entrance on that
career at Oxford, which only terminated with his death,

cannot fail to have been accompanied with a strong
feeling of enlargement and emancipation. Yet considering the combination of enterprise and caution, of
moral intrepidity with constitutional shyness, of eager
interest in life with the most delicate refinement and
sensitiveness, which was inherent in his nature, one
cannot suppose that his freshman's term at the University
was altogether unclouded. And the difficulties of beginning life at Oxford were sensibly increased for him
by the fact that, notwithstanding the Scholarship and
the liberality of the Mercers' Company, in comparison
with the public school men amongst whom he found
himself, he was decidedly poor. His first anxiety was
to gain, if possible, the Hertford University Scholarship
for Latin, and for this purpose he felt the need of extra
tuition. An unexpected gift of £20 from an anonymous
donor enabled him to read with Edward Massie of
Wadham, a Shrewsbury man who had taken the Ireland in
1828, and was known to be a successful 'coach.' Jowett
won the Hertford, to the disgust of his competitors,
who, as one of them [1] says, could not bear to be beaten by
'a little puny, boyish, chubby-faced youth.' This was in
Lent Term, 1837, the same year in which A. P. Stanley
obtained the Ireland.

Jowett's first success, with the accompanying circumstances, produced a marked effect upon him, and was the
beginning of the earliest, and for a time the most intimate,
of his Oxford friendships. His benefactor proved to be
W. A. Greenhill, a Rugby man, Stanley's senior by about
two years, who was at this time studying Medicine. He
afterwards practised as a physician at Oxford, and married

---

[1] Dr. Frederick H. M. Blaydes, the well-known editor of Aristo-phanes, &c. He was the winner of the Hertford in the following year, 1838.

Miss Ward, a favourite niece of Dr. Arnold. He has since been known as a learned writer on the history of Medicine. The following letter, written while the giver was unknown, shows the feeling with which the gift was received :—

OXFORD, *January* 31, 1837.

DEAR SIR,

I gratefully avail myself of your wonderful and un-expected goodness. I do so with the less hesitation as I am persuaded from the letter with which it was accompanied that it was really meant. It will give me the opportunity of obtaining what I have long wished for and could not other-wise have had.

May I venture to hope that I shall one day have the pleasure of thanking personally my unknown benefactor. Should I fail in the ensuing contest (and I feel persuaded such will be the result) I trust he will believe that this want of success has been owing to no deficiency of exertion on my part. With the most sincere gratitude for your kindness, and the *manner* in which it was offered,

Believe me to remain, my dear Sir,

Ever yours most truly and respectfully,

B. J.

Should I not hear from you to the contrary, I will leave a letter for you at the Post Office on March 1, directed to X. Y. Z.

May God bless you for your kindness to me. I never thought much about religion till a few days before your letter came, [and] it has left an impression which I trust I shall never forget.

Many years afterwards (in 1867), when Professor Jowett was corresponding with Dr. Greenhill on the subject of Plato's *Timaeus*, he referred with characteristic grati-tude to this long-past kindness, adding that he had himself known the pleasure of helping others in a similar way.

Before proceeding further with the narrative, some attempt should be made to imagine Balliol College as it was when Jowett entered it. The Scholarships had been thrown open to competition in 1828, Richard Jenkyns having then been Master for several years. This was a most important step, for which G. A. Ogilvie, one of the Tutors[1], was largely responsible. The list of Balliol Scholars, previous to 1836, already held distinguished names, and the Scotch contingent, supplied chiefly by the Snell foundation, had long since been an acknowledged source of strength. Adam Smith, John Lockhart, and Sir William Hamilton, not to mention others, were Snell Exhibitioners in their day. Archibald Campbell Tait, who, when Jowett began residence, had recently been appointed Tutor, was both a Scholar and a Snell Exhibitioner, having been educated at the Edinburgh Academy and Glasgow University. The bond of friendship with him, thus early formed, was strained by later events, but never broken.

Another of the Tutors to whom Jowett owed much as an undergraduate, was Robert Scott, part author of the famous *Lexicon*, who in 1854 became Master of Balliol. The Mathematical Lecturer at this time was W. G. Ward[2], the importance of whose influence over Jowett for a brief period will shortly appear.

Arthur Penrhyn Stanley was now entering on his third year at College, and, as his custom was, took out the junior Scholar from time to time for a walk in the afternoon. On the first of these occasions he is said to have reported that he never met with such a disputatious

---

[1] Afterwards Professor of Pastoral Theology.

[2] See *Life of Dean Stanley*, vol. i. p. 169, letter to C. J. Vaughan.

FISHER'S BUILDING AND END OF 'RATS' CASTLE,' BALLIOL COLLEGE

Copied from a print in an old Oxford Guide

youth. His surprise was not unnatural. For many years
after this Jowett's appearance was juvenile in the extreme,
and it was long remembered that he first came to College
in a round jacket, and with a turned-down collar. This
gave to his animation in argument the greater piquancy.
What subjects were discussed between the two young
men, whose friendship was destined to be so closely
cemented afterwards, we can only guess; but it is difficult
to imagine any discussion at Oxford, in those days, that
did not turn on matters theological. The subscription
to the Articles; Dr. Arnold's influence; the observance
of Sunday; J. H. Newman's sermons; Clericalism and
Evangelicism; the relation of Catholics to Protestants;
the admission of Jews to Parliament; the Divinity
Examination at London University: any or all of these
subjects afforded ample matter for controversy, and had
more fascination for young Oxonians than those eternal
arguments on 'Foreknowledge, Will, and Fate' in which
Milton's fallen spirits lose themselves. But the event
which had most interested Stanley's mind in 1836 was
the appointment of Dr. Hampden to the Regius Professorship of Theology, and the disputes that followed.

Some others of Jowett's College contemporaries may
be here enumerated. Edward Cardwell[1] had taken his
degree in 1835 and was now a junior Fellow. John
Moore Capes, who afterwards became a Roman Catholic,
was a graduate of the same year. James Lonsdale[2] had
been elected Scholar with A. P. Stanley. W. C. Lake[3],
Benjamin C. Brodie[4], E. M. Goulburn[5], and Hay S.
Escott, were Jowett's seniors by a year; also senior

---

[1] Afterwards Lord Cardwell.

[2] Rev. James Lonsdale. See his
Life by Duckworth.

[3] Afterwards Dean of Durham.

[4] Sir Benjamin C. Brodie, F.R.S.,
Professor of Chemistry, Oxford.

[5] Head Master of Rugby; afterwards Dean of Norwich.

to him were John Wickens[1], Hugh Pearson[2], Samuel
Waldegrave[3], E. Hobhouse[4], and P. S. H. Payne (who
died in 1841). His immediate contemporaries, who must
have been freshmen with him, were F. C. Trower[5],
Stafford H. Northcote[6], and Reginald Hobhouse[7]. His
juniors while he was still an undergraduate were T. H.
Farrer[8], W. Rogers[9], Arthur Hobhouse[10], Arthur H.
Clough[11], Constantine Prichard[12], Frederick Temple[13],
and John Duke Coleridge[14]. Oxford contemporaries
not at Balliol, who became distinguished in after life,
were W. F. Donkin[15] of University College, Richard
W. Church[16] of Wadham, James Fraser[17] of Lincoln,
James A. Froude[18] of Oriel, Richard Congreve[19] of
Wadham, R. R. W. Lingen[20] of Trinity, Henry Halford
Vaughan[21] of Christ Church, Bartholomew Price[22] of
Pembroke, Henry W. Acland[23], Christ Church and
All Souls, John Ruskin[24], Christ Church, and George

---

[1] Vice Chancellor Wickens.

[2] Vicar of Sonning and Canon
of Windsor.

[3] Bishop of Carlisle.

[4] Bishop of Nelson, New Zealand.

[5] Bishop of Glasgow, afterwards of Gibraltar.

[6] Lord Iddesleigh.

[7] Rector of St. Ives and Archdeacon of Bodmin.

[8] Lord Farrer.

[9] Rector of St. Botolph,
Bishopsgate; Canon of St. Paul's.

[10] Lord Hobhouse.

[11] The Poet.

[12] Fellow of Balliol, son of
James Cowles Prichard, the
author of *Natural History of
Man*, &c.

[13] Head Master of Rugby;

Bishop of Exeter, 1869; Bishop
of London, 1885; Archbishop of
Canterbury, 1896.

[14] Lord Chief Justice.

[15] Savilian Professor of Geometry.

[16] Dean of St. Paul's.

[17] Bishop of Manchester.

[18] The Historian.

[19] The Founder of English
Positivism.

[20] Lord Lingen.

[21] Professor of Modern History,
Oxford.

[22] Sedleian Professor of Natural
Philosophy, Master of Pembroke
College.

[23] Sir Henry W. Acland, Bart.,
M.D., Professor of Medicine,
Oxford.

[24] The well-known Author.

Butler[1] of Exeter. Mark Pattison [2] of Oriel, afterwards
Fellow of Lincoln, was **already a young** graduate when
Jowett came into residence at Balliol. These names may
suffice **to indicate to those who recall** their many associations, the sort of *milieu* into which the **reserved, town-bred**
youth, eager **and yet shrinking,** dutiful and **adventurous,**
was suddenly **plunged.** There was the Eton set, brilliant
and careless, full of gentlemanly prejudices, **but also of**
boyish fun. There were the Scotchmen, in striking **con-**
trast to these, **not** less noisy perhaps, but plodding and
industrious, and bringing with them more of metaphysics
than of classical learning. **And there** were the Rugby
men, full of enthusiasm **for Dr. Arnold, in** whose unpopularity they gladly **shared.** **They knew more of**
history than the **rest, and** were eager **to** break **a lance in**
theological **controversy.** That was already filling the air
to the detriment of other studies ; and grave **dispassionate**
elders lamented the **decline** of scholarship **in the Uni-**
versity **of Musgrave and Elmsley.** Young Jowett kept
his head, we may be sure, but while proving all things,
was taking impressions from all. **In these early** days he
was eagerly observant, but more receptive **than critical ;**
and in the pursuit of scholarship, which was his **main**
business, he made rapid **progress, though he did not**
immediately come **quite to the front.** **Indeed** he was
very little known in his earlier **years at** Balliol, and did
not see much of any one, even **in his own College,** except
when he **met his** brother Scholars daily in Hall. There
was **always a good deal of conversation at the** Scholars'
table, **and it is easy to imagine how the** novice, after
listening **long in silence,** would strike **in from time to**
time with **some unexpectedly** pertinent **remark.** **His**

---

[1] Canon of Winchester.   [2] **Rector of Lincoln College.**

circumstances forbade his entertaining any one, and he took no part in athletic exercises, although on rare occasions he indulged himself with rowing in a solitary skiff on the river[1]. He took long walks, was fond of bathing, being a fair swimmer, and, like his friend A. P. Stanley, took part in visiting the poor[2]. By degrees, however, his love of conversation and his social nature made for him an inner circle of companionship drawn from all the various sets in College, in which the figures of Arthur Hobhouse, Benjamin C. Brodie, H. S. Escott, E. M. Goulburn, A. H. Clough, Stafford H. Northcote, and W. Rogers are still clearly discernible.

In picturing the life of an Oxford undergraduate of sixty years since, it is necessary to bear in mind that athletic sports were less developed, and there were stronger lines of demarcation between the reading, the boating, and the hunting men, than at a later time. It was in one of his rare sculling excursions that Jowett first came in contact with one of the Bunsen family. Henry Bunsen of Oriel[3] happened to be passing by at the moment when Jowett's skiff was upset in one of the lower reaches of the river, and he always spoke of Bunsen as having acted the part of the Good Samaritan on that occasion. No friendship formed in Jowett's undergraduate days was more lasting than that with W. Rogers, a boating man from Eton.

The following reminiscences have been kindly communicated by surviving contemporaries. I take first the narrative of Lord Hobhouse, who seems to have been

[1] He took part in a College sculling race in June, 1838. See p. 71.

[2] He pointed out to Dr. Evelyn Abbott a house in the neighbourhood of Hinksey, where he had visited a poor woman.

[3] Eldest son of Baron Bunsen; Vicar of Lilleshall, Salop; afterwards Rector of Donington. He was educated at Rugby, under Dr. Arnold.

brought into specially close companionship with Jowett when both were undergraduates [1] :—

'I went to reside at Balliol in Oct. 1837, being then under eighteen years old ; and I made acquaintance with Jowett, who was a Scholar of the House, and had commenced his residence a year before. I do not remember how our acquaintance began, but it must have been very soon after my arrival ; probably through Northcote (Lord Iddesleigh), an old Eton friend, who won a Scholarship a year later than Jowett. The Scholars dined at a separate table ; and, not being one, I missed that stimulus of intimacy which is got by companionship at meals. On the other hand, I was thrown in with Jowett in this way. The top floor of the staircase on which he lived was shared between his rooms and those of a man of his own standing named Vaux. This Vaux was very fond of taking to his rooms some congenial soul, or it might be more than one, to imbibe tea, and indulge in talk *de omnibus rebus*. He often so received me ; and occasionally his neighbour Jowett would come in ; and, again occasionally, Jowett would make tea for us, or for me alone, in his own territory [2].

'So there sprung up, quickly as is the case with lads, a mutual attraction, and such intimacy as our natures and

---

[1] I am bound to insert here the words in which Lord Hobhouse deprecates the publication of the contribution so kindly made by him ; although I think the reader will agree with me in considering his doubts unnecessary. 'Reviewing my intercourse with Jowett I cannot think that anything I have to say is fit for publication or for more than casual talk across a tea-table. It is pleasant enough for me to conjure up old pictures shining in the soft light of other days ; but to those who have not that light the case is different. I conceive that my remarks are worthy of the blessed repose of the waste-paper basket. But of that you, who are writing the biography, are the best judge, and not I. So I will throw such light on your subject as I can.' — L. C.

[2] His poverty was so evident, that A. H. scrupled even to accept his invitations to tea, but his doing so gave B. J. manifest pleasure. 'It was difficult to draw him away from his studies, but when once you had him out of his shell he was pleasant to talk to.' (From conversation with Lord Hobhouse.)—L. C.

circumstances permitted. I may mention in this connexion
that to the end of Vaux's life, through good fortune and
through ill, which he did not escape, Jowett never forgot the
regard for him which existed in these early days.

'I have heard men say that one of Jowett's foibles was to
be too much taken by successful or prominent men. I am
by no means sure of that; but I am sure that he was a man
of rare fidelity in his attachments. I have known him come
to like adversaries; I have never known him turn away from
or forget one whom he has called his friend.

'Jowett never joined in our games; not from any dislike,
I think, for he always took due interest in the doings of the
Balliol boat, in which I then pulled an oar. The only exercise
beyond a walk, which I ever enjoyed with him, was swimming[1],
to which we were both addicted. I do not know, but believe,
that in the matter of games, as in other things, such as chess
and entertainments, the necessity of a rigid economy kept him
from doing what was done by others in easier circumstances.
That his means were narrow before he won a Fellowship, was
evident; but he never spoke to me on the subject. Indeed
he was very reticent on all things connected with his personal
life, either in his school or in his family. It was natural that,
seeking to know more of one to whom I was attracted, I should
invite information on such matters, as in the case of other
friends. But beyond the fact that his anchor was for the
present cast in Bath, I learned little. He would give but
a bare answer to a question; and of course I soon abstained
from broaching subjects on which he was not communicative.

'The part of Jowett's character which was most attractive
to me was his perfect simplicity, truth, and originality. Behind
his pretty, girlish looks, quiet voice, and gentle, shy manner,
one soon found that there lay a robust masculine understanding, which would not accept commonplaces as true or
mere authority as a guide. I think that most boys of eighteen
are apt to repeat without testing what they have been

---

[1] 'Jowett took readily to the water and swam well. The bath-ing was at Parson's Pleasure.' (From conversation with Lord Hobhouse.)—L. C.

accustomed to hear, to fancy that what they see in print must be true, and to accept for gospel what comes to them accredited by the authorities of their little world. Certainly that was the case with me. And then I came into contact with one who, not flippant nor irreverent nor specially fond of paradox, nor specially desirous of victory in a discussion, yet insisted on seeing everything with his own eyes, and refused to utter a proposition until his own judgement was sufficiently in accord with it. I looked upon Jowett as the freshest and most original mind I had come across; and I still think that I have never held converse with any one who was more thoroughly original, or more careful to say only what he made his own. Among the living influences which compelled me to think and tended to invigorate my thoughts in the plastic age between eighteen and twenty, I put as chiefest the lectures of Archbishop Tait and my intercourse with Jowett. Of course there were many others playing on a ripening mind, not then realized in any distinct way, and now impossible to disentangle; but in looking back and trying to take stock of my earlier life, I have always attributed the most powerful effect to the hard-headed rationalism of these two, combined with their steady love of truth and their sympathetic natures. Probably the parts they played in after life will go far to justify my estimate. Jowett's fearless, and apparently passionless, tenacity under the storms which, at least during the first half of his working life, blew with great violence round the heads of the few who dared to think for themselves and to say so; his abstinence from anything like triumph when he made his position good—all these things seem to me the natural healthy outgrowth of the twenty-year-old boy, whose resolute questionings startled, posed, interested, and attracted me.

'I have just called his tenacity passionless, and his victory one without triumph. Of course in the immature time with which I deal, qualities of this sort are not brought out or tested by circumstances. But one of his characteristics which impressed me even then was his calmness when opinions differed; that he did not, as other men are wont, get heated or argue for victory in a wordy war, but contended only when he had something to say which he believed to be true.

'Not that he was wanting in feeling; he had warm feelings and sympathies; and he valued sympathy very much. Indeed I don't know why he should have regarded me with any favour except from feeling that I liked him. One expression of his I recall because it touched me at the time, and has always remained with me. In the spring of 1838 he stood for the Ireland Scholarship and was defeated. The successful man, if I rightly recollect, was the present Lord Lingen. Jowett had hoped to win and was much mortified. Probably, besides the pleasure of success, the emolument would have been a great help to him[1]. I went to his rooms and sat with him for some time. On parting he thanked me warmly, and added, perhaps with a little bitterness, "There are plenty who come when one wins, but you are a losing friend." I don't say that he was right, but such was the man, quickly responsive to sympathy, hurt if he thought it was withheld.'

Dr. Holden, whose account of Jowett's appearance among the candidates for the Scholarship has been quoted in the previous chapter, continues his narrative as follows:—

'As I was three years his senior we did not attend the same College lectures, and consequently did not regularly meet, except at the Scholars' dining table in Hall. But there I can well remember his quiet, unassuming manner, when the elder and more advanced Scholars led the conversation, and sometimes laid down the law for the juniors in politics or theology, subjects, at that stirring time, very warmly discussed in Oxford. . . We little thought that the retiring, unobtrusive young Pauline was about to develop into a Hertford University Scholar in the following spring (1837), and in the year after that (November, 1838), while still an undergraduate, to be elected over the heads of all the senior Balliol Scholars and a score of others, First Class men from other Colleges, to the high distinction of a Balliol Fellowship.'

[1] 'He was much disappointed when he found that the Hertford Scholarship which he had gained was only for one year, and he was also greatly disappointed at missing the Ireland.' (From conversation with Lord Hobhouse.)—L. C.

The following recollections of the Rev. Hay S. Escott
may be compared with the preceding. His account of
the teaching at Balliol about this time is especially
valuable :—

'At the period of Jowett's election the undergraduates of
the College numbered about eighty ; but this small number
had in it a very large amount of intellectual power and energy
of life. It was rather sharply divided into sets, and even
at the tables in Hall, open to all, this division was generally
preserved. But still the borderers in each set were more or
less also members of the adjoining set, and a man might have
friends in other sets than his own. But it was the stirring
activity of the College which most struck the new members
as they joined it. Of course in this vigorous life the Scholars
took the lead ; but it was not confined to them, and the
presence of such men, so intellectual and so studious as
Lonsdale, Stanley, Goulburn, and Lake, may well be supposed
to have kindled and stimulated many minds of less conspicuous power. But much was also due to the authorities
of the College. In Dr. R. Jenkyns[1] (afterwards Dean of
Wells) it had a Master, according to his light, thoroughly
devoted to its interest. He was not a man of a great and
large mind—and width of thought was neither cultivated nor
affected in his day—but he was eminently practical, and
possessed of shrewd common sense, though deficient in
delicacy of touch when handling minds more complex and
more sensitive than his own. His dignity may have been
somewhat pompous, and his energy bustling, but he honestly
exerted all his powers for the improvement of the College,
considering no part of its machinery beneath his notice ; and
the result of his exertions was seen in the character of the
men he gathered round him, first as Scholars or Commoners,
then as Fellows and Tutors, by whose agency the prestige
of Balliol was so rapidly and greatly raised. At the time
of which we write, Moberly had just left Oxford to become
Head Master of Winchester, and afterwards Bishop of Salisbury.

[1] See Oakeley's 'Balliol under Dr. Jenkyns,' in *Reminiscences of
Oxford*, Oxford Historical Society, 1892.

The Classical Tutors were Oakeley, Chapman, Tait, and immediately after (in the Lent Term of 1836) Scott, and the Mathematical Lecturer was Ward, of the *Ideal*. Oakeley, an excellent man, but speculative and dreamy, is more remembered as Catechetical Lecturer than as Tutor, though his lectures on Lucretius were highly spoken of. Chapman— a truly good man, full of kindness and gentleness—usually took the lectures to freshmen, and the more elementary part of the work, dividing the Divinity lectures with the other Tutors. But the nerve and backbone of the teaching lay with Tait and Scott—and with the former even more than with the latter. Of Tait, tried and approved as he afterwards was in the highest position, it may seem superfluous to speak. But in enumerating the influences to which Balliol undergraduates were then subject, it is important to notice the impression made by him, as we know, on some at least of his pupils. There was in him a charm—a union, perhaps, of manliness and kindness, which won for him the affection and respect of the more susceptible. He seemed to understand character, and to deal with the individual less according to any trifling occasional error, than according to what he knew to be his main purpose and aim. He had that dignity which was natural to his talents and his official position, but because it was natural, unstudied, and unassumed, he could exchange it for perfect equality with an undergraduate in social intercourse. Then, as a Lecturer, he had the remarkable gift of clearing up obscurities, and of leaving some definite idea in the minds of his pupils where all had appeared hopelessly confused. He could take up some intricate passage, over which an inexperienced translator was sorely perplexed, and at once, apparently without effort, elicit a satisfactory meaning and produce it in idiomatic English.

'Scott had not these gifts. Truly good and kind, and in pure scholarship immeasurably in advance of Tait, his learned and careful lectures left comparatively little impression on the mind. His manner did not commend him, and he was deficient in tact, and in those qualities, so conspicuous in Tait, which give influence over others and call forth affection and respect. Yet to those intimate with him he was, we believe, as lovable as he was talented; and in young Jowett—fonder then of the literature than of the philosophy of Greece—he had a pupil after his own heart, whose accurate scholarship he could at once admire and enrich [1].

'Besides those already mentioned, a senior Fellow of the name of Carr [2] occasionally looked over the weekly Essay, dividing the work with the Master. For the "Essay" was then in existence, written alternate weeks in English and Latin. . . . At times a copy of English verses was accepted instead of an Essay. . . . And as the final schools drew near, it was allowed to substitute for original composition a translation of a passage of English into Latin prose.'

With reference to the same period the Rev. John L. Hoskyns, Rector of Aston Tirrold, writes:—

'I was never intimate with Jowett when at Balliol. He was a shy, retiring student, quite a recluse, and I was not one of the magic circle of the Scholars and their immediate friends.

'. . . But I can never forget the deep impression that the general aspect of things in College made upon me. The scene in Chapel, Hall, Lecture Room; the countenances of the men—of Tait, Scott, Oakeley, Chapman, Ward; the Scholars' table, and high table; the twos and twos going out for their constitutionals, live fresh in my memory after nearly sixty years. It was a marvellous time, and a most interesting set of men.'

[1] In his reminiscences (*W. G. Ward, &c.*, p. 115), Professor Jowett says: 'I must not forget the late Dean of Rochester, afterwards Master of the College, *who was very kind to me in early life.*' The lectures of both these distinguished men had effects for their youthful listener which they were far from contemplating. He wrote as follows in one of the notebooks, dated October, 1875: 'I think the Dean of Rochester's Lectures on Niebuhr first aroused in my mind doubt about the Gospels, and that the Archbishop of Canterbury first aroused in me the desire to read German theology.'

[2] See *W. G. Ward, &c.*, loc. cit. The Rev. John Carr, afterwards Rector of Brattleby and an Honorary Canon of Lincoln.

'The twos and twos going out for their constitutionals,' recall a feature almost unknown to a more athletic generation, the 'long walk with a friend,' which Jowett has often recommended as a recipe for low spirits [1].

His failure for the Ireland Scholarship in 1838 may have been partly due to grief or anxiety for his sister Agnes, a year younger than himself, who died about this time. In the same Term, however, he again surprised his friends, by winning the Powell Prize at Balliol, then awarded for proficiency in English literature. His father wrote as follows to Mrs. Irwin :—

'During the present term, Benjamin has been trying for the Powell Prize at Balliol, for English Composition. I wondered very much at his venturing, as it was quite out of his line—at least, so I should have concluded. We knew nothing about it till he had obtained it. . . . We were glad to find his English had been respectable enough to carry him through.'

A greater and more joyful surprise was in reserve. By a statute of the College the Balliol Fellowships were open to all Bachelors of Arts of the University *and to Scholars of Balliol*. On one previous occasion, it was believed, an undergraduate Scholar had been elected. In November, 1838, there were four vacancies—an unprecedented number—and Jowett was urged by some of his companions, Goulburn in particular, and it is said also by his Tutor, Robert Scott, to try his luck.

The biography of Dean Stanley has thrown a curious light on the conditions of election to a Balliol Fellowship in those days. Arthur Stanley was induced to try for a Fellowship at University College in July, 1838, because his 'supposed theological opinions' had rendered his

[1] M. Arnold's *Scholar Gipsy* and *Thyrsis* enshrine reminiscences of this familiar habit. Cf. *Letters of Matthew Arnold*, vol. i. pp. 38, 191.

election at Balliol in November very improbable[1]!
Amidst the searchings of heart which he went through
before taking that decisive step, the last thing to occur
to his mind would be, that in changing his College he
would be leaving the coast clear for the admission of his
younger friend. Yet so it was; and we may safely infer
that Jowett had not as yet fallen under suspicion
either for liberal or Tractarian sympathies. In point
of fact, as appears from the letters to W. A. Greenhill,
while Evangelical prepossessions had been to a great
extent already discarded, he was looking keenly round
him with a suspense of judgement very uncommon in
one so young.

The circumstances of his election may best be told in
Dr. Holden's words:—

'As this is an achievement only once before[2], I believe,
recorded in the annals of Balliol, some particulars may be
interesting, especially as coming from one who was himself
a candidate. Four vacant Fellowships were to be filled up
by examination; all B.A.'s were eligible. The undergraduate
Scholars of Balliol had also the peculiar privilege of being
eligible, as the Master of the College, Dr. Jenkyns, used sometimes to remind them. It was current at the time that the
Rev. Robert Scott, afterwards Master of the College for sixteen years, and who had himself been elected Fellow from
Christ Church just two years before, had persuaded the young
Hertford Scholar, the most promising pupil in his lecture
room, to avail himself of this privilege and to offer himself
as a candidate for one of the four vacant Fellowships[3]. It is

[1] Stanley's *Life*, vol. i. p. 195.
Among the candidates was Mark
Pattison: see his *Memoirs*, p. 177.
The Master, Jenkyns, was a stern
foe to innovations; Tait's ante-
cedents were not Anglican; Scott
and Ward were not originally
Balliol men; and neither Ward

nor Oakeley had as yet become
known as followers of Newman.

[2] In the case of Jenkyns himself (so tradition says).

[3] A contemporary letter names
E. M. Goulburn and John Turner
as 'the persons who with great
difficulty induced him to en-

said also that when speaking of this pupil to his brother electors, he often used the words *non res sed spes* (promise not performance) [1].

Jowett was out of College when the result was declared. The names had been read out in Chapel, and the Master and Fellows were waiting to confirm the election. Jowett was not forthcoming. Men rushed to his rooms and the rooms of his friends. He was not to be found. W. Jenkins, the Blundell Scholar [2], by whom this incident is told, 'chanced to be going out of College, and when the gate was opened ran full tilt against him.' 'Jowett,' he exclaimed, 'you are elected.' 'Nonsense,' was the answer. 'You *are* elected, they are waiting for you in the Chapel.' Even then he could hardly be persuaded —till on his entering the gate other friends confirmed the tidings.

The spirit in which Jowett took his success appears from the letter which he wrote to his father at the time. It has been preserved in a long epistle of Mr. Jowett's to Mrs. Irwin in Australia, to whom he confides what was probably hidden from those more nearly concerned, his exultant pride and delight in the success of his son, and the ambitious dreams which it awakened in him; but also his fear of spiritual dangers which this might involve to Benjamin. There is no trace, as yet, of any constraint in the intercourse between the father and the son.

BALLIOL COLLEGE, *Friday Morning.*

My DEAREST FATHER,

You will be amazed and delighted to hear that I have been elected a Fellow of Balliol. There were four vacancies,

[1] Immediately after the election Scott reported the fact to roll his name among the candidates.'

his colleague in the work of Greek lexicography. Liddell then heard of Jowett for the first time.

[2] Late Rector of Fillingham.

and the four successful candidates are Woollcombe of Oriel, Lonsdale, Lake, and myself. The whole number of candidates was twenty-nine; of whom about eighteen had taken a First Class. I can never be sufficiently thankful to Providence for giving me the ability to obtain it, or for putting it into their minds to give it me. The expenses of getting in here are about £35. What the value of the Fellowship is during the probationary year I do not know, probably about £60 a year, and afterwards nearly £200. Scott (one of the Tutors) has, with his usual kindness, advanced me the money of his own accord. If repaid in a month it will be sufficient. Pray write to me by return of post, as your joy at my success is half the joy of having succeeded.

I am sorry to think of the unsuccessful candidates. One man whom they rejected, Wickens, is probably the ablest man in the University, and I should think *facile princeps* in the examination. The Master confesses that the only ground for it was his irregularity, not in moral conduct but in matters of discipline, when an undergraduate[1]. For Holden, whom you remember, I am also exceedingly sorry; he wrote a most affecting letter to Wickens which the latter showed me this morning. He said he could not but feel being beaten by one to whom he had been in the stead of a Tutor, 'the old man beaten by the boy.' Street's brother is another of the rejected candidates. I fear I must conclude, as I am engaged for a walk with Massie, &c. &c.

Believe me,

Yours affectionately,

B. Jowett.

PS. I should have written last night, but was really unable. A few lines to Mamma I scribbled off, but was sent for before

---

[1] Dr. Richard Congreve, who knew Wickens 'at home,' tells me that the Master said to the disappointed candidate, 'Mr. Wickens, we have elected in preference to you—a little child.' Wickens is the accredited author of the often-quoted repartee:—*Dr Jenkyns.* 'Mr. Wickens, I never stand at my window, but I see you passing.' *Wickens.* 'Indeed, Master, I never pass but I see you standing at the window.'

I had finished them.   Remember me to Mr. Turner, Johannes,
Aunt Courthope, Uncle, and all others.

That his letter to his mother should have remained
unfinished is not wonderful, considering the excitement
which his election had caused amongst his comrades.
This is recorded in a letter from James Sandham,
Commoner of St. John's (also transcribed by the glad
father):—

'Nothing has been talked about here so much for a long
time.   It is thought to be, as it is, a most wonderful achievement.   "Little Jowett" was nearly pulled to pieces when his
success was known ; one man shaking his hand with all his
might and two or three others contending for the other, till at
last, being hoisted above their heads, he was carried in triumph
round the quadrangle[1].'

When Jowett was Vice-Chancellor, one of his contemporaries whom he happened to be entertaining at
luncheon said, referring to this election. 'I then thought
you four the happiest people going.'   'So we were,' said
the Master in a cheerful tone.

A word may be added here *à propos* of 'little Jowett.'
The undergraduates of his own time seem to have shared
this impression with those who twenty years afterwards
loved to talk of 'little Benjamin their ruler.'   Yet it
was only partly justified.   Jowett was not 'little' in the
sense in which Dean Stanley and Dean Johnson of Wells
were little men.   He was really middle-sized, with rather
sloping shoulders, and a chest not broad but deep.   His
boyish countenance, like Milton's,

'Deceiving the truth
That he to manhood was arrived so near,'

---

[1] Cf. Mr. L. A. Tollemache, *Benjamin Jowett*, p. 43: 'He at once testified his joy by leaping as high as he could, and he was carried round the quadrangle on the shoulders of his friends.'

his delicate complexion, high-pitched voice, finely taper-
ing hands, and small well-moulded feet, contributed to
strengthen the illusion.

By a custom which prevailed for some time after
Jowett's election, the lessons in Chapel were read by
the two junior Fellows, and the undergraduates were
interested and perhaps amused to see this function
assumed by one of themselves [1].

The Long Vacation of 1839 began sadly. Much of
it was spent at home. His sister Ellen, who had long
been in failing health, died at Tenby on July 1 in that
year. Jowett's grief was silent but very deep. He wrote
of it at the time to his friend Greenhill; and in more
than one letter written during the last years of life he
spoke tenderly of those of his family whom he had
lost as being never absent from his thoughts.

The name of Benjamin Jowett appears in the First
Class *in Literis Humanioribus*, Michaelmas Term, 1839, in
the same list with Stafford H. Northcote of Balliol, and
James Fraser and William Kay, both of Lincoln College.

Before taking his degree he had engaged in private
tuition, and among his first pupils—not counting his
brothers Alfred and William Jowett, whom he had
tutored in the Long Vacation of 1838—were T. H. Farrer
of Balliol [2], who took honours in Easter Term, 1840, and
his brother Oliver, who appeared in the same Class List.

Lord Farrer's reminiscences contain the best record of
the impression which Jowett produced on others at this
time, and may fitly conclude the present chapter:—

---

[1] W. L. Newman and Charles
S. C. Bowen (Lord Bowen) are the
only undergraduate Scholars who,
since Jowett, have been elected
to the Fellowship. The Scholars' privilege was abolished in
1857.

[2] Lord Farrer.

'My first acquaintance with Jowett was as an undergraduate.
He gained the Balliol Scholarship in 1835, and I went up to
Balliol after Easter in 1837.   His youthful person, his round
hairless face, which in later years made that mother of nicknames, Mrs. Grote, call him "the cherub[1]"; his low shoes
and white stockings ; his brisk, tripping, almost childish gait ;
made him a noticeable figure in Balliol quad ; and they are
still present to me as a vivid image of what he was in early
youth, and the more so since the characteristic features of that
image remained traceable in him to the end.   He did not
at that time, I think, give any promise of the power which
he afterwards became.   I did not see much of him beyond
an occasional walk together, for he joined in no games ; and
though never an ascetic, or absorbed, as Clough was, in the
theological mists of that polemical time, he was absolutely
devoid of athletic propensities, and was I believe too poor
then to indulge in the hospitality which in later years was
so great a pleasure to him and to his friends.   To him, to
Brodie, to Hugh Pearson, and one or two others, I owed
a mental stimulus which was not to be found in the general
healthy, but not intellectual, society of the Eton and Harrow
men with whom I mostly lived.   Towards the end of my time
at Oxford, I lost the good coach—Elder—with whom I was
reading for my degree, and betook me to two Balliol men
equally kind, and perhaps equally well-read, but very different
in their effects on a pupil's mind.   One, who shall be nameless, made Aristotle's *Logic* as unintelligible to me as confusion
of thought in the interpreter can make the work of a great
master.   The other, Jowett (I really cannot remember what
he taught me), managed to make everything he taught suggestive and productive of thought.

'Indeed, if I were to attempt to characterize in a few words
the effect which Jowett's personality had upon me through

---

[1] She was anticipated, if I mistake not, by Mr. Edward Pigott
in the *Leader* (weekly) newspaper,
who wrote of him, in the early
fifties, as 'the middle-aged cherub.'

Another creator of nicknames,
Mrs. Ferrier of St. Andrews, used
to speak of him some years afterwards as the 'little downy owl.'—
L. C.

life, in our latest visits to one another as well as in those early days at Balliol, I should say that it was stimulating rather than formative. His instruction was not the explanation of a system of thought or the communication of cut and dried propositions, but the opening of a vista which you were to follow up yourself. He had the Socratic art of saying to youthful eagerness, "Are you sure you are right?" but of saying it in such a manner as to develop zeal in the pursuit of truth. He discouraged dogmatism, he encouraged thought. Perhaps this temper of mind was at a later period fostered by what I always felt to be his somewhat equivocal position with respect to the Church and Church doctrines; a relation which, whilst in some respects it gave him great power, I have often wished otherwise. But however this may be, I have always felt from those early undergraduate days down to the last visit I paid him in Balliol in 1893, that his effect on me was one of the most invaluable services one man can render to another, viz. the stimulation of mental and moral energy—of ἐνέργεια ψυχῆς κατ᾽ ἀρετήν, and he would have gladly added himself—ἐν βίῳ τελείῳ ("in a complete existence").

'I remember at one of the Balliol gatherings of which he was so fond, when going through his old friends in his after-dinner speeches, his referring to those old undergraduate relations between us by saying of me—"And then comes my old friend Farrer, of whom I may perhaps say, that something more might have come of him if he had not been my first pupil." I prize those words for their kindness, not for their truth.'

LETTERS, 1837–1839.

To W. A. Greenhill.

Cowes, 5 Trafalgar Place,
September 15, [1837].

. . . I went to call on Waldegrave. He was in Ireland with his father's ship, but his mother received me very kindly, so that I was really glad to have had an opportunity of seeing her. She almost did as much to dispel my prejudices against the Evangelicals, as the Welsh clergyman had done to increase them. Indeed I hope I see more and more the necessity of not proscribing any order of men, however widely we may differ from them in opinion.

There is a text very often quoted which it is hard to realize in its full meaning—'they that do the works shall know of the doctrine.' In the present state of the Christian world, especially at Oxford, it is a great consolation to think of this, if we do but begin at the right end by doing our duty first.

To W. A. Greenhill.

Ilfracombe, *August* 26, 1838.

You will be surprised at receiving this letter from me from the place from which it is written, but before I tell you anything about my doings, I must beg you to forgive my long silence, which has been caused by close employment in reading, and teaching my two brothers.

Whether you think this apology sufficient or no, I most sincerely hope that you will not interpret my neglect into unkindness or ingratitude.

You do not like my saying much on the latter head—the obligation to you—which I have never sufficiently felt, and in comparison with which all your other kindness however

great is as nothing—I mean your endeavour to keep me in
the right way [1].

. . . I came here three days since, and shall remain till the
end of the week. Before I leave I purpose walking along
the coast to Clovelly and back again, and from Linton to Bridg-
water. We had a terrible passage here by the steamer, which,
although the distance is but 80 miles, lasted two days. After
lying to the greater part of the first day we attempted to
proceed in the evening, but had not gone above a mile when
we were struck by a Welsh steamer. The carrying away of
the figurehead was the only injury we received, but as the sea
was running high the captain was afraid to proceed. We
arrived here after a stormy passage at six o'clock the next day.

. . . Speaking of Newman, there is an article in the last
Edinburgh on the life of Froude [2] in which, though gross injustice is done to the subject of it, there are some striking
and useful remarks. It is evidently written by a religious
man, and would I think please, and certainly not displease
you. How full religious people's minds are of what they
term the popery of Oxford—their violence against it being
in exact proportion to their ignorance. I do not either agree
with or understand many of Newman's principles, but cannot
help thinking that they will have on the whole a salutary
influence on the Protestant Church in bringing back men's
minds to a class of duties which have been too much neglected.
I fancy that in the ordinary divinity of the day, far too much
stress is laid on words; there is a sort of theological slang,
if I may be excused the expression, a religious phraseology,
in laying aside which you are supposed to be undermining

[1] More than fifty years after
this, in writing to Dr. Greenhill,
who had congratulated him on
his recovery from the almost fatal
illness of 1891, he referred to
their intercourse at this time:
'I shall always remember with
gratitude your great kindness to
me when I was a youth. I was
very weak and wayward in those
days, and had troubles to which
I was unequal, though I ought
not to have been so. . . . This
College has been a haven to me
for fifty-six, or, since I gained
a Fellowship, fifty-three years.'

[2] *Edinburgh Review* for July,
1838, 'Remains of Richard Hurrell
Froude.'

the fundamentals of the Christian Faith. Thus, if you do not draw a very distinct line between faith and works you are supposed to be unsound in doctrine, a distinction which seems to me to have arisen very much from a wrong application of St. Paul's words, referring to the works of the law and the principles of the Gospel, an opposition which I do not understand when applied to the faith and practice of the Christian covenant.

St. Paul's was not, I think, decided when you left. Kynaston was the successful candidate[1]. One circumstance gave me great pleasure. I was assured by an impartial person, that by far the best testimonial sent in was one for Massie, given by the Bishop of Llandaff without his application or knowledge.

To W. A. GREENHILL.

TENBY, *July* 2, 1839, *Tuesday Morning.*

I should have written to you before this, but the two last days have been so full of trouble and anxiety that I am sure you will excuse it.

My beloved sister is gone to her rest, nevermore to be disturbed by the cares and sorrows of this sinful world. The last two days of her life, it was the saddest scene I ever witnessed. At the beginning of the week there had been a great improvement, all symptoms of the disease having subsided. On Saturday morning a great change took place and the last struggle began. I am most thankful it is now all over; although I never saw death before, I do not think it can be often seen in so dreadful a form.

From the very beginning of her illness, with far more to attach her to life than most young persons, she did not wish to recover. We dwell very much on everything she said, as, from her being almost insensible during the last few weeks, she was unable to bear much testimony to the power of religion. While in health she read the Scriptures and prayed regularly, latterly visiting among the poor, and this gives me a far surer confidence than a few rapturous expressions on

[1] Kynaston succeeded Sleath as High Master of St. Paul's School, in June, 1838.

a death-bed would have done. On Sunday afternoon she became more sensible, and after reading two prayers from the Visitation of the Sick I asked her if she felt happy; she replied faintly that she did. I asked her to assure my mother that she was so (as the latter had made herself needlessly unhappy about it). She said she could hardly venture to do so. On Saturday, when in the greatest pain of body, she remembered the servant girl who waited upon her, requesting my elder sister to talk to her and have her taught to read the Scriptures.

I could tell you a great deal more about her, but my heart is too full to go on. When I remember her form and disposition, such as I never saw united in any one else, I feel persuaded that I can never again be so happy as I was before. I do not repine against Providence, but pray God that the scene of the last few days may for ever dwell in my mind and be a continual motive to love and serve Him. To me who feel my own weakness more and more contemptible, her strength of mind was quite extraordinary. But I feel I am running away into what I can hardly trust myself to speak of. Out of a family of nine there are now only five remaining, and I thank God that He has hitherto been pleased to take those who were best fitted to serve Him in heaven.

Since these pages were in type, the following entry from the Balliol Boat Club Records has been supplied by the kindness of the Hon. A. Henley and Mr. A. L. Smith :—

Saturday, June 2, 1838. Sculling sweepstakes at 2s. 6d. each, at 2 o'clock, from the top of the Long Reach, round the Island, up to Iffley. Order in rows, numbered as they came in.

1		2		3		4		5	
C. Sumner	11	Moberly	17	Davy	18	Estcourt	8	Powys	4
Swayne	12	Garnett	7	J. Sumner	13	Trower	9	T. Farrer	10
Jowett	14	Brodie	16	E. Hobhouse	15	Holbeck	3	Pocock	1
Moncrieff	2	Hardinge	19			R. Hobhouse	5		
						Northcote	6		

1st Prize, £2 10s.; 2nd Prize, £1 10s.; 3rd Prize, £1; 4th, recovered stake.

Each row had an umpire, who arranged by lot the place of his men—the starting-posts 10 paces apart—boats started with their heads level with the post.

N.B. 10 paces seemed barely enough.

CHAPTER IV

(Aet. 23-29)

THE years from 1840 onwards, though outwardly uneventful, were fertile in consequences. Jowett's increasing intercourse with Ward and Stanley, both of whom in different ways were leaders of the theological agitation then at its height, the commencement of his Tutorship, his own independent studies and reflections, to which the prospect of Ordination gave practical significance—all tended to promote the growth and consolidation of his mind. Friendships with younger men were also formed, which lasted to his latest breath. Through Stanley he already came into contact with the great world. An influence of which no one anticipated the extent or depth had its commencement here.

In the years which immediately followed his degree he seems to have spent part of the vacations in solitary

rambles;—accepting lifts from bagmen, stopping at way-
side inns, visiting Cathedral towns, and conversing with
all and sundry as occasion served him. His familiar
knowledge of English topography often surprised those
who had only known him in the retirement of his study.

Meanwhile in his own case that 'other work of
education[1]' of which he wrote in 1860 had begun. This
may be roughly dated from the completion of his Latin
Essay, which won the Chancellor's Prize in the spring of
1841. Stanley's efforts in favour of a large toleration had
his entire sympathy, and their intercourse, even in the
earlier years of Jowett's Fellowship, was pretty constant.
But a more intense albeit temporary influence was
working within the walls of Balliol. The strange and
powerful individuality of William George Ward had
not yet taken its final bent, and the communication
of his questionings and mental struggles in many
a dialectic argument produced a strong effect upon
young Jowett's mind. To Ward more than to any
other man he probably owed his first initiation into metaphysical inquiry. It is true that the Scotchmen,
especially John Campbell Shairp[2], brought with them
some Kantian enthusiasm, and that the prose writings
of S. T. Coleridge were already attracting attention in
Oxford; but the fervid and incessant talk of a senior

---

[1] 'As he grows older he mixes more and more with others; first with one or two who have great influence in the direction of his mind. At length the world opens upon him; another work of education begins; and he learns to discern more truly the meaning of things and his relation to men in general.'—'Essay on Interpretation,' *Epistles of St. Paul*, 3rd edition, vol. ii. p. 57.

[2] Principal Shairp used to tell how he had brought with him from Glasgow a copy of Kant's *Metaphysic of Ethic* (probably in Semple's translation) and lent it to Jowett, who afterwards went stamping about the quadrangle, as if to assure himself that the solid earth was beneath his feet.

colleague so vivacious as Ward must have been far more influential. In a conversational intercourse that never flagged, difficulties raised by Bentham, John Stuart Mill, or Auguste Comte were laid by the authority of the Fathers. Such were the strange cross-currents of the time. Years afterwards Jowett used to speak of Ward as a kind of Silenus-Socrates, whose delight it was to deliver young men of their doubts. For a brief while his influence drew Jowett powerfully in the direction of Newmanism [1].

'I sometimes think,' said Jowett once (about 1856), 'that but for some divine providence I might have become a Roman Catholic. I had resolved to read through the Fathers, and if I found Puseyism there I was to become a Puseyite. It is not unlikely that I might have found it, but before I had gone through my task the vacation ended, and on returning to Oxford we found that Ward was going to be married! After that the Tractarian impulse subsided, and while some of us took to German Philosophy, others turned to lobster suppers and champagne. They called that "being unworldly."'

Those words were lightly spoken, and at a later time. But in the early years of his Fellowship, with Ordination in prospect, theological difficulties had a serious practical import, especially in connexion with the then burning question of the meaning of Subscription. Tract XC

---

[1] Some years after this, January, 1849, he wrote to Stanley from Bonn, with reference to young Cruickshank (see above, p. 21): 'I think there are two classes of persons who turn Roman Catholics: one, the rationalizers like Capes and Ward, of whom my present type is a student or rather Ph. D. who comes here to teach us German, and who considers human nature to be a sign of interrogation which finds its answer in the Church: and the other, just the opposite class of persons, whose feelings are too deep for them ever to get on in the highways of the world, and who find the Church a home for the lonely.'

appeared on January 25, 1841, and was immediately
followed by an outburst of controversy. Jowett had
formed the habit, recommended by Locke, of tabulating
reasons for and against disputed propositions; and on
May 20 of this year he began a series of notes on the
question of Subscription, which still remain amongst
his papers. They are in pencil, and in a neat upright
hand, not unlike that of his sister Emily. While
reflecting much of the intellectual perplexity that was
rife in the Oxford of that day, these observations, which
would occupy about four pages of small print, bear also
the clear impress of an independent and finely balanced
mind, and of the intrepid determination to thrash out
the subject, not blinking any aspect of it, and to reach
a decisive judgement as a basis of action. On the whole
he seems to have been at the moment in favour of getting
the Articles simplified and reimposed by the authority
of the State.

'This seems really the practical thing to struggle for. If it
be said, it would drive many good men from the Church, it can
only be replied, that good men were driven out at the Restoration, and that we are apt to estimate the evil to religion by the
extent of evil to our personal friends. . . .'

'The Articles may include as many as they do now—only
without danger to men's consciences—those which are ambiguous now may be omitted—the Articles at present are
a sort of movable fence which may be shifted as far as you
please—the restraint they impose is purely imaginary. This
ideal restraint may be really useful, until men begin to push
at it; afterwards it is worse than useless.'

Under the existing conditions it seemed equally impossible to admit a strict construction or an indefinite
latitude.

'The original framers were not at one with themselves, or

with the second revisers, or with the Convocation which
sanctioned, or with the last revisers who put forth the
Articles.'

'It may be said—"Why not take them, as all good men do,
in their obvious sense?" Because this is impossible. The
Articles are irreconcilable with the Liturgy if both are taken
in their most obvious sense : both being equally imposed on
the clergy.'

'Again, it may not be denied that some licence is allowable—
it cannot be supposed that all the propositions in the Articles
were to be taken in their fullest sense. But where can we
draw the line about this licence, especially as every man sees
the Articles through his own spectacles?'

Once more, supposing the Articles to be imposed by the
State—

'We should be only obliged to take the test in the letter as
we should obey a law. . . . No one can say we are bound to
carry out in its full spirit a law we conceive to be indefensible.'

These notes are immediately followed by other discussions, which throw considerable light on this transition
phase of a cautiously comprehensive mind.

On the Relation of Tradition to Scripture.

'There seem to be several views on this subject.

'1. Of the extreme ultra-Protestant, who takes the Bible
and the Bible alone, without note or comment either of Fathers
or any one else, and professes that by the agency of prayer and
of the Holy Spirit he shall be guided into all truth.

'He would urge that the most ignorant people are capable
of receiving the saving truths of the Gospel and getting
comfort from them. And most truly so : but it must be
remembered as one of the most wonderful parts of Christianity
that it is a scheme which adapts itself not only to different
ages, but to different ranks of mind and education. The poor
man does not need a complete doctrinal system, and therefore

does not want the helps towards forming them from Scripture[1] ;
but the educated man does, and ought to, form such
a system. Further, it is impossible to say how much all men
through very different channels get of tradition.

'2. Of those who consider the Bible as the only inspired
writing, but think that for the right understanding of it
the same ordinary assistances are required as for the understanding any other moral or religious system.

'(The second view would give quite a sufficient authority for
all the doctrines and observances of the English Church.)

'3. Of the Anglican, who holds the Bible to be in the
highest sense inspired, but that the oral teaching of the
Apostles has been preserved by the Fathers of the Church,
whose writings, for this reason, have a claim to a secondary
kind of inspiration. That their only authority springs from the
preservation of Apostolical fragments, and that one only test
of this original doctrine is its catholicity—" Quod semper, quod
ubique, quod apud omnes "—counting the first three centuries
as preferable to all others, because nearer the fountain-head.

'(The objection to this view seems to be the doubt whether
such genuine remains can be traced ; they would be rather
found in the form of the Church itself than in creeds and
writings.)

'4. The view of the Romanist, that the decrees of the Church
represented by the Pope and a general Council (says the
[Cismontane]), of the Pope singly (says the Ultramontane),
are the sole authority for the interpretation of Scripture, as
well as an independent source from which new truth may flow.

'5. There is an opinion which may be placed between these
two, which denies the co-ordinate authority of the Church,
but places no limit to the interpretation of Scripture. The
Church may draw an important truth from a metaphor,
a similitude, a single word, any of the various senses which
a particular passage might be made to bear. This seems only
to differ from the former view in being dishonest ; it has the
appearance of reverence to Scripture while it only perverts it.

[1] This sympathy with the religious wants of the poor is a
feature which reappears prominently in the book on St. Paul.

It may prove purgatory from "every sacrifice, &c.," papal supremacy from the two swords of Peter, &c. This is a very different thing from the use of Scripture to prove Episcopacy.

'(Anglo-Catholic says that his view differs in an important respect from the papist, because it leads to the study of Scripture. Such a view would be grounded chiefly on the interpretation of the Old Testament by St. Paul and the practice of the early Fathers.

'It might be urged against the Romanist that he gives much less weight to S. S.[1] than the early Fathers, to which he would reply that S. S. stands in a much less important place in respect to the whole body of revealed truth, now than then.)'

These notes sufficiently indicate his attitude at the moment towards the Tractarian School. Another entry, 'On Strauss's Theory of Christianity,' shows how far his mind was opening to speculations of a different nature.

'Strauss considers Christianity to have been the offspring of a mythical age, enlightened indeed by revelation but forming a slender groundwork of facts into a mythic history. (The *a priori* truth which is supposed to be self-evident and which all these systems are intended to support is the subordination of Christianity to German philosophy.) A malefactor named Christ who was put to death for religious enthusiasm might undoubtedly have existed ; he was brought into the mythic scheme of the Jews, just as Xuthus into the Pelasgic mythology, but the attributes given to him were not those of a person but of a principle : he became the embodied representative of a new system of belief. (*Note.* A much more plausible theory would speak of Christianity as an inspired myth.) The Gospels were written many years after his death : they are full of miracles and supernatural appearances which the common sense of mankind has agreed to reject. Moreover they bear traces of two schools of mythic lore, a Jewish and a Greek, and for this reason are as full of discrepancies as any confused mythology of the Ancients. The doctrines are the dry core of truth which they contain.

[1] Scriptura Sancta.

These may be separated from the facts, as they rest too upon an internal evidence which the other cannot have.'

A brief note on the evidence of prophecy[1] further indicates the direction in which his thoughts were moving :—

'It is worth while considering in what the real evidence from prophecy consists—not certainly in the exact fulfilment of minute details giving occasion for all sorts of phantasies *à la* Prideaux and Newton, nor in the application of most of them (except those referring to our Lord) to a particular individual or time ; but in their general applicability to the Phenomena of the world in these latter days. They may be interpreted on large and liberal principles, as the words of Him "with whom a thousand days are as one day, and one day as a thousand years."

The same note-book contains the heads of similar discussions on 'The Respect due to our Mother Church,' 'Prayers for the Dead,' 'Transubstantiation,' 'Internal and External Evidence,' 'Romanism and Rationalism[2],' 'Romanism and Evangelicism,' 'The Patristic System,' 'The Power of the Keys,' 'Absolution,' 'The Via Media,' &c., all showing the drift of his thoughts and the resolution to let no doctrine pass unchallenged. It is evident that when, through his intercourse with Ward, he was most powerfully drawn towards Tractarianism[3], he was thinking actively and independently. The attraction was a strong one, however. Ward's influence in stimulating theological inquiry was not the less poignant and invasive, because of the many-sided activity of his

[1] Cf. *Remains of Rev. J. Davison,* author of *Discourses on Prophecy.*

[2] 'Both Romanism and Rationalism are founded in a great measure on metaphysical speculations, one of the Schoolmen, the other of German Philosophy.'

[3] There is little evidence of Jowett's having ever come directly under the spell which in these years J. H. Newman exercised over many minds.

intellect.   Readers of that delightful book *William George Ward and the Oxford Movement* will not readily forget either Professor Jowett's recollections therein embodied (pp. 112–114, 428, 439) or the picture of Ward as improvising a *ballet d'action*, in which he impersonated the Master (Jenkyns), mimicking the well-known voice and demeanour and 'pirouetting[1].'

It was probably to one who literally could have 'acted Falstaff without padding,' that Jowett owed his more intimate acquaintance with Shakespeare which began about this time.   He certainly always knew his Shakespeare best upon the comic side, seldom quoting any serious passages except from the *Tempest*[2], and now and then a familiar phrase from *Hamlet* or *Macbeth*. His junior contemporary John Duke Coleridge was also noted as a Shakespearian scholar and reciter.   But the enthusiasm of Coleridge, Shairp, and other friends for Wordsworth[3] and Tennyson, had in these earlier days little effect on Jowett.

After long separation, he met his old friend at Freshwater, in the Isle of Wight : this was about 1868, during one of his many visits to Farringford.   He was delighted,

---

[1] *W. G. Ward, &c.*, p. 40. Jowett's words to Stanley a year or two after Ward's admission to the Church of Rome, call up a picture of the man : 'I cannot resist the charms of the fat fellow whenever I get into his company.   You like him as you like a Newfoundland dog.   He is such a large, jolly, shaggy creature.   Though he is not yet changed into an Italian greyhound, the shagginess is beginning to wear off with the influences of a Southern climate.'

[2] On September 5, 1846, he wrote to R. R. W. Lingen : 'I have been reading Shakespeare daily.   The *Tempest* strikes me as one of the most remarkable and least understood plays.   Is it not a sort of English *Faust* ?'

[3] He said of one who was known amongst his comrades as 'the poet' (1846) : 'He is a very clever fellow and with considerable powers of mind, but obscured a little by the haze of Emerson and Wordsworth.'

as he told me, to find that his former comrade cherished warmly the recollection of earlier days. Mr. Lecky, who was present, witnessed the joyous eagerness of their re-greetings.

'He (Ward) reminded me,' says Jowett, 'that I charged him with shallow logic, and that he retorted on me with "misty metaphysics." This perhaps was not an unfair account of the state of the controversy between us[1].'

An outlet for the intellectual activity with which Jowett was brimming over at this time was afforded by a small debating society called the Decade. This is mentioned in a letter of George Butler's in 1841[2], which throws a welcome light on Jowett's relations with other contemporaries and on his position in the University. It appears that Jowett had proposed that Butler should be a member of this little club.

'I see Jowett occasionally; I like him very much. He is very quiet in manner, and does not show off to advantage in a roomful of men, but he is a very agreeable companion. He has made me an exceedingly kind offer, which I think you would like me to accept. He is a member of a debating society called the "Decade." I think there are twelve members now. They meet at each other's rooms for discussion on a subject previously announced. Among the members are Jowett himself, Lake (a Fellow of Balliol), Arthur Stanley (son of Bishop Stanley and Fellow of University College), Coleridge, Prichard, Matthew Arnold (eldest son of Dr. Arnold), Blackett[3], and a few others. They elect members without their knowledge, and then ask them to join the society, which precludes all canvassing. I am pleased beyond measure at the prospect of getting into such an excellent set, consisting, as you may see, of the picked men of the University.'

---

[1] *W. G. Ward, &c.,* p. 438.
[2] *Recollections of George Butler by his wife, Josephine Butler,* p. 31.
[3] John F. B. Blackett, Fellow of Merton, afterwards M.P. for Newcastle. He died in 1856.

In the summer of 1841, Jowett made what seems to
have been his first foreign tour, in company with a friend
whose initials are J. P. Entering the Continent at
Ostend, they visited Antwerp, Brussels, Malines, Ghent,
Liége, and other Cathedral towns in Belgium, Trèves and
the valley of the Moselle, Coblentz, the Rhine, Mayence,
and Heidelberg. He makes careful notes of the architecture of the Cathedrals, the sculptures in wood and
marble, the chief pictures, and the religious habits of
the people; also of the Roman remains at Trèves; and
he gives a picturesque description of the scenery of
the Moselle. He had already commenced the serious
study of Political Economy, and one page is filled
with observations 'On the state of the poor—Schwal-
bach.' On another page there is a list of works on
Political Economy to be got for the College Library, and
also a series of acute general remarks on the New
Science, on the Industrial Revolution which had given
rise to it, on the importance of the subject, its relation
to morality, and the uncertainties attending it.

Two extracts from the notes of this tour may serve
to show how his speculative thoughts were balanced
with an active habit of intelligent observation:—

'The Moselle, a muddy, rapid stream running between hills
clad with vines and underwood—sometimes rugged and pre-
cipitous—sometimes shelving down in layers to the water's
edge—at others opening into a sort of amphitheatre, at the
foot of which the river takes its winding course. In many
places it has the appearance of a lake seeming to spring from
the successive ranges of hills which cross one another until
lost in the vista. Sometimes scenery varied by the cornfields
which wave on the very top of the steep. The vines in many
places stretch as far as the eye can reach.

'Low down on the river the rocks become more craggy and
terrible, gradually closing in so as to conceal the river from

view : the ruins of old castles raised on eminences greatly increase the picturesqueness of the scene.

'Another feature of the river is the villages with which the bank is studded — each with its church and school and picturesque houses with wooden frameworks.'

'The Church of St. Paulinus (Trèves). Italian architecture, the sides of the interior ornamented with pilasters terminated by coloured capitals with projecting entablature, intended to harmonize with the painted roof, a very curious piece of work executed about a hundred years ago. It is intended to represent the martyrdom of 40,000 Christians who perished at Trèves in the Diocletian persecution. At one end of the picture the work of slaughter has commenced, the waters of the Rhine are flowing red : about the centre Christ and the Father are represented with the cross.'

When he returned to Balliol in October, 1841, although not yet Tutor, he began to take a share in the teaching of the College. This is evidenced by notes for lectures on Aristotle and Butler, long strings of questions, and subjects for essays, and other hints for classical instruction, in the note-book of which so much has here been said. He appears as 'Assistant Tutor' in the Oxford Calendar of 1842 (brought up to date for December, 1841).

In 1842 he took Deacon's Orders. From the dry light of speculation which shines through the disquisitions above quoted, it is not to be inferred that, at this time, his emotional nature was not also deeply stirred. The truth comes out in his letters to his friend Greenhill (inserted at the end of this chapter), with whom for a time he seems to have indulged in an interchange of 'religious sympathy.' There are traces in them of some inequalities of health and spirits—perhaps also of inward struggles.

A sentence in the letter from Bonn, June 28, 1842 [1], in which he deprecates further correspondence on this subject, is characteristic and biographically important.

Like every act of his life, his Ordination vows were realized by him with deep intensity. This was manifested not only by increasing devotion to his pupils, but by single incidents, in which he boldly broke through conventionality, in accordance with the spirit of his profession, and overcame his natural shyness.

From that moment, and to the end of his life, he was in the truest sense a 'son of consolation.'

Sir Henry Acland has favoured us with the following account of a fact in his own experience which exemplifies this :—

'I first saw Mr. Jowett in 1844 at the country house of Sir Benjamin Brodie (Betchworth, Surrey [2]), the grandfather of the present Baronet.

'Mr. Jowett was a close friend of the eldest son, afterwards Professor of Chemistry here, and was on a visit to Sir Benjamin. I was weak and ill, and one night when Jowett heard I was sleepless, he came quietly into my room, sat by the bedside, and said in that small voice, once heard never to be forgotten, "You are very unwell, I will read to you": and he read in the same voice the fourteenth chapter of St. John, and said, "I hope you will feel better," and went away, and often, often have I thought of this during Oxford controversies.'

His sense of his vocation in another aspect may be illustrated by the following anecdote. When staying at a country house, amongst men of great literary reputation, when the host, then but slightly known to him, made use of some Rabelaisian expression—unaware perhaps for the moment that he was entertaining a clergyman—

---

[1] See p. 109.
[2] Broome Park, Betchworth, Surrey, was the seat of Sir B. Brodie, M.D., the first baronet, who died there in 1862.

Jowett said quite simply, ' Mr. ——, I do not think myself
better than you, but I feel bound to disapprove of that
remark.' This attitude was maintained consistently in
later life, but with differences of method, in accordance
with his increasing knowledge of men and things. At
a Scotch shooting lodge, somewhere in the sixties, he
insisted on going down to the smoking-room with the
others at a late hour, and when the conversation of the
younger men took a doubtful turn, the small voice that
had been silent hitherto, was suddenly heard—' There is
more dirt than wit in that story, I think.' Once again,
in the eighties, when at Balliol after dinner some old
companion ventured on dangerous ground, he quietly
said, 'Shall we continue this conversation with the
ladies?' and rose to go [1].

From this epoch also may be dated a marked expansion of that cheerful helpfulness which had always
characterized him, but received a new impulse from
his Ordination vow. No minister of Christ ever more
fully realized the precepts, 'Strengthen thy brethren,'
'Support the weak,' 'It is more blessed to give than to
receive.' Many of his best thoughts on Law, Political
Economy, Statesmanship, the management of an estate,
the conduct of a public office, were drawn from him by
his practical sympathy with friends whose position was
most unlike his own, and whose opportunities, difficulties,
and responsibilities he sought to understand in order to
advise them better. His own work, already sufficiently
heavy, was often multiplied by taking on himself the
duties of others who were temporarily disabled.

A letter to B. C. Brodie, written in October, 1844, shows
his feeling on the subject of religion in the years following
his Ordination. Brodie's scientific studies had led him

[1] Cf. *Benjamin Jowett*, by L. A. Tollemache, p. 116.

to express opinions which to Jowett's mind savoured
of materialism :—

'What appears to me to make the greatest gulph between
us, is not your taking a rationalistic or mythic view of the
Bible, or difficulties about miracles, or even prayer, but that
you do not leave any place for religion at all, so that although
you may hold the being of God as the Author of the Universe,
I do not see how you would be worse off morally if Atheism
were proved to demonstration. What would you lose but
a little poetry, which is a very weak motive to holiness of
life?   And having shut yourself out from any moral relation
to God as an incentive to Duty, does this moral Atheism
satisfy human nature ?'

Behind all ecclesiastical obligations, all speculative
difficulties, were the realities in which he afterwards
summed up the influences of religion—'the Power of
God, the Love of Christ, the efficacy of Prayer[1].'

And at the centre of his religious life, both then and
afterwards, was his conception of the Person of Christ, the
divine image of the Father, the Elder Brother, the Sinless
One, the Friend of sinners, who went about doing good ;
never sparing rebuke, yet to whom all would soonest go
for confession; who called His chosen ones not servants
but friends, and having loved His own, loved them to
the end.

The Summer Term of 1842 seems to have been spent in
Paris, where he passed much time in the great libraries,
pursuing eagerly an ambitious course of study.   From
Paris he went to Bonn with a pupil, and made the
acquaintance of Nitzsch, the great Homeric scholar.   It
was here that he received from A. C. Tait the news of
Dr. Arnold's death.   He had been greatly impressed with
Arnold's inaugural lecture in the previous December,

[1] *Epistles of St. Paul*, 3rd edition, vol. ii. p. 126.

and had also seen him in the Balliol Common Room,
where he witnessed the meeting of Arnold with W. G.
Ward after some passages of arms between them [1].

These visits to Paris and Bonn prepared the way for
his parents' residence in the Rue Madeleine from 1846
onwards, and their temporary retirement to Bonn during
the disturbances of 1848.

In October, 1842, soon after Tait's appointment to
succeed Dr. Arnold at Rugby, Jowett became a Tutor of
the College.   The old Master hesitated about giving the
Tutorship, vacated by Lonsdale [2], to so young a man.
But he was prevailed upon by the urgency of Woollcombe.

The standard of a College Tutor's work at Oxford had
been considerably raised since the commencement of the
century [3] : first by the Tutors of Oriel, amongst whom were
Richard Whately [4] and J. H. Newman, and still more
at Balliol by Jowett's predecessor, Archibald Campbell
Tait.   The following entry from Tait's private Journal [5]
speaks volumes as to the ideal which he had set before
him :—

'*Nov.* 16, 1839. *Memorandum.*—What can be done . . . to
make more of a pastoral connexion between the Tutors and

[1] *W. G. Ward and the Oxford
Movement*, p. 438.

[2] Earlier in the same year
Lonsdale had written to his
mother: 'You laugh at my pope
Jowett, but really I know of
nobody so clever. Several here
look upon him and Stanley as
quite the cleverest persons here.
The only fault in them both is
that they are too purely intellectual, and rack their brains
from morning to night' (*Life of*

James Lonsdale, p. 23).

[3] Cyril Jackson (d. 1819), who
preferred the Deanery of Christ
Church to a Bishopric and did
so much to promote the Oxford
Honours system, seems to have
stood almost alone amongst his
contemporaries as an educator of
young men.

[4] Afterwards Archbishop of
Dublin.

[5] *Life of Archibald Campbell
Tait*, 3rd ed. 1891, vol. i. p. 72.

their pupils? What can be done for making the Tutor more fully superintend his individual pupil's reading, without mere reference to the Schools? What for reviving provisions to enable the lower classes to profit by the Universities, as they did when Servitorship existed[1]?'

Jowett entered upon the task, as thus conceived, with all the freshness and ardour of youthful devotion. But some time passed before he began to reap the reward of his labours. In the years from 1841 to 1844 inclusive, Balliol was not very fortunate in the Schools. For whatever reasons, both Arthur Clough and Matthew Arnold were placed in the Second Class; and the only Balliol Firsts of these years, in eight Class Lists, were Constantine Prichard in Michaelmas Term, 1841, and Frederick Fanshawe and Frederick Temple in Easter Term, 1842.

Jowett's power as a teacher did not at once fully assert itself. His reputation in those early days rested more upon Scholarship than on Philosophy. All admired the beauty of his Latin prose, and generally the felicity and grace of his literary expression. It was only towards the end of the period now under consideration, that he commenced those lectures on the History of Philosophy which first revealed to a select number of his pupils the larger scope of his thoughts. This was probably after his return from Germany in 1844. Such men as Clough and Matthew Arnold were too conscious of their own powers to see what lay beneath their youthful teacher's quiet but rather peremptory manner; and in return, while Clough's personality certainly impressed him, for he reverted to it in his last days on earth, it was not until long afterwards that he learned to take

[1] On the position and work of an Oxford Tutor in 1825-1835, see Mozley's *Reminiscences*, vol. i. p. 33 ff.

Matthew Arnold seriously. His closer intimacy with
F. Temple dates from somewhat later, when Temple had
become a Junior Fellow.

From the Easter Term of 1845 onwards Balliol Scholars
again take First Classes, as a matter of course; and it is
at this point that Jowett's success as a College Tutor
becomes established. The honours gained by James
Riddell and Edwin Palmer[1], both in 1845, mark the
commencement of a fresh series of Balliol successes; and
the degree in which this was referable to Jowett may be
gathered from Archdeacon Palmer's reminiscences[2].

Jowett's position amongst his colleagues appears from
a recollection of Lord Lingen's, who had been elected
to a Fellowship in 1841, and was present at a College
meeting in 1844, when plans for the rebuilding of the
College, sent in by Pugin and other architects, were
under discussion. The Master (Jenkyns) had given his
opinion in a knock-me-down style, and Lingen imagined
that no one was likely to 'take the bull by the horns.'
His surprise when the youthful Tutor began to speak
was equalled by his admiration of the calm, firm, and
clear manner in which Jowett expressed an opposite
opinion.

If this period begins with Ward, it ends with Arthur
Stanley. It appears from Ward's Life[3] that while preparing his *Ideal of a Christian Church* in 1844, he
had withdrawn from close habitual intercourse with
the more liberal amongst his former friends. In the
summer of that year Jowett joined with Stanley in a tour

[1] The late Venerable Edwin Palmer, Archdeacon of Oxford.
[2] See p. 102.
[3] p. 438. Jowett, in referring to their intercourse, says, 'I am speaking chiefly of the years between 1840 and 1844.'

to Germany [1]. An entry in one of the Master's note-books, shortly after the death of the Dean of Westminster, records the fact that at this time, more than ever before or afterwards, he poured out his whole heart to Stanley. They had already been reading Hebrew together, and Stanley mentions that in the course of the journey the travellers 'supported their weary minds by alternate reading, analyzing, and catechizing, on Kant's *Pure Reason*.' Jowett's familiarity with German is clearly shown by his writing more than once in that language at some length to Arthur Stanley, out of mere playfulness, in 1844-6. The interest of the tour did not culminate for both companions at the same point. Not the Holy Coat at Trèves nor the antiquities at Nuremberg, but the Congress of Philologers at Dresden—'one of the most uninteresting places,' says Stanley, 'that I ever saw '— made the deepest impression upon Jowett's mind. To converse with Gottfried Hermann [2], with Lachmann, Immanuel Bekker, and Ewald, made an era in his intellectual life. It was probably here also that the two friends consulted J. E. Erdmann of Halle [3], the Hegelian disciple, on the best manner of approaching the works of Hegel. The introductions which Stanley had brought with him, due to the friendship between Dr. Arnold and the Chevalier Bunsen, must have greatly facilitated all such intercourse. Nor is the performance of the *Medea* before the Philologers, presumably in Greek, to be regarded as a wholly insignificant circumstance.

---

[1] *Life of Dean Stanley*, vol. i. pp. 326 ff.

[2] To Stanley from Bonn, January, 1849: 'Do you know, Hermann died last week, "der frische lebendige Mann"?' At Bonn Jowett made the acquaintance

of Nitzsch, Brandis, and Dörner.

[3] Erdmann was born in 1805. His *Geschichte der Philosophie* was in course of publication at this time, and the Jubilee of his Professorship at Halle was celebrated in 1889.

In a letter to B. C. Brodie, where he sums up the impressions derived from the tour, he mentions this congress as especially memorable:—

'*November* 5, 1844.

'I hardly know whether our tour will much interest you: it went as far as Vienna, and with some disagreeables was eminently successful. An infinite quantity of talk was one result, for which there was some excuse, as we had nothing else to do. . . . We returned by Dresden, where we saw old Hermann, who seemed to be undergoing a sort of apotheosis at the hands of a great Philological Association who dined and fêted him in every possible way. Various others, Zumpt's *Latin Grammar*, Thiersch's *Greek Grammar*, Wunder's *Sophocles*, Lachmann's Greek Testament, who were formerly supposed to be myths, also sprang up into life and reality.'

Though Stanley was the more enthusiastic traveller, his companion appears to have had a chief part in planning the details of the tour. Stanley would have spent the whole of every day in sight-seeing, but Jowett insisted on reserving certain hours for study: he had brought the still recent Liddell and Scott amongst his luggage; Stanley nicknamed this 'the monster grievance,' in allusion to a phrase of O'Connell's, and dubbed his friend 'the inexorable Jowett.'

Although the posthumous influence of Hegel in his own country had already culminated and was beginning to decline, it was still powerful with many students of Philosophy, and had begun to exercise a wide influence upon Theology. The complete edition of his works and his Life by Rosenkranz had lately appeared, and from this visit to Germany, repeated in the following year, Jowett's more intimate acquaintance with this special phase of German philosophy may be dated [1]. For several

[1] Professor W. Wallace remembers Jowett telling him how he once stood on a bridge at Mainz absorbed in Hegel's Preface to the *Encyclopädie*.

years after this he remained an ardent, though still an independent, student of Hegel[1]. How critically he studied the philosophy even when most absorbed in it appears, however, from a letter to Stanley of August 20, 1846, in which he says :—

'Hegel is untrue, I sometimes fancy, not in the sense of being erroneous, but practically, because it is a consciousness of truth, becoming thereby error. It is very difficult to express what I mean, for it is something which does not make me value Hegel the less as a philosophy. The problem of ἀλήθεια πρακτική, Truth idealized and yet in action, he does not seem to me to have solved ; the Gospel of St. John does. Hegel seems to me, not the perfect philosophy, but the perfect self-consciousness of philosophy.'

Dr. Whyte's Professorship of Moral Philosophy was vacated by Sacheverell Johnson in the autumn of 1844, and Jowett allowed his name to be sent in for the post : 'Because I feel,' he writes[2], 'that it would suit me better than any other Chair.' He does not consider himself a serious candidate if H. H. Vaughan should stand : 'I would much sooner hear him than teach myself.' But he thinks that Vaughan's theological opinions may possibly stand in his way. The Chair was ultimately conferred on H. G. Liddell, who held it only for a year.

In the excitement which followed Newman's retirement to Littlemore and the publication of the *Ideal of a Christian Church*, Stanley and Jowett were intimately associated, and while the elder man took the more active part, as at this time his position in the University was much more prominent, he found no small support and help from consultation with Jowett, who in November,

---

[1] 'One must go on or perish in the attempt, that is to say, give up Metaphysics altogether. It is impossible to be satisfied with any other system after you have begun with this.'—Letter to B. C. Brodie, September 28, 1845.

[2] To B. C. Brodie, October 15.

1844, was already assisting him in the preparation of a
Protest on the subject. They were together at the scene
of the degradation of Ward in February, 1845 [1]. The
events of that day have often been described, but no-
where more graphically than by Dean Stanley and in
the Memoir of Dean Church, who, as Junior Proctor, took
a memorable part in the proceedings. The latter work
contains a graphic piece of description at first hand
which may be quoted here.

'Mr. Church's youngest brother, then an undergraduate at
Oriel . . . had stationed himself at a window in Broad Street,
in order better to view the proceedings ; and he recalls the
excitement of the moment, the sight of the crowd, which still,
after the procession had entered, lingered round the railings
that enclose the Theatre—the dull roar of the shouting which
could be heard at intervals from within the building itself—
and at last the appearance of the assemblage streaming out
through the snow, the big figure of Ward emerging among the
earliest, with his papers under his arm, to be greeted with
shouts and cheers, which passed into laughter as, in his hurry,
he slipped and fell headlong in the snow, his papers flying in
every direction [2].'

The scene within the Theatre was vividly described by
Jowett in a letter to Brodie written a day or two after
the great event :—

'. . . The 13e Février came off last Thursday, a most tragic
scene which the inclemency of the weather contributed to
heighten. 1300 wild country parsons are calculated to have
come up to do battle on the occasion : the Theatre was crammed ;
Ward in the rostrum with Oakeley for prompter. The V. C.
and Hebdomadals take their places. Ward requests leave
to speak in English, which is granted ; and then began an
oration containing some of the unpleasantest words to the ears
of country clergy that were ever spoken. He supposed there

---

[1] *Life of Dean Stanley,* vol. i.   [2] *Dean Church's Life and Let-*
p. 340.   *ters,* p. 55.

were men of all parties present—High Church, Evangelicals, &c., and compared the first with the Articles, the second with the Liturgy. Their difficulties were obvious, but neither party had the least conception of them. He then supposed the Evangelical to become High Churchman—in what a new light all things would present themselves!—his view of the Articles would vary with his opinions. He himself took the Articles in a non-natural sense, as they all did, and what he wanted to show was that they were not all dishonest but all honest together. The rest of his speech was a complaint of the unfitness of the Court, and the impossibility of making any real defence before them. In conclusion, he warned them of the present state of the Church of England, which might last as a framework to hold them all, but if they pulled out a single stone would fall together.

'I cannot give you any idea of his manner. He was as much at home with his audience as he is in the C. R.[1] after dinner. He read a passage from a pamphlet of Maurice's to prove some point, which spoke of himself in a manner far from complimentary, interjecting—"He means me, he has no very good opinion of me, he says he would rather go to a dame's school and be a dustman than do what I have done." Another time he threw in a parenthesis—"Believing as I do the whole cycle of Roman doctrine"—which threw his audience into a titter by the extreme simplicity with which it was said. At the end he stood forth with prophetic voice and told us of what was to happen in "the latter days."

'The vote of censure was passed by a majority of 770 to 380. Ward again made a short speech in arrest of judgement, but he was condemned by 570 to 510. Only the drawing and quartering was remitted. For the "Horrendum Carmen," a fragment preserved in the statute *de degradatione*, runs as follows:—

> Heréticum vicecancellárius iúdicet.
> Si ad convocatiónem provocátur
> Provocatióne certánto,
> Si vincent, pileum exúito:
> Capúceum, tógam detráhito:
> Combúrito íntra vel extra Universitátem.

[1] The Balliol Common-room.

'We returned home with the feelings of men who had witnessed an execution or rather had themselves been executioners at an *Auto da Fé*. Perhaps you will wonder at my levity in treating of the whole affair, but it is the only way I can revenge myself for having looked upon it seriously a week ago.

'The tragedy is now at an end, and the comedy or what I must call the tragi-comedy is about to begin; but the curtain is not yet drawn up for the public. Do you remember the end of the *Beggars' Opera* where, after the feelings of the spectators are wrought to the highest pitch, a sort of [dramatic revolution] takes place and by poetic justice the execution is turned into a WEDDING? Between the first and second acts of the above-mentioned tragedy, letters were brought to the prisoner in his cell, written in a fair Italian hand,

> And whiter far than that whereon it wrote
> Was the fair hand that writ.

'In a word, our Confessor is going to be married.

'I do not of course blame Ward for this in itself, but I think he is very much to blame for recklessly writing a book which has thrown us into confusion and then doing precisely the thing most inconsistent with his own principles, and lastly, instead of retiring from the contest as he ought under the circumstances, he has fought it out to the last. Either he felt himself called to announce a high and important truth or his book is absolutely indefensible. A man in love is not exactly the person to breathe the spirit of Hildebrand or Innocent. I believe he has not the least conception of the ludicrous point of view which he will present to a mocking world, and am truly sorry for it for his sake.'

Stanley always claimed for the little band of Oxford Liberals, including himself, Jowett, Donkin, and Greenhill, the merit of having moderated the violence of that day's proceedings, not only by the moral support they gave the Proctors (H. P. Guillemard of Trinity and R. W. Church of Oriel) in the courageous act of vetoing the condemnation of Tract XC, but still more by their strenuous

opposition to the proposal 'that the Vice-Chancellor
should have power at any time to require a member of
the University, in order to prove his orthodoxy, to subscribe the Articles in the sense in which they were both
first published and were now imposed'—which motion
was withdrawn within a few days of the meeting of
Convocation, partly in consequence of an opinion of
counsel which Stanley and others had obtained[1]. This
claim on Stanley's part was admitted thirty-one years
afterwards by the person most competent to speak of it,
when Dean Church wrote to Dean Stanley in 1876, ' It was
a very generous as well as wise action on your part and
that of the men who joined with you[2].'

With what alacrity Jowett had thrown himself into
this course of action, what part he took both in stimulating and guiding it, how he realized the full significance
of the situation, especially as it affected the future of
the Church of England, is made apparent by a letter to
Stanley written in the Christmas vacation preceding the
event, which vividly reflects both the sanguine eagerness
of the writer and the persons of most account in Oxford
at that critical time. It will also be observed that the
chief stress is laid, not on Ward's danger, but on the
principle involved in the ' New Test.'

' It is difficult to choose out of the medley of opinions you
sent me. I am glad that Liddell signs.—In a sense I agree
with them all.

' I agree with Milman in thinking that the short protest
might advantageously be worked up into an eloquent document, when you have felt the temper of the people who are
going to sign it. Meanwhile in its prosaic form it is already
printed. I should send it round in MS. to likely persons as
something like the document in its poetic form which they

[1] *Life of Dean Stanley,* vol. i. p. 335.   [2] *Life of Dean Church,* p. 58.

are hereafter to have. This latter it would be an appropriate compliment to Milman to ask him to assist in writing, as he seems to have ideas upon the subject.

'I think persons innumerable should be written to with respect to the Test exclusively. What Lake says is quite true—Ward's case is comparatively unimportant and very unpopular. Besides the protest there are clearly only two things to be done, a shower of pamphlets to be written by all sorts of persons putting the matter in every different light— also private letters to all one's old College friends, &c. Will you write to Blackett, Congreve, and Donkin, urging them to canvass against the Test immediately; also to Tait, dropping the Wardian part of the question?

'Could any Oxford Bishop, Longley, or Denison, be got to express his opinion on the Test before it comes on? Would it not be worth while to write to Hamilton[1] and put a view of the case before him? Get Lake to write to Burrows and Trench—and so ascend to Archdeacon Samuel[2]. . . . Write to H. Vaughan[3]. Might he not be got to write something?— it ought to touch heterodox laymen to the quick. I trust we shall never have any more agitation. I suppose it to be a duty, but, as I have often said, I feel peculiarly unfit for it and, what is more, people think that I am going out of my place, which is not the case with you.'

In the Long Vacation of 1845, after visiting Lake in Germany[4], he again travelled with Stanley, whose sister joined them at Ischl. The two friends had spent some weeks together at Berlin, where Jowett observed curiously the state of Prussian politics, the King's 'idea of government being to tread in the steps of Frederick the Great and preserve Prussia as he had raised it, by

[1] Afterwards Bishop of Salisbury.

[2] Samuel Wilberforce became Bishop of Oxford in 1845.

[3] Henry Halford Vaughan, afterwards Professor of Modern History.

[4] A letter from E. Bastard to F. T. Palgrave, July 20, 1845, mentions that Lake was in Germany on account of health, and Jowett had joined him there, 'much to his comfort,' as he had been very solitary before.

a military despotism.' There also he had the interviews
with Schelling and Neander of which he afterwards
spoke. He wrote to Brodie (September 28):—

'I must say I was very much pleased with the old "twaddler"
Schelling. He was exceedingly kind, and thoroughly modest
and unassuming. We saw him several times, when he talked
about Coleridge, who he said was unfairly attacked for
plagiarism from himself in *Blackwood's Magazine*. He struck
me as having more of the poet than of the philosopher about
him—and far more genius than strength of character. I do
not know anything about his philosophy, and to judge from
Schelling's face it is probably somewhat dreamy, but it was
evident that there is so much party spirit that it was impossible
to form a judgement of what you heard, and it is in his favour
that Steffens, who was universally respected, was his follower
to the last.'

With reference to this tour Mrs. Vaughan (then
Catherine Stanley) writes (1894):—

'My sister and I went out alone to Ischl—where we met
him and my brother—and where we remained with them
a fortnight. After which, we went on our way—but what
that "way" was, I am ashamed to say I cannot remember.
I know we went across Bohemia, and we were most anxious
to get into Italy by the Stelvio; but were prevented by my
brother's inability to get up early enough to accomplish it in
the only time at our disposal. He and B. J. were deep
in those days in the study of Hebrew, and could hardly
be persuaded to look up from their books and contemplate
the beauties of the scenery through which we passed. We
used to exclaim, "Oh, do look! how beautiful!" and they
would hastily raise their eyes, cry out, "Yes, very fine," and
as hastily return to the contemplation of their Grammar. In
those days B. J. was, as I have said, the most charming friend
and companion it was possible to have: never out of temper,
never depressed, never looking weary or discontented—always
full of the most interesting subjects of conversation. He was
delightful.'

The *Hebrew Grammar*[1], with Jowett's name written in ink over Stanley's in pencil, and with pencilled annotations by B. J. (chiefly a running analysis of the Hebrew syntax), is now in the possession of Lady Lingen, to whom Jowett gave it when he had himself relinquished the study at the end of 1846, finding that to be a critical Hebrew scholar required more time than he could give. He always said that even a smattering of Hebrew was worth while: 'it gave you a new idea of language.' He was studying the Hebrew Bible in the autumn of 1846, when, according to a letter of E. Bastard to F. T. Palgrave, he had been working very hard at Hebrew :—

'The day he went away from here, he was reading (as we afterwards heard) the Hebrew Bible as he went along,—and ended by leaving it in the coach[2].'

Shortly before this, while working at Ewald's *Hebrew Grammar*, he had written to Stanley, 'I am hard at work at Hebrew and really begin to find some enjoyment in reading it.' But at the opening of 1847 he wrote, 'I find Hebrew too trying to the eyes to be pursued to any great extent, and am accordingly reading the *Republic* for lectures next Term.'

His letters to Stanley, a few of which are appended to this chapter, make it manifest that the influence of the elder upon the younger friend was more than reciprocated. When Stanley was preparing his sermons on the Apostolic Age, Jowett was consulted at every step, and his letters reveal in a remarkable way the character and working of his own mind.

He was ordained priest in 1845. Earlier in that year, he had been occupied in writing some Theological Essays;

[1] Gesenius, ed. Rödiger, Leipzig, 1845.
[2] Bastard was one of Riddell's reading party who visited Jowett and his pupil at Beaumaris, August 16, 1846.

and in 1846 his systematic study of the New Testament was stimulated by an idea which Stanley had suggested to him, that he should contribute a series of Essays to the volume which his friend was preparing for the press. This particular design was not carried out, as Jowett ultimately declined to publish in this way; but it was agreed that they should produce a joint work in Theology at some future time. Meanwhile, in what he afterwards called their 'furious' correspondence he communicates his anxious thoughts on New Testament criticism.

Stanley, in his Life of Dr. Arnold (1844), had laid special stress on the importance which his master attached to the critical study of Theology, and his intention of setting on foot a 'Rugby Edition' of St. Paul's Epistles under his own superintendence[1]. There can be no reasonable doubt that the work now undertaken had some reference to this unfulfilled design of the great Head Master. In one of their afternoon walks, the two friends were caught in a heavy shower of rain and driven to take refuge in a quarry. It was under these circumstances, as Jowett afterwards told W. L. Newman, that in eager conversation the plan of the work was sketched in outline. Nine years elapsed before the publication in part of what was then projected. The plan was more than once modified after its main outlines had been agreed upon, and at one time it was enlarged to a scheme for a complete work on the New Testament. In a letter of 1846, Jowett writes to Stanley :—

'I have been thinking a good deal about our Opus Magnum, and trust that by God's blessing we may be able to bring it to some result. I propose to divide it into two portions, (a) the Gospels, and (b) the Acts and Epistles, to be preceded respectively by two long prefaces, the first containing the hypothesis

[1] *Arnold's Life and Correspondence*, p. 163 of sixth edition.

of the Gospels, and a theory of inspiration to be deduced from it; the second to contain the "subjective mind" of the Apostolic age, *historisch-psychologisch dargestellt.* I think it should also contain essays on such subjects as "eschatology," "the demoniacs," &c., which cannot be properly effigiated in notes.'

In the autumn of 1846 he had a vision of a 'flight to Ireland with Stanley, to examine into the constitution and Revenues of Trinity College, &c.,' which was broken off by some change in Stanley's plans. The letters to Stanley belonging to this period which are preserved are very numerous, and they dwell on many points of merely temporary interest. But those not here included contain some morsels which it would be a pity to lose : as this on self-improvement (1846):—

'Can any summary rule be given more than this, every day and every hour to frame yourself with a view to getting over a weakness? How a person does this can only be learnt from experience, not, I think, to be intruded on by others. But the line you quote in the Preface to Arnold's Life, "That moveth all together if it move at all¹," seems to me ever to be borne in mind in all these things. If a defect be anything more than a trick, character is too elastic to admit of any mechanical contrivance for getting rid of it.'

Or again this passing remark on the words 'I, if I be lifted up from the earth,'—' Does it not seem as if the Crucifixion and the glory of Christ were absolutely identical in St. John's Gospel?'

From another letter (December, 1846) it appears how much he built on having Stanley at his side in Oxford :—

'I am delighted to think that you are committed to Oxford, as you say : σύν τε δύ' ἐρχομένω² makes one independent at least. Where shall we be at the end of the year? Perhaps not living ;

---

¹ Observe that Wordsworth is only quoted at second hand.

² 'Two going on together.'

otherwise, much where we are, getting a little deeper and filling up a little more in speculation,—and reforming the kitchens of University and Balliol.'

The position of Jowett in Balliol and his growing credit as a teacher may be further illustrated by the following reminiscences contributed by the late Archdeacon Palmer:—

'Balliol College in 1842, when I came into residence as a Scholar, was in many respects very unlike the Balliol of the present day. The Chapel and the Hall and more than half of the other buildings have been erected since that time, and a College Garden has been created by the union of two gardens, then walled off for the use of the Master and of the Fellows respectively, with an irregular piece of ground called the Grove, which was absolutely devoid of beauty, though covered with trees. Moreover the number of Commoners in the College is at least twice as large now as it was in my day, and the number of Scholars and of Exhibitioners has been doubled also. But these differences, however striking, are only superficial. In more important respects the College has preserved a uniform character for a good deal more than half a century. Its Masters, Tutors, and Lecturers have devoted themselves ungrudgingly to its service, and among its undergraduates the proportion of reading men to idlers has been greater than anywhere else in Oxford. But I am asked to set down briefly my own undergraduate recollections.

'In Michaelmas Term, 1842, when I first came up, there were only four undergraduate Scholars in residence, four besides myself, James Riddell, Matthew Arnold, Edward Walford, and C. S. Lock. Lock was a Blundell Scholar from Tiverton. The rest of us came from public schools of greater name. Indeed, this was the case with all the open Scholars who were elected from 1838 to 1845 inclusive, except William Young Sellar. He was a Snell Exhibitioner from Glasgow University. Of the other fifteen Scholars elected in those eight years, five came from Rugby, three from Shrewsbury, three from Charterhouse, two from Eton, one from Harrow, and one from Winchester.

Yet no preference was given by the statutes, nor any favour shown by the electors, to public school men. The emoluments of a Balliol Scholarship were reckoned in those days at £30 a year or thereabouts. Scholars were exempt from tuition fees, and had an allowance for maintenance of 10s. a week during actual residence. The competition, however, for these Scholarships was at least as great as for Scholarships at any other College in the University, although at some Colleges (such as Trinity, for example) the emoluments were much more considerable. The Snell Exhibitioners, then as now, formed an important element in the College. There were ten of these Exhibitions, and there were usually five or six undergraduates holding them in residence. I may mention among my own contemporaries, John Campbell Shairp, after-wards Professor of Poetry; H. A. Douglas, afterwards Bishop of Bombay; William Young Sellar, afterwards Professor of Humanity at Edinburgh; Francis Sandford, and Patrick Cumin, who filled successively the post of Secretary to the Committee of Council on Education. Many or most of the Commoners were public school men; Eton in particular was largely repre-sented. Not a few were reading men, whose pursuits and ambitions were similar to those of the Scholars and Exhibi-tioners. In consequence, the Scholars and Exhibitioners did not form a distinct set, although the Scholars had a table to themselves in Hall. There was a fast set (as we called it), which consisted of ten or a dozen men, whose amusements were more expensive than those of the rest; but there was no hard line of demarcation even here, some of the reading men were more or less intimate with the members of the fast set. There were also a few men who, for one reason or another, did not mix much with their neighbours. So far, however, as I remember, the bulk of the College, some forty men at least, Scholars, Commoners, and Exhibitioners, associated freely together. Breakfast-parties and wine-parties, small or great, at which we all met (though seldom all at once), went on every day. It is my impression that I myself rarely breakfasted alone, and rarely failed to pass an hour or more after dinner in company. But our breakfast-parties broke up at ten, and the amount of wine drunk at our wine-parties

was inconsiderable; and consequently our social habits did not
interfere with the reading of those who, like myself, wished to
read.   The men of whom I speak—they were too numerous
to be called a set—were the representatives of Balliol in
the eyes of the University at large.   It was by them that the
reputation of the College was maintained in the Schools, on
the river, and in the cricket-field.   Football was not yet played
at Oxford.   It is an illustration of the union between Scholars
and Commoners that there was almost always a Scholar in the
College boat.   Before I began to reside, Balliol had become
conspicuous for success in University examinations and in the
competition for prizes.   My own generation carried on this
tradition.   It was not, however, till somewhat later that
Balliol Commoners were found in the First Class as often as
Scholars or Exhibitioners.

'I pass from undergraduates to dons.   Dr. Jenkyns, who was
Master from 1819 to 1854, though the subject of many stories
which represent him in a ridiculous light, was a remarkably
efficient and successful head.   We laughed much at him ourselves, but we also liked him much.   He had the interest of the
College thoroughly at heart, and the success of each individual in
it was a matter of concern to him.   Moreover, he had a great
amount of practical shrewdness.   Edward Cooper Woollcombe,
William Charles Lake, and Benjamin Jowett were our Tutors.
Frederick Temple was our mathematical lecturer, and sometimes lectured in other subjects also.   Lake, Jowett, and
Temple all began to teach in Balliol in October Term, 1842—
the Term in which I came up.   Woollcombe had been Tutor
along with Archibald Campbell Tait and James Gylby Lonsdale during the previous year, in which Dale had been mathematical lecturer.   In those days each undergraduate was
assigned to one special Tutor for the whole period of his
residence, but it was only for Latin and Greek composition
that he went, as a matter of course, to his own Tutor; for his
lectures he went to this or that Tutor, as the Tutors might
arrange among themselves.   Undergraduates had then no
choice in the matter.   On an average each undergraduate was
required to attend two lectures every week-day.   There were
no off-days but Sundays.   We had abundant evidence that all

our teachers were thoroughly in earnest, and that they not
only desired to make us work, but also worked hard themselves.   I was one of Jowett's pupils.   So was James Riddell,
who was already known for his remarkable scholarship, and
in after years had no superior in Oxford in that department.
Jowett did not spare his labour in preparing us both for
University Scholarship examinations.   I had to bring him
during my first year Latin or Greek composition three times
a week.   I believe he would have made me come to him still
oftener, if he had not been aware that I was working for the
same examinations with a private Tutor, Mountague Bernard,
who was then a B.A. Scholar of Trinity.   Just before the
Christmas vacation, 1842, Jowett put into the hands of Riddell
and myself a plan of work for that vacation which must
have cost him a considerable amount of time and thought.
Numerous pieces of composition, prose and verse, Greek and
Latin, were prescribed [1]; selected portions of Greek and Latin
authors were to be studied or learned by heart; one or two
books on philological subjects were to be read.   Whether
he gave the same holiday task to other pupils at the same
time I do not remember.   I believe that Riddell and I followed
out his plan completely ; I know that we did all the composition
prescribed, and that Jowett looked it all over with us at the
beginning of the next Term.   In dealing with composition,
it was his method to criticize rather than to correct.   Of
course he pointed out flagrant errors, but else he did not go
much into detail.   He looked rather to the general style, and
(when the composition was original) to the treatment of the
subject.   He took great pains also with the criticism of his
pupils' prize compositions.   It was the practice then (strange
and indefensible as it now seems) for College Tutors and other
friends to see and comment upon compositions which were
to be sent in for the Chancellor's prizes or Sir Roger Newdi-
gate's.   Such comments must often have given a material
advantage to those competitors whose fortune it was to have

---

[1] The list includes a large proportion of original subjects for
Latin letters, Greek dialogues,
Latin Odes, &c., and passages for
verse translation from Shakespeare, Milton, and the Bible.

good advisers; but at that time nobody thought the practice unfair. I remember that in my first year Jowett condemned absolutely a Latin poem of mine, and made me write another. My second attempt, however, did not please him better, and ultimately the first draught went in, with such improvements as I was able to introduce. I am bound to add that its failure justified his unfavourable opinion. Jowett's pupils always felt that they were in the hands of a good scholar, but I do not think that we attributed to him pre-eminence in this respect over other good scholars in the University. The same thing may be said as regards his College lectures generally in those days. They were the lectures of a well-read and able man, but they did not give us an impression of learning or of power to teach which was singular either in kind or in degree. Indeed, I have a livelier recollection of lectures which I heard from other teachers in Balliol during my first two years. One thing I remember, however, which was peculiar to Jowett among our Lecturers, and it is a thing which distinguished him through life. It was inventiveness. He was fertile in experiments. At one time he made a select class turn Johnson's *Rasselas* into Latin before him without preparation; at another, he made us construe Demosthenes' speech against Midias at sight. He tried his hand at the explanation of Sophocles' Choric Metres. He introduced us to Wolf's Homeric theory. He took the Septuagint as his text-book for a lecture on the Old Testament, Greswell's *Harmony of the Gospels* for a lecture on the New. It may have been my own fault, but I cannot remember any particular advantage which we derived from these various experiments. A time came, however, at last (I am unable to fix the exact date) when Jowett began a course of lectures which made upon me and others a very different impression from any which he had made upon us before. His subject was the Fragments of the early Greek philosophers; but the lectures did not close without a mention of Socrates and Plato. They were delivered to a class which consisted of ten or twelve men—Scholars, Commoners, and Exhibitioners. We had never till then heard him lecture on any philosophical subject. We were struck by the insight which he showed into the speculations of ancient thinkers, and by the felicity of expression which enabled him to make them intelligible to us. These lectures gave him in our eyes a position all his own. I believe myself that his interpretation of Greek philosophy, of which this was the first specimen, was the true foundation of his greatness in the eyes of Balliol men and of the Oxford world. I suspect, moreover, that his success in this department brought to himself a consciousness of power which gradually unlocked his tongue, so that later generations of pupils were able to enter into his thoughts and feelings more than the men of my time could do. His popularity followed the growth of his intellectual reputation ; it did not precede it. No doubt the pains which he took with his early pupils showed kindness as well as conscientiousness, but his manner in dealing with them was such as to repel rather than to attract. During my undergraduate years he was singularly silent and undemonstrative. To shy men he was positively alarming. I remember myself one occasion on which he invited me to take a walk with him. The number of words exchanged between us during that walk was incredibly small, and I believe that it was a relief to both when we regained the College gate. The experiment was not repeated, nor did I ever feel at home with him before I took my degree and became a Fellow. Others less shy than myself may have found less difficulty in understanding him ; but I do not think he would ever in those days have been described as a popular tutor. Something of this early taciturnity remained with him through life, though it grew less and less as years went on. Meantime, however, opportunities multiplied for the display of his kindness in other ways than the promotion of his pupils' studies ; and that kindness was always ready, always unstinted. It made an impression upon those who were least able to appreciate his intellectual gifts. His independence of mind, his originality, his fullness of resources, attracted to him the abler men. At last even his fits of silence came to have a charm of their own, and to give weight to the pithy utterances which succeeded them.

'I remember Wall saying of Jowett in 1854, "It is to him that the College owes its constant supply of Firsts in Greats." '

LETTERS, 1840–1846.

To W. A. GREENHILL.

Good Friday [1841].

I send the books for Dr. Arnold[1], also the five pounds which you kindly lent. I have not thanked you for the note which you sent with them, but have often thought of it since. I can never forget the way in which our acquaintance began more than four years ago, and only hope that if you are ever in need you will put me to the proof. You may be quite sure you never can be in my debt.

Wishing you a happy Easter,

I am, yours ever,

B. JOWETT.

To W. A. GREENHILL.

34 LEE ROAD, BLACKHEATH,
April 21, 1842.

. . . I was very much pleased by your kind note on my birthday, although, considering how evil the last two years of my life have been, it is unpleasant to be reminded how old one has grown. In about a week I am going to bury myself in Paris—it is rather a relief to me to get away from people, and I still build up dreams of steady reading and devotion. This, you will think, is rather a misanthropical strain, but I do not mean to indulge any such feelings. I hope the study of the Greek Testament and regularity in diet, &c., may bring me into a better state of mind and body. Change of scene does not seem to me of much use, but I mean to go to Paris to be quiet and get away from all agitating subjects :—

'Est Ulubris, animus si non te deficit aequus.'

This is rather like spinning a letter ' out of one's own bowels,' but as the subject may possibly be not so agreeable to you as it is

[1] Dr. Arnold was Mrs. Greenhill's uncle.

natural to me, I will say nothing more about it. We are very busy in getting my brother[1] ready for India, as he is to start in about three weeks. I think it is a nice prospect for him —his pay is quite sufficient to support him, and it is a great advantage of the East India service that his prospect of rising depends almost entirely on his diligence and ability. He is very much pleased himself, and notwithstanding your pithy remark that it was a better employment to cure than to kill, considering his disposition, I think he has made the best choice.

I am sorry to hear you are so downcast at Mrs. Greenhill's absence; it is one of the misfortunes of married life, I suppose— just sufficient to let you know your happiness.

Will you kindly give me any introductions you can at Paris[2]? You mention M. Miller, which may be of real service to me in case I am unable to get an introduction to the library from my other friend.

To W. A. GREENHILL.

BONN, *June* 28, 1842.

. . . One chief reason I have for writing at this moment is that I have just received in a letter from Tait the news of Arnold's death. It must have thrown you and Mrs. Greenhill into overwhelming trouble. I was quite shocked to hear of it—so very sudden, and a man who seemed so made to enjoy this world that you might wish him long life for its own sake. No person could see him without feeling an interest about him. I shall never forget his noble appearance in the Theatre at the inaugural lecture. It is pleasing indeed to remember that he was the first person who really conducted a public school on Christian principles. I should as soon doubt the truth of religion itself as doubt that such a man had gone to receive his reward.

One reason, I would just hint, why I don't write to you oftener is that I do not like writing about religion; and it seems so cold and prosy to write to an intimate friend about

---

[1] William Jowett.

[2] Greenhill had been pursuing his medical studies at Paris in 1840. See *Life of E. B. Pusey,* vol. iii. p. 7.

anything else. I doubt not that there may be many persons
to whom religious communion with one another is of great
good; for myself, I fear that I have received all the good that
I can gain from it. For the future I would rather go on my
way alone, and, to avoid self-deceit, trust to God only.

Your introduction to M. Miller was of great use, as it enabled
me to go to the library and read. What little I saw of him he
seemed a very learned man, but he was so much engaged that
this was not much, and the medium of communication between
us was so imperfect that I am afraid he thought me something
strange. . . . A French officer with whom I used to dine, and
two or three Oxford men, were quite enough society for me.
Upon the whole I am very glad that I went to Paris, where
I was getting a great deal better, and should be so at present if
I had not, like an ass, tired myself with walking along the
Moselle last week, and have not got over the effects of it yet.
Nothing can be more delightful than our present situation at
Bonn—all our windows command a view of the Drachenfels.
I never was in any place I liked so well. The professors here
seem disposed to be very kind. Yesterday, on the strength
of Tait's acquaintance with him, I went to call on the
illustrious Nitzsch. I always find myself struck dumb in the
presence of a great man, but Nitzsch was so very kind it was quite
easy to get on with him. He talked a good deal and very well
about the English Church, though from not being able to read
English he has but an imperfect idea of things. Afterwards
I went to see Böcking, who most kindly gave me an introduction
to another professor who, he said, spoke excellent English.
They were both shocked and grieved to hear of Arnold's death.
Böcking seemed quite affected by it.

. . . I suppose you are too much a man of peace to tell me
anything about the new Hampden row [1]. The tumult has by

[1] In May, 1842, the Heads of Houses proposed to repeal the Statute depriving Dr. Hampden of his right to vote in the nomination of Select Preachers, &c. In the interval before the meeting of Convocation, 'Dr. Hampden delivered a lecture which Stanley strongly condemned. "But," he adds, . . . "I still vote for him." The proposed repeal was rejected by 334 votes to 214.'—*Life of Dean Stanley*, vol. i. pp. 310, 311.

this time dwindled to a calm, and left you in the quiet of
a Long Vacation. From all accounts Hampden's conduct seems
to have been very bad. I hope that Newman and his friends
will become more liberal—or perhaps 'charitable' is the right
word—not only towards individuals, but in their own views
of parties; if so, I think the work they will have done will
be almost one of unmixed good.

To B. C. Brodie.

BALLIOL, *November* 24, 1844.

. . . Various new things have happened here since I wrote
last. In the first place, the report about Newman's leaving
the English Church is not immediately true, though it was
generally believed, and I incline to think that it is founded on
fact. A committee of Heads of Houses are sitting on the fat
fellow's book [1], who seems likely to have hard measure dealt to
him if the inextricable confusion of the statutes does not save
him. The Heads of Houses are not over scrupulous either
legally or morally in their method of proceedings. Whately
has been backing them, which, considering his liberal views, is,
I think, a mistake. It has been much discussed among us
whether Stanley shall write a pamphlet on the occasion.
Maurice [2] of Guy's Hospital was anxious that we should draw up
a genuine Liberal protest against persecution of the Newmanites,
in which he says he himself, Archdeacon Hare, &c., will join.
The said protest we wish to represent as coming from
F. Maurice himself. Honestly confessing that I am rather
proud of having helped to draw up a document abounding in
Liberal sentiments, I will send it you if it ever gets into print,
which is rather uncertain, as matters are only in embryo yet.

I must tell you another thing which is to me a matter of
great interest. Yesterday I went to dine with Coleridge: just
such a dinner-party as you and I were at together six months
ago. Froude was there, as on the former occasion; but I was
greatly amazed to find that he has become regularly Germanized,
and talked unreservedly about Strauss, miracles, &c. Of course

[1] W. G. Ward's *Ideal of the Christian Church.*
[2] Frederick Denison Maurice.

you will not mention this (a caution which it seems useless to give at Giessen [1]). I cannot quite tell how entire his change of opinion is ; he seemed to take such a very artistical view of things that his conversation gave me no satisfaction, and, if I do not do him injustice, a want of the earnestness natural to a person who feels what an aweful thing it is to disbelieve all he has formerly held and believe something new. I am told that he justifies his *Lives of the Saints* and the mythic view of the miracles contained in them by saying that he did it to realize to people the absurdity of their belief. Therefore what you heard him say at dinner was εἰρωνεία. Newman has disowned the editorship of the tract [2], so that I suppose he is aware of all this.

This is regular gossip, I fear very uninteresting to you. It is too bad to make your sublime spirit, soaring with Prospero in a world of its own creation, descend to the commonplace of Oxford life. *À propos* of Prospero, as a lady would say who did not know how to connect the next sentence of a letter, I went to see Charles Kemble read the *Merchant of Venice*, from which, in comparison with Macready, one did not get much. It struck me that there was a good deal of difficulty in explaining the character of Shylock—a sort of Italian Jew (the Jew perfect, and Shakespeare seems to have seized what Newman hints at in one of his sermons, the ideal of Jewish character in Jacob), Iago-like malignity and cunning, vulgar simplicity, and violent passion, and withal something of 'the form left to pine away amid an altered world' which arouses one's sympathy for him. There is something very deep in the idea of strict law as opposed to justice, the only notion of morality which the Jews appear to have. In the trial scene this is admirably brought out. I wish theologians understood the relation of Judaism and Christianity half as well.

. . . Your friend Charles Vaughan is a candidate for Harrow— rather late in the field, so that if the Trustees have not great discernment he will be beaten by Jelf, whom people here consider the winning man.

---

[1] Where Brodie was studying.
[2] i.e. J. A. Froude's contribution to the *Lives of the Saints*.

To B. C. Brodie.

BALLIOL, *December* 23, 1844.

I was very glad to hear from you, and find that you were
happily settled at Giessen.   For solitariness I am almost as
lonely as you can be, as there is not a living creature in
College, except the cats, who are wild with hunger.

The politics of the place have been developing themselves
rapidly since I last wrote. About the middle of next Term the
country clergy are to be summoned to Oxford, red with anger,
fiery hot with Protestant zeal, to vote (1) that certain passages
of Ward's book are objectionable, (2) that Ward is to lose
his degrees, (3) that all gentlemen of suspicious character shall
be summoned by the Vice-Chancellor to sign the Thirty-nine
Articles 'in eo sensu quo et primitus editos fuisse constat et
universitas imposuit.'   It seems probable that the rage of the
said country clergy will carry the two first, but perhaps the
common sense of the residents may prevail against the test.
The Heads of Houses λαβεῖν ἀμείνους εἰσὶν ἢ μεθιέναι[1] ; that is
to say, more fond of getting than resigning a power.   I strongly
suspect, however, that they will find themselves mistaken in
this mischievous and unjust attempt.   No deprivation of
degrees can take away the Fellowship, which is what they seem
to be aiming at, and without this it is a mere *brutum fulmen*.
They might have put him in the Ecclesiastical Court, or in the
Vice-Chancellor's Court, so that there is no excuse for trying him
by Convocation.   He is allowed to be heard in his own defence.

I cannot quite agree in the serene view you incline to take
of the sufferings of the Newmanites.   I am quite aware that
I have not very much in common [with them], except so far as
every person who wishes to be in earnest has with every one
else who has the same wish.   I think of course that you must
guard against being made a cat's-paw of, and perhaps their
principles would not allow them to do anything of the same
sort for a Latitudinarian[2] ; moreover, they showed a very
ugly spirit about Hampden ; but nevertheless it seems but
right to see justice done to conscientious men, and very
expedient when it is the dominion of Ogilvie and the Heads

[1] Aeschylus, *Persae*, 690.   [2] See pp. 237 ff., 306, 309 ff.

of Houses which is to be feared, and not of the Newmanites, who are beginning to scatter like sheep without a shepherd.

I mentioned to you a book which I had been reading[1] in praise of J. M. Turner on landscape painting. I have read it all through with the greatest delight; the minute observation and power of description it shows are truly admirable. His theory in general is that landscape painting must be true, and not a mere romance; and considering the infinite variety of nature and the individuality of the minutest section, the only way in which true effects can be given is by suggestion, not by distinct drawing, which can never produce in the mind the idea of infinity always found in nature. There is a great deal on the form of clouds, &c., which gives one, so to say, some true principles not only of art but of nature. Since I read it I fancy I have a keener perception of the symmetry of natural scenery. The book is written by Ruskin, a child of genius certainly.

. . . Is there any chance of your being found at Rome on St. Peter's day next summer? I think, as the Long Vacation is a temptation, I am very likely [to] be there. I sun myself with the thought of an Italian sky all the year round; it would make life happier to have seen Rome and stood on the Tarpeian Rock and under the dome of St. Peter's.

Concerning the 'Heilige Rock[2]' about which you make merry, I do not quite see the cause of your mirth unless you believe it to be an imposture, which is very improbable, even though there are twenty-four of them. I think it would be more probable to account for the whole twenty-four on a Straussian hypothesis than to suspect imposture in this particular case.

Stanley is writing a pamphlet, Donkin is writing a pamphlet, Ward is writing a pamphlet, Eden is writing a pamphlet, F. Maurice is writing a pamphlet, Hussey is writing a pamphlet; in short, all the world are pamphleteering.

Concerning matters serious allow me to say one word. I feel very deeply that one cannot live without religion, and that in

---

[1] *Modern Painters*, by a Graduate of Oxford.

[2] The Holy Coat at Trèves.

proportion as we believe less, that little, if it be only an aweful
feeling about existence, must be more constantly present with
us ; as faith loses in extent it must gain in intensity, if we
do not mean to shipwreck altogether.   I go about from one
subject to another just as if we were talking together, and am
well aware how feeble and unmeaning my words are to bring
us to any further agreement on these subjects, but I cannot
help often thinking about you, and sometimes—it is at least
a harmless superstition—remembering you in prayer.

To A. P. Stanley.

Bowness, *January*, 1845.

Concerning your pamphlet[1] I have spoken to Tait, who
thinks that he cannot possibly judge without reading it.   I do
not think his opinion of much value in such a matter.   Ask
Donkin or Price[2] or Clough, if you want a good opinion.

All vulgar reasons seem to me in favour of publishing.   It
will be a hit ; even the Newmanites will be propitiated :—'We
have read with pleasure Mr. Stanley's most seasonable pamphlet,' will be the leader of the next week's *English Churchman.*

The Bishop of N.'s son and Dr. A.'s biographer cannot be
worse off than he is with reference to suspicions of Latitudinarianism.   The 'gens Newmanica' possesses in an eminent
degree the virtue ascribed to our Master in the Statutes, 'saga-
citer odorat,' sc. Hereticos.

Also, there are many persons like Donkin, Mr. Myers of
Keswick, and myself, who would be glad to see what they feel
and think, well said for them.   I do not doubt that it would
have a great sale and gain its author much honour if it
were published.   My reasons against are—the greatness of
the subject, which I quite believe you will one day have the
opportunity of putting out in a better form.   A pamphlet is
inadequate to such an extensive work, which should be the end,
not the beginning, of a life.   I think you may mar it in some

---

[1] See *Life of A. P. Stanley,*
vol. i. p. 335. The pamphlet
was not published, but seems
to have furnished some of the
materials for Stanley's article on
the Gorham Case in *Edinburgh
Review,* July, 1850.

[2] Bonamy Price, afterwards
Professor of Political Economy
at Oxford.

measure by publishing now, and cannot imagine you will regret it [the delay] ten years hence, if you keep the same purpose steadily in view and do not let yourself fall back into listlessness and inactivity. Moreover, the question now is rather legal than constitutional, whether it is consistent with the law of the Church of England to hold Roman doctrine. The inexpediency of deciding the question cannot alter the fact when decided.

. . . In the last five years, if they had not fallen into a maze of casuistry, they[1] would have brought things exactly to the point most favourable to the real interests of the Church as well as of themselves. They have never given up No. 90, and if they did so now, it would seem like an attempt to draw the Anglo-Catholics to Rome who were caught by it. And 'honesty *versus* casuistry' is a point I am very unwilling to give up directly or indirectly in favour of Protestantism. The legal ground, or expediency ground, is one that Oakeley does not distinctly take, but clings to Bishop Montague and Ward's sophistical explanations. Also, I am persuaded that Ward and Oakeley are almost certain to go in any case, and would soon cease to have any practical idea of doing good in the Church of England. Oakeley's distinction of holding as distinct from teaching[2] is not to be tolerated for a moment, and yet it is the only way in which his Romanist subscription could possibly be allowed.

All this would strongly determine me in your case to do nothing. 'In quietness and confidence shall be your strength.' I hope you will not think what I have said harsh. The evils of Newman's going I think very great—it would be a mournful fact in the history of the Church of England[3]. Still, the assault from without would be so much stronger that it could hardly bring us back to the days of orthodox misrule.

---

[1] The Tractarian party.

[2] Oakeley of Balliol, Ward's chief supporter, and contributor to the *British Critic*, at this time minister of Margaret Chapel, London, had written a pamphlet (*The Subject of Tract XC Historically Examined*) defending his position as an Anglican, which he shortly afterwards abandoned to join the Church of Rome. His article on Jewel was 'a landmark in the progress of Roman ideas' (Dean Church's *Oxford Movement*, p.322).

[3] J. H. Newman joined the Church of Rome in October, 1845.

This is the end of my prose, which you must receive with all possible suspicion, as coming from a person who feels daily how unfit he is to advise anybody, and has a natural prejudice on the side of 'quiescence.'

To B. C. BRODIE.

. . . I have been reading Hegel's Lectures on the History of Philosophy, which, although I only half understand, seem to me to give a deeper and more continuous account of philosophy than any book I have seen. The manner in which he traces the growth of self-reflection and the progress of mental analysis is admirable. The other day I had to give a lecture on the Atomic philosophy which recalled to my mind what you told me of Faraday's doctrine of forces. To get rid of the infinite divisibility of matter he must make abstraction of matter, space, &c., but the idea of cause which remains seems so abstract that I do not see how to get back again into the physical world. . . . 'Si quid habes imperti.' I did not understand you at the time, but suppose something of this kind must be meant, only I wonder that any physical philosopher should hit upon this method of solving the difficulty.

To B. C. BRODIE.

BOWNESS [ON WINDERMERE],
March 28, 1845.

The country here you probably know, so I will not describe it. A week ago there was a severe frost, the sky I think the clearest I ever saw in England, so that the lake seemed quite like an Italian landscape. There is nothing in the way of natural beauty I admire so much as the clear Italian sky, which you seem to look through, not *at*, and into which all objects seem to project. The lake here is very beautiful on a small scale, especially towards Ambleside, where you have rich outlines of the mountains and shadows. On Monday I went over to Fox How and saw the Arnolds, and am going again in a few days, when I hope to get a sight of Wordsworth.

I quite agree in what you say about Pimlico churches and modern Luthers. I wonder people do not feel the curse of having no old to entwine with the new. The said Pimlico structures very soon become cracked and show the stuff they are made of. For my own part I get rather to hate logic, certainly when applied as it usually is to these subjects, and hope there is a point of view in which you may place yourself above it without being a fool or a madman. I think it is one of the chief charges against the Church of Rome, that it has defined, and subdefined, and deduced, and subdeduced until religion has come to be something absolutely different from the religion of the Bible, not merely as to the things believed, but as to the mode of believing. Systematized theology they put in the place of the philosophy of religion.

You see I am obliged to have recourse to a kind of shady dissertation to fill up my letter. Old Ward's marriage you will have seen by the papers is known to all the world— sonnets are addressed to him, the country newspapers have *impromptus* on the subject, the matter has ended in a universal roar of laughter. I am afraid it is a bad thing for him, which it would not be on your view, if he would resign himself to his better nature and become a domesticated animal. This, however, he is not disposed to do. I fear he will go on despised by all the world—'Hildebrand the married man'— with the worst effect on himself if not upon others.

To A. P. Stanley.

September, 1845.

I have read part of Ewald and part of Bunsen's[1] work. 'Give me a bit of paper and a pencil, and I'll sketch you a plan of a church. It won't take five minutes, I assure you.' It seems to show a great ignorance of the truth, 'Ecclesia nascitur, non fit.' Surely it must be an idle attempt to construct any outward form of a church which is not simply an expression of religious tendencies in the people. . . .

. . . Ewald I like much better than I did at first. About

---

[1] *Die Verfassung der Kirche der Zukunft,* published in 1845.

the miracles it may be said that if there is such uncertainty
about the common facts, you cannot possibly have evidence
sufficient to warrant you in believing the miracles. But is
not this unfair, because the history and the miracles mutually
support each other? The miracles, however improbable in
themselves, make the history probable. And is it not rather
the general question of the probability of miracles in such an
age and dispensation than the *evidence* for particular miracles
with which we are concerned? Whether, e.g., it is not
natural that these 'vestiges of creation' might be perpetually
going on until the spiritual world were set forth in Christianity?—whether it would not be contrary to analogy that
the God who was believed to dwell in the thunder should
not show Himself in the thunder? Does it seem consistent
to suppose such vast changes in men's minds and feelings
about religion, and to suppose no changes in the laws of nature
corresponding to it, but a harmony of subject and object which
consists in the ceaseless play of the subject around a never-
varying object? This seems to me the strongest and the
real ground of defending the Old Testament miracles.

To A. P. Stanley.

1 Great George Street,
December, 1845.

I return Donkin's letter, which entertained me much. May
I venture one or two criticisms [1]? If a certain friend of ours
saw that passage about the resurrection of our Lord, would
he not at once say, 'How can I be responsible, in what appears
to me defect of evidence, for not believing a fact?' To which
I imagine the only answer would be that this fact is so in-
separably connected with certain doctrines that approve themselves to our moral and religious sense, that you must take
the fact with the doctrine. Suppose him to answer—I do not
see this connexion; you may be right, but you only prove a
lack of historical or metaphysical faculties in me for not agreeing
with you. Can that be essential to Christianity, the unbelief

[1] On a writing of Stanley's, probably based on the pamphlet
referred to on p. 115.

of which does not imply any moral guilt, but a want of acuteness and good sense? I have not any tendency to doubt about the miracles of the New Testament, but this seems to me a very difficult question. May not the answer perhaps be that of Erdmann, that the ideas are the essential, and that the facts are a manifestation of the ideas? If so, and I think this is partly true at all events, it *does* matter very much what we believe, even though we doubt about our Lord's resurrection.—Concerning Hegel, I doubt not that Donkin's ignorance is far more than my knowledge. I have only a glimpse of his meaning, but feel restless until I can get deeper into it. Erdmann's advice, if you remember, was to read first the *Phänomenologie*, then the *Logic*, and then the *Philosophie der Religion*. The *Logic* I have been toiling at since I came back, but it is almost impossible to get any idea of it in the details without first getting an idea of the whole. I thought the *Geschichte der Philosophie* gave me great help at first. As a history I suppose it is bad, because it sees Hegelianism everywhere, and brings all systems under its categories. It is an exposition of himself *stufenweise*, his philosophy being the result of all former ones, which are subordinated as 'moments' and are ever in process of transition. Without the history of philosophy in which to realize them, his abstractions and concretions would seem quite unmeaning.

To A. P. STANLEY.

DULOE, LISKEARD, *December*, 1845.

Samuel of Oxford is not unpleasing, if you will resign yourself to be semi-humbugged by a semi-humbug. He was very kind, and would do great good if he could but be persuaded to keep off speculative matters. In the latter respect Mauricianism, diluted by Trench, and still further watered by himself, seems to be the prevailing tone. But he is a man of the world and a gentleman, and above all 'head-of-a-house' delusions, and exactly agrees with us about the College for poor students. Nevertheless, with all his practical ability he shows weakness of character—e. g. he said he would print his charge if we wished it; but some of us did not wish it, so the charge was not printed.   I must tell you of a conversation that occurred between Trench and one of the candidates [1].

Scene I.   *The Garden, Cuddesden.*

Trench. Has Newman's book [2] produced much effect at Oxford?

Cand. Yes, a great one.   Very able, do you not think?   How very striking the last page is!

Trench. Humph!   Yes, touching.   The chief thing that strikes me about the book is the aweful amount of scepticism it discloses.   It will do great good, the publication of it.

Scene II.   *Palace, Cuddesden.*

The Bishop.   One of the Candidates.

Bish. The Irvingites use this passage ('He gave some Apostles') to prove the institution of a sevenfold ministry.   How would you answer such an argument?

Cand. It refers to an accidental state of the Church; there was no regular ministry at the time.

Bish. You do not believe, then, that the Episcopal Order existed from the beginning?

Cand. No; but that it sprang up gradually.

Bish. (*Here followed a speech which lasted five minutes.*)   Let me hear what you say in answer to this?

Cand. Bishop and Presbyter are used convertibly in the New Testament.   This place shows that there was no regular ministry.   There is no mention of Bishops in the Apostolical Fathers; and it seems more natural that it should grow up, like other institutions, gradually.

Bish. But might not the thing be older than the name?   It may be in human things that it is more natural institutions should grow naturally, but not so in divine.   And Ignatius—

Cand. Have you seen the Syriac Version?

Bish. And did you see the places at the end which confirm from the Syriac the authority of the other Epistles?   (*This is a mis-statement.*)

Bish. One more question I wish to ask.   In what sense do you sign the Articles?   Certain modes I consider dishonest, without at all wishing to narrow their limits.

Cand. (*A pause.*)   In Paley's sense.

[1] What follows is clearly autobiographical: cf. p. 240.   Jowett took Priest's Orders in the winter of 1845.   Every Fellow of Balliol was bound by statute to be ordained within four years of his M.A. degree.   Richard Chenevix Trench (afterwards Archbishop of Dublin) was Bishop Wilberforce's examining Chaplain.

[2] *The Development of Christian Doctrine* (1845).

Bish. What does Paley say?

Cand. That it is an absurdity if the Legislature meant to say that you assented to four or five hundred disputed propositions. It only meant that you were an attached member of the Church of England.

Bish. No, I don't mean that I require assent to four or five hundred disputed propositions, &c. &c.

Cand. One question I should like to ask. Do you think that Dr. Arnold was justified in signing them?

Bish. Yes.

I have omitted the civilities, but the candidate informed me that nothing could be more bland and amiable than the Bishop's manner to him.

Scene III. The Tea Table, Cuddesden.

Bish. Sir R. Peel's scheme when he went out of office is said to have been a total repeal of the Corn Laws, Malt Tax, Sugar Duties, &c. This would be a great sacrifice for the landed interest, &c. But the poor would be the gainers by it.

Cand. The clergy, my Lord, would be great sufferers.

Bish. Yes, I am afraid they would ; in all changes they suffer.

Cand. But if the poor are the gainers, the clergy ought not to complain.

To complete the portraiture of Samuel of Oxford, I will add two extracts from his sermon :—

'All saving truth is contained in Scripture, not the germ of it, not to be developed out of it, but is *in it*. If you go to the Primitive Church or to Fathers or to Councils, there is no amount of superstition to which you may not be led on.'

'Scripture is to be interpreted by the Creeds and Catholic consent.'

. . . The Bishop is an excellent man, overflowing with goodness ; but I doubt whether anybody can do him perfect justice who has not a spice of humbug in his composition and therefore a sympathy with the sort of thing.

To A. P. Stanley.

Sonning, [1846].

I am here in that 'temple of peaceful industry' at Sonning. I do not know whether 'indolence' might not partly express it too.　It is a charming place, and the vicar[1] is full of virtues and kindness; it is delightful to see him get on so well with his people and with all the world.

I stopped a night in London, first with Lingen, second with Brodie and Vaughan[2]; the latter greatly pleased me.　I am afraid we are on different tacks in Moral Philosophy, and though I cannot compare with him in power and originality, I doubt whether he is in the right.　The truth is he is 'The Sheepskin' still—works alone, thinks alone, would analyze the origin of our moral ideas in the individual rather than the world at large[3].　He will write a more striking book for not having read German, and certainly a more readable one, which will be a real accession to English Philosophy; but unless a man could, like Descartes, pluck out one by one the ideas he already has, I do not see what gain there can really be in travelling alone, and probably losing the way on the same ground with the German thinkers.

PS.—I have forgotten to mention a sudden revolution in my plans.　Last Thursday Scott appeared, and seeing that he is blind and solitary, I thought it would be better to go and

[1] The Rev. Hugh Pearson, a great friend of Stanley's and of Jowett's. See vol. ii. p. 195.

[2] Henry Halford Vaughan (see p. 97, note 3). He was a man of whom great things were expected. He wrote a metaphysical work, of which the MS. was destroyed in some mysterious way before it could be published. He left behind him three volumes of emendations on Shakespeare. 'The Sheepskin' is a nickname for him, which recurs several times in the correspondence, perhaps suggested by his rough shock of lightish-coloured hair. He was acknowledged to be the most brilliant of all Dr. Arnold's pupils.

[3] This is repeated in a subsequent letter: 'Did I tell you that I saw H. H. V. in London and had a talk with him? He looks upon morality as having its roots in pleasure and pain, the flower which it bears being the work of imagination or reflection on those first impressions. His great object seemed to be to find out the origin of our moral ideas—looking for them, however, only in the individual, not in the history of the world.' Dean Liddell, to whom portions of the work were read in MS., understood it to be an attempt to trace the upward growth of morality in human history, finding its consummation in Christ.

see him for a few weeks, as my presence is not absolutely
necessary at 'the seat of war [1].'

To A. P. STANLEY.

[1846.]

About the Evangelical Alliance I do not know anything,
but the views of all parties concerned in it must be so essentially sectarian that it can hardly hold together very long.
I suppose it is a sign that the Dissenters, like the Church,
are getting out of their shallow formalism and ceasing to
declaim about the State Church, as we on our part about our
venerable Establishment. A more interesting question to me
is the more general one—What is the real cause and what
the future fortunes of the English Dissenters? . . . One
fancies it [Dissent] must be some kind of cross between
Puritanism, formalism, Anglicanism, political liberty, and
Church authority, &c.; its constant degeneration into Uni-
tarianism, and never into Latitudinarianism, is a remarkable
feature. A small admixture of *religio sceptici* would greatly
improve it; at present it is equally tenacious of all, from the
Beast in the Revelation down to 'John the Immerser came
preaching in the wilderness.' It is evidently a good deal
shaken at present, and getting out of place like the Church
itself. . .

[1] Balliol.

CHAPTER V

ATTACHMENT of his pupils to him—His interest in their works —Hegel and Comte—Lectures in Political Economy—Plato at Oxford—Paris in 1848—Conversation with Michelet, &c.—Theological Essays—Long Vacations—The Oban reading party—Alexander Ewing, Bishop of Argyll—Notes on the Romans—Death of William Jowett— A pupil's record of conversations—Letters.

THE preceding years have witnessed the formation and ripening of opinion and character. It is only now that these begin to be fully realized in action.

Jowett's ascendency in Balliol reached a new stage about the year 1846. In the Long Vacation of that year, spent partly in helping Scott, his former Tutor, who had lost his wife some months before, and partly in charge of a pupil at Beaumaris, he was more isolated than heretofore[1]. From Scott's rectory of Duloe, near Liskeard, he wrote to Stanley :—

'Many thanks for all your kindness, to which I am not at all insensible ; perhaps it is better and more useful that we should work alone sometimes. It cools the nervous fever of intellectualism. I have already begun to form projects for next Long Vacation.'

[1] The solitude at Beaumaris was broken by a visit from James Riddell and his Balliol reading party on August 16.

Amongst his pupils of the next few years there was a little inner circle, whose relation to him, partly because they most needed his support, was peculiarly intimate. Chief among these were William Y. Sellar, Alexander Grant, T. C. Sandars, W. S. Dugdale, F. T. Palgrave, Theodore Walrond, R. B. D. Morier, and H. J. S. Smith. It was within this group that there sprang up what outsiders designated a sort of 'Jowett-worship'; but it will be seen by-and-by how little there was amongst them of the spirit of what is called 'the mutual admiration society.' They were on the best terms of good fellowship, and devotedly attached to Jowett as their teacher and friend, submitting to his insistent criticism only because of his evident good will towards them. His devotion to his pupils was, at this time, something unique at Oxford ; and it was rendered more effective by the singular personal charm which made him irresistible to younger men, and the candour of his judgement, in which he always sought to take in the man as a whole, without regarding minor points of position, conduct, or opinion. More valuable than all was the penetrating sympathy with which he discerned the individual wants of his pupils and the critical points in their mental history, and the eager promptitude with which he came to their aid unasked in difficulties which his sagacity had divined.

Sellar was one of the Glasgow men, but, unlike most of them, had come up before he was nineteen, and had gained the Scholarship in addition to the Snell. He had crowned a brilliant Oxford career by taking an open Fellowship at Oriel. With great vigour both of mind and character, he had the temperament of genius ; and in the year following his degree he suffered from a nervous reaction after the long intellectual strain. Jowett's

resolute and self-denying kindness was of lasting service
to him ; and a life-long mutual attachment was the result.
At his home in Artornish, Sellar used to talk of 'the
divine Jowett.'

Grant was the heir to a baronetcy, whose expectations
had been reduced by misfortune. Of all the men of his
time he was most generally looked upon as having made
Jowett his ideal. His note-books, from which some
quotations will presently be given, attest the eagerness
with which he drank in every word of the teacher.

Dugdale was a man of fortune, who gained a First
Class, married, and died comparatively young in a mining
accident, where he had risked his life for the sake of
others [1].

Palgrave's intimate relation to Jowett and their early
intercourse will be amply shown by the letters and
reminiscences which he has contributed to the present
work. His love of poetry and art was one great bond of
intellectual sympathy between them.

Of Morier, Mr. Palgrave says—

'He had come up to Balliol a lax and imperfectly educated
fellow, but Jowett, seeing his great natural capacity, took him
in the Long Vacation of 1848 and practically "converted him"
to the doctrine of work. This was the turning-point in
Morier's life, and the warm friendship between them continued
until from his own deathbed (in Switzerland) Morier wrote to
the Master, who himself was then either dying or dead.'

Of Jowett's attachment to this younger friend, who
was then unknown to me, I was myself a witness. One
day in 1852, when I had taken him some work, he

---

[1] He was attempting to rescue
the miners who were buried in
one of his own pits. See the
tablet to his memory in Balliol
Chapel. The inscription there is
Jowett's, as appears from several
drafts of it in one of his note-
books.

turned round from stirring the fire—an habitual action with him—with a brighter look than I had ever seen in his face, and said, 'Morier is coming[1]!'

Henry Smith had been a pupil of Highton's at Rugby, but before obtaining the Scholarship had been travelling with his family on account of health. He gained the Ireland and Senior Mathematical Scholarships, but his work had been again interrupted by illness before taking his degree. Jowett wrote to him urging an extended absence in a letter full of wise sympathy, which was treasured by Smith's mother until her death, but has been unfortunately destroyed. In earlier years he was equally distinguished as a Classic and a Mathematician, but latterly he became absorbed in the special branch of mathematics on which he has left his mark. He remained to the last a steadfast friend, and his untimely death was deeply lamented by Jowett, one of whose latest writings was a short memoir of his former pupil and junior colleague[2].

The careers of these and other friends who had been his pupils cannot be separated from the course of Jowett's own existence. Their interests both in private and public are as coloured strands, which appear and reappear in the texture of his life. If he gave them support and strength, they were his 'wings,' to use the quaint phrase of Niebuhr. He read their books in MS.; he followed every step of their success or their discomfiture; he formed close friendships with their wives and children. With

---

[1] It was on some such occasion, on the return of an elder pupil to Oxford, that he gave the entertainment in Common Room to which Mr. Tollemache refers (*Benjamin Jowett*, p. 113), when Jowett enacted the Chinese exe-cutioner. I remember the scene. There was certainly a touch of light-heartedness unlike his bearing in after years.—L. C.

[2] *Memoir of H. J. S. Smith*, prefixed to his collected works. See vol. ii.

Sellar he renewed his knowledge of Lucretius and
Virgil ; with Grant he saw how Aristotle had absorbed
the ideas of Plato and 'stamped them with logic '; with
Morier he took a bird's-eye view of continental politics ;
from F. T. Palgrave he sought to gather new impressions
of German and Italian art. Something of the same kind
was true also of younger contemporaries, who were not his
pupils. While Lingen, ' sensitive to every breath of truth,'
was studying for the Bar and writing for the *Morning
Chronicle,* he received many a 'prose' from Jowett on the
philosophy of law and on various questions of the hour ;
and when in 1847 the same friend obtained a secretaryship in the Education Department under J. Kay-
Shuttleworth, the office of the Committee of Privy
Council became a centre of sustained interest to Jowett[1].
Lingen was followed thither by Temple, Sandford, and
several other Balliol men, all friends of Jowett's, while
M. Arnold became private secretary to Lord Lansdowne,
who was President of the Council. And to ffolliott
of University, the heir to an Irish estate, whose acquaintance he made through Morier, Jowett expatiates on
the whole Irish question in its bearing on the duties
of a landlord, as well as on farming, the breeding of
cattle, &c. It was thus, through sympathetic (and yet
critical) intercourse with other minds, that his more dis-
cursive thoughts took shape. Meanwhile his own studies
were pursued, above all in vacation time, with greater
assiduity than ever. In company with Temple, his junior
colleague, he now made a close and serious study of
Hegel. They had translated a good deal of the *Logic,*
when this task was broken off by Temple's being summoned away to practical life. Jowett was for the time

---

[1] He was keenly interested in Lingen's Report as a Commissioner on Education in Wales in the autumn of 1847.

powerfully attracted by the Hegelian philosophy. 'Men
call a page of Hegel difficult,' he said; 'that is because
they do not sit down to it as to a problem in mathematics.'
In a lecture once, on Jowett's statement of the doctrine
that 'Being both is and is not,' one of the undergraduates
present could not repress a laugh. 'You may laugh,
Mr. Dugdale,' the teacher is reported to have said, 'but
you will find it true.' But however strongly impressed,
his mind was too elastic and too onward-moving to be
long absorbed in any system. He 'could not be holden of
it.' In speaking, as he sometimes did, of the educational
value of metaphysics, especially of German metaphysics,
he would add, 'The philosophical movement in Greece
was far more important.' He would sometimes dissuade
a pupil from the study of Kant, 'because it takes so
long to see what these fellows would be at.' And even in
these earlier years he was fond of observing that no old
man had ever been a metaphysician. 'Hegel is a great
book,' he would say, 'if you can only get it out of its
dialectical form.' That is heresy, I imagine, in the ears
of a true Hegelian.

In one Long Vacation, about 1850, he made a special
study of Auguste Comte[1]. That which always seemed to
him most valuable, both in Comte and Hegel, was the
historical method which they pursued in different ways,
and the idea of an orderly evolution of the human mind,
which had not been clearly expressed before their time
—even in Lessing's suggestive essay on the education
of the human race. On recovering from the impression
which Comte made on him, he said, 'The world will
not be again deceived by a metaphysical system.—Comte
has such great knowledge of the world in one way,

[1] In 1882 he re-read Comte and made many annotations. See
vol. ii. p. 187.—E. A.

so little in another.' A later epigram of his may be quoted here: 'Comtism destroys the minds of men; Carlyleism destroys their morals.'

For his pupils at the time now spoken of, especially for Alexander Grant, his philosophical teaching had a peculiar charm. The course of lectures on the History of Philosophy, mentioned in the last chapter, became from year to year more comprehensive. It had no immediate relation to the examination system as then constituted, but helped to quicken men's intellects, and gave them larger views about the books they were reading. The kind of talk about the *Ethics* and Butler which had 'paid' hitherto no longer satisfied either examiners or examinees.—Single sayings of the great Tutor passed from mouth to mouth, such as 'Logic is neither a science nor an art, but a dodge'; and 'The efflorescence of art is the bloom upon decay.' Another quotation, probably apocryphal (though some may think it prophetic), was to the effect that 'Education is the grave of a great mind.'

He now also gave a course of lectures on the 'new science' of Political Economy, which he had been studying since 1841. Henry Smith was amongst his auditors [1]. The lectures were renewed from time to time, but a few years after this he was wont to observe that Political Economy, like Benthamism, had done its work, except that there were problems connected rather with the distribution than the accumulation of wealth which had to be settled in the future [2]. A sentence in one of his letters to Lingen (September, 1846) is significant:—

'All the world are become Political Economists, and there

[1] See the *Economic Journal* for 1893, p. 745.

[2] It may be mentioned as an instance of his foresight, that he had counted upon the inevitable-ness and also the difficulty of the *land* question before the subject had been broached by any British statesman.

is almost as much reason to fear the application of these abstract principles to Ireland as there was formerly [to fear] their utter rejection.'

But the most substantial and permanent addition made by Jowett in the early years of his Tutorship to Oxford studies, was the introduction of Plato's *Republic* as a book to be taken up for the Schools. Hitherto, in Greek Philosophy at Oxford, the *Ethics* and the *Rhetoric* of Aristotle had been all in all. By lecturing on Plato, Jowett infused new life into the study of Greek and of Philosophy. He had been doing so at least as early as the Lent Term of 1847, although the practice of 'professing' the *Republic* became general only with the inauguration of the new system in 1853.

In 1846–1847 he was still subject to occasional fits of depression. His letters contain some curious reflections on this subject. To a friend, who had owned to the same weakness, he wrote half humorously in May, 1846 :—

'This malady to which we seem both subject, as far as my experience goes, begins with the stomach, extends itself to the head, where it dries up the fountains of the intellect, and is not wholly unconnected with the weather. This, in the language of Hegel, is its reality. But its ideality embraces a higher field : life, death, eternity, &c. The misfortune is that the world see it from the outside, whereas to yourself it generally retains its sublimer aspect from within.

'But joking apart (you must attribute what I am going to say to a headache or not), I feel every day what a serious thing it is, and that there is far more truth in its ideal side than in the other. It is a most painful thing to fancy that you have no moral nature, or power of fixing your own character ; no stamina that seems as if it could last you through life. I think one wants more resignation and more determined living on a system—to avoid excitement and all ecstatic efforts.

'. . . It must depend on oneself whether all this self-experience and over-sensibility ends in a morbid consciousness and dependence on others, or in a real self-sufficient knowledge of human nature. Let us be of good cheer, and trust that when the sky clears we may have life and spirits to enjoy it.'

In August, 1847, he 'made acquaintance for the first time' (as Boswell would say) with Selden's *Table-talk*, a copy of which, in the neat Pickering edition, then first published, was given to him by his friend Lingen. Two phrases of John Selden's became 'household words' with him: 'The best translation in the world' (of the English Authorized Version of the Bible), and 'Rhetoric turned into logic' (of some theological notions).

In April, 1848, the Revolution and the flight of Louis Philippe, which drove Jowett's parents for the time from Paris to Bonn, was the occasion of his excursion to Paris in company with Stanley, Palgrave, and Morier, of which a vivid account is given in the *Life of Dean Stanley*[1]. It there appears how Jowett's encouragement had rendered the scheme feasible by overcoming his companions' irresolution; and, according to Mr. F. T. Palgrave's diary of the expedition,

'It was Jowett who, on their arrival, at sight of the Tricolor and Tree of Liberty, expressed the feelings of the whole party, when he said, "How absurd all fears seemed now." . . . We turned a corner, and there was the long line of the Tuileries, with the Tricolor flying from the central dome—the deepest sign of the great change. . . . The Arch of Triumph in the Court of the Tuileries was guarded . . . not as of old by lofty gens d'armes, but by two young, resolute fellows of the Garde Mobile, in blouses and muskets. . . . Everywhere these soldiers of the people are on guard; they are at present the police of the town, and are said to do their duty in good earnest, and to the great preservation of public order. . . . Jowett, however, allows that he does not pass them without a shudder. One thing, Morier said, that seemed to

[1] Vol. i. pp. 390 ff.

have struck the people most, among the great events of the three days, was the discovery of the picture of *Christ* in the chapel of the Tuileries. Everything was being smashed *de fond en comble* by the people, when suddenly they reached this picture. Some one cried out that "every one should bare his head." The crowd at once did so, and knelt down, whilst the picture was carried out through the most utter silence— "you might have heard a fly buzz"—into a neighbouring church. Then the suspended wave of destruction rolled on. . . . Jowett says Paris is now *attristée*—the people in the streets remind one of London.'

Stanley brought from Matthew Arnold an introduction to the veteran historian, Michelet, who told them they had come too late or too soon : 'C'est l'entr'acte,' viz. between Revolution and Counter-revolution. Mr. Palgrave says :—

'S., J., and I chiefly sat and listened whilst Michelet went on from one thing to another for more than an hour. He seemed to anticipate much from the Chartist demonstration to-day (April 10). *J.*—"It will be of little consequence." *S.*—"Ireland will be our revolution."'

Besides Rachel's singing of the *Marseillaise*, they heard the people's stormy eloquence in the clubs, visited St. Cloud and Versailles, and fraternized with individual citizens. Lacordaire's sermon in Notre Dame Jowett thought far more eloquent than any English preaching that he knew of. But the most thrilling spectacle in which they shared was the distribution of colours to the troops of the Republic.

'*April* 20. . . . The day began in rain, but advanced to gleams of sunshine, which, passing up and down the long stream of bayonets that poured for twelve hours incessantly from the distant Tuileries or Place de la Concorde, lighted up the waving lines like a silver cornfield. There was every variety of colour in the advancing thousands, troops of the

line (saluted with cries of "Vive la Ligne!") mixed with the
dark uniform of the National Guard; then a splendid cavalry
regiment; then the ragged, but bold and soldier-like, Garde
Mobile, *enfants de la Révolution*, with green boughs and
flowers stuck at their musket ends. Stanley, Jowett, and
I joined one regiment and marched round close before
them, with bare heads, to the sound of drums and shouts of
"Vive la République!"

'. . . The members of the Government frequently passed
between the platform and the stairs which led downwards in
front of the gallery under the arch ; . . . and when Dupont de
l'Eure, aged, and dreamily looking out on the scene, or Arago,
or Cremieux, or Ledru-Rollin passed out, they had a free
way between the spectators. But when Louis Blanc, small,
piercing-looking, and thought-wearied, came out, there was
a cry and a rush, and all crowded about the little *ami des
ouvriers* with enthusiasm ; far more so when Lamartine, tall
and noble, with thoughtful and care-worn looks, passed among
us, with loud shouts of "Vive Lamartine!" There was one
rough fellow in a blouse who offered him a rose-bud, an
"offrande pour la patrie," to cheer him through the long,
weary day.'

I have transcribed this record because of its intrinsic
interest. On the whole it seems improbable that the
events of 1848, either at home or abroad, had any
important influence on Oxford politics or on Oxford
studies. As Canon North Pinder well observes :—

'The University at that time had not emerged from the
theological stage, and secular politics attracted comparatively
little interest. The best of the Dons were for the most part
Tractarians, and hated Liberalism of every shade as strongly
as Newman did, while the iron heel of the old Hebdomadal
Board crushed out every germ of liberal aspiration. . . .
Excitement in the February of 1848 there was in plenty ; but
it was not of a very intelligent kind, nor had much seriousness
about it. Christian Socialism was taken up ardently by the
few, who for a testimony were content to wear strange
patterned and ill-fitting trousers, made in the workshops of

the C. S. tailor. Foremost among these was John Conington, then Fellow of University, and a friend of Richard Congreve's. A. H. Clough was just then leaving Oxford, or he would doubtless have been a powerful factor in the new movement[1].

Yet a mind like Jowett's, although, as appears in the above narrative, he thought little of Chartism, could not remain unaffected by a great European change which had come immediately under his view.

With the exception of this excursion to Paris, his journeys abroad, after 1845, were less frequent and less extensive than they had been. His responsibilities were becoming more grave, and the φιλοθεάμων (lover of sight-seeing) was yielding to the φιλόσοφος (lover of wisdom). His desire to visit Rome, so keen in 1846–1847, was never gratified, although in one of those years, with ffolliott or some other friend, he went as far as to Florence. An occasional run to Switzerland might follow the annual visit to his parents at St. Germains (1849), or Fontaine-bleau (1850); he is known to have been at Chamounix in 1851; he took short tours with ffolliott, and visited him more than once in Ireland; but the bulk of the vacation was divided between Oxford and some country place, where he pursued his own studies while assisting those of some undergraduate friend. His thoughts became more and more concentrated on Theology. There are still extant amongst his papers some theological essays, most of which were probably composed when Stanley was preparing for publication his *Apostolical Age*, although, as mentioned in the last chapter, Jowett eventually declined to publish them in that volume. An examination of the essays in question may justify the conjecture that this refusal was partly due to a consciousness that

[1] Clough gave up his Fellowship at Oriel in 1848, against the earnest remonstrances of Jowett and other friends.

his opinions on Theology were not yet sufficiently matured.
The essay 'On the Person of Christ,' for example, is
an extremely subtle but hardly a satisfactory piece of
work.   It has the charm of Jowett's most finished style ;
but if he ever read it afterwards, he must have recognized
in it a moment of transition.   Traditional orthodoxy is
sublimated and held in solution by an application of
Hegelian method.   The feeling with which, on hearing it
said that Christ was merely human, he answered ' I shall
never say that,' is there in full intensity, but is expressed
in forms which retain a savour of scholasticism.   The
' golden haze' is still surrounding him ; he does not
yet 'look out on the open heaven.'   The essay on the
motive of Judas Iscariot in betraying our Lord turns on
a bold conception of the complexity and range of human
character.   To the suggestion of Whately and others,
that Judas acted from the disappointment of a mistaken
patriot, Jowett replies that in Oriental natures there
appear to be depths of treachery and perfidy which cannot
be measured by ordinary standards, but spring suddenly
into full activity no one can tell from whence.   A curious
speculation about angels under the title of ' Angelo-
phania ' is very characteristic of the transition phase of
which I have spoken.   A great step forwards in the
formation of his theological opinions appears to have
been made in the Long Vacations of 1846 and 1847,
especially the latter.   By this time the more comprehensive work on the New Testament, to be executed by
Stanley and Jowett in common, had been definitely
planned.

In 1848 began that long series of vacation readings
with Balliol pupils, of which Mr. F. T. Palgrave says :—

'During my Oxford time, and for years after, despite his
heavy work during Term-time, and the friends ready to welcome

him **during** vacation, he would constantly devote some weeks
of the Long to study in some pleasant place, with any
undergraduate he had noticed as of promise, though disposed
not to make the most **of** himself. These efforts, of course,
were not always enduringly successful. **Yet there** must be,
or have **been,** not a few, perhaps, who **could** look **back** to
these vacations as forming, more or less, **a** critical moment in
their lives, a "choice **of** Hercules." This, **indeed,** throughout
his own life was (it **has always** seemed **to** me) one of **the**
most admirable points in **his** character. **The** kind counsel—
wise, if not always applicable—to work while yet it was day,
to do all that a man could—a **doctrine wherein** he may
have been encouraged by **Dr. Johnson's** example—friends
old and young never failed **to receive from him at** all times
and seasons. One might sometimes **have been tempted** to
pray that his precious balms might **not break one's head,** if
the clear candour, good sense, and deep affectionate **interest
of** the adviser had not been always obvious. **Even Tennyson,
between whom and** the Master there was equal love **and
reverence for some forty** years, although he surely had **done
a** complete **man's work,** Jowett would still urge, after **the**
Idylls had appeared, **to** attempt some new and greater song.
Let us now whisper "**Requiescant** in pace."'

Jowett's **stay at Oban with Morier,** in 1848, unlike
some tutorial engagements **in previous years, was a** purely
voluntary arrangement on both **sides. They had** been
together at Paris in the previous spring, witnessing scenes
of revolution, and their life-long **friendship was** already
begun. They were again together in the **Long** Vacation
of 1849, occupying a farm-house at **Grange in** Borrowdale ; but the season **was** unpropitious, **and** Jowett began
to lose faith in the refreshing qualities of the Lake
country in comparison with Scotland. Accordingly, **in**
August, **1850,** he returned to Oban, this time with a party
of four, comprising Arthur Peel[1], T. Fremantle[2], **Henry**

[1] Lord Peel.   [2] Lord **Cottesloe.**

H. Lancaster, a Scotch Exhibitioner, and Donald Owen, a Blundell Scholar.

Jowett delighted in Oban, the scenery, the bathing, the walks and climbs, and also in the congenial society which he found in the neighbourhood. He had been originally drawn thither through his friendship with Alexander Ewing, Bishop of Argyll, whom he visited at Duntroon in successive years, and with whose daughter Nina (afterwards Mrs. Crum) he formed one of many child-friendships which have left a life-long impress on the friends so made. Finding her somewhat vague as to the use of money, he insisted on sending her small sums from time to time, of which he required from her a strict account. The value which the Bishop set on his conversation is manifest from several passages in the *Memoirs of Alexander Ewing*, by A. J. Ross. Reference is there made to an occasion when **Jowett read** the prayers, and **Stanley preached, in the** upper room which took the **place of an** episcopal church at Oban; **and the** Rev. H. B. Wilson, afterwards of *Essays and Reviews* celebrity, seems also to have been in the neighbourhood that summer. Jowett lent the Bishop a copy of Mr. Myers' *Catholic Thoughts*, printed for private circulation[1], a fact which, says the biographer, 'had a very important bearing on the Bishop's mental development.' The memoir records long and intimate conversations with Jowett at Duntroon in June, 1850, on many subjects, especially Christian evidences and the nature of revealed religion, also on the nature and development of the religious life. Jowett was charmed with the Bishop's simple, genial ways, and wrote to Stanley, 'He is some-

---

[1] Published some years afterwards. Jowett's copy was probably obtained through Stanley, from whom he had an introduction to Mr. Myers at Keswick.

times almost mad with fun.' This was the year of the wreck of the *Orion*, and a sermon of Jowett's on the Resurrection preached at the time seems to have produced a remarkable impression. The Bishop says, 'I felt as if, for me, the sea had given up her dead.'

Lord Peel has told me (December, 1895) of an incident that happened during the stay at Oban. The four pupils crossed one day in an open boat with one boatman to the island of Kerrera. While they were enjoying themselves there, the sky began to threaten, and the cautious Highlander warned them to return while it was light. With the recklessness of youth, they disregarded his advice, and when they started homewards the sea was rough. The boatman asked if any of them could row, and Peel, who had rowed at Oxford, took an oar. They made some headway, but when the middle of the strait was reached, a big wave laid the boat on her beam-ends. The man called out to them, 'Jump for your lives!' But at that moment the boat righted, and after much labour they got home. They found Jowett sitting alone at work. He insisted on their bathing their heads with spirits to counteract the chill; and when they had changed their dripping garments, taken some food, and recounted their adventure, he said quietly, 'Don't you think we had better have prayers?' They all knelt down, and he offered up an extempore thanksgiving for their deliverance.

Of all the pupils of this time there was none with whom his friendship afterwards became more intimate, or was more constantly maintained, than William Young Sellar, whose work on the Latin Poets will long remain a monument of critical erudition. He wrote of Sellar (after his death in 1890):—

'I shall always think of him as long as I live. He was so

simple and kind, so free from jealousy or ambition or self in any form, so "transparent," and so fond of his friends, and himself so unlike others, that we cannot help mourning when we think that we shall never see him again. . . . I remember also more than forty years ago his coming up to stand for the Scholarship and the old Master remarking on his handsome youthful look. The five or six men who were elected in that set were a remarkable band :—Sandars, Grant, H. Smith, and a year or two previous Riddell and M. Arnold. I am pleased to think that they stood together and had a strong affection for one another through life[1], and that Balliol College was accidentally the centre of this connexion.'

Meanwhile the notes on the Epistles for the projected joint work with Stanley were in progress, and Jowett's theological position was becoming more clearly defined. The study of philosophy had loosened the bonds of ecclesiastical tradition. As he says himself in his reminiscences of Mr. Ward[2], he had 'put away casuistry and was determined to place religion on a moral and historical basis.' 'Really, I think,' he writes to Stanley, 'one must give up admiring or looking for help from others in Theology.' The writings of the Tübingen theologians, headed by F. C. Baur, were at this time the last word of modern criticism, and in his own work, of which he felt the increasing magnitude, Jowett availed himself largely of their suggestions : but he could never be reckoned as a close follower of any school. In all that he has written, there is the note of first-hand inquiry and original thought. And throughout the confusion

---

[1] A proof of this appears in Matthew Arnold's letter to Shairp of April 12, 1866:—'It gives me great pleasure that you and Sellar like *Thyrsis* : . . . the voices I do turn to are those of our old set, now so scattered, who, at the critical moment of opening life, were among the same influences and (more or less) sought the same things as I did myself' (*Letters of M. A.*, vol. i. p. 326).

[2] *W. G. Ward and the Oxford Movement*, p. 434.

of the years which followed on the collapse of **Newmanism he held firmly to the** pursuit of the 'practical **ideal,'**
standing jealously aloof both from scientific materialism
and from mere literary and artistic self-culture.

In a letter to Stanley (1847) he remarks, '**It strikes
me that the German** theologues get more and more
drawn into the whirlpool of philosophy, and that all
their various harmonies are but faint echoes of Schelling
and Hegel.'

In **F. C.** Baur, however, **he found a** critical spirit that,
while following in the footsteps **of Hegel, was able to use
the** weapons of philosophy **freely and without pedantry.**
This flashed upon him with **the light of a new discovery**
at the end of the Long Vacation of **1848** ; **when,** in the
same letter in which he urges Stanley **not to** refuse
the Modern History Chair if offered, although **he still
looked to their** joint work on the New Testament **as
the source for them both** of 'many happy years,' he
writes : '**Baur appears to me** the ablest book I have
ever **read on St. Paul's** Epistles : a remarkable combination of Philological **and** Metaphysical power, without the intrusion of Modern Philosophy.'

Another **letter to Stanley of January 10, 1849, gives**
a welcome glimpse of his literary work **at the time :—**

'**I have** to apologize for much **seeming** indolence about
the Commentary. It has been really unavoidable. . . . This
vacation **I** shall have completed my **translation of** Hegel's
Logic, and, I hope, my part of the work **on the** Universities[1].
Then **I** have a **short** paper to write on **Kant and** Hegel, for
the Moral Philosophy Society. Then, lastly, I desire to write
a short review of your Sermons[2] in the *Edinburgh,* which has

---

[1] See p. **177.**

[2] Stanley **seems to have been**
cast down about the effect of **his**
Sermons. Jowett wrote to him :

'Why do you call your Sermons
unfortunate ? *Fortunati nimium!*
. . . A suspicion sometimes comes
over you that your work is and

long been in my mind: after which I shall expatiate in boundless freedom[1].'

The letter to **Dr. Greenhill** appended to the last chapter[2] shows his resolution to 'consume his own smoke,' **and** to keep his religious feelings to himself. **The** present labour afforded an **outlet in** which some part of his personal **religious life** became absorbed. He said long afterwards **to a friend** who had purchased his book **on the Epistles, 'I** am grateful to every one who reads **that** book; I put so much of myself into it.' It should **be borne in** mind that this work had been preceded **by a** close study of the Gospels, which had been included **in** the original scheme. In the **autumn** of 1846 he **had** written to Stanley :—

'I am still at work **on the three** Gospels, **and** am trying to make a careful comparison **of them** throughout ; **a** work of much time with little to **show.** I think it may be proved that there is **no passage of** four or five verses in length, where there is not **either** discrepancy or over-close resemblance for independent **writers.** If this can be brought home, it **blows** away attempts at chronology, harmony, arguments from style, &c. I mean to read over a part of the Septuagint, to examine the variations in **the** MSS. and see whether anything analogous can be detected.'

The first trace of the concentration of his labours on will be in vain. Nothing but the thought of this can make it so. **No one** can tell what will be the **effect of** these Sermons on the minds **of** Heads **of Houses** and country parsons, but it cannot be irretrievable or make you "forfeit beyond recovery **the** confidence of the Church of England." Moreover the sort of ambiguous orthodoxy of Hare, Maurice, and Bunsen must surely be a great evil.'

[1] In these years he wrote much which never saw the light, and planned more :—for example, an *Edinburgh Review* article on the Hampden Controversy of 1847. An Essay on Pascal, which I remember seeing on his table about 1850, may have been published, **but I know** not where.

[2] p. 109.

St. Paul occurs in a letter to Stanley in the autumn of 1847: 'I have to-day finished a short essay on Romans i. 17 about Natural Religion.' He adds:—

'I hope you will always rest assured that I feel it to be the greatest blessing and happiness to me to bear a part with you in this work. I feel that I could not do it alone. It has done more to cure me of nervous headaches, &c., than any Long Vacation trip I ever took.'

In 1850 William Jowett died. The two brothers, William and Alfred, had just agreed to make a handsome remittance to their mother, and to relieve Benjamin from a moiety of the burden which he so long had borne. The amount of that burden, long studiously concealed, was made known to Dean Stanley when the salary for the Greek Chair had been at last secured in 1865. It was then stated at £400 a year [1].

In a letter to John ffolliott, he says:—

'First, of my dearest brother, whom as long as I live I shall remember. I have the pleasantest recollection of him possible, and his cheerful happy ways amid the trials we had to undergo in his early life. He left us eight years ago to go as a cadet to India, and as far as I can learn during all this time he acted rightly amid many temptations and was universally beloved. Perhaps I exaggerate my recollection of him—it is hard not to do so when a person is taken from us—I was always proud of him and used to think that I never knew in a young fellow a greater union of manliness and gentleness and good sense. I hoped when he came back in two years' time to introduce him to my friends: therefore let me talk of him to you now, as it pleases me to do so, if it does not bore you.'

I have reserved for the following chapter the movement towards University Reform in which both Jowett and

---

[1] See chap. x. *sub fin.* Yet in 1849 he was assisting a poor man to emigrate: and in 1852 he proposed to contribute £50 a year to the support of a 'Balliol Hall.' (See p. 213.)

Stanley took an active part from the spring of 1846. This went on simultaneously with the activities which have now been described, but an historical question of such importance requires consecutive treatment.

This chapter may conclude with some extracts from a note-book of Sir Alexander Grant's, in which, while an undergraduate, he recorded conversations with Jowett :—

1846. 'We hear people talk of a "free" translation and a "literal" translation. This is a false distinction. There can properly be neither the one nor the other. A translation is only good, and only to be called a translation, when it exactly conveys in our language the feelings expressed in the foreign language. To translate well from Greek is as great a work and requiring as much practice as to turn a piece of English into Greek.'

'To give oneself up to "Scholarship" is much the most useful thing while an undergraduate. To be able to turn a piece of English into good Latin is a better sign of power, and gives more promise than knowing the whole of Tennyson and Wordsworth, and all such books.'

'None of those people who were about Coleridge have left us a good account of him. Gillman died before the second volume was published—the *Table-talk* does not do him justice at all, for though it tells us what he said, yet it does not give us any idea of that stream which used to flow on so uninterruptedly—as for instance it is said of him that, on one occasion, he talked for a whole night without stopping, in a drawing-room, about Kant's metaphysics, and made the ladies listen. There are some remarkable points in his character, as for instance, his extreme egotism, and his want of truthfulness in certain things. That case of his taking a whole paragraph of Schelling as his own, is excused by some on the ground that he had it copied out among his own papers, and that, as he himself tells us, there were certain writers who had contributed to form his mind and were virtually part of himself. But altogether we must look at this and other acts as different in him from any one else. He seems often not to have known what he was doing. We must separate men like him from common persons, and look at them partly as though they were madmen. But he was a great man, and we must be thankful for what he has done for us. In his theological writings he was always truthful and fair ; but his political views seem very warped ; that essay on international law in the *Friend* goes on a very distorted view of morals. His character of Pitt is full of a personal bitterness which perhaps later in life he might not have felt. His gradual conversion to a right belief is to be attributed partly to his gaining sounder views of philosophy, partly perhaps to his bad health, which, coming upon him as it did, would dispose him to seriousness. At Berlin I talked to Schelling about Coleridge's plagiarism ; he seemed very good-natured about it, and said that Coleridge had expressed many things better than he could himself, that in one word he had comprised a whole essay, saying that mythology was not allegorical but tautegorical.'

'*Sunday, February* 20, 1848.—B. J. sent for me to ask me about Harrow. I could not give him much information. I was leaving him, but I could not open his outer door. After trying in vain we called for Herbert[1] and sent for a blacksmith. I sat down for about half an hour. I tried to draw him into conversation. He answered by detached sentences, and of course as I could not enter into his thoughts sufficiently, we could not get thoroughly interested, so as to flow on spontaneously.'

[Jowett's detached sentences are represented in the following notes.]

[J.] 'I like the Sundays at home much better. The parish service is so much nicer. If we had music in our chapels I should like it better ; the singing and the heartiness of the congregation at home adds so much. Newman's influence in University preaching is exaggerated. There used to be perhaps twenty-five undergraduates in the gallery ; very few cared about him or went to hear him. There was, in all his practical earnestness, an undercurrent of his own peculiar views. A remarkable instance of that was a sermon on

---

[1] The College servant in the Fisher Building.

Elijah—in which to the uninitiated nothing would have appeared remarkable, but which was in reality a claiming for himself to remain in the Church on the same terms as Elijah had remained under an unregenerate Kingdom in Israel.—High Church principles can never be really impressed upon the poor. Sewell has gone far to produce that very doubt and scepticism and want of an objective standard of which he himself complains. It must unsettle people to hear men like him talking so rashly and positively about things which they have been accustomed to hold most sacred.—The verbal inspiration of the Scriptures was necessary to the mystical interpretation of them, such as the Fathers employed, therefore those who hold to the one must hold to the other. It was never doubted before this century. Christian Evidences must vary much at different times. Some people find the argument of miracles—some the indications of a Creator —some the internal evidence—some analogy, most convincing. Perhaps a time may come when we shall see them all combined. Paley's argument must not be pressed too far : it consists of two propositions, (1) that the miracles are evidenced by the Apostles dying in vindication of them ; (2) the miracles of the fourth century, &c., have no such evidence. But the first limb will not stand, because Paul can hardly be said to have "counted all lost " for the sake of the miracles alone. It was rather Christianity as a whole, all he had seen and heard and felt, that impressed him, so that he would even lay down his life. No more will the second limb, because, whether true or not, we believe that Loyola would quite have died to vindicate what he believed to be miracles.'

LETTERS, 1846–1850.

To A. P. Stanley.

Beaumaris[1], *August 1*, 1846.

. . . Have you read Hook's Pamphlet[2], and how do you like it? All Liberals, of course, do : at the same time the text of it seems rather to be, 'Let us teach Church principles without the bore of having to teach children to read.' It is surely a great 'Schiefheit,' that anti-Hegelian mode of distinguishing religious and moral and secular education. One might much more truly say, 'You cannot teach reading without teaching morality,' and then, of course, teaching morality is a sort of infidelity without teaching religion. Upon Dr. Hook's plan the secular education must be absolutely mechanical—the better it is, the worse it is —no more morality must be allowed than is absolutely neces- sary to teach people to read. And then the tickets that the children are to bring to prove attendance at the Church or Chapel School before they can be allowed to go to the secular —and in a free country ! And the squirearchy guardians of education ! . . . Fancy the Squire, especially if he is the Parson of the Parish, considering impartially the claims of his 'Dissent- ing brethren.'

I think there are only two ways in respect of Education which are worth considering—a national scheme of general religion, i. e. in what men of the world and thoughtful men acknowledge the essentials, leaving the Sunday Schools untouched, whether Church or Dissent ; in short, a 'gigantic scheme of unbelief' as

---

[1] Beaumaris in Anglesey was near to Penrhyn, where some of Stanley's relatives lived.

[2] The Rev. Walter Farquhar Hook, Vicar of Leeds, afterwards Dean of Chichester, published in 1846 a Letter to the Bishop of St. David's, *How to render more efficient the Education of the People.*' See *Dean Stanley's Letters*, p. 106 (letter of August 4, 1846).

Evangelicals and Puseyites would call it—and the giving money
to each sect separately to apply as they please. Government
Inspectors ' in plain clothes ' might be stationed in the distance,
who should gradually approach nearer and nearer until the clergy
at length discovered that they had taken the whole into their
custody. Any scheme of education . . . must be done by some
great doer of the age, who is able to act out the discovery of
a truth through all its stages, and who does not get too soon
convinced of the whole truth.

The only thing to be thought of in favour of **Dr. Hook's** plan
as it seems to me, is whether secular education will not of itself
break up sectarianism.   But one does not like to lose so great an
opportunity for moral and religious good.   Look forward thirty
years, and all Dr. Hook can hope for is twice as many Puseyites as
at present, twice as many Evangelicals, and the great solid mass of
the world with its many virtues external to the Church—utterly
unimpressed—with twice as much education as at present,
with twice as many newspaper and railroad influences. . . .
How Arnold would have blown his trumpet !

To R. R. W. Lingen.

Beaumaris, *August* 7, 1846.

. . . I have been working lately at the three first Gospels, to
try if possible to find out the manner in which they came into
their present form.   Nothing can exceed the absurdities which
the orthodox English divines have talked about this subject.
They very nearly all believe that by attentive and accurate
observation of facts, the three Evangelists, without any concert,
were led to describe them in the same words.   If you have any
curiosity about this, which is a most curious question for lawyers[1],
you will find a *résumé* of the opinions in Horne's *Introduction*
(Vol. ii. p. 2, at the end), whose only zeal is, of course, how to be
most orthodox.   I would sooner believe that every Cross in
Christendom is of the wood of the true Cross, than that such
a miracle as their theory requires had taken place.   So much
seems clear, but the problem is so hopelessly complex, where

---

[1] Lingen was at this time studying for the Bar.

you have the power of assuming *ad libitum* Aramaic documents and oral Gospels, that I think the only thing to be done is to prove it insoluble except in a general way. . . .

To A. P. Stanley.

Beaumaris, *August* 17, 1846.

. . . A thought has struck me often during the last few weeks, which is, I think, comforting about one's vocation in life. Considering how little sympathy I have with the clergy, for I never hear a sermon scarcely which does not seem equally divided between truth and falsehood, it seems like a kind of treachery to be one of them. But I really believe that treachery to the clergy is loyalty to the Church, and that if religion is to be saved at all it must be through the laity and statesmen, &c., not through the clergy. Is there any reason to think that if the clergy with their present intolerance, ignorance, narrowness and love of pious frauds, could succeed to the utmost of their wishes, they would produce any other revival than such a one as seems to be going on in France at present, four out of five women made semi-Catholics, four out of five men made semi-Infidels?

What I mean is, that I do not see that one need look upon one's occupation as gone because the usual routine is very much shut up. It is in reality a higher work that opens, trying to make the laity act up to and feel their own religious principles. Surely it is a surprising thing what a much higher tone they have of late years taken, e.g. in the House of Commons, &c., while, at the same time, the old talk of the clergy about sacrilege, &c., Irish Bishoprics, Penal Acts, divine right of education, has been gradually exploding. While Arnold was chiefly known among the clergy, he was reviled and despised : I doubt whether, even now, there are a hundred clergymen over forty who feel any sympathy with him ; but the laity ' rose at him.'

His theory of Church and State seems to me chiefly a mistake, because it is for making a work outward and external which should be inward and spiritual, and also because it implies that Church and State is a device of statesmen or of Churchmen, and not a natural dualism, which except among angels who are above this world or infidels who know of no other, must ever be. It involves two impossibilities, to destroy one Church and build up another.   I think too that in his way of speaking it was wrong to imply that we, and especially the clergy, were so very bad and corrupt.   Altogether, whatever truth there was in it seems to have been inconsiderately expressed.   If there should ever be a second Reformation we shall not say ' Lo here or Lo there.'

... I find rest here a good thing, and my pupil works hard and is very considerate.   About September 20 I am free.   It has struck me you might like to go over to Ireland for a fortnight about that time, see Dublin, ' Derrynane Abbey,' &c.   Would not this be more relaxation than hovering about the coast of Norfolk ?   Therefore come to Ireland ; shake hands with the Liberator [1] ; see Roman Catholicism in a new form, get a nostrum to cure Irish evils, and qualify yourself to talk with country gentlemen all your life on the subject.

To R. R. W. LINGEN.

BEAUMARIS, *August* 18, 1846.

... The Aristocracy is too long a subject to discuss in a letter. You seem to me to imagine this oligarchy to be a much more narrow thing than it really is.   It cannot do without wealth— it is liable to become a jest :—it cannot do without education, for [then] it is robbed of more than half its associations.   And in this way the Plutocracy and the aristocracy of talent, the latter partly through the professions, are ever blending with it, and as it seems to me becoming greatly improved by it.   It may sound natural to say 'I value a man at what he really is'; but can you separate a man from circumstances in this way ? ... If you say 'No, but I will resist artificial distinctions'—this seems to me the very point—does not all experience show that this is a natural distinction ?   If it were true that there is no sense in which the aristocracy are better than shopkeepers, is it conceivable that in these days they could keep up a merely feudal distinction ?   No distinction lingers so long in a revolution or so soon returns.   Is it not true that the gentlemanly virtues (I do not mean real worth) exist tenfold among the aristocracy for one 'gentleman by

[1] O'Connell.

nature' you find among the middling classes? A gentleman's motto ought to be regardlessness of money except in great things and as a matter of duty—a tradesman's motto ought to be, 'Take care of the pence and the pounds, &c.' And when one remembers what a hold this principle must get, I do not think we can afford to give up aristocracy as an element of National Education. . . .

To R. R. W. Lingen.

BEAUMARIS, *August* 24, 1846.

. . . I confess it is the priestcraft of S. Oxon. I am most afraid of. Coming the Bishop of Oxford is, I am afraid, likely to be a much more successful game than coming the Bishop of Exeter over the world. Think of a man who always looks good, out of whose mouth Christian charity flows like rivers of oil, equally respected by old women and prime ministers, who never for a moment loses sight of spiritual in his search after temporal things. . . .

To A. P. Stanley.

August, 1846.

. . . You have everything to encourage you both in the past and the future, if you would but bring yourself to believe that you have the power of self-improvement. I sometimes think that you indulge a kind of fatalism about character; there are no faults intellectual or otherwise which may not be got rid of, if the right methods are used—sometimes fighting them, sometimes flying from them. Let us think of journeying on until seventy in these kind of pursuits; the thought, perhaps you will say, is oppressive. But let us try and 'victual ourselves for such a voyage as this.'

There is something impertinent in this sort of 'subjective' letter, even between two intimate friends; therefore excuse it. It is needless to say that I know a thousand times more folly in myself than these defects in you—I mean, indecision and premature theorizing. I have been anxious about it for a long time, and as your letter gives me an occasion, say what I feel once for all.

To A. P. STANLEY.

August, 1846.

. . . About publishing them [1] in your book I scarcely know what answer to give. It would be pleasant to have them put with your Sermons and would, perhaps, get them readers, and might give me some note, good or evil. I have often dreamed of this, and feel most sincerely that it is truly kind of you to give me a chance I might never have again of putting myself ' in oculis hominum.' But, for reasons that do not in the least degree apply to you, I must, however reluctantly, say No.

. . . I do not ever wish or desire or think it possible that the clergy should be done away ; their institution is 'a supply to the imperfection of our nature,' and though essentially imperfect may ever approximate to something better. The Woods and Hansards must give up sectarianism, keep their common sense, and get more if they can. A sort of instinct, it may be hoped, will make them retire from debateable ground. I think that the position of the clergy is only melancholy where it is neither speculative nor practical. If Biblical criticism spreads they will be driven, as many of them have been by Puseyism, into the practical, and cease to give such an account of the visitation of Ahab's sins on his posterity as I heard last Sunday from Mr. Blomfield [2], a true younger brother of the Bishop ; or such an account of the internal evidences of religion as he favoured us with to-day. Really, I never hear a sermon of which it is possible to conceive that the writer has a serious belief about things— if you could but cross-examine him he would perjure himself every other sentence. Morality is, for the sort of men you speak of, a great light ; they must bury themselves in their parishes and learn humility and drink no more the dregs of Orthodoxy. If they could get rid of Theology altogether and learn the New Testament, especially the Gospels, by heart, it would be well. From the side of Christian charity, too, they are quite accessible. Politics, Maynooth Grants, Education questions must with or without them be settled

[1] His Theological Essays.

[2] Rev. G. B. Blomfield, Rector of Stevenage, Hants, Prebendary of Chester, and Rural Dean.

in the next ten years, and unless they are prepared for an irreconcilable war with the course of events they will sit down and be 'rationally pious.' There seems good hope, I think, that what has already taken place in politics among statesmen will take place among Churchmen—plain matter of fact people in a matter of fact country will honestly look about them and see what wants doing.

About Arnold's theory I do not quite agree. Its fault is not simply, I think, that it is too concrete, but that it does not acknowledge the true *concreteness* of the Church as it is. When it gets out of the Ideal, it is not merely impracticable, but a falsehood. Men must have religion, but they are not all equally religious; their inward requires an outward; but external institutions are not things of degrees, they cannot represent shades of feeling and opinion. And therefore when you say, 'If they must have a Church externally, this is the true external,' I cannot consent, because it is leading men to expect an outward form of the Church which never can be while human nature remains, and drawing them from the true form which we have at present and [which] may ever approximate towards the spiritual, although the dualism will still remain :—

> Was ist wirklich, das ist vernünftig:
> Was ist vernünftig, das ist wirklich.

Granting the truth of Christianity, the opposition having lasted 1800 years is a tolerable proof that it is 'wirklich.'

No, it is not the system, but the ἦθος[1] of the English Church, which is distasteful to me. The change of this ἦθος ought to preserve, not destroy the system. If we could once get out of the pious fraud line, Englishmen would not soon relapse into it, whereas Germans are, I think, ever liable to returns of the malady.

Your two last letters gave me great delight. I feel every day of my life that if one is ever to be of any good, idiosyncrasies, eccentricities, irritabilities, excitements, self-consciousnesses, follies of all sorts must be got rid of. No more subjectivity, but I hope you are going on your way rejoicing.

---

[1] The moral tone.

To A. P. STANLEY.

Saturday, August, 1846.

. . . Another *Tablet*[1] came to-day—one still missing. Number one I like better than number two. The beginning conciliates me; but it really makes me sick at heart to think of the past, to find *mutatis mutandis* the same thing going on still on a humbler scale, a self-deception so uncommonly like truth, and so all-pervading. Is it possible that a man of his great activity of mind, with all his recollections of Arnoldism, Whatelyism, as well as of his deep faith in the weaknesses of Puseyism, can remain as he is with nothing short of 'vera sunt vera,' &c.[2]? It is not Catholicism I care about, but he is such a monstrous unnatural Catholic, not like Pascal giving up human learning, or like the Hermesians throwing up a sort of Pantheistic outwork, but distorting every kind of human knowledge which he does not ignore. Many a sceptic there must have been in the Roman Catholic Church who has died humbly receiving the Sacraments, and believing in eternal possibilities, but this is very different from this concentrated scepticism with its ponderous front of dogmatism, which not only does not believe, but is incapable of believing because it believes everything. With Pascal or Newman I cannot help feeling the deepest sympathy; they do not say it, of course, but you feel they are clinging to it as a last resource, if the mercy of God may accept them now that they have given up the strife. With the lusty orthodoxy of Ward I have no sympathy; he is too flush and full-blown, and too light in condemning others, considering all the past.

[1] W. G. Ward, having become a Roman Catholic, was now writing a series of articles in the *Tablet*.

[2] See *W. G. Ward, &c.*, p. 115, note 1: 'One of his (John Carr's) inventions which I happen to remember, is worth preserving: "Vera sunt vera ac falsa sunt falsa. At si Ecclesia dixerit vera esse falsa ac falsa esse vera, tum vera sunt falsa ac falsa sunt vera"' (True things are true and false things are false; but if the Church should say that false things were true and true things were false, then true things are false and false things are true).

'This oracular saying he brought out with great seriousness as a quotation from Bellarmine.'

For John Carr see above, p. 59.

To R. R. W. Lingen.

Beaumaris, *September* 5, 1846.

. . . It is impossible that we can have the faith of our fathers, because the light will be always breaking in upon us. . . . Religion, it might be said, has become more a matter of reason . . . more extended, less concentrated, not one belief but an equilibrium of all the elements of belief. . . . A man may live in a happy valley with respect to religion ; the misfortune of which is, that he excommunicates his neighbours ; but if he looks out into the world East and West, *in hac immensitate longitudinum latitudinum*, &c., of speculative truth, it is impossible that his views of Christianity should not be modified ; and one man will think that he is defiling the simplicity of Christ, and puffed up with knowledge falsely so called, while another might fancy that there may be here something of the wisdom which St. Paul or St. John, living now, would have spoken among those that are perfect. Think of how many unpleasant truths there are that remain untold about Christianity and Christendom, and yet we all give an implied assent to interpreting the Gospel by the course of the world. . . .

To A. P. Stanley.

Beaumaris, *September* 6, 1846.

. . . What a grand fellow the new Pope [1] seems to be ! What say you to this as a politico-historical prophecy for 1856 ? I mean, worthy to be the picture at the beginning of Moore's Almanack and nothing more :—Italy an ecclesiastical Republic, Pansclavismus with one arm reaching into Poland become an independent province, and the other in Bohemia ; two great German kingdoms, Protestant and Catholic, the first advancing on Denmark with a navy on the Baltic, the second looking upon Switzerland as though it loved it ; Spain a sort of dependent on France, which should have moved onward to the Rhine ; America with towns and ports all along the Pacific, and England steaming it over the whole world, a great Steam Navigation Company with stations at Oceania,

[1] Pio Nono.

New Zealand, Australia, India, the Cape, &c. There should be railroads, too, intersecting India, and 'British Capital' should have cut through the Isthmus of Darien; mountains being blown up by some unknown Warner[1] invention, and locks made sufficient to support the weight of an ocean. Here I am getting out of my latitude and shall therefore stop, but I think you must allow that the plan for Europe is about as good as the treaty of Vienna, if it were only possible. My balance of power should be Protestant against Catholic Germany, France and England against Panslavismus and despotism; Germany a debateable ground, and the Pope without reference to nice distinctions of doctrine looking simply to the question of how he might best keep his head above water.—I find reading prosper here and therefore purpose staying about three weeks longer, when I wend my way probably to the Lakes, Durham, York, Lincoln, Peterborough, Cambridge;—a Cathedral tour, you see. . . .

To R. R. W. Lingen.

BEAUMARIS, *September*, 1846.

. . . Just now persons who are at all thoughtful about things do seem strangely solitary, 'wandering about in sheep-skins and goatskins': at first sight there might seem no limit to scepticism in speculation, and that practical changes were getting altogether unmanageable. I do not think this is so really. Is not the sin of infidelity in a great measure despair about the course of the world?

. . . The *Vestiges of Creation* I have read. The way in which it was attacked by Sedgwick disgusted me. I dare say it is all wrong, but cannot see that there is any religious interest against it any more than against science in general. All science tends to demonstration, to lock up the world under a series of causes and effects. It is no use to make religion fill up the interstices of science which are merely accidental; I mean, to seek the freedom of the will, for example, in the denial of materialism. As to revelation, you are retreating

---

[1] Warner's Explosive Force: first widely known through an experiment in Shoreham Roads, July 20, 1844. See *Times* for July 22, 1844.

inch by inch from before astronomy, geology, linguistik, history, and criticism in general. As to natural religion, the German metaphysicians would all find a place for materialism as a complete though one-sided account of the world. Sedgwick and Co. do unmixed evil by making that the battleground, on which they must be beaten.

To R. R. W. Lingen.

March 10, 1847.

. . . What is to be done about Ireland? a question every day becoming more aweful.

Dufferin of Christ Church, who seems a most excellent tuft, went over to Skibbereen about a fortnight since and brings back, as you may expect, the most horrible accounts. He says that the dead from starvation and fever are about one-third, that a regular cart goes about like the descriptions in the plague, that the men who are *employed* on the public works can scarcely stand from their meagre food and diet, &c. Lord Lansdowne told M. Arnold the other day that he expected 1,000,000 of persons would die before it was over. Notwithstanding the £200,000 subscription it is difficult to persuade oneself that enough is doing in England. I do not quite understand why 1,000,000 of people should die with a free trade in corn and an income in this country of £300,000,000 a year: it could not cost more than about £6 a year to keep them alive per head. Is it absolutely impossible for persons who have the greatest knowledge of Ireland, to hit upon some method between public works and mere charity which might apply £6,000,000 usefully? Now, it does seem to me, has come the time for England to repay all her debts to Ireland and lay the foundation of a new connexion between the countries. There is of course the double difficulty how to get it and how to use it—English credit and Irish corruption; but I can hardly think insuperable. Such a mistake as the Government have made about the public works is, surely, without excuse, although civil things are said about it in the House of Commons. It must have been easy to foresee, that the small farmers without money or means of subsistence would be driven on the public works instead of cultivating their own land.

It is against all the rules of Political Economy to be in favour of a poor law, but in the present case, does it not seem as if the barbarous nature of the people and the interests of the landholders are leagued against it equally? Suppose the rental of Ireland £36,000,000, and one-third of it to have been collected, why not reduce the landholders a little and make them understand that the crisis of their country requires a little more than 'giving up pastry'? Unless Ireland makes much greater sacrifices it is impossible to persuade England to make the necessary sacrifices.

To A. P. STANLEY (ON HIS RETURN FROM SPAIN).

[OXFORD, *April or May*, 1847.]

Ὦ μακάριε καὶ τρισμακάριε καὶ μακαριώτατε [1], ut sis vitalis metuo [2] : but think you may possibly recover from this historical surfeit.

. . . This is only to greet you ; it is a waste of time writing as you return to these bustling scenes so soon. 'Had it not been for the battle of Tours,' Oxford might have been Granada, St. Mary's a mosque, you exegetical professor of the Koran, giving equal offence both to the Sonnites and Shuites.

I am delighted to hear of the prosperity of your tour, although I was not there to plan it. I hope I shall live to see the East some day and (not in Moses's company) 'make a pilgrimage to the Holy City.'

There is nothing to tell here ; *stagnant omnia*. With your Sermons and my Essays I have done nothing; the last, because I found it so difficult to rewrite them.

I have been reading the Counter-Reformation in Ranke. How strange the causes which religious changes depend upon ! At one time scarce any Catholics in Austria, at another all France on the point of joining the Huguenots. At Gratz in 1596 all Protestants, 1598 all the Lutheran Ministers expelled ; compare Oxford 1844 to 1847. 'If you mark the history of the Popes well, look you, the history of the Heads of Houses comes indifferent well after it [3].'

---

[1] 'Happy, thrice happy, nay most happy!' Cf. Ar. *Eccl.* 1129.

[2] 'Too happy to live long.'— Horace, *Sat.* II. i. 60.

[3] Cf. Shakesp., *Henry V*, iv. 7. 35.

To R. R. W. LINGEN.

DULOE, NEAR LISKEARD,
August 21, [1847].

I have got so transcendentalized lately with reading Schelling's *Systems of Nature* that it is quite a blessing to get back again to the outward world. I confess I begin to look upon metaphysics rather as a necessity than as a great good—the air is too rarefied to breathe long, and you are like a balloon, a good deal at the mercy of the currents. Yet the spiritual world is so much like the ideal one that it is impossible to stir a step in theology without them. . . .

. . . Do you think that the existing state of opinions in morals, theology, &c., will 'break up before we are yet old men'? Looking at the progress of criticism and of physical science, at the plasters we have been applying to theology, I fancy that a second Reformation is not impossible even in our time. I hope that whatever comes of it will not be egotheism—which seems a compound of indomitable egotism with the artistic love of truth—but some real and practical good. I notice in several persons whose opinions on many things are much to be respected a great tendency to this artist-like perception of right and wrong—Truth under the image of a beautiful statue, a naked statue too, stripped bare of the garment in which education has clothed her. I greatly lament I cannot myself get more practical; one has such a weak hold on the world or on other people—you acquire a sort of feeble intelligence of everything and lose force of mind and character. . . .

To A. P. STANLEY.

[*August*, 1847.]

. . . I think we ought to do more towards it [the book on the New Testament] than we have done in the last two years, if we are to live to see it finished. I wish we could read through the New Testament together, to begin with : otherwise there will be no sort of unity in what we write. I know very well how ignorant one of the commentators is, who has been spinning cobwebs for the last four years instead of arranging facts and gaining real knowledge.

My own wish would be, if it is to your taste, to work at it together, something in the same fashion that Liddell and Scott did at their *Lexicon.* We might read separate series of authors, and if our work could be made to square with the Lectures it would be a great gain. Next Term I could read the Epistles with you three or four evenings in the week, if you are not alarmed by such a proposal.

What think you of making a paraphrase of the Epistles, like Locke? I wish there were any one to whom we could look, like Arnold, for advice and assistance, but it is no use to lean upon broken reeds.

. . . Do you know Selden's *Table-Talk*? If you have not got it, I will order it and make you a present of it. 'All the best commentators on hard texts of Scripture have been laymen.' 'Now oaths are so frequent they should be taken like pills. If you chew them they are bitter : if you think what you swallow, it will hardly go down.' Bishop Wilkins, editor of Selden's works, cannot believe them [1] to be genuine.

Where are you going after September 22? I must go to Paris first of all to see my father and mother ; but for the last fortnight or three weeks I would gladly meet you in Normandy or at Paris, if you liked a short French tour.

To B. C. Brodie.

1 *Great George Street*, [1848].

I hope it will not seem to be from any unkindness that I have not seen so much of you as formerly. It grieves me to think how very much we disagree in opinion, but I trust we have still the 'common ground of conscientiousness' of which you once spoke to me. I do not like to say anything more about these subjects, because I shall only seem to condemn you, and show myself inconsistent. The strongest feeling that I have is that no merely artistic religion or morality has any real truth or usefulness, or can have any hold on the minds of men

[1] Viz. the sayings recorded in Selden's *Table-Talk.*

in general.   Do let me urge you to be as serious as you possibly can in considering these things, which, if not aweful realities, are still very aweful when we think of our absolute ignorance about them.

To A. P. Stanley.

Oban, [*September,*] 1848.

My own feeling would be that you should not refuse a position [the Chair of Modern History] for which, without flattery, you are fitter than any one else who could be found.   I do not like to urge your standing for it, considering how we are circum-stanced with the Commentary, out of which I look for us both for many happy years' work : ὅπερ οὐκ ἐνδέχεται πάρεργον εἶναι[1]. But, if it is offered, I would not refuse. . . . Any scheme of University improvement would be greatly aided by your having the Chair.

Many thanks for your letter, which amused me greatly. Le gros Citoyen[2] and ffolliott (who is here and speaks of you in the kindest manner) desire their best regards.   I am just returned from Staffa and Iona. . . . Baur appears to me the ablest book I have ever read on St. Paul's Epistles : a re-markable combination of the philological and metaphysical power, without the intrusion of modern philosophy as in Usteri.

To F. T. Palgrave.

Duntroon, Loch Gilphead,
April 14, 1849.

. . . I have been reading with great pleasure Schelling's *Verhältniss der bildenden Kunst zur Natur.*   I wish you would get it and read it, as the German is not difficult. It shows a mind 'sensitive to every breath' of beauty, and combining with this the highest metaphysical power.   I should think Schelling was the only one of the German Philosophers who had any true feeling for art.

---

[1] 'Which cannot be made a secondary task.'   [2] Morier.

To F. T. PALGRAVE.

BORROWDALE, *August* 21, 1849.

I quite agree with you in thinking Malvern one of the most beautiful places I ever saw.   The style of country I like much better than this, which is not open enough, or grand enough, or fresh enough to suit me, though there are magnificent views in a few places.   Scotland is a far finer country than this to my mind, with brighter colours, and richer skies, and a fine line of coast.

I have been simmering over my notes to the Romans ever since I have been here: the mere notes I think I could complete in a few months.   But there are so many other subjects, such as the Text of the New Testament, the 'Lehr-begriff' of St. Paul, the language of the New Testament in relation to Philo and the Alexandrians, and the 'Analoga' in the present day or in history to the state of things for which St. Paul wrote, &c. &c., that I hardly venture to think of the end of my work.

To A. P. STANLEY.

BORROWDALE, NEAR KESWICK,
[*August*, 1849].

I should be glad to know whereabouts you are, and whether there is any chance of your coming into this part of the world.   I hope the Eastern tour is finally settled.

I have been reading Baur, and confess myself a convert to his view of the 'Christus-partei' as a matter of probability, which is all that can be attained to on such a subject.   *Was haben Sie dagegen einzuwenden?*   It strikes me a good deal, however, how uncertain and unpromising any Niebuhrian attempts are on ecclesiastical history.   The Fathers and the heretics between them have so sophisticated matters, and the circumstances are so new, there being no analogy to guide us, that the end of all inquiries is almost an even balance of probabilities about the first century.   If the Fathers were right, the heretics were wrong: if the heretics were right, the Fathers were wrong.   It seems to me absolutely necessary to place oneself at some higher or lower point of criticism or scepticism, if we are to do anything more than add another guess to the many already made by *Genus Theologicum.* I was very sorry to hear of De Wette's death : an honest man and a great critic.

Last night I read a good part of the *Apostolical Fathers.* It is difficult to imagine how anything so poor and so miserably rhetorical could have been written so near the Apostolical Age and the writings of the New Testament.

Müller[1] and Morier are here with me—the first busy with his book on 'the Arian nations before their separation, as traceable in language.' The book is in many parts interesting, but requires a much more artistic working up. . . .

I am sorry to see the democratic cause falling so low : there is still a hope 'of the Prince of Wales being King of England.' I would sooner live in the backwoods than in Cossack Europe. Whether the democratic party or the despotic aristocratic party is uppermost is almost equally bad. Chartism and Protectionism, Legitimist, Socialist, Church and State, Manchester and Almack's, wealth and birth, should balance each other, and all be regulated by education, common sense, and Sir Robert Peel.

One is especially sorry to see Germany in its present state, seeming to fulfil all the worst prognostications of Tories and bigots, and destroying all faith in ideals. . . .

To R. R. W. Lingen.

KESWICK, [*September* 8, 1849].

What an extravagant value for human life seems to be springing up, seen in Peace Congresses and Rush[2] petitions, such as would have been despised in an ancient state. I don't like to see the military spirit of a people destroyed in this way. And as to Rush petitions :—to give the poor wretch time to repent, who has lived all his life in the moral sink of Field

[1] Mr. Max Müller had recently come to Oxford, introduced by the Chevalier Bunsen, and was preparing the *Essay on Comparative Mythology* which appeared in 1856. Jowett had tried to get him made a Fellow of Balliol, but the negotiation ended in his becoming a Student of Christ Church under Gaisford's headship.

[2] i. e. for the reprieve of the murderer of that name.

Lane and St. Giles's, with uncleansed sewers, for whom Society
has done nothing—to come in at last with this sentimentalism
about repentance, &c., seems disgusting. People will find out at
last that there is something more valuable in the world than
human life, as they are beginning to find out that there is
something more valuable than the abstract idea of freedom
on the Slavery question. It strikes me that one might make
three divisions of practical questions which have a bearing on
the morals of the community. (1) How to make the worst
better ;—Prison Discipline, Juvenile Offenders, &c. (2) How to
raise all up to a certain fair level of morals and education—the
Education question, the business of Kay-Shuttleworth and his
heirs or assignees. (3) How to make the decent intelligent
member of Society into a real high-minded Christian, rising
above the ordinary tone and rules of Society—the business of
the clergy.

To R. R. W. Lingen.

BALLIOL, *October* 16, 1849.

. . . This is 'the busiest time of all the busy year,' and
therefore I hope you will excuse my sending you only a few
lines. I heard from Palgrave this morning that Temple had
just left for his holiday. The *John Bull*, I see, has been attacking
'the Infidel College[1].'

It would be a strange thing to collect together all the evils
that have sprung from religion, not merely from downright
persecution, but from the prejudices and narrownesses which
in the mass of men seem inseparable from it. How seldom
you meet with a religious man who is quite sensible also—as
politicians, most are almost insane. When anything touches the
very name of religion, εὐθὺς μάχεται[2] and becomes so stupefied
and isolated in his prejudices, that it is impossible for him to
understand the real state of the case. One cannot give up the
hope of better things, but there is small sign of them at present.
At Oxford persons are considerably excited just now by a sermon
of L——'s, which, if it was truly reported to me, seems to have
been very bold indeed, implying that he desired to get rid of

---

[1] University College, London.   [2] 'He is ready to fight.'

the definitions of the Trinity, Sacraments, &c. It was a discovery that in the progress of time had been made, that these things were undefinable.

.I should be glad to hear from you, though, as you knew long ago, I am a very bad correspondent. You must take care of yourself and let your mind be at rest or your body will never flourish. I think one is often oppressed with a sort of nightmare of work and anxiety and trouble which disappears tho instant we attack it vigorously. There is a great truth in that verse, 'Casting all your care upon Him, for He careth for you.'

To A. P. Stanley.

[October, 1849.]

. . . The difficulty about St. John's Gospel is, first, the general difficulty about so short a work, which cannot be verified from our other knowledge of the writer: second, the silence of about a century, which must be taken in connexion with the other fact of its being the one book which all Christians would naturally have sought for, appealed to, and thought about: third, from the silence of Justin, a writer of the same tendencies, who knows the ideas of the Gospel, but not the Gospel itself: fourth, what Baur urges, the question which cannot be excluded, of its relation to the other Gospels and to authentic history, as viewed from the internal evidence: lastly, the cumulative force of all these points together, if they can be all proved.

On the other side, the spirituality of the Gospel is a testimony to its being no fiction—nay, to its inspiration, in almost any sense of the term. And its general reception and recognition by heretics and orthodox alike about the year 160, say, is an immense difficulty on the Tübingen hypothesis. . . .

To A. P. Stanley.

October 23, 1849.

I could not help feeling pained at the latter part of your very kind letter[1]. I know well how much better and wiser I ought to be at all to be worthy of that high opinion you express. It

[1] Cf. *Letters of Dean Stanley*, pp. 138, 139.

will always be a motive with me to try and make myself very different from what I am. I think it is true (and I am glad you mentioned it) that we have not had the same mutual interest in talking over subjects of theology that we had formerly. They have lost their novelty, I suppose : we know better where we are, having rolled to the bottom together, and being now only able to make a few uphill steps. I acknowledge fully my own want of freshness : my mind seems at times quite dried up, partly, I think, from being strained out of proportion to the physical powers. And at times I have felt an unsatisfied desire after a better and higher sort of life, which makes me impatient of the details of theology. It is from this source only I can ever look for any 'times of refreshment.' Had I always done rightly, my life would doubtless have been happier and my mind clearer.

I think sometimes we have been a little too intellectual and over-curious in our conversations about theology. We have not found rest and peace in them so much as we might have done. As to the other point you mention, I am quite sure you cannot be too independent. Your supposed want of judgement is a mere delusion, and if it were not, and I were really able to guide you, it is the greatest absurdity for one man to submit his will to another, merely because he has the power of sympathizing and has greater energy at a particular moment. I think I see more clearly than formerly that you and I and all men must take our own line and act according to our character, with many errors and imperfections and half-views, yet upon the whole we trust for good. We must act boldly, and feel the world around us as a swimmer feels the resisting stream. There is no use in desultory excitement, of which perhaps we have had too much : steady perseverance and judgement are the requisite. And Oxford is as happy and promising a field as any, such as we are, could desire.

I earnestly hope that the friendship which commenced between us many years ago may be a blessing to last us through life. I feel that if it is to be so, we must both go onward : otherwise the wear and tear of life and the 'having travelled over each other's minds,' and a thousand accidents, will be sufficient to break it off. I have often felt the inability to converse with you, but never for an instant the least alienation. There is no one who would not think me happy in having such a friend. We will have no more of this semi-egotistical talk : only I want you to know that I will do all I can to remedy the evil, which is chiefly my fault.

To A. P. STANLEY.

BATH, *December*, 1849.

. . . I am staying here for a day or two (until Thursday) with Morier. Mr. Morier has much to tell of battles of Leipsic, of the Congress of Vienna, &c. . . .

Get Newman's new volume of Sermons [1]—most remarkable. I don't know whether it is old association, or not, but his writings certainly have an extraordinary power over one. I think that Romanism was never so glorified before. No one ever mixed up such subtle untruths with such glorious truths. It is like the old Sermons, only aggravated in beauties as well as defects.

To JOHN FFOLLIOTT.

BALLIOL, *January* 20, [1850 ?]

I have just been reading Cicero to revive if possible a lost faculty of writing Latin prose, and may as well add an extract :—

'Omnium rerum ex quibus aliquid exquiritur nihil est Agricultura melius, nihil uberius, nihil homine libero dignius.' You have the Text. Let me add another passage which I am not quite sure exists in all the MSS.: 'Nihil procuratori aut villico mandandum nisi tute ipse intersis.'

Let me say first a word about your taking Orders. I confess I think it is a desertion of your post. It would compel you to leave your home and family, nor is there any point of view in which you could do as much good as a clergyman, as you might being a layman. It might be that from taking to it with thorough good will, you would devote yourself to it more successfully from feeling that you were suited to it ; but, on the

[1] *Discourses addressed to Mixed Congregations*, 1849.

other hand, I doubt whether you are suited to many of its duties, as for example that of writing a weekly sermon ; and also, I fear, you would always reproach yourself for having left Ireland and neglected the peasantry on your father's estates. I ventured to mention it to Temple, and no one else.   You will see from the enclosed what he thinks.   But indeed, I understood when you last talked about it that you yourself had given it up and thought it inexpedient.

'Well, and what has your confounded πολυπραγμοσύνη[1] got to suggest next?' you exclaim.   I want you to be an agri-culturalist, a cattle-breeder (don't laugh), a model Irish squire, beloved by the finest ' pisantry ' in the world.   I do not think you are right in looking forward to a time when your estates will be worth nothing.   Is it not possible to contrive that the time shall never arrive?   Is not the one duty tolerably plain, to save yourself from ruin and the people from starving? I do not in the least doubt that you see this, yet forgive my impertinence for repeating it—things sometimes strike us more when said by another person.   To effect this is the business of a life, spent in enduring all the disagreeables of Ireland, the dulness of society, the bore of the landlords, the perversity of the tenants, the idiot farming of the peasantry, who may possibly, but not probably, turn out ungrateful after all.

. . . If you wish to become an agriculturalist, I fear you would find it a mistake to begin with chemistry.   Any real knowledge of such subjects requires so much bookwork and also so much experiment, that you would find it, I fear, very difficult and irksome ; also, the practical result too dis-tant to be of any use.   I do not mean to doubt its use as a means of general improvement and a subject of great interest, but merely that I do not think any one is very likely to make two blades of wheat grow where one grew before by the study of it.   The first point in a farm must always be economy and good management.

. . . Well, I hope you will forgive me for saying all this. I will not trouble you again.   Indeed I know, especially in

[1] Meddlesomeness.

Ireland, that every one must judge for himself, and it would not at all surprise me if you felt it right to disregard everything I have ventured to say.

To John ffolliott.

Balliol, *February* 12, [1850 ?]

Many thanks for your kind letter. I am sure I never meant to say that you were incapable of writing a sermon (I don't doubt that you could write a very good one), but only that you were not one of those 'regular posters' who could accomplish two sermons per week with comfort to yourself. I could give, I think, exquisite reasons for this, but dare say you would not wish to be further bored by the subject.

No letters from 'Joe[1],' but only tidings through Müller, now at Paris and soon to be at Oxford, that the said Joseph is diverting himself at Berlin, where he thinks of remaining for some months. Warburton is here ; also Stanley. Goldwin Smith is to have a Fellowship, under whose auspices 'Floreat magna Aula Universitatis.'

I hope you will write and tell me whether you find 'farming concerns' thriving and interesting. Free trade I fear will press more heavily on Ireland, as there is no great manufacturing interest which is proportionably benefited. I should not think it was likely any degree of protection would be restored either for cattle or grain, for, as Lord John Russell said, the moment it was clearly seen that a part of the increased value of cattle or corn went to raise rents, it was impossible to maintain this state of things even if good in the abstract. It is said, or more strictly it was told me by a man who said he heard it from Lord Charles Russell, that the Ministry had considered the proposal of an eight shillings fixed duty, that Lord John Russell was in favour of it, Lord Grey against it ; but that the idea was finally given up on finding that the leaders of the Free Trade party would not hear of it, that none would consent to more than a five shillings duty, and Lord John Russell thought that the Ministry would lose more by this than the agricultural interest could gain.

[1] R. B. D. Morier.

I will inquire about the carols to-morrow, as I ought to have done long since, and send them to you in remembrance of the Christmas Eve which we spent together.

Respecting farming, Shairp tells me that an excellent Scotch bailiff may be procured for £100 a year. I fear you will find the responsibility irksome, if you have the management in your own hands. There is a good article respecting 'Draining' in the last *Quarterly*—deep draining for all soils whatever appears to be the writer's theory.

. . . Fare you well, and do not forget the line—

> Who feeds fat oxen must himself be fat.

To A. P. Stanley.

OBAN, *August* 12, [1850].

. . . I hope you are placable about letters, and do not think I have less regard for you than four years ago, when we had a furious correspondence.

. . . Get to Italy if you can, and look upon the blue waters of an Italian lake—it is a sight that refreshes one for the rest of the year. I think I shall hardly rest another year without getting a sight of one myself.

. . . I have four pupils here, Fremantle, Owen, Lancaster, and Peel. What I have seen of the latter I decidedly like—he is very manly and intelligent. I hope something may be made of him.

My sermons make some progress[1], and I have written a weekly one for the congregation here. A zealous member of the congregation asked how many Presbyterians we had converted. I was happy to assure her that there was no danger of our converting any.

There is a poor young lady here (an Episcopalian) who is dying. I have been to see her several times, as there was no one else here. It is a strange sight to see a person so entirely resigned to death, saying with the greatest placidness, 'I wonder whether I shall be alive the day after to-morrow.'

---

[1] He was now Select Preacher.

CHAPTER VI

UNIVERSITY AND CIVIL SERVICE REFORM. 1846-1854 [1]

W. D. Christie, M.P.—Sir J. Kay-Shuttleworth—Roundell Palmer
—Goldwin Smith—The University Commission—East India Civil
Service Examinations—Lord Macaulay's Committee—Letters on
University Reform.

THE movement for reform at Oxford, which culminated in the Act of 1850, was the result of long-
continued agitation both without and within the
University. The first beginnings of it may be traced
to Sir William Hamilton's articles in the *Edinburgh
Review* of 1831-1834. The external pressure was directed
to the nationalization of the University through
the admission of Dissenters, while the earliest efforts
from within aimed rather at the revival of the Professoriate, and the abolition of obsolete restrictions.
Early in 1839 a motion had been introduced in Convocation by the Hebdomadal Board [2] proposing to institute
new Professorships, and to require the attendance of
all undergraduates at Professors' lectures. This proposal
was rejected at the time, but its principles were embodied

[1] Cp. vol. ii, chap. v.
[2] It proposed a revision of the Statute ' De Lectoribus Publicis.'

in an important pamphlet, which was drawn up that autumn by Archibald Campbell Tait with the help of Arthur Penrhyn Stanley[1]. In this it was proposed to institute what would have amounted in effect to a system of post-graduate Professorial teaching.

The practical reforming spirit was eclipsed for a time by clerical reaction and the excitement which followed the publication of Tract XC. But Stanley, who had already done good service in the cause of reform, began a new crusade when the ecclesiastical ferment was abated. This appears from several letters in the Stanley-Jowett correspondence of 1845-6. On April 10, 1845, Mr. W. D. Christie, the public-spirited member for Weymouth, who had previously championed the cause of the Dissenters and of the University of London, brought forward a motion for a Royal Commission of Inquiry[2]. He said in an able speech of the following year[3], 'he believed that some of the most eminent and distinguished men in the University would rejoice if such a Commission were issued.' Two references to Mr. Christie occur in Jowett's letters to Stanley of the year 1846. In one he says lightly, 'Think of a Parliamentary Committee at which . . . everybody should tell tales of everybody.' The other is more serious, being in fact an elaborate draft of questions that might be submitted by such a Parliamentary Committee to Heads of Houses and other persons in

[1] *Life of Dean Stanley*, vol. i. pp. 230, 418; *Life of Archibald Campbell Tait*, vol. i. pp. 69-71. Several other pamphlets on the subject appeared in the same year —one by the Rev. P. S. H. Payne, a Fellow of Balliol.

[2] Hansard, vol. lxxix. p. 393. This was the first attempt in Parlia-

ment towards a comprehensive measure. Sir Robert Inglis, as member for Oxford, was the strenuous opponent of all such legislation.

[3] Hansard, vol. lxxxvii. p. 1242. Debate on Mr. Ewart's motion for the education of the people.

Oxford. This document is crossed with a memorandum in another hand, 'from Stanley for Mr. Christie, 25/2/1846[1].' From 1846 onwards movements were proceeding simultaneously from within and from without. In the autumn of that year a scheme for the reform of the Examination Statute was proposed by F. Jeune, Master of Pembroke[2], in a Committee of the Heads, but never got beyond the Hebdomadal Board. In September, 1846, Mr. Horsman proposed to advocate the cause of University reform in Parliament, and in 1847 J. Kay-Shuttleworth visited Oxford to obtain further information with a view to legislative action. But Jowett was not minded to leave the matter in the hands either of Dissenting members of Parliament or the Education Department. In a letter to Mr. Roundell Palmer[3] he urged him to represent the views of the Oxford reformers in the House of Commons. His letter exhibits clearly the scope of the writer's aims at this time, while the scruple which withheld his correspondent from acceding to the desire sufficiently indicates the general state of opinion[4]. On March 4, 1848, a Memorial signed by two-thirds of the Tutors, proposing a revision of the Examination Statute, was presented to the Hebdomadal Board. It maintained the principle of an intermediate examination. This was immediately followed up with an anonymous pamphlet[5], of which the 'advertisement' is dated March 13, 1848. A letter to Lingen of April 3 shows this pamphlet to have been the joint work of Jowett

---

[1] About the same time Dr. Pusey was interested in a scheme for the extension of University education through the foundation of Halls or Colleges under Church authority. *Life of E. B. Pusey*, vol. iii. p. 79.

[2] Afterwards Bishop of Peterborough.

[3] Afterwards Lord Selborne.

[4] pp. 188–192.

[5] *Suggestions for an improvement of the Examination Statute.* Oxford, 1848.

and Stanley[1], and both the preface and several of the
suggestions are unquestionably Jowett's.

The following sentences are curiously characteristic
of him :—

'Our only defence against attacks from without is to build
up from within, to enlarge our borders that we may increase the
number of our friends.   We have no one to fear but ourselves.
At this moment, to use the language of an eminent writer,
are we not living "behind our dykes" in fear of the German
Ocean?   There may be enemies from whom it is right to
fly, but the tide of opinion cannot be escaped in this way.'

One peculiarity of these *Suggestions* was the inclusion
of a School of Theology (both Pass and Class) side by
side with the subjects of Philosophy, History, and Philology.—When a Theological School was founded under
different auspices in 1867, Jowett, though Professor of
Greek, was excluded from the Examining Board!—In
recommending the study of theology in the spring of
1848, he employed arguments which are strangely familiar
to readers of his work on St. Paul:—

'Religious persons feel that the evidences of Paley or
Lardner are not the reasons of their belief, or the answers to
their difficulties.   Can it be truly said that much has been
done in this place during the last twenty years for Scriptural
interpretation, which seems to be the most hopeful mine in
theology, and strangely enough the least explored?   It would
hardly have been an unreasonable hope that the meaning of
Scripture, like that of any other book, might by this time have
become fixed, and raised above the fancies of sects or individuals.'

The discussion of the new Examination Statute came
on in the following autumn, and it was passed in 1849.
The result was not altogether in accordance with Jowett's
views, which had aimed at something like the old final
examination to come at the end of the second year, after

[1] p. 193.

which undergraduates should be encouraged to specialize within certain limits. This would have been in effect to carry out the principle of Tait and Stanley's pamphlet of 1839. As a preparatory step, Jowett suggested a plan for courses of lectures to be given in the Schools by distinguished graduates, which might serve as a temporary substitute for a Professorial system[1]. But in this as in some other schemes, by which he sought to lure back friends to Oxford, and make them sharers of his own labours there, he was disappointed[2].

From the facts above stated it appears how distinctly in the reforming movement at Oxford, which is commonly dated from 1848, Stanley and Jowett were foremost in the field.

By the autumn of 1848, however, several other eminent men had joined in the agitation; amongst whom were Mark Pattison, Richard Congreve, John Conington, and Goldwin Smith, who became Secretary to the Executive Commission of 1854. The whole movement appears to him to have grown out of Newmanism through a reaction. He writes (1894):—

'Newman's romantic picture of the mediaeval Church carried away the young, who had before seen nothing but high and dry Anglicanism, with its social and political accompaniments. But Newmanism, though ecclesiastical and reactionary, was at the same time revolutionary in its way.

[1] See p. 31 of the *Suggestions*: 'It would only be acting up to the spirit of our own institutions if the liberty which at present only exists in the Statute book were practically recognized and encouraged by allowing (under such instructions [*sic*] as were thought necessary) the free use of the public Schools as lecture rooms for any Master of Arts, or Doctor of Theology, Law or Medicine, to deliver lectures on any branch of knowledge which fell within his sphere or capacity.'

[2] It is worth remembering that a Cambridge Syndicate was working at the same time and preparing the way for the *Moral Sciences* and *Natural Sciences* Triposes.

It was a revolt against the old high and dry *régime*. It cut
active minds loose from their traditional moorings and launched
them on a sea of speculation over which they at last floated to
a great diversity of havens. Nor was Newmanism politically
conservative. On the contrary, it sneered at conservatism, which
was closely connected with Protestant orthodoxy, and a particular object of its hatred and contempt was Peel. Ward, if
I remember rightly, professed himself a Radical. Then came
the crisis, brought on by the condemnation of Ward, which
was followed by the secession of Newman. Those who
refused the leap recoiled more or less from the brink. Some of
them, such as Mark Pattison, recoiled, as you know, the whole
length of thorough-going Liberalism. They by degrees tacitly
coalesced with the knot of original Liberals, though they
were rather liable to mental irresolution and to recurrences
of asceticism in a new form.

'In some of us Liberalism soon took the practical shape of
an effort to reform and emancipate the University, to strike off
the fetters of mediaeval statutes from it and from its Colleges,
set it free from the predominance of ecclesiasticism, recall it
to its proper work, and restore it to the nation.'

In 1848-9 Jowett and Stanley were actively engaged
in preparing a joint work on the Universities to which
others were to have contributed, but before it could
be published the Commission had been issued. The preparation of the book, however, laid the ground for
Jowett's evidence and for Stanley's memorable Report.

While efforts towards reform had thus been ripening
from within, the attacks on the existing system from
without became more and more clamorous; the Nonconformists insisting on the admission of Dissenters, and the
advocates of Natural Science, Modern History, and 'useful
knowledge' deprecating the narrowness of the old curriculum. The curriculum, indeed, had been already
widened by the change in the Examination Statute; but
the new regulations had not yet taken effect.

The crisis came in 1850, when, on April 25. Mr. Heywood, the Radical member for North Lancashire, moved in the House of Commons a long resolution requesting the issue of a Royal Commission of Inquiry into the state of the Universities. This was strongly opposed by Mr. Gladstone, Mr. Roundell Palmer, and Sir Robert Inglis. But Lord John Russell, as Prime Minister, while declining to vote for Mr. Heywood's resolution, promised on behalf of the Government that a Royal Commission of Inquiry should be issued. The Commissioners were, Samuel Hinds, Bishop of Norwich; A. C. Tait, Dean of Carlisle; F. Jeune, Master of Pembroke; H. G. Liddell, Head Master of Westminster; J. L. Dampier, M. A.; Baden Powell, Savilian Professor of Geometry; G. H. S. Johnson, Fellow of Queen's; with A. P. Stanley, Fellow of University, as Secretary.

A copy of the following unpublished document, which was addressed to Lord John Russell, has been furnished by the kindness of the Very Rev. W. C. Lake, late Dean of Durham :—

'We, the undersigned, Tutors of Colleges in the University of Oxford, beg to thank your Lordship for the intention you have expressed, as Head of Her Majesty's Government, of advising Her Majesty to appoint a Royal Commission to inquire into the state of the Universities, and for the friendly terms in which your intention was announced. We do not think it desirable at present to address your Lordship publicly, but we wish to express our belief that changes are necessary which can only be made by the assistance of Parliament, and in the confident hope that the proposed inquiry will be carried on with a real desire for the good of the University, we are ready to give the Commissioners every information in our power.

B. JOWETT	W. C. LAKE
A. P. STANLEY	GOLDWIN SMITH.'

Those who in Oxford bore the name of reformers had
not all precisely the same ends in view. They were
agreed that the constitution of the University must
be altered, that its benefits must be extended, restrictions abolished, and the Professoriate strengthened. But
Oxford would not have been Oxford, if individuals had
not widely differed as to the particular changes required.
As usual, there were many who thought more of their own
rights than of educational needs. Resident members of
the University were naturally jealous of the non-resident
vote, and sought to revive Congregation, i. e. the House
of Residents, for legislative purposes, in place of Convocation, i.e. the body of M.A.'s at large. They would
have transferred the initiative from the Heads of Houses
(whose action in the Tractarian controversy had pre-
judiced their cause not only with Liberal reformers,
but with High Churchmen of the newer school) to the
whole body of residents. College Tutors were made
uneasy by the increasing importance of private tuition ;
and opinions differed greatly as to the best way of
making the University a national institution.

Jowett's evidence before the Commission sets forth the
points which at this time he considered at once desirable
and practicable. His views as there expressed are anything but revolutionary : far less so, for example, than
those of Mr. Robert Lowe, who had recently returned
from Australia.

Jowett sought to strengthen what he found existing [1].
For example, while proposing to enlarge the Professoriate,
he emphatically approved of the Tutorial system.

---

[1] 'What I want to see is the
Universities made somewhat more
dependent on the State, so as to
become a real link between
Church and State, instead of
representing the worst half of
the clergy.'—Letter to A. P. S.,
1850.

'In foreign Universities,' he says, ' the Professoriate system has been resorted to, not from choice, but from necessity. Our wealth gives us the means of combining the two, and of carrying out the spirit of each more perfectly.'

Nor does it appear that he was, as yet, in full sympathy with those who anticipated the extension of the benefits of the University to non-Collegiate students. In other ways his evidence is not that of a violent reformer. He would have limited the powers of Convocation without extending the powers of Congregation or constituting an elective Hebdomadal Board. He clearly foresaw the evil that was likely to result, when the unobtrusive performance of College duties would give way to the excitement of debates in Congregation. This would probably ' have the effect of plunging us into a perpetual state of agitation.' Instead of giving Congregation the initiative, as had been proposed, he would have simply added the Professors, whose number was to be increased, to the Hebdomadal Board. He says, 'The changes at present required are such as have become necessary from lapse of time in institutions that have not the power to amend themselves. We are not to infer from this that the University needs to continue for ever legislating, or that it is well to form a constitution which will give the greatest facility for such an object.'

For University extension, he looks to improvements in College management, rather than to private lodgings or 'independent Halls,' but suggests that noblemen and men of large fortune might be allowed to reside with private Tutors in the town; referring to the advantage which Lord Palmerston and others had received from such residence in a former generation, at Edinburgh.

'The benefits of a University education cannot be thought to consist merely in the acquirement of knowledge, but in the opportunities of society and of forming friends; in short, in the experience of life gained by it and the consequent improvement of character. With many, a College is their first means of introduction to the world. Advantages of this kind cannot be wholly secured to the poorer student, although he most stands in need of them, yet they should not be completely lost sight of. . . . The poor student should be scrupulously treated as a gentleman.'

When, however, the Commissioners proposed a scheme for establishing new Halls in connexion with the Colleges, he approved of it and looked upon such Halls as a useful occasion for the gradual admission of Dissenters, 'so getting rid of the scandal of requiring youths of eighteen to sign the Thirty-nine Articles.' At this time and long afterwards, Jowett had little sympathy with Nonconformists, but he regarded their admission to the University as an essential part of any national scheme, though 'their admission on the Foundations would upset things too much [1].'

He thinks that sinecure Fellowships are doomed, but is strongly in favour of removing the existing restrictions upon Fellowships, including the clerical restriction. He does not explicitly touch the question of the marriage of Fellows. He treats very lightly the scruple about Founders' intentions, which had been twice already overridden[2]. For the extension of the Professoriate he suggests the addition of Professorships of Latin, English Literature, Ethnology, Comparative Philology, and Geography; also additional Professorships in Greek, Latin, Ancient History, Modern History, Ancient Philosophy, Modern Philosophy, Logic, the Physical Sciences, and Hebrew.

In establishing new Professorships (not Theological), he says :—

[1] From a letter to R. R. W. Lingen in 1846.

[2] i. e. once at the Reformation, once in the time of Laud.

'It appears to me unnecessary that religious tests should be required. There seems to be no reason to fear in scientific men any peculiar hostility to our ecclesiastical institutions; while, on the other hand, their habit of mind renders them averse to such restrictions. In this way only can we fulfil the injunction which Sir H. Savile lays upon his Trustees, that they should seek for the fittest persons out of the whole world. It would be of little use to multiply professors of physical science, if such men as Liebig or Faraday were liable to be excluded.'

One object which he alleges for the extension of the Professoriate is 'to encourage persons resident in the University to carry on their studies with the view of hereafter filling Professorial chairs. The College Tutor, who is in most cases waiting for a living, has no inducement to study beyond what is necessary for the preparation of his lectures.' Jowett is in favour of a Theological School, in preference to the establishment of Theological Colleges. And, lastly, he sees no harm in the system of Private Tutors, characteristically adding: 'The evils arising from the excessive use of Private Tutors can only be corrected (1) by College Tutors getting up their lectures carefully, and rendering private assistance themselves, (2) by the manner in which the Public Examinations are conducted.' About the time of the nomination of the Commissioners he wrote to Stanley[1]:—

---

[1] At a still earlier time, he had written, with reference to their joint work on the Universities: 'I should be almost inclined to make a fight for open Fellowships and Professorships only. I am afraid the necessity of getting rid of the Heads is the same as the necessity for getting rid of Charles I, that he was so per-fidious, nobody could trust him. . . . The natural first step would have been the revival of the Professorial system, and the second, the stimulus of examinations: only we have inverted the order, because one could be done without the assistance of Parliament, the other not.'

'. . . I hope the Commissioners will chiefly rely on themselves and not on the witnesses whom they examine. . . . We have long ago settled, I mean as our own opinion, that open Fellowships, Professorships, modification of clerical restrictions (certainly), change in the constitution (probably), should be the great topics. To which I would be glad to add "Poor Students" and "Expenses" (although there are difficulties in the matter); first, because it is a most popular topic —the University educates 1,500, why not 3,000? Is it a sufficient οὗ ἕνεκα [1] of a national institution that in the nineteenth century it educates 1,500, two-thirds of whom are the sons of country gentlemen and clergymen? Jeune will be lukewarm in this matter, but I hope you and Tait will take it up. If the object of the Commission is only to make a more intellectual aristocracy, this may be good, but will hardly command much sympathy. Secondly, unless the Universities are to be wholly separated from the Church it is of the greatest importance that poor clergymen should be educated at the University and not at Theological Colleges. The poor student clergy have always a tendency to High Church views, because they give them a position which they had not before. This tendency would, I think, be very much diminished if the University became their home more and its Professors their teachers.

'The general principle I would be guided by in reference to the Commission is to ask oneself plainly what changes have taken place in the country in the last 200 years, and then as far as possible transfer them to the University. If the relation of one class to another is different, if the subjects of knowledge are different, the University must receive corresponding changes sooner or later before it can return to a natural state; only remembering that it is a place of education chiefly, and that education clings naturally to the past. . . .

'I feel that I do not agree either with Vaughan's intellectual aristocracy as the idea of a University, nor with the "gentlemen heresy" that appears to be partially entertained by Jeune and by G. Smith. I hope that the small numbers

---

[1] '*Raison d'être.*'

educated at a University will be prominently urged by the Commission—it is an effective topic. And although it can do no good to force men to Oxford who are unfitted by previous education, it is of the greatest use to awaken in people's minds a sense of the necessity of a liberal education for more than the numbers contained in Harrow, Winchester, Eton, &c. The abused Grammar-school and Charity foundations supply abundant means. . . .'

Although the Commissioners issued their Report in 1852, the Universities Act embodying their recommendations was passed only in 1854, when it received the active support of Mr. Gladstone. It established Congregation, but instead of giving the initiative to that body, created an elective Council[1] representing Heads, Professors, and resident M.A.'s; and, what Jowett always regarded as more important, it provided for the abolition of many local restrictions upon Fellowships, and opened them to general competition. Before the measure left the House of Commons, Dissenters had been admitted to Matriculation and to all degrees lower than M.A.

Jowett was anxious to impress upon his pupils his conviction that life at the University would be much the same after the reforms as it had been before. Meanwhile his part in the whole business brought him forward, and made his real position better known to public men. He was one of the first set of Public Examiners under the new system[2], and was recognized along with Mark Pattison and J. M. Wilson as one of the leaders of the Liberal party, an estimation which earned

[1] This appears to have been partly due to a suggestion of Dr. Pusey's. See *Life of E. B. Pusey*, vol. iii. pp. 391–393.

[2] Richard Congreve had been nominated by one of the Proctors who was a Wadham man, and though he declined the office, he was touched by the generosity of Jowett, who had said that he would not take the post if Congreve were passed over.

for him the suspicion of the older Tutors and of the majority of the Heads of Colleges.

His position at Oxford led to his being consulted with regard to educational movements of a wider scope, such as that for opening to competition posts in the Home Civil Service and in that of the East India Company, in which Sir James Kay-Shuttleworth and Sir Charles Trevelyan severally took a leading part. Two sayings of theirs recorded by Lord Lingen, may be repeated as illustrating the courage of public servants in those days, of which posterity now reaps the benefit. Sir J. Kay-Shuttleworth had said to Lingen, who was serving under him, with reference to some change, 'Get it done; let the objectors howl.' Sir Charles Trevelyan said, 'The Civil Service requires as much pluck as the Military.' A letter from the Rev. B. Jowett (January, 1854) is printed together with the Report on the *Organization of the Permanent Civil Service*, by Sir Stafford H. Northcote and Sir C. Trevelyan, dated November 23, 1853. The reformers in the Civil Service were turned into ridicule by Anthony Trollope in his novel of *The Three Clerks*, where Sir Charles Trevelyan figures as 'Sir Gregory Hardlines,' and an imaginary caricature of Jowett appears as 'Mr. Jobbles.'

It was perhaps through his friend Lingen, who was now at the head of the Education Office in London, and also through Sir Stafford Northcote, that Jowett came to correspond with Mr. (afterwards Lord) Macaulay and Sir Charles Trevelyan about the Indian appointments. He gave an eager welcome to the plan, not only on general grounds, but because he saw in it a new stimulus for the Higher Education in England. Thus commenced his life-long interest in the public service of India; and he was thenceforth actively engaged in the promotion of measures which had no less far-reaching consequences even than the Oxford reforms. The correspondence led to his nomination as a member of Mr. Macaulay's Committee under the India Act of 1853 for opening to general competition the appointments of the Honourable East India Company's Service.

The Committee held its sittings in 1854, and reported in November of that year. Macaulay drew up the Report, but some passages bear the stamp of Jowett's mind.

For example :—

'We believe that men who have been engaged up to one or two-and-twenty in studies which have no connexion with the business of any profession, and of which the effect is merely to open, to invigorate, and to enrich the mind, will generally be found, in the business of every profession, superior to men who have at eighteen or nineteen devoted themselves to the special studies of their calling. The most illustrious English jurists have been men who have never opened a law-book till after the close of a distinguished academical career; nor is there any reason to believe that they would have been greater lawyers if they had passed in drawing pleas and conveyances the time which they gave to Thucydides, to Cicero, and to Newton. . . .

'We propose to include the moral sciences in the scheme of examination. . . . Whether this study shall have to do with mere words or with things, whether it shall degenerate into a formal and scholastic pedantry, or shall train the mind for the highest purposes of active life, will depend, to a great extent, on the way in which the examination is conducted. We are of opinion that the examination should be conducted in the freest manner, that mere technicalities should be avoided, and that the candidate should not be confined to any particular system. . . . The object of the examiners should rather be to put to the test the candidate's powers of mind than to ascertain the extent of his metaphysical reading.'

LETTERS ON UNIVERSITY REFORM, 1846–1848.

To R. R. W. LINGEN.

BEAUMARIS, *September* 5, 1846.

. . . I am very glad you have made acquaintance with Horsman, of whom I have heard Stanley speak highly. If he is up to the speaking part of it I should think he was a very fit person to take up University reform. The Universities seem to me a more promising nucleus for education, if we could but educate them first, than Dr. Kay-Shuttleworth and Privy Council schemes. If you and I and Stanley were Canons of Christ Church, I wonder what difference it would make in the perspective of our view. In what increased ratio, think you, should we feel the responsibility of change? Not of course in the gross palpable form of as 200 : 1200—but in some remote corner of the mind a maturer wisdom would spring up, and we should say of the efforts of the juveniles, 'This also is vanity.' After all, men not systems might seem to be wanted. *Quid ultra tendis.* Here are we. . . .

To R. R. W. LINGEN.

BEAUMARIS, *September*, 1846.

. . . About University reform, I fully agree in the necessity of getting practical suggestions ready for the opportunity when it occurs. The greatest change within, the least without, nothing unprecedented, nothing without regard to the better spirit of the place, seems the conservative side of the question. What is the feeling among lawyers respecting Corporation property? I suppose to save additional theories as much as possible and class it all with private property. If so, to assert a constitutional against the legal view is the *indoctrination* to be instilled. Something may be made of the anomalous character of the University, neither national, ecclesiastical, nor private, but all three together : to a case so complicated, it might be urged, it is impossible to apply the simple principles which regulate either corporate or private property, and College property might be isolated from the general fear about vested interests.

To R. R. W. LINGEN.

BALLIOL, *Sunday Evening*, [1847].

Your master, 'master Doctor Caius¹,' not the French Doctor, paid a visit of inspection to our Normal School yesterday. You can guess his object.

The particulars you can hear from Temple. . . . My purpose in writing is to say for myself and for Stanley that we are quite willing to be guided by your judgement in the matter. Shuttleworth's name is I think an omen of success in the scheme, at the same time he is as unfit as the two barbarians Hengist and Horsa to reform the University, and the prospect of good is really how far he will be advised by others.

We think that if we and others undertake the somewhat invidious part he assigns to us, we ought to have some understanding with the Ministry that they are to support us, time and opportunity favouring, with a friendly measure of University reform ; in other words, that we are not simply made a cat's-paw of by Kay-Shuttleworth in a private speculation of his own.

We have, I think, provided this sort of assurance were given, a sufficient respect for K.-S.'s usefulness to be willing to act with him in such a cause, unless you dissuade.

To ROUNDELL PALMER, ESQ., M.P.²

BALLIOL, *November* 15, [1847].

MY DEAR PALMER,

I take the liberty of writing to you under the idea that you are half an M.P. for the University of Oxford. I have heard several persons lately speak of University reform,

¹ J. P. Kay-Shuttleworth, M.D., head of the Education Department. He received a Baronetcy on retiring in 1849.   ² Lord Selborne.

and express a strong wish that you could be induced to turn your attention to the subject. They were Clough, Lake, Lingen, Temple, Stanley, T. Arnold, and others whom you probably do not know. Their feeling was that there was no one so well acquainted with the question, or so likely to take it up in a fair and friendly spirit, or who was more really sensible of the great and increasing intellectual deficiencies of the place. They seemed to think, and I heartily agree, that, for many reasons, the subject would be far better in your hands than in those of Gladstone.

Excuse this exordium, which looks like flattery, but is not meant so. The immediate occasion of my writing to you is as follows. Mr. Horsman was intending to take up the matter and bring it before the Ministry, but owing to the representations of Lingen, Stanley, and Clough, who thought that he was going to fight the battle 'nec dis nec viribus aequis,' although not in an unfriendly spirit, he has been induced to give it up and will now confine himself to seconding Christie's motion. What we hoped was that you might be induced in good time to take the question out of their hands, and prevent much evil and gain for us many things which would be a great boon.

Perhaps I am assuming too much in supposing that you would favour any movement to assist the Universities from without. Let me ask what chance is there of reform from within. It is now twelve years since the Duke of Wellington answered Lord Radnor's question in the House of Lords about University reform, that the Colleges were reforming themselves, and since then I do not think a resident in the place can point to any change, except perhaps the abolition of the oath to the Statutes, which touches our real abuses. It is nobody's fault—we cannot reform ourselves. To say nothing of the stationary nature of the place—the close Fellows are interested in keeping up close Fellowships. Merton and All Souls desire to hand down their privileges to posterity οὐκ ἐλάσσω ἢ αὐτοὶ παρεδέχοντο [1]—the true *Filius Aedis Christi* has a theory ready to show that the Christ Church method of

---

[1] In no less measure than they received them. Cf. Thuc. i. 71.

giving away Studentships is the sound and right one, although out of a hundred students it is continually found impossible to choose distinguished men to fill the Tutorships.

These things are so invidious, that although they are strictly true I am almost ashamed to state them. It would be great injustice, too, not to acknowledge that there are a great many persons in all those societies who are sincerely anxious about altering the present state of things. Only what fills me with despair about these internal reforms, [is that] partly from the want of power, partly, as I think, from a too narrow view of duty, they involve some crotchet which mars the practical good : for example, a return to some obsolete Statute which won't work or which works mischievously, when the *consuetudines* of the College would have formed a much better basis for a useful reform, and so the real and crying evil remains untouched.

There is nothing I wish less than to see Oxford turned into a German or a London University. On the other hand, is it at all probable that we shall be allowed to remain as we are for twenty years longer, the one solitary, exclusive, unnational Corporation—our enormous wealth without any manifest utilitarian purpose; a place, the studies of which belong to the past, and unfortunately seem to have no power of incorporating new branches of knowledge ; so exclusive, that it is scarcely capable of opening to the wants of the Church itself ; and again, the mere funds of which considered as a trust fund can by no means be said to have been administered with strict conscientiousness for the promotion of 'virtue and good learning'? And the good done here, which is certainly very great, [is] not of a kind to be paraded before the public, οὐ λόγῳ τιμώμεν' ἀλλὰ τῇ συνουσίᾳ πλέον [1], though we readily admit it in talking to one another ; while the abuse and inefficiency is flagrant.

You will perhaps excuse, if you do not agree with me, for writing all this. I do not wish to make a paper constitution for the University. If Parliament interferes, should

---

[1] 'Honoured, not in story, but in the hearts of those who know it best.'—Soph. *Oed. Col.* 62, 3.

not the effort be to limit the interference to one or two great and simple points, such as the opening of the Fellowships and providing by an effectual system of visitation, and perhaps by a declaration on the part of the electors like the Simony Oath, for their being honestly given away? Second, the establishment of Professorships which might be formed out of extinguished Fellowships (which would, perhaps, if they were thrown open be too numerous), and might be attached as a sort of compensation to the Colleges from which the Fellowships are taken. To which, third, I would add a pet crotchet of my own, to raise the value of the Scholarships (to make them really Demyships) from the same source,—to provide the means for many more persons of the middling class to find their way through the University into professions.

I think at present the close Fellowships work very badly, especially in holding out the prospect of a provision for life, which provision is generally not obtained until a man is twenty-seven or twenty-eight, when it would be better for him to leave the University altogether and settle in a parish : to say nothing of the evil of superannuating in Oxford so many men who are not fitted by nature for a student's life.

As to the Professorships, there is not at present a single well-endowed one for any of those subjects which form the staple of the University course, except Theology. There is no inducement for any College Tutor to carry on his reading of Aristotle beyond the routine of his lectures, as far as prospects of this sort are concerned. Does not this in some measure account for our not having yet settled the province of Logic ? Is it likely that we can expect the process of simply converting Butler into Aristotle, and Aristotle into Butler, and making them both mean pretty much what we believed before, can lead to any permanent good ? The great evil at Oxford is the narrowness and isolation of one study from another, and of one part of a study from the other. We are so far below the level of the German Ocean that I fear one day we shall be utterly deluged.

I must again apologize for writing in this desultory manner to you about these matters. If you were disposed to take up the question it would be a great pleasure to Stanley and myself to assist you in every possible way, not of course that we expect you to agree in our suggestions.

Believe me, my dear Palmer,

Yours very truly,

B. Jowett.

Note by Lord Selborne.

[N.B.—My answer to this letter, declining to undertake the question as suggested, was mainly grounded upon the impediment arising out of the oaths which I had taken on my election to my Fellowship at Magdalen. On this subject there is in print a letter, which I addressed in 1853 or 1854 to a Fellow of Magdalen.—R. P.]

To R. R. W. Lingen.

BALLIOL, *December* 3, 1847.

. . . Last Saturday R. Palmer came down here to talk over University reform. He was liberal as one could wish, but has some difficulty in stirring about the matter himself from the oath he has taken at Magdalen—he does not consider the oath binding himself, but as the terms of it are very explicit he dislikes the scandal it would make. This I mention in confidence. He is quite willing however to present a petition for open Fellowships and Professorships, and to speak in its favour. He is not sanguine at present, and thinks with you that enough has not been done to bring the matter before the public : our best chance, he said, would be to get the ear of some one of the Ministers, especially if Campbell's[1] father[2] were made Lord Chancellor, which is a possible event.

To R. R. W. Lingen.

OXFORD, *February* 20, 1848.

. . . We are getting up a petition to the Heads from Tutors of Colleges in favour of Jeune's scheme or something like it. The main objects are three: (*a*) to get the 'Little Go' placed

---

[1] W. F. Campbell, afterwards Lord Stratheden.

[2] Lord Campbell, made Chancellor in 1850.

so early as to stand in the place of a University Matriculation ; (β) to extend the studies of the place so as to give passmen something as well as Latin and Greek which may interest them ; (γ) to place the present 'Great Go' at the end of two years, somewhat contracting the number of books, and allowing the third year [of residence] for separate studies, as Theology, Mathematics and Physics, History and Law. I do not expect that nearly all this will be gained, nor see how the University could be carried on if it were at present, but something useful will probably come of it.

. . . I have not heard anything about the Price[1] schemes ; I quite admit that the plan mentioned above does alter the character of the place, but not objectionably. At present for the greater part of the passmen it is little more than a place of brute discipline, where they may be drawn out by their companions and amusements, but certainly not by polite literature. The chief fear is lest we fritter ourselves among too many things.

To R. R. W. Lingen.

OXFORD, *April* 3. 1848.

I send herewith a pamphlet[2] which is a joint production of Stanley's and mine. As there is a good deal of talk about these things at present, it may perhaps survive into the next Term, and reappear in an enlarged edition. Will you look through the scheme carefully and see if you can suggest amendments and alterations ?

I am going to attack you about another scheme, which as far as I can see at present I shall pursue tooth and nail. It is the formation of an association to give a course of lectures in the Schools on all principal subjects connected with our present examinations. Stanley would lecture on Herodotus and early Greek history, Clough on Livy, myself on the history of the Greek Philosophy. We hope that Scott and Vaughan would be induced to give lectures in Scholarship and Moral Philosophy respectively, also G[oldwin] Smith.

---

[1] Bonamy Price.   [2] See above, p. 174.

Now here lies the point : do you think you can assist us, by giving, say, twelve lectures in a year on some philological or general subject, something which might be the τέλος[1] of all your *dilettante* work during the year? Latin literature or Homer or Aeschylus would upon the whole be the most useful. I mean something of this kind, in which the University has been always weak.

The first step we propose is to request the sanction of the V.-C. (not the permission) for the use of the Schools, to which as Masters we have a right—this memorial to be signed by all those who are going to take a part in the plan. A fee of a pound to be required from every one who attends.

The great object as you will see would be to form a nucleus for a Professorial system, to give a better standard of lectures, also to construct a little from within in expectation of changes from without.

Well! the Deluge has come in our time. I think of going to Paris at the end of the week[2], and shall call at the Privy Council Office to see you, as I come through on Friday.

To R. R. W. Lingen.

Balliol, *November* 17, 1848.

. . . The reform of the Examination Statute progresses very badly. The second examination is to be in 'words,' in the third men are to give up words altogether and return to things. This is the final form in which the Statute is to be proposed, nothing but Philology to the end of the second year —and no Philology afterwards. It would be surely better to keep our present system to the end of the second year and then commence separate studies not excluding Philology. Love to Temple.

[1] 'End and aim.'   [2] p. 133.

CHAPTER VII

WIDENING social horizon—Bunsen—Sir C. Trevelyan—Tennyson—
Tutorial methods—Vacations—Mr. W. L. Newman's reminiscences.

AS we turn from these public activities to resume the
tenor of his life in Oxford, we may take occasion
to observe the expansion of Jowett's social interests,
which were scarcely ever separated from his educational
and other labours. His pupils of some years back were
about to enter public life : his friends and colleagues
were rising to positions where they could help him in
pushing the fortunes of younger men. Lingen became
Head of the Education Department in 1849, and in
appointing Examiners and Inspectors relied on Jowett's
recommendation more than on that of any other of the
Oxford Tutors[1]. C. J. Vaughan, Stanley's brother-in-
law, was Head Master of Harrow, and Balliol men
became assistant masters there. Temple, in whose conversation Jowett delighted more than in that of any
other man, had gone to be the Head of a training
college for workhouse school teachers, which had been
recently founded at Kneller Hall in the neighbourhood
of Twickenham ; and in 1858 succeeded Goulburn at
Rugby.   At Jowett's recommendation, Temple took
Palgrave to be his lieutenant at Kneller Hall. Morier,

---

[1] W. H. Thompson of Trinity was similarly Lingen's mainstay at
Cambridge.

after spending the years 1851 and 1852 at the Education Office, became attached to the Diplomatic service at Vienna and afterwards at Berlin.

Through Stanley Jowett was introduced to the Chevalier Bunsen—Baron Bunsen—who spoke of him to his son Henry as the deepest mind he had met with in England. Henry de Bunsen's own impression of him, as he told me afterwards, was that of a man who lived intimately with a few friends, but was shy and retiring in general society.

William Young Sellar had gone to assist his old teacher, Professor William Ramsay, in Glasgow, and there became engaged to Miss Eleanor Dennistoun, whom he married in 1852. That home was thenceforward a centre of growing interest for Jowett.

Lingen, too, had married Miss Hutton in 1852, and they often received him at their house in Gloucester Place, Hyde Park. Mrs. Lingen [1] was greatly struck by the 'joyousness' of her husband's friend. He used to rally her on the strictness of her Politico-Economical principles, with which, at that time, he agreed. They took him to a theatre, where the after-piece turned on disputes between husband and wife. At this he laughed heartily, not, as Mrs. Lingen thought, without a spice of side-long malice.

Lord Lingen writes (1895):—

'He has left on me the impression of being in those years lighthearted and gay: and this impression agrees with the earliest portrait of him, that by Richmond, to which, let me add, his likeness after death returned with striking reality. I was constantly seeing him during those years, and we talked unreservedly about everything, being orthodox and rather advanced Liberals of the time both in Church and State—such as Oxford Toryism had made us. His visits, generally unannounced, are among the pleasantest recollections of my life. Punctual as he was to the last in business and duty, there

[1] Lady Lingen.

was a humorous irregularity about his social observance of hours.   I shall never forget our frequent anxieties, in which he never shared, whether he would really catch the ten o'clock train to Oxford, on which he was bent, with his breakfast to finish, and our servant packing his things.   Then, as up to the end of his life, he always carried with him papers which he had in hand, and would work at them upstairs and down, and at all spare times.'

The question of competitive examinations for India led to an intimacy with Sir Charles Trevelyan and his family, including the present Lady Knutsford and Mrs. Dugdale.   At their house he had opportunities of personal intercourse with Macaulay.   Sir George Trevelyan says, 'I remember a period of one or two years, when the question of Civil Service reform was at its height, during which Mr. Jowett constantly came to us at Westbourne Terrace, and used to sit through the evening, as my boyish recollection goes, quite silent.'

At Harrow he made the acquaintance of Mrs. Vaughan's cousin Rosalind Stanley, now Lady Carlisle, then a child of eleven, who rated him soundly—much to his delight—for not having read the *Arabian Nights*, and commanded him to do so without delay[1].   And he had many a friendly battle on theological subjects with Mrs. Vaughan —Catherine Stanley—his fellow-traveller of 1845.

Meanwhile he kept up his correspondence with still older friends.   He writes to James Lonsdale, who had lost his mother:—

'No one who had known ever so little of her could help seeing that she was just one of those persons who spread light and peace over their homes.   Stanley has several times mentioned her to me as what he termed . . . one of his three pattern ladies: . . . her grace and goodness were admired by others as much as they were appreciated by her own children.'

[1] Mrs. Vaughan is my authority for this.—L. C.

Jowett's intercourse with Tennyson, which like
a golden thread ran through the whole of his remaining
years, began in the following way. In 1852 Tennyson
resided at Twickenham ; where both Temple and Palgrave, then at Kneller Hall, saw much of him. When
Jowett visited his two friends, they invited Tennyson to
meet him. He came, and the poet and 'philosopher' were
charmed with each other. After settling at Farringford,
the Tennysons invited Jowett to stay with them. When
the invitation had gone forth, Tennyson humorously
confessed to Palgrave his apprehensions at the thought
of entertaining a cleric and a don, but was assured that
Jowett was, after all, a human being. Mrs. Tennyson was
delighted with her guest's discourse upon high subjects,
such as the freedom of the will[1].

It may be mentioned in passing that Jowett examined
more than once at Durham University, where James
Lonsdale was one of the Tutors for a time.

Men have been known to rise to high places in Church
and State by taking advantage of such opportunities
as now opened for Jowett in the great world,
to the neglect of more immediate duties. That was
not Jowett's way. The Balliol Tutorship was still
his main employment, and he laboured in it as if
it were the sole purpose of his life; turning all
other interests to account in ennobling and enriching
this. It might without exaggeration be said of him in
relation to his pupils, that 'all things were for their
sakes.' With each new batch of undergraduates there
came an accession to those living influences, whose
fountain seemed inexhaustible and which flowed onward

---

[1] Grant, also, and William
Sellar, soon became frequent
guests at Farringford, through
Grant's connexion with Mr. Cotton
of Afton, Tennyson's neighbour at
Freshwater.

throughout the remainder of his career. The freshmen used to be assigned to the care of the several Tutors by some arrangement of a College meeting; but those whose promise and aspiration were above the average, if they had not the good fortune to be Jowett's pupils, were only too glad to avail themselves of the permission which he readily gave them, to bring essays or pieces of composition to his room, in addition to the regular work with their Tutor. He treated them, in such cases, as if they were really his pupils, and the work done for him was entered into with greater eagerness and delight than the ordinary College exercises. It was not that he spent more pains in looking over such attempts than other Tutors did; his remarks were brief, and he seldom rewrote a sentence, but, somehow, his merely saying of a copy of iambics, 'That is not so Greek as the last you did,' had the effect of sending one off upon a quest of higher excellence, the craving for which was not to be satisfied at once [1]. He seized upon what was best in one's attempts, and showed a way in which the whole might have been better.

He managed always to direct the study of language so as to promote literary culture. The pieces set by him for composition were choice specimens of classical English, which prompted higher efforts, and led to a closer intimacy with great writers, than such passages as used often to be prescribed. And he impressed upon his pupils an idea which was new to most of them, that in translating from Greek or Latin classics into English, as much of time and labour might be usefully spent as in turning an English passage into Latin or Greek.

---

[1] A contrary instance should perhaps be quoted. Somewhat earlier than this a Scholar of the College brought him a set of Greek verses. He glanced over them and, looking up rather blankly, said, 'Have you any taste for mathematics?'

His criticism in those days stimulated without discouraging. In setting before the mind a lofty ideal, he implied a belief in powers hereafter to be developed, and the belief seemed to create the thing believed in. But the intellectual stimulus was not all. He seemed to divine one's spiritual needs, and by mere contact and the brightness of his presence, to supply them. If he was ready to repress conceit, he was no less ready to bestow encouragement on the diffident, and sympathy upon the depressed ; not without timely warning, when he saw that danger or temptation was at hand. His intimate knowledge of his former pupils' lives was applied to heal the errors of their successors, and his own experience of early struggles also had its effect. He ignored trifles, but never let pass any critical point.

The mornings were of course spent in the Lecture Room. This was the larger of the two rooms in the Fisher Building which he then occupied. The lecture list, like the choice of Tutors for the men, was a matter of College arrangement. The subjects were distributed amongst the Tutors and Lecturers, the division of labour being, however, less minute than it became afterwards ; and attendance on the prescribed lectures was supposed to be compulsory.

Although Jowett had made his early reputation by Latin scholarship, it has been observed that he seldom if ever lectured on a Latin subject. His favourites were Sophocles, Aristophanes, Thucydides, and the *Republic* of Plato. There was no listlessness at any of his lectures, and often one man would remain after the rest to discuss a difficulty. If there was less of exact scholarship imparted by him, than, for example, by James Riddell, the whole subject was surrounded with an air of literary grace and charm which had a more educative effect. As

an interpreter, and above all as a translator, he seemed
to his pupils to be unrivalled. He was never satisfied
with any interpretation that could not be expressed in
perfect English. There were also Divinity Lectures on
the Epistles of St. Paul, and the History of Philosophy
Lectures already referred to; also a Logic Lecture (for
Moderations) in the Hall of the College, of which
Aldrich's *Logic* was still the text-book, though we were
expected to read Whately too; but the commentary
was diversified with many suggestive remarks and illustrations, especially on the subject of fallacies. Jowett
would suddenly ask for a quotation from English poetry,
which, if given, he would make the pupils analyze, and
recast in logical form. It was a sort of conversational
lecture. Besides all these, he now and then gave
a special course on Political Economy to a few
volunteers, and at one time held a very useful composition lecture for half an hour between morning Chapel
and breakfast-time, in which men were expected to turn
a piece of classical English, taken down from dictation,
extemporaneously and viva voce into Greek or Latin.
He would read out a passage, sentence by sentence,
inviting first one and then another to improvise a version
in Greek or Latin, welcoming any improvement of that
version from other members of the class, and settling
the ultimate form by general consent.

When it came to Jowett's turn to be Dean, some
men looked for a slack *régime* in regard to morning
Chapel, as Jowett himself, being a sound sleeper, and
studying late at night, was not always regular in his
attendance. They soon discovered their mistake; every
defaulter was immediately sent for, and instead of being
admonished for his failure in religious observance, was
told that morning Chapel was a rule of the College. In

case of continued delinquency, an imposition was inflicted and inexorably required. The Warden of Merton
(the Honourable G. C. Brodrick) says:—

'One morning several of us, including Jowett himself, were
just too late and found the door closed. Nevertheless he sent
for the absentees as usual and anticipated the allusion to
his own misfortune which I was on the point of making, by
asking shortly, "Why were you not in Chapel, Mr. Brodrick?"
and adding in the same breath, 'It's no use saying that I was
late too, for it was very wrong in both of us."'

No business of this kind really affected his relation
to his pupils. If his anger ever showed itself, it was
momentary, and left no trace on after intercourse.

In special cases he was lavish of his time and energy,
already, it might be thought, only too fully occupied.
If a promising but unequal scholar seemed to him to
have a chance for the Ireland, he would say, 'Bring me
a piece of composition every evening till the examination.' The evenings after Hall were given up to
interviews of this nature; the afternoons were often
spent in walks with undergraduates. His summer
reading-parties had made for him a little nucleus of
friends in College, to whom the extension of his influence
was largely due.

The Warden of Merton, who was an undergraduate at
this time, has made some valuable remarks which include
the period now under review:—

'In my opinion Jowett's heroic industry, during his Tutorial
career, has never been fully appreciated. At almost all hours
of the day, and up to a very late hour at night, his door was
always open to every man in the College seeking help, and,
though I was never among his chosen disciples, I continued
after taking my degree to bring him answers to questions
at my own request, which he looked over and criticized as
carefully as ever. No other Tutor within my experience has

ever approached him in the depth and extent of his pastoral supervision, if I may so call it, of young thinkers ; and it may truly be said that in his pupil-room, thirty, forty, and fifty years ago, were disciplined many of the minds which are now exercising a wide influence over the nation.'

Even amongst the Balliol undergraduates, however, Jowett was not universally popular. He had no false dignity, but he had an adequate sense of his position [1], and his native shyness had not worn off. His long silences were felt as an awkward bar to conversation by those who did not understand that he himself was hardly aware of them, as the intervals were filled with active thought. He was apt to disclaim this when taxed with it, and to declare that he was thinking of nothing [2], but the fact was often proved by the pregnancy of the few words that followed the silence. It seemed as if the thought had to make a long circuit through his capacious brain before the result, brief, terse, and pointed, was evolved [3].

To interrupt this silent process by starting a fresh topic was often to provoke a snub. This was partly due, as a friend remarks, 'to his absorption in his work, but also to a natural shyness and aversion to the commonplaces of society. As he never made an unmeaning remark himself, he was impatient of unmeaning remarks from others.'

In an early letter to Stanley he speaks of the 'idiosyncrasy' which led to these awkward silences :—

'Cromer is such an immense distance that it rather appals

---

[1] He was said to have rebuked Riddell for being too familiar with the undergraduates.

[2] *Life of J. A. Symonds*, vol. i. p. 227.

[3] A shrewd observer remarked long afterwards on his conversation at high table : 'Everything he said had an edge on it ; and was so perfectly expressed as to seem final. This made the give and take of conversation difficult. He seemed to be holding up an ideal, but one could not breathe freely in that high air. It was true elevation however, and not the donnishness of an academical *poseur*.'

me, but to say the truth, I would go there after your kind
letter, were it not for some idiosyncrasy that makes me, at
times, very unwilling to be among strangers, which it would
probably involve. I hardly like to mention it: it looks so
like affectation. But somehow or other I get thinking about
matters speculative or otherwise, and, when not perfectly well,
they get such a hold that I cannot relax, and one becomes a
sort of ἰδιώτης, wrapped in selfish care and out of tune with
ordinary life.'

Another thing that somewhat hampered his intercourse
with younger men was his fastidiousness on the score of
language, which he regarded almost as a sacred thing,
making it part of his vocation to impress this feeling upon
others. Hence the abhorrence of slang, which some undergraduates thought a piece of donnishness. With one of
his child-friends in the country he took a singular way
of enforcing this lesson. He insisted on giving her
a shilling every time she used the word 'awfully,' and so
shamed her out of the habit.

He never flinched from acts of necessary discipline,
although when anything severe was done, his intimate
friends knew well how his heart bled for the youth whose
prospects were affected. On the other hand, it was indirectly known that he had stoutly resisted what appeared
to him unnecessary harshness, and some of his chief
friends, as Mr. W. L. Newman observes, were amongst the
'unsteady ones' whose lives he was insensibly guiding.
One who appears to speak with feeling writes: 'Though
he did not spare you in private, he stood between you and
harm in public. He would send for you, and you found
him sitting, poker in hand, before his fire. It would
be many minutes sometimes before he would speak,
but when he did speak, it was to the purpose.'

His appearance at this time was still very youthful,
but at moments, at least to younger men, his personality

was very impressive. The look of great refinement, yet of manly strength, of subtlety, combined with simplicity; his unaffected candour, tempered with reserve, could not fail to attract even when it baffled observation. His soft wavy locks were already touched with grey, beginning to recede from the temples, so as to make more prominent the expansive brow, in which phrenologists would say that 'idealism' was balanced with 'comparison' and 'causality.' His full grey eyes spoke of the clearness of the mind within, yet had a dreamy wistful look, sometimes increased by a slight twitching of the eyelid. His mouth in repose appeared full and slack, but the expressive lips were under absolute control. He was always clean-shaven except the scanty whiskers, and the small chin seemed hardly to promise the strength of volition which lay concealed within. The effect of his sloping shoulders was rather enhanced by the black dress coat of fine broad cloth which he always wore. His waistcoat disclosed a faultless shirt-front and white neckerchief loosely tied about the upright collar, which he continued to wear long after it ceased to be the fashion. He never wore a great-coat before 1859, when he purchased one of roughish cloth for travelling purposes, described by J. A. Symonds as 'a barrel-bodied great-coat.' In walking about Oxford, if the cold happened to be extreme, he would propose to his companion to run for warmth. He seldom wore gloves, but when he did so they were of cloth, not kid. His hands seemed the only parts of him that were sensitive to cold. When cap and gown were discarded he wore a soft wideawake, which he called his 'cap.' In writing, if there was no chair at hand, he would kneel at a table. Those who knew him only in late years, would have been surprised to see his slight figure racing about the Balliol quadrangle, or to hear him, as he often did, hum or whistle, as he came back to his room, some broken phrases of a familiar melody.

He had still some lessons to learn in the management of men; and his advice to other Tutors at a somewhat later time probably reflects his own early experience: 'Young men are so sensitive. You will find one burning with indignation for some neglect of which you were profoundly unconscious. It will not do to speak roughly to them.' Yet it was often observed how as with a silken thread he put a check on those whom others found unmanageable. The frankness of his dealings with them, even when they had left College, may be illustrated by the following extract from a letter which is too intimate to be quoted at length :—

'There are many things which must give you, as all of us, pain in your past life. In your case they come rather under the head of weaknesses than of faults. You are now a man, so must put away childish things. . . . God has blessed you hitherto in your Oxford course, but you have been wanting to yourself. You have many friends looking on, and hoping that you will not allow egotism, or any mental or bodily weakness, to get the better of you. Forgive me for mentioning these things.'

This is a specimen of what some used to call 'a paternal from Jowett.'

A peculiarity which impressed many undergraduates was the beauty of his delivery, especially in reading Scripture. Mr. Isambard Brunel, who came to Balliol in the fifties, says that he and others used to make an effort to go to morning Chapel when it was known that Jowett was likely to read the Epistle and Gospel. Though rather high-pitched, his voice in reading had a richness in its tones, as of a silver bell, which charmed the ear; and the absence of mannerism, the sincerity

and reverence of the expression, and the perfect rendering
of every shade of meaning, without undue emphasis,
made an entireness of effect unlike anything that could
be heard elsewhere.   Poor young D'Arcy[1], a scholar of
genius, and of a deeply religious turn, remarked to me
after one Communion, how devoutly, in administering
it, Jowett had said the sacred words.   There were no
sermons then in Balliol Chapel, the institution of the
Catechetical Lecture having taken their place.   But
during the week before Communion, it was the practice
for each of the Tutors to give a short discourse to his
pupils.   Jowett's addresses were much valued by those
who heard them.   When they had assembled quietly in
the Lecture Room, he would come out of his inner room,
with the ink still wet upon the notepaper, and read
what he had prepared.   Two subjects are especially
remembered : 'Rejoice, O young man, in thy youth,' and
'Let me die the death of the righteous.'   In one he
spoke plainly of the temptations to which young men
were liable at College; 'All this,' he said, 'because
young men are weak.'   In another address he made
some subtle remarks on social difficulties, observing that
the secret of true influence was not conscious effort,
'nor sympathy, which may be weakness, but a consistent
life.'   In the sermon on death he dwelt on a favourite
topic, of which he had lately been reminded by conversations with Sir Benjamin Brodie, the great surgeon,
that the current notions about death-bed scenes were
an illusion, and that the desire of life often failed with
life itself[2].   One sentence in that sermon still remains

---

[1] He died in his second year at
College.

[2] See Brodie's *Psychological Inquiries* (1855).   Another impression which he took from converse
with Sir Benjamin was that 'the
force of specifics can go only a
little way.'

with me: 'God will not judge of men by what they know; yet to have used knowledge rightly will be a staff to support and comfort us in passing through the dark valley.'

Jowett's voice as a preacher was so long silent in Oxford, that there is a special interest in recalling the few occasions on which he is known to have occupied the University pulpit. Besides the Assize Sermon in the autumn of 1849, there were some which he delivered as Select Preacher in 1850-51. Of one of these he writes to ffolliott, October, 1851 : 'My sermon was greatly admired—by the wooden benches, who found something in it exactly adapted to the ecclesiastical position which they had taken up. It was an animating sight to see them; they echoed every word that was said.' But there are some who still remember an impressive discourse on the text, 'The hairs of your head are all numbered,' treating of the Reign of Law; and Mr. Gladstone, in a recent letter to P. Lyttelton Gell, spoke of a discourse which he had heard from Jowett about this time, on the contrast between faith and experience, as 'epoch-making.'

The small hours were given, when not demanded by special calls upon his attention or sympathy, to the systematic study of St. Paul.

Stanley's departure from Oxford in 1850, and his appointment to a Canonry of Canterbury in 1851, were events of trying significance for his chief Oxford friend. Their paths in life were sundering; they could no longer work at the New Testament together [1], and the dream of a visit to the Holy Land could only be fulfilled for one of them. The Homeric ideal of σύν τε δύ᾽ ἐρχομένω, 'two going on together,' became for the time unrealizable

[1] See p. 160.

in Oxford. Jowett was more than ever isolated in the
studies of his choice, to which he held on with unremitting tenacity [1].

Theological agitation had died down at Oxford;
Tractarianism was no longer persecuted, and though
increasingly influential in country districts, was at
a standstill in the University. No onslaught had as
yet been made on liberal thought: the Broad Church
had hardly even been named [2], yet suspicion was rife in
certain quarters. Mr. Henry Bristow Wilson's Bampton
Lectures in 1851 (*The Communion of Saints:* an attempt to
illustrate the true principles of Christian union) sounded
the first clear note of a demand for freedom in theological
inquiry, a demand which was destined to grow and
strengthen for years to come.

The challenge was not taken up. The High Church
party felt that their 'strength was to sit still.' The
moment was inopportune for active measures: the
Gorham judgement had been a severe discouragement,
and the two chief powers on the orthodox side, Dr.
Pusey and 'Samuel of Oxford,' were in sharp contention
concerning the Eucharist and the Confessional. But
that Pusey at least was on the watch appears from
his letter to the Bishop, dated May 5, 1851:—

'Mr. Stanley . . . has been forming a school, known as
the Germanizing school. . . . The present Bampton Lecturer,
Mr. Wilson, of St. John's, has been preaching such doctrine

[1] Already in 1846 there had
been some questionings as to
'Arthur's future,' and Jowett
had written earnestly to Mrs.
Stanley in favour of the Oxford
career.

[2] This Saxon equivalent for
'Latitudinarian' was first brought

into general vogue by an article
on Church Parties in the *Edinburgh Review* for October, 1853,
where it is employed to include
Arnold and his followers, Julius
and Augustus Hare, Frederick
Denison Maurice, and Bishop
Jackson.

as has much scandalized many of the Heads of Houses. . . . You will be asked why they are allowed to officiate, I forbidden [1].'

Nor did the 'great Tutor,' as Sir Robert Inglis called Jowett, escape calumnious strokes. 'He reads Plato on Sundays' (the *Phaedo*, for example!), said the simpler Evangelical sort amongst the Oxford youth. But the imputation of 'Germanism' cut much deeper. Readers of Arnold's Life will remember the interest awakened in his mind by the impulse which the genius of Niebuhr had given to historical criticism, an influence which about this time reached the abler minds at both the Universities, through the translation of Niebuhr's *History of Rome*, by Julius Hare and Connop Thirlwall of Trinity, Cambridge. There were some who foresaw that the same spirit would not ultimately be warned off from the sacred territory. Milman's historical writings were already giving proof of this, and Pusey, who had himself at one time hoped much from such moderate theologians as Tholuck and Neander, was beginning to fear that the more recent visit to Germany of Stanley and Jowett might bear such fruit as would deepen the remorse he felt for his own former interest in German theology. It is idle to suppose, because Jowett had not yet published, and was therefore not openly attacked, that he was not suspected. His complaint in 1855, that men in private conversation would listen with apparent assent to opinions which they were ready to denounce when published, is enough to prove that he had given some cause for suspicion. In his lectures he was freely putting forth the interpretations which were afterwards embodied in his writings. And his letters to Stanley show quite clearly that as early as 1846 he was disturbed by accusations of heresy.

[1] *Life of E. B. Pusey*, vol. iii. p. 335.

'What you say about —— does appear to be some reason for telling people what you think. I have been very cautious for the last two years past, so that —— has no reason for his charges, except reports of my lectures which he gets from —— and misrepresents. . . . He takes those things from —— and distils them. . . . He talks about my atrocities, which, considering I have not spoken to him for the last two years on these subjects, is rather cool : nor can I ever remember to have held an "esoteric" conversation with him.'

That he had read Lessing and Schleiermacher, and had studied Hegel, could not but be known to the younger men, and less than this was enough to compromise a clerical reputation in the early fifties.

I have spoken of special calls on his attention which interrupted his private study. Amongst these the duties of the Bursarship, which he had undertaken in 1849, must have occupied an important place. To the surprise of some who then regarded him as a dreamy, speculative thinker, he displayed administrative abilities of no common order. Not only were the accounts kept with a lucidity and precision which had not always been observed[1], but the work of pulling down and rebuilding the north-west angle of the College, known as the Caesar Building, was now projected, and was carried out largely under his superintendence. He stayed up in vacation time for this purpose, and kept things going in spite of the obstructive tactics of the Master, of which he writes to ffolliott:—

'We have got a very beautiful plan, but that little fellow of whom you must have heard many stories which ought to have been true, all of them falling far short of the truth, makes a stout resistance, and valiantly takes his stand upon his brewhouse, which he disputes our right to pull down.'

Jowett took a pride in making suggestions to the architect, some of which were adopted. Other practical

[1] *W. G. Ward and the Oxford Movement*, p. 436.

schemes were already germinating, two of which, at least, were ultimately realized.

First, that of a Balliol Hall for out-College students. This, although mentioned by him in confidence to two persons only, was a practical idea which he had very warmly at heart for some time before the Report of the Commission in 1852. He even indulged himself in a fond vision of bringing Stanley back to Oxford as the Head of such a Hall. A letter to Stanley on this subject is of sufficient interest to be embodied here :—

Rugby, *June* 6, 1852.

I am going to trouble you with a scheme for University Extension, 'cujus tu pars magna es.'

While other people are writing pamphlets and reports and theorizing about 'caste,' and trying to meet on paper difficulties that can only be got over in practice, might we not attempt the thing itself?

I remember proposing it to you at Christmas : you did not encourage it then—and I would not like to annoy you by pressing it again. But your taking part has struck me so strongly since as likely to be for the great good of all and also for your own good, that I hope you will consider the following points, and if you feel hearty in the cause we may work together in it.

1. I think it may be fairly urged against us University reformers that we are unpractical. S—— can raise —— and —— which fall to pieces again from his folly and Tractarianism, and we who ' being the children of this world imagine ourselves wiser than the children of light,' sit still and do nothing. M—— will be deluging the Church of England with his straight-coated buttonless clergy, and no one is ready to show the same energy and self-denial in a better cause. As religious men I think we can give no account of our indifference to such an opportunity. As University reformers we must appear to the world rather as seeking to make an intellectual aristocracy or, to express it more coarsely, to form good places for ourselves out of the revenues of the Colleges, than earnest

about anything which the world in general cares for or which can do any extensive good.

2. This appears to me true of all of us—myself included of course—with the exception of Temple. Let me add a few reasons why I would rather see you than any one else at the head of such a move. (1) You have a far greater name and distinction than any one else. (2) You have independent means. (3) Such an attempt would come with especial good grace from the Secretary of the Commission. (4) If, as I should expect, we had a lower class of men at the proposed Hall, I believe you would be one of the few persons who would treat them and make others treat them with perfect kindness and consideration. It is a blessed use to be able to make of aristocratic birth and family.

I think, if in this way you could be connected with Oxford, you would be brought back to us in the most honourable way, and you would not only have deserved your Canonry as everybody allows, but you would work for it. . . .

The scheme is, shortly, a Hall attached to Balliol College with intercommunion of Lectures ; Tuition to be free. Room rent also free—the total expense to be reduced (by common meals, &c.) to the lowest point, say £50 a year. Of such a Hall I should hope you might be induced to become Principal, with Walrond perhaps for Vice-Principal. . . .

I should propose to begin by renting houses. The necessary funds for furnishing them and paying the rent, and also for salarying the Vice-Principal, might, I think, be easily raised by subscription. I would endeavour to give £50 a year, and I think we should have many warm supporters.

Suppose you were to make the application before going to the East. I do not think it need interfere with your journey, if you thought of entering on the plan. In your absence Temple and myself and others might set the thing afloat to commence a year hence.

I have not mentioned the matter to any one excepting Shairp, and shall not do so until I hear from you.

The position I am anxious to see you take is not that of a drudging College Tutor, but one quite consistent with a Professorship and with the completion of our book, also one which would not require residence of more than eighteen weeks in the year, and one in which you would be perfectly independent instead of being vexed as at University with —— & Co.

Ever yours affectionately,

B. Jowett.

Some years afterwards (January, 1855) he wrote :—

'I am sorry for the annoyance which that and similar counsels of mine may have caused you. I should not care about it with any one else, but I am aware that those sort of things give you pain. No one's position is more justifiable than yours : I only wish that we had some additional tie to connect you with Oxford.

Twenty or thirty years of life and leisure with the power of writing is a grand prospect, enough to make a man's heart leap within him.'

It would seem that Stanley had been hurt by the implied reflection on his enjoyment of a clerical sinecure, and that Jowett's heart smote him (after his own repulse for the Mastership) for having 'made sad' the mind of his friend. But an earlier effect of that friend's refusal to undertake the work so eagerly pressed on him, was to call forth a long and elaborate letter on the Reform of Cathedral Establishments, beginning 'How may Cathedral Institutions be made to teem with life at every pore?'

The second scheme above referred to was the acquisition of a convenient Cricket-field for the College. The late Archdeacon Palmer wrote in 1894 :—

'It may be of interest to record that some years before the University purchased the land which now forms the University Park, Jowett asked me to accompany him and Chitty (now Lord Justice Chitty), who was then a Balliol undergraduate or a new B.A., through the fields on the west side of the Cherwell, in search of an eligible piece of ground for a Balliol Cricket ground. We entered them near Holywell Church and made our way northwards at least as far as the northern fence of the park. Nothing came of this, but it may serve to show

how early Jowett had conceived the idea which was realized in the establishment of the Balliol Recreation Ground. This search must have taken place in 1851 or 1852.'

The Public Examinership, which came to him in 1849, and was renewed under the changed Statute in 1851, compelled him to relinquish the Bursarship for a while. This was another serious interruption to study; although the burden of the Examination was less heavy then than it is now. Jowett felt the responsibility of reorganizing the Final Examination in Classics, especially in the direction of encouraging the study of Plato, the History of Philosophy, and the illustration of Ancient Philosophy by Modern.

On March 6, 1854, the old Master died, and was buried at Wells, of which he had held the Deanery since 1845. He was one of those men whom, when placed in authority, their juniors at once like, and laugh at. In his reminiscences of Ward, Jowett has given a vivid picture of his eccentric predecessor [1]:—

'He was a gentleman of the old school, in whom were represented old manners, old traditions, old prejudices; a Tory and a Churchman, high and dry, without much literature, but having a good deal of character. He filled a great space in the eyes of the undergraduates. "His young men," as he termed them, speaking in an accent which we all remember, were never tired of mimicking his voice, drawing his portrait, and inventing stories about what he said and did. . . . His sermon on the "Sin that doth so easily beset us," by which, as he said in emphatic and almost acrid tones, he meant "the habit of contracting debts," will never be forgotten by those who heard it. Nor, indeed, have I ever seen a whole congregation dissolved in laughter for several minutes except on that remarkable occasion. The ridiculousness of the effect was heightened by the old-fashioned pronunciation of certain words, such as "rayther," "wounded," (which he pronounced like "wow" in "bow-wow"). . . . It was sometimes doubted

[1] *W. G. Ward, &c.*, p. 440 ff.

whether he was a wit or not ; I myself am strongly of opinion that he was. . . . He was short of stature and very neat in his appearance ; the deficiency of height was more than compensated by a superfluity of magisterial or ecclesiastical dignity. He was much respected, and his great services to the College have always been acknowledged. But even now (1890), at the distance of more than a generation, it is impossible to think of him without some humorous or ludicrous association arising in the mind.'

The 'old Master' had served Balliol long and faithfully, and his loss was sincerely mourned. Jowett was one of those who represented the College at his funeral.

The following reminiscences of Mr. W. L. Newman, the editor of Aristotle's *Politics*, who was a Scholar of Balliol from 1851 to 1854, when he was elected to a Fellowship, like Jowett, while still an undergraduate, bear reference to the period now described :—

'When I went into residence at Balliol in October, 1852, I became one of Jowett's pupils. He then occupied rooms in the Fisher Building, which have since undergone alterations. The outer and larger of the two sitting-rooms has been parted from the inner one, and has been assigned to another set of rooms. Jowett used his outer sitting-room for many of his lectures, till on the completion of the Salvin Building he moved them all to the upper Lecture Room there. The inner sitting-room, under the window of which the well-known inscription " Verbum non amplius Fisher' is still to be seen—he used as his living-room, and for seeing his pupils. I well recollect one or two of the engravings which hung on the walls—in the outer room an engraved portrait of Niebuhr, the face of which always had a charm for me, and in the inner one an engraving of Sir Joshua Reynolds' " Age of Innocence," which also delighted me [1].

'Jowett himself, though only thirty-five, was already grey-haired, and he was altogether much more unlike other people than he

---

[1] There was also an engraving of the companion picture of 'Simplicity.' It was a proof before letters, and the title was written on the under margin in Jowett's hand.—L. C.

became in after years. I despair of conveying to any one who did not know him then anything like an exact idea of what he was. He left on me a stronger impression of genius at that time of his life than at any other. Moments of musing and abstraction were allied in him with a singular alertness and rapidity of mind, meditative power went hand in hand with keen insight.

'I well remember his ways. When one took him composition, he used commonly to seat himself in a chair placed immediately in front of the fire and close to it, and to intersperse his abrupt, decided and pithy comments on one's work with vigorous pokes of the fire. Occasionally he would lapse into silence, and say nothing whatever perhaps for two or three minutes ; but, if one rose to go, one often found that his best remarks still remained to be uttered. The silent interval had been a time of busy thought. The same thing sometimes happened on the walks which he often took me ; I remember one day when we walked for some miles in the Cumnor direction side by side without exchanging a word ; then I said something which caught his attention, and roused him, and for the rest of the way we talked eagerly and without intermission. He always had a dislike for small-talk and trivialities, and never talked unless he had something to say. I have heard of his excusing his silence and saying : "If I say nothing, it is not because I am out of temper, but because I have nothing to say." His occasional abstraction or apparent abstraction—now and then accompanied by the half-unconscious " crooning " in a low voice of a kind of tune—never disguised to those who knew him his real alertness or the keen watchfulness of his interest in his pupils. In later days all this passed away, not altogether unregretted by some of us. The intervals of silence also became rarer ; I remember a half-jocose remark of Pattison's about him towards the end of the sixties, " Now there's affability."

'I liked his abrupt and peremptory, yet always serene and kindly ways. " I want you to do this or that," he would say, poker in hand. He was good as a critic of composition, and especially as a critic of Latin prose. He had a quick instinct for what was Ciceronian and what was not, perhaps rather in connexion with the flow of the sentence than in matters of diction. He never gave me fair copies, an omission which I often

regretted ; I do not know whether he ever gave them. He
certainly did not spoil his pupils. He was most kind to them,
but he expected them to work hard, and he set them the example
himself. I have often taken composition to him at half-past
twelve at night. He was, in the days when I was his pupil,
rather severe as a critic of his pupils' work. I have been told
on good authority that in earlier days than mine he always had
high praise for Riddell's composition, but for that of hardly any
one else. As to Riddell he was unquestionably right. No
doubt his strict criticism was a wholesome discipline for us. One
of his many useful remarks has remained in my memory ; there
is nothing, perhaps, particularly new about it. He used to say
that in good English writing—he illustrated his remark by the
practice of Macaulay—one sentence always leads on to the next.

'College lectures were in those days smaller and more conversational than they have since become, and much of the hour they
occupied was spent in listening to construing. I remember two
lectures of Jowett's in my first Term, if I do not mistake
(Michaelmas Term, 1852), one an elementary lecture, at which
we used to sit round a table in the Hall with Jowett at the head,
and pull to pieces the fallacious arguments collected for that
purpose at the end of Whately's *Logic*, and another on the
Agamemnon of Aeschylus. Jowett was little given to enthusiastic comments on what we read, but I think I recollect that
he dropped half a dozen emphatic words at the end of one lecture,
to the effect that the scene with Cassandra was the finest in any
tragedy. Later on I attended his lectures on Plato's *Republic*,
in connexion with which I specially recall the grace and felicity
of a kind of paraphrastic analysis (if I remember right), portions
of which he used to read to us, and also an excellent lecture on
Political Economy, in which he often broke off his remarks to
address questions to some of us which occasionally led to an
argument or even a discussion. One or two of my contemporaries were very useful to the rest of us on these occasions.

'Jowett's lectures were not in my experience of much direct
use for the examination Schools, they were hardly systematic
enough for that—but they showed us how to state and handle
questions, and, as Green [1] once said to me, they "gave one

[1] Professor T. H. Green.

glimpses." In those days the University was not as much in the grasp of its examination system as it has since come to be ; we kept the Schools in view, but they were not the Alpha and Omega of our reading as undergraduates. Jowett's lectures were very useful to me ; I found them a welcome addition to the teaching of others and to the books which one read for examination or otherwise.

' But I think that his conversation was even more useful. He often took his pupils for walks and invited them to breakfast, and I am sure that I learnt much from this familiar intercourse with him. In those days he was quite unconventional, and his occasional intervals of silence may have been baffling and dis-appointing to some, but no conversation was more stimulating to thought than his. It did not stimulate to research or to learned inquiry, but to thought. The value of a conversation with him arose partly from the fact that he listened as well as talked, and often made one's own remarks the starting-point of what he said. Indeed it was frequently necessary for his companion to set the conversation going ; I think he rather liked those who were useful in that way ; I remember his saying once how much he appreciated the company of a friend, "he starts so many hares." The remark which gave the first impulse to the conversation was commonly of little value in itself, but it elicited comments and additions from him which were of the greatest value. His quick apprehension and ready sympathy were encouraging ; one felt sure that if there was anything whatever in what one had to say, more than justice would be done to it. He was himself quite candid and very ready in comment, and one learnt much from the pithy sense and subtle insight which were never lacking in what he said. He was at his best when some observation threw him into a momentary reverie ; he would be silent for a minute or two, and then would say something which went to the heart of the matter. His strength lay especially in quick perception —quick perception of fact, quick perception of character, quick perception of the best thing to be done. His insight into character was very keen and was aided by his ready imaginative sympathy. No one was more alive than he was to the subtle mingling of good and bad in human nature, to the frequent com-bination in it of characteristics apparently opposite and incompatible. As Sir A. Grant, one of his earliest and most attached pupils, once observed to me, his talk was less remarkable for knowledge than for thoughtfulness.

'Nothing, however, in his relation to his pupils pleases me more in retrospect than the fatherly vigilance with which he watched over able but unsteady young men. He was untiring in his efforts to keep them straight, and when he failed in this, to set them on their feet again. He cared for them as few fathers care for unsteady sons, saving them from themselves and persevering in the face of disappointment.'

LETTERS, 1850-1853.

To A. P. Stanley.

August 22, 1850.

This is dated Oban, though I am really at Duntroon, spending a day with the Bishop. His powers of entertainment are as good as ever—indeed, he is at times quite mad with fun. I have left off assisting in the affairs of the Scotch Episcopal Church, which he does best in his own peculiar fashion.

I work with my pupils of an evening, and for an hour in the morning. The sermons make some progress. I still find ghostly comfort in reading Plato and Hegel and Bacon, after Mauricianism, Niebuhrism, Bunsenism, &c., have departed, and the shades of German divines begin to vanish. Many thanks for your account of Neander. I wish he had lived to finish his history. Yet it is not *the* Church History—how different in command of his subject when compared with Gibbon! It is uninteresting and uncritical, and yet too critical to retain a religious or devotional interest.

To A. P. Stanley.

Oban, *September* 9, 1850.

Manning and Co. have issued a circular to the Clergy to the effect that they never intended by taking the Oath of Supremacy to imply that the Queen could decide spiritual questions; and requesting to know the opinions of others. The whole question is getting to a very false position. Five years hence let us imagine the possible issues. 1. A free Church with spires reaching to heaven, deriving its succession from H. Exeter or S. Oxon., or haply from a poor Scottish sister, ornamented with the bust of St. Barnabas, and with the virtues of Bennett, Manning, Wilberforce; having as many priests as people, with clerical Colleges for the study of the schoolmen, like the primitive Church in every respect but one, that it preaches to the rich.

2. Bennett, Manning, Wilberforce are already Romanists, preaching 'extra Ecclesiam nulla salus,' winding themselves in and out of society, pulling hard at the pockets of the aristocracy, and also at the opinions of the clergy, upon whom they will make a much greater impression than Newman did, whose influence decreased as he was better understood. Notwithstanding, the huge creature goes on its way for a time apparently uninjured.

3. The last act of the history of the Church of England. Convocation has met: they are revising the liturgy: the Bishop of Oxford is addressing them: by a final vote they are going to settle who is to keep possession of the Establishment.

What a system of terrorism it is with people about 'Regeneration'! Twenty years ago no bishop or clergyman would have hesitated to take it in a non-natural sense: now every one seems 'mum' for fear of the letter of the law. Formerly the High Churchman was the black sheep.

FROM MRS. JOWETT TO HER SON ALFRED, IN INDIA.

April, 1851.

It is a great pleasure to hear from you, dearest Alfred, you are such a comfort to us. Benjamin often speaks of it. He is such a great fag at College, we seldom hear from him; for he says, though he thinks of us often, when he is so tired, he cannot settle his mind to write, so you must not wonder if he does so to you. I can truly assure you it does not arise from forgetfulness or want of affection. I hope you have reached safely your destined station and that you like it; the most minute details in your letters are acceptable; what would be nothing to a stranger is everything to us. I have passed a better winter than usual, and am quite as strong as I can expect to be for sixty years old. In my next I shall have some-

thing to tell you; little or much, I must write.   I wish I had
done so oftener to others[1].   Emily says I must send the letter.

To W. Y. Sellar.

BALLIOL, *October* 26, 1851.

Grant told me that you wished to hear from me.   Indeed,
my dear fellow, I wish I could say anything to comfort you.
I do not doubt that it is well with your father after his long
and honourable life.   There is another world too, in which he
will be as happy as in this, though we are unable altogether
to conceive its nature.   'The souls of the righteous are in the
hand of God, and there shall no evil touch them.'   I think
we cannot help turning to ourselves as we see the dying, and
asking what lesson the sight of them conveys to ourselves.
Can it be anything but this, that we should find our true
comfort in leading a higher life, such a life as makes death
and life indifferent to us and raises us into communion with
them?   They leave us alone, and yet the world is not lonely
if we look upon it as the scene in which duties are to be
performed and work to be done, ere after another generation
we follow them to rest in peace.   I hope you will feel it to be
a duty you owe to your father to nerve yourself for your
new post.   Could he live to see it, there is nothing that
would give him so much pleasure as your success in it.   I was
very much struck more than a year ago with what your father
told Harvey, 'that he had lain awake at night thinking of your
illness, because he fancied that he had encouraged you to
overwork at Glasgow.'   You only need a small portion of his
energy and decision of character to give you success in life.

To F. T. Palgrave.

[LUFFENHAM], *June* 8, 1852.

Many thanks for your long letter, which I was very glad to get.
I am on the way to Durham and lingering for a day at Scott's.

I am sorry of course not to agree with Temple and Lingen
and you respecting Gladstone, and really feel half inclined to
sign.   But though not of very much importance I think it would
be a mistake.   We should obtrude ourselves on the public and

[1] William Jowett had died in the previous year.

show our weakness in numbers. I don't at present intend to vote for Gladstone, because not agreeing with him either about University reform or Church and State. Also I feel a strong dislike to that over-conscientiousness of his, which, instead of walking in the great highway of political truth and honesty, is always winding round to his own interest and coming out at odd places where nobody expects him. Were it not for this I think him a noble fellow : at present he is too good to be trusted. I dare say, however, that Temple is right in seeking to tie him up with the coil of his own tail.

I have been thinking for some time past of a Balliol Hall and University Extension. At present it has only been mentioned to one person. If anything can be made of it I will write to you and Temple and tell you, but it is difficult to manage, as some of the Fellows and the Master would oppose it, and others only desire to carry it out on a Puseyite model. Meantime don't mention it, please.

. . . I am sorry, very sorry, to hear of Lady Palgrave's sad state. When I saw her she used to strike me as a wonder of patience and cheerfulness and thoughtfulness for others amid her own great sufferings. Remember me most kindly to her. I thought last time I had sent the last message there would be an opportunity of sending—may she be spared to you yet for long.

Scott's children for the last half-hour have been trying to make me come out for a walk, and as their patience is now exhausted I must conclude [1].

To F. T. Palgrave.

CANTERBURY, *August* 11, 1852.

Many thanks for your note. I am very sorry to hear that one for whom I had so much regard is gone.

The last time I saw her was about a year ago. She was as cheerful and pleasing in conversation, and as much interested about others, as if she had been in health. I remember her repeating several passages of Wordsworth. She said that she

---

[1] Scott was now at Luffenham, having exchanged Duloe for this rectory in 1850. He had married again in 1849.

wished to tell me, as I was a friend of yours, what a comfort you had been to her in her illness. She also mentioned the pleasure it had given her to be able to continue writing your father's history.

I cannot think any death otherwise than happy in which the mind so completely triumphs over suffering. I do not doubt that she is with God, and that all this has not passed away, though what this means I cannot tell. I do not wish for any other end than hers, notwithstanding the pain she must have endured.

Do not think that there is a blank or solitude because she has departed. There are many pleasant memories of the dead come back upon us if we keep them daily in the mind's eye. They seem to urge us onward to do something in life before the end which is so near.

To F. T. Palgrave.

BALLIOL, *December* 13, 1852.

It is very good of you and Temple to want me to come to Kneller for Christmas; at present my face is set in another direction, to Malvern; like Gabriel Grubb I am going to dig while others are making merry.

Owing to a great many interruptions my work has not prospered this Term. I am anxious to get one volume completely finished before the Schools begin.

It often strikes me as a doubt (independent of defects in the execution) whether the book will not be too heterodox for the orthodox to read, and too orthodox for the heterodox. If the world is divisible into these two classes I see not where the readers are to be found. . . .

When is your article coming out? I hope you and Temple rejoice with us in the Class List[1].

PS.—Don't think I am indifferent to your kindness. The only reason you have for calling me a Don is that I won't smoke and talk aesthetics in the tower[2], and don't like to hear people, especially my friends, run down.

[1] Balliol had four Classical Firsts in the list for Michaelmas, 1852.

[2] A room in the tower at Kneller Hall, which was used as a smoking-room by the subordinates.

To Mrs. Greenhill.

. . . I am here alone at this place, and have had no one to speak to for a fortnight. It is not unfavourable to composition. Fortunately I am two miles from the Water Cures, and therefore have no temptation to dilute my intellects in that way. But when I think upon how many merry parties and Christmas children dancing round trees and playing at flap-dragon there have been, I fear I am a fool for my pains, and feel like Charles Lamb bursting into tears when he gave away his aunt's nice cake to a worthless beggar in the streets.

Give my love to Kate, and tell her to learn more songs, and to paste up the enclosed piece of red paper in her bedroom as a remembrance of me. It is a New Year's Gift.

Remember me most kindly to Dr. Greenhill. I hope his practice flourishes and increases. There is nothing I desire so much as to see him a rich man. Don't let him go to church on week-days too often, for no one will imagine that he has a large practice if he does, and no one would go to Esculapius himself unless they thought he had a large practice. *I* should not object to Dr. Greenhill being called out of church every Sunday morning by a flunkey, but I know his high principles would revolt at this.

I hear of Stanley from Marseilles and Alexandria; he is enchanted, as might be expected, with Eastern life, and seems quite bounding with delight. His mother and sister came back a few days ago.

Oxford, you see, is bustling with two elections. I hear Gladstone is to be opposed by the Marquis of Chandos.

I always thought his election for Oxford would end like Peel's. He will go through one more 'conscientious' betrayal of his friends, one more 'conscientious' resignation of office. What a pity it is that the most religious and in many ways high-principled man in the House of Commons should have got himself with all mankind the character of being the least straightforward!

CHAPTER VIII

THE EPISTLES OF ST. PAUL.   THE PROFESSORSHIP OF
GREEK.   1854–1860

(Aet. 36–43)

POSITION in Oxford and elsewhere—Repulse for the Mastership—
Epistles of St. Paul—Greek Professorship—Vice-Chancellor Cotton—
Endowment withheld—Work of the Chair—Isolation—Death of his
brother Alfred and of his father—Second edition of the *Epistles*—
Portrait by G. Richmond—W. L. Newman's reminiscences (continued).

AMONG the 'stately homes,' where Jowett had now
become a welcome guest[1], was Ockham Park,
Surrey, the seat of Dr. Stephen Lushington, Judge
of the High Court of Admiralty, whose son Godfrey had
lately passed from Rugby to Balliol. It was several
years after this that Dr. Lushington became Dean of the
Court of Arches, and thus had jurisdiction in ecclesiastical
causes. No shadow of events to come fell between the
elderly lawyer and the young divine. He was also
a visitor in Dr. Lushington's house in London. Here,
amongst other interesting persons, he met Brunel, the
engineer, then engaged in the construction of the *Great
Eastern*. Jowett had always been an admirer of the
Thames Tunnel and the Great Western Railway, and
this meeting must have been a delight to him[2]. He

---

[1] e. g. The Limes, Hurstmonceux, Broome Park (Sir Benjamin Brodie's), &c.

[2] It may have been in conversation with Brunel that he was first struck with the idea which so long haunted him, that of draining the Thames valley so as to improve

delighted also in the ripe and varied experience of his host, who had vivid recollections of the state of England at the beginning of the century. Dr. Lushington, when in Parliament, had advocated the abolition of capital punishment, and used to describe the feelings of the peasantry in the home counties, who, when a relative went up to London, regarded him as literally doomed to the gallows. Jowett often repeated this. To the young people at Ockham, their father's guest appeared as a mild and amiable cleric, in whom they saw no promise of great things to come.

Hitherto Jowett's relations to those about him had been almost uniformly friendly. Some may have thought him opinionated, but there is no trace of any actual discord.

He goes to visit Scott in his country parish, and does duty for him when he is 'blind and solitary,' relinquishing pleasant plans for this purpose ; he stays with him again under altered circumstances, rejoicing in his new prospects, and the children insist on his coming out to walk with them. He looks up Lake, when on the Continent and out of health, as if they had not enough of one another in Term-time ; reads Trench's *Hulsean Lectures* aloud to him with frank comments [1], and works in his favour when a candidate for the Head Mastership of Rugby in 1849. He presses Henry Wall's claims

the climate of Oxford. Some years afterwards he told a party of guests that a great opportunity had been lost in making the G.W.R., when this had been part of the great engineer's original plan, but had been opposed by the Heads of Houses, with two exceptions—Wynter of St. John's, and Harrington of Brasenose.

[1] The substance of these is repeated in a letter to Stanley : 'Is there one theological writer of the present day who can be said to be morally and intellectually truthful ? And if so, the mournful fact forces itself upon one that there is no elder person in whose footsteps one can tread, however little or nothing it is possible for us to do.' (1846.)

for the Registrarship of the University. To Lonsdale he gives unstinted help and sympathy. His friendship with Stanley is the closest possible ; with Temple he is on an intimate and affectionate footing, and when his friend goes to London and engages in practical work, urges upon Lingen the advisability of procuring for him a higher salary. He is pressing forward every man's interest except his own. When he goes with the Lingens to see a review of the troops at Chobham, they meet Bishop Wilberforce, who is on horseback, while they are on foot. He greets them cheerfully, with a jesting remark on the Church Militant.

In London the Oxford Tutor is respected and esteemed by public men, such as Macaulay, and he is a contributor to Dr. William Smith's *Dictionaries of Antiquities* and of *Classical Biography*, in which the first scholars of the country took part from 1842 to 1849. On the whole he is swimming with the stream[1]. But a time was approaching when these waters were to be troubled, and his powers as a 'strong swimmer' would be put to the test.

After the death of the old Master, Jowett seems for a time to have looked upon the succession to the vacant office as an open question, in which he had no immediate concern. A letter of his to James Lonsdale—in which he tries to rouse his friend's dormant ambition by saying, 'Perhaps you may be our new Master ; who knows? It would be a great happiness to me if you are[2]'—is sufficient evidence of this. But in the course of a few weeks, he found enough of favour amongst his colleagues

---

[1] Lord Lingen says (1895): 'Up to 1855, his life was one of growing honour and success, which shed its light over his presence among his friends.'

[2] *Life of James Lonsdale*, p. 45.

to awaken his own hopes. Nearly half of the Balliol
Fellows, by this time, had been his pupils, and the
self-devoted labour of twelve years and more had had its
effect.   It was largely recognized that no College Tutor
had worked so well.   And it became apparent that, of the
residents, he had the strongest chance.   This is proved
by the fact that his opponents adopted the expedient
of bringing up a candidate from the country.   Robert
Scott had taken a College living, Duloe near Liskeard,
in Cornwall, in 1840, before Jowett's work as a Tutor
had begun, and in 1850 had exchanged this for Luffenham, in Rutlandshire.   He was an accomplished scholar,
and his lectures had been valuable (this Jowett himself
had found), but he could not be described as a 'great
Tutor,' and his one distinguished service, namely, his
share in the production of Liddell and Scott's *Lexicon*,
did not clearly mark him out as fitted for the control and
guidance of younger men.   But he was orthodox ; and
the opposition to Jowett, of which the strength was
proved by the event, found in him the most likely card
to play.   Not that the objections taken to Jowett were
wholly theological.   There were those who resented
the firmness of his attitude in College controversies,
and did not choose to place him in authority.   The
parties were nearly balanced, and all depended on one
or two waverers, who on general grounds were thought
likely to be on Jowett's side.   It is not necessary to
mention names ; but two votes, on which Jowett had
counted, went the other way.   One of these may have
been influenced by family associations.   The other, who
really turned the scale, was said to have been talked over,
at the last moment, on theological grounds, by a disciple
and friend of Dr. Pusey.

The bitterness of the repulse was aggravated by the

reasonable confidence of success which had preceded
it. That Jowett resented it long and deeply, although
silently, there is no reason to doubt. His feeling on
the subject appears not only from his letters to Palgrave of April 7, 1854 [1], and to Stanley on April 12,
but also from the sympathy which he afterwards expressed in writing to a friend who had met with a
similar disappointment. The language then used appeared
exaggerated, but revealed what had passed in his own
mind many years before. In later life, however, he felt
that this rude check had not been wholly a misfortune.
He said to a friend on one occasion, ' I should not have
been fit for the Mastership then. I did not know enough
of the world.' Severely as he felt the blow, it produced
on him a very different effect from that which a similar
rejection had upon Mark Pattison. Instead of para-
lyzing his energies, it roused him to renewed efforts. He
went straight from Oxford to the Vaughans' at Harrow,
where he remained six weeks, and devoted himself to the
work of finishing his book ; and on returning to College
in the summer, he threw himself more than ever into
his labours for the undergraduates. He again became
Junior Bursar, the Senior Bursarship being retained by
H. Wall. While keenly resenting his defeat, he was
sensitive to every breath of sympathy. 'It gave me real
pleasure to-day to hear that Johnson the Observer had
said that " he did not agree with me in opinions, but
that there was no one whom he would sooner have
seen Master of Balliol."'

In June, 1854, he went for a short walking tour in
Derbyshire with F. Temple, who was still Principal of
Kneller Hall. Temple wrote to F. T. Palgrave, July 1,
1854 :—

[1] p. 277.

'We walked up the Derwent and down the Dove, and managed to make out a very pleasant tour . . . discoursed of every conceivable subject ; sometimes "making picture-galleries of our friends " ; sometimes settling the destinies of the University ; sometimes examining the genuineness of the Pastoral Epistles ; most often, I think, comparing the scenery with other that we had seen, or trying to recollect all that books of any sort had said about it. The Philosopher has only two faults ; he walks too slow and too unevenly, and he prefers tea or even ginger-beer and biscuits to more generous meat and drink.'

He must have frequently visited London as a member of Macaulay's Committee, referred to on p. 186.

In the autumn, a majority of the College, headed by the Master, passed a by-law requiring every Scholar to declare himself a member of the Church of England. This attempt to violate the spirit of the new Statute was vetoed by the Visitor, to Jowett's great relief.

Two other matters may be mentioned here. His friend Brodie was repeatedly in difficulty about the subscription to the Articles which was still required for the M.A. degree. He wished to obtain leave to have recourse to an obsolete process of 'incorporation,' and so to obtain the degree without subscription. Jowett clearly saw this to be impracticable. His advice to Brodie is marked by a singular union of calm moderation with serious apprehension of the gravity of the position :—

'I think you will rouse the "Odium Theologicum" without any grounds to justify you in the eyes of the public. . . . I cannot see any reason to suppose that this process of incorporation was intended in the case of members of the University to relieve men from any of the forms gone through at the time of taking the degree : but only from the residence and exercises at that time required for a superior degree : . . . much as I wish that you should come here, and dislike subscriptions of this sort, I could not think the Vice-Chancellor wrong for interposing his veto.'

He was also consulted by Dr. Bagot, Bishop of Bath and Wells (and formerly of Oxford), on the legal intricacies of the famous Denison case[1]. Through Stanley's introduction he stayed with the Bishop (who had ordained him Deacon) at Wells, from whence he wrote to Stanley:—

'There is more difficulty in the Denison case than I thought, owing to the wretched state of the law. It appears to be really doubtful whether the Archbishop has any option to refuse Ditcher : there is little or no doubt that the Bishop *has* under the peculiar circumstances of George Anthony Denison's living. But this is merely an accidental power, which the law could hardly have intended to give.'

Thus matters proceeded in an even tenor, though not without discouragement, until the appearance of the book on St. Paul early in June, 1855[2]. He had been consulting Stanley, as far as he found it possible, until the last, showing no small solicitude even about the form of the page. In a letter written in the summer of 1854, he defends an interpretation which Stanley had questioned, and asks for reflections on eight different points:—

1. Scepticism. 2. Christian Society. 3. Interpretation of Scripture. 4. Greek of the New Testament. 5. Controversy. 6. Observance of the Sabbath. 7. Prayer. 8. On a future life. To this he adds: 'On the last subject I am most anxious. One cannot but have a solemn feeling in endeavouring to handle it. What between figures of speech and idealism, and the contrast between the universal acceptance of it in words, and the common indifference to it in fact, and the interest of it to us all

---

[1] Ditcher *v.* Denison; see Brodrick and Fremantle's *Ecclesiastical Judgments*, p. 156.

[2] *The Epistles of St. Paul to the Thessalonians, Galatians, Romans, with critical notes and dissertations:* by Benjamin Jowett, M.A., Fellow and Tutor of Balliol College, Oxford. In two volumes. London : John Murray, Albemarle Street, 1855.

as we get older, it seems to me the most important
and most difficult of all theological questions.'

As has been told elsewhere [1], his two volumes and
Stanley's on the Corinthians appeared on the same day.
A common spirit was perceptible in both works, but
Jowett's Essays went far more deeply into the heart
of theological questions. This was felt immediately by
friends and foes. Stanley's book, though it soon came
to a second edition, was comparatively little noticed,
while that of Jowett at once became the centre of
animated discussion [2]. The literary excellence of some
parts was highly praised, especially the Essay on Natural
Religion, and the Fragment on the Character of St. Paul.
This last inspired an ideal work of Woolner's, a reproduction of which, presented to Jowett by Palgrave, is
the subject of an interesting letter of October 24, 1858 [3].

Very different was the fortune of the book in theological circles. Grant truly apprehended the situation
when he spoke of the work as ' a miracle of boldness.'
Religious prejudice was especially aroused by the Essay
on the Atonement, in which the moral objections to the
popular Evangelical doctrine were stated with a passion-
ate vehemence, that broke through the habitual serenity

---

[1] In my Preface to the third
edition of *St. Paul's Epistles, &c.*

[2] Lord Lingen writes (December, 1895) : ' It is an interesting
subject of inquiry why the religious outcry was so much louder
against Jowett than against Stanley, whose published opinions
were not very different. One
reason, said to be given by Stanley
himself, was "because my name
is Stanley." There may be something in that. But I am disposed

to find a further explanation in
the characteristics of the men.
Both were fearless, honest, well
informed of their subject, and
of commanding address; but
Stanley was, perhaps by temperament, Roman rather than Greek,
Ciceronian rather than Socratic.
The Master, like Socrates, asks
provoking and unexpected questions, which are easier to resent
than to answer.'

[3] p. 286.

of the style. As the first edition has long been out of print, a few sentences may here be quoted :—

'No difference between God and Man can be a reason for regarding God as less just or less true than the being whom He has made. He is only incomprehensible to us because He is infinitely more so.

' It might seem at first sight no hard matter to prove that God was just and true. It might seem as if the suggestion of the opposite needed no other answer than the exclamation of the Apostle, " God forbid, for how shall God judge the world ? " But the perplexities of the doctrine of the Atonement are the growth of above a thousand years ; rooted in language, disguised in figures of speech, fortified by logic, they seem almost to have become a part of the human mind itself. . . . One cannot but fear whether it be still possible so to teach Christ as not to cast a shadow on the holiness and truth of God. Whether the wheat and the tares have not grown so long together that the husbandmen, in pulling up the one, may be plucking up the other also.'

Then, after a statement of the doctrine of human guilt, as commonly expounded, he continues :—

' Were we to stop here, every honest and good heart would break in upon these sophistries, and dash in pieces the pretended freedom and the imputed sin of mankind, as well as the pretended justification of the Divine attributes, in the statement that man necessarily or naturally brought everlasting punishment on himself. No slave's mind was ever reduced so low as to justify the most disproportionate severity inflicted on himself : neither has God so made His creatures that they will lie down and die, even beneath the hand of Him who gave them life.'

He then states the doctrine of vicarious satisfaction, which he criticizes with equal warmth, and adds :—

' We are trespassing on holy ground. There will be many who say it is good to adore in silence a mystery that we can never understand. But there are "idols of the temple," as well as idols of the market-place. These idols consist in human reasonings and definitions which are erected into Articles of Faith. We are willing to adore in silence, but not the inventions of man. The controversialist naturally thinks that in assailing the doctrine of satisfaction as inconsistent with truth and morality, we are fighting not with himself, but with God.'

These passages are quoted, not as fair samples of the Essay, which, like every part of Jowett's book, is full of spiritual thought and far-sighted suggestion, but as helping to explain the acrimony of the assaults which followed. There was no mistaking what this man meant. He was one to reckon with, and could not be safely ignored. In some quarters, however, the work was being estimated on its merits. The Chevalier Bunsen had been recalled from the Prussian Embassy in London, and was residing in the neighbourhood of Heidelberg, where his house, which he had named Charlottenburg, was hospitably open to English visitors. One of these, a pupil of Jowett's, had the privilege of introducing the volumes to the Chevalier, whose own copy had not yet arrived. He remarked emphatically, ' Das Buch muss seinen Weg machen ': but added that he had heard incidentally that the Archbishop of Canterbury ('though otherwise pleased,' as he diplomatically phrased it) had his doubts about the Essay on the Atonement. Partly fired by Bunsen's encouragement, the young Oxonian wrote a review of the book, which Henry de Bunsen recommended to the *Times*, through a friendly channel. The article was printed, but not published, having been crossed by counter-influences, which are thus characterized in a letter of Stanley's to Jowett, referring to Dr. Lightfoot's able review in the *Journal of Classical and Sacred Philology* (vol. iii. pp. 81–121) of March, 1856 :—

'I must say I was pleased, more pleased with the good he said of you than displeased with the evil he said of myself; and in a man of his turn of mind, I think it specially creditable not to have been deterred from saying this much by the popular clamour which has hounded on the Conybeares, Goulburns, or Wilberforces, and has *muzzled* the *North British*, the *Edinburgh*, and the *Times*[1].'

As late as September 24, 1855, Jowett was fully possessed with the idea of continuing his work on St. Paul. He then wrote to Stanley :—

'I propose in a few days commencing regularly with the Ephesians and Colossians, and think with health I might get them out by this time next year. When you see Murray, will you sound him about it? If he likes, it may be advertised at once as preparing. Are you of the same mind touching the Philippians and Philemon? If you are, I shall be glad; if not, I shall try them myself. What do you propose for what you once called the final work of life?'

The Regius Professorship of Greek had been vacated by the death of Dean Gaisford in June, 1855, and Jowett was singled out by Lord Palmerston's Government for the appointment, which was made before the end of the vacation. His reputation as a College Tutor and University Reformer, and his public services in the cause of higher education generally, may have naturally drawn attention to him, and the first impression produced by his book on competent judges had confirmed the opinion of his exceptional erudition. There can be no doubt that Stanley, now a Canon of Canterbury, with whom Jowett stayed in the beginning of 1855, exerted

[1] *Life of Dean Stanley*, vol. i. p. 476. It must suffice here to refer in a note to the candid and able critique of Mr. J. Llewellyn Davies in his pamphlet entitled *St. Paul and Modern Thought*. This pamphlet and Dr. Lightfoot's article formed marked exceptions to the general run of comment.

Balliol
Oct. 16.

Many thanks for your most kind
Congratulations

My dear Campbell

I have delayed too long
in answering your most kind
letter and must now beg
you to excuse my doing so
very hastily

Upon the whole I am
clearly of opinion that you
should first get a fellowship
and then settle down in
whatever line of life you shall
best   Numerous fellowships
will be thrown open & Institution

during the next year Exeter
Lincoln Pembroke certainly;
also Merton & probably others
a fellowship is such a "pièce
de resistance" all through life
that it is worthwhile to
Sacrifice a year to obtain it
if indeed it can be called a
Sacrifice to have an additional
year of study & reading.

. . . .

Ever yours
B Jowett

much influence on his friend's behalf, and H. G. Liddell, Gaisford's destined successor in the Deanery, to whom in point of fact the Chair was in the first instance offered, was also believed by Jowett to have given him valuable support [1].

Most fortunately the appointment had been made and confirmed before the 'cross influences' had had time to work; and the announcement greeted us at the commencement of the October Term. Jowett said at the time, that he preferred this to any other Professorship 'except one of Theology.' The impossibility of this latter aspiration was soon to be made manifest.

In a previous chapter it has been seen that the action of the young Oxford Liberals in 1845, and of Jowett amongst them, in opposing the institution of a new test, was regarded by Dean Church, who was the Junior Proctor on that occasion, as 'a very generous as well as wise action on their part [2].'

In the measure now meted out to Jowett, there was not much generosity, though there may have been something of 'the wisdom of the Serpent.' The Vice-Chancellor at this time was Dr. Pusey's brother-in-law, R. L. Cotton, D.D., the Provost of Worcester, a dry little

---

[1] The following is Dean Liddell's own account (1895):—'The death of Dean Gaisford left the Professorship of Greek vacant. Lord Palmerston, who was then Prime Minister, offered to recommend me for the place. I declined it for reasons that it is needless to specify. He asked me to furnish him with names of scholars whom I thought competent to fill the office. I gave him several names with my opinions upon the qualifications of each. In the end he recommended Jowett to Her Majesty, and he was appointed.' Amongst the names under the consideration of Lord Palmerston were Charles Newton (afterwards Sir Charles Newton) and Robert Scott, co-editor of the *Lexicon* and Master of Balliol. Newton could not have afforded to take it, and it was thought better not to appoint the Head of a House.

[2] p. 96.

wizened man, whose notions of theological '*soundness*'
were undoubtedly strict, but would hardly have moved
him to act thus of his own accord[1]. The real actor was
said to be the Rev. C. P. Golightly, with Dr. Pusey and
Bishop Wilberforce in the background. Mr. Golightly,
whom some witty Newmanite had re-christened 'Agag,'
was a local clergyman, of Evangelical principles and
restless activity, whose *bêtes-noires*, of about equal black-
ness to him, were Newmanism and Germanism. He had
raised the storm against Tract XC[2], and it was he who
now stirred up this trouble. Acting upon a section in
the University Statutes[3], dating from a time when the
term *Fides Catholica* included dogmas which the Thirty-
nine Articles explicitly condemn, two members of Convocation, J. D. Macbride[4] and C. P. Golightly, denounced
Jowett to the Vice-Chancellor as having denied the
Catholic Faith. The powers of the Vice-Chancellor in
such matters, even under the revised Statute, although
rarely exercised, were virtually unlimited, and Jowett
was summoned to appear before Vice-Chancellor Cotton
and to subscribe the Articles anew. This act of discipline, it will be observed, was in the spirit of the
proposal which, when aimed against the Tractarians,
had been withdrawn in consequence of the opposition
of Jowett and other Liberals, ten years before.

The only preparation for this contumely had been a note
from Pusey to Jowett, to which he made no reply, but,
apparently while the matter was still pending, enclosed
it to Stanley with the remark, 'I was very much affected
by it at first, but since reading it I have seen too much

[1] He had been one of the most stubborn opponents of the University Commission.
[2] *Life of Dean Church*, p. 29.
[3] Tit. IV. 3, subsection 2. It had been originally enacted in the time of Henry VIII, at the instance of Cardinal Pole.
[4] D.D., Principal of Magdalen Hall.

of the writer to be capable of being affected by what he says: of whom I have much to say to you when we meet.' He thought less bitterly of Pusey afterwards [1], but it is right that the first impression produced on him by these 'gentle cruelties' should be recorded here.

Jowett appeared in answer to the summons, and Vice-Chancellor Cotton began to address him solemnly on the 'awfulness' of his situation. Jowett cut him short with the words, 'Mr. Vice-Chancellor, I have come to sign the Articles.' Dr. Cotton recommenced his harangue, but was again interrupted. Tradition has it that Jowett simply asked for a new pen [1]. He was always very particular, in beginning any writing, to have a quill pen ready made, and was a proficient in the art of mending them. But the anecdote has been treasured as indicating his perfect coolness on the occasion. And such truly was his demeanour outwardly. But in reality he was much perturbed, and on returning to his room, where a friend awaited him, his first words were, 'They have done me harm; but I shall live it down.' And then he added: 'I hope my friends and pupils will not care for what is said for or against my book, but study the Scriptures for themselves.'

Jowett's own account of the matter to Stanley omits some of the preceding details, but is more unquestionably authentic, and may be inserted here:—

December 14, [1855].

MY DEAR CANON,

Your letter was most welcome. Since I made up my mind what to do, I have been quite at rest about the whole subject. You will perhaps have seen in the newspapers that I have taken the meaner part and signed. It seemed to me

---

[1] This is recorded in Cox's *Reminiscences of Oxford*, and has been often repeated since.

that I could not do otherwise without giving up my position as a Clergyman.

Scene. *Vice-Chancellor's Study.*

A domestic picture of Dr. and Mrs. C. . . . Enter Hereticus —'I am come to comply with your request.' 'Will you write your name on this sheet of paper and on that?' Done. Vice-Chancellor turns over letters from Golightly and Heurtley[1], mumbling something in an undertone of voice. But before the words are out, Hereticus says 'Good morning' and escapes.

It grieves me to have been put to this sort of schoolboy degradation, and also to think that such things are possible nowadays. I don't intend to write a single word in reply to the attacks on me. Without taking any notice of them, I shall enlarge the Essay on the Atonement in a second edition; also some of the other essays in the Long Vacation, and then all the help you can give me will be most welcome. Liddell has been most kind. I often think of a sentence in a sermon of his which you repeated to me: 'No man can enter into controversy without being sorry for it: many reasons might be given for this, but I prefer to repeat it,—No man, &c.'

There is a text in the Psalms which often comes into my mind in these troubles: 'Happy is the man that hath his quiver full of *them*[2]: he shall not be ashamed when he speaks with his enemies in the gate[3].'

It was shortly after this that he ceased from dining in Hall and attending Common Room. He said, 'I have no pleasure in looking forward to my lectures now,'

[1] The Rev. C. A. Heurtley, Margaret Professor of Divinity, 1853-1895.

[2] i. e. of friends.

[3] The writer of an article in the *Leader* (weekly) newspaper for December 22, 1855, on 'The Regius Professor's Submission,' after exhorting laymen to take up the study of Theology, concludes as follows:—' Mr. Jowett's case shows that no clergyman, not even the strongest pietist and a man of the highest religious character and influence, can venture so far to depart from ecclesiastical tradition and clerical forms of belief as to admit, even in such an age as the present, that God is not unjust.'

and he gave no inaugural address; but opened at once with a course of lectures on the *Republic*, which were delivered in the Hall of Balliol College (now the Under-graduates' Library). I was present at his opening lecture; and well remember how, after a few sentences of critical prolegomena, he continued, 'And now having, as it were, blown off the dust from the outside of the Volume, let us proceed to examine what I may call *the greatest un-inspired writing.*' The lectures drew, and continued to be well attended, at least for several years. Three years after this, Grant wrote to his *fiancée*, 'Jowett's lectures have still a crowded attendance.' In 1862 Jowett himself made a similar report to Stanley[1]; and in 1865 the Hall was filled with undergraduates from various Colleges.

He had again been thwarted in his career: the path of Theology which he had marked out for himself was found to be beset with thorns; and the academical appointment in which he gloried had been made the occasion for an humiliating rebuff. But the effect was once more to redouble his labours. Gaisford had sus-tained the reputation of the Greek Chair by a series of critical editions of Classical books—the Greek Minor Poets, Stobaeus and Suidas—which are still valuable. But he had not lectured, and it might be counted as a sufficient excuse that while his emoluments as Dean of Christ Church were considerable, the salary attached to the Greek Professorship was only £40 a year. To many in the University it appeared that the Chair was a mere ornament to decorate a specially deserving Tutor. But such was not Jowett's view of the situation. It had been a capital point in the Reform of the Uni-versity to strengthen the Professoriate and to render it more efficient. And with regard to this particular

---

[1] p. 325: cf. p. 312.

Chair, when the Commission had applied to the Dean and Chapter of Christ Church with a view to their contributing to Academical purposes, they had replied that the most proper object for such benevolence on their part was the endowment of the Professorship of Greek. This was in 1854 [1]. But after the death of Dean Gaisford and the appointment of his successor, this virtuous intention was not fulfilled. The cause of such a change of front is somewhat obscure. So much, however, is tolerably clear. In December, 1856, the Chapter were in the midst of their dealings with the Executive Commission [2], and at the same time Dean Liddell was attacked by a severe illness, which compelled him to winter in Madeira. During his absence one of the Canons was examined before the Commission, and on his representing that Christ Church already supported several Professorships in the University, it was agreed that two canonries should be suppressed, and their emoluments applied to the improvement of the Studentships as rearranged.

The truth was that the authorities at Christ Church had become aware of the difficulty of their position consequent upon the opening of Fellowships and Scholarships in the other Colleges, and by strengthening their own Studentships sought to improve the relative status of the College as an educational corporation. Stanley, although only a Canon elect, having been recently appointed to the Chair of Ecclesiastical History, was already using his influence on Jowett's behalf; but he

---

[1] *Correspondence respecting the Proposed Measures of Improvement in the Universities and Colleges of Oxford and Cambridge*, 1854, p. 46.

[2] Jowett wrote to Stanley on December 14, 1856, with reference to the Dean's illness: 'Christ Church at the present moment is "full of stirs, a tumultuous city," and they are in the midst of their dealings with the Commission. This must be very irritating to him.'

had no vote in the Chapter until March, 1858, and the Christ Church Ordinance by which the question was determined had appeared on January 9 in that year. On coming into residence, therefore, Stanley at once began to moot the subject in the University at large, but he could only do so indirectly until he was himself elected a Professorial Member of the Hebdomadal Council in November, 1860.

The course which Jowett took under these circumstances was to work the Professorship in addition to the Tutorship, and on the same lines[1], without asking for reward. He would not even exact the Statutory Fee. Not only were his lectures *gratis*, but he invited all who attended them to send in exercises to be personally looked over by himself. A special duty which was fulfilled about this time, was, in conjunction with Liddell, the new Dean of Christ Church, to make regulations for the Greek Composition Prizes, which had been established by subscription as a Memorial to Dean Gaisford. The examination of the exercises sent in by competitors for these prizes, and the arrangement of the subjects, was another piece of work which came in annually, and was entirely gratuitous. It appears also from a letter of Mrs. Jowett's, that in order to do his work as Professor, he again relinquished the College Bursarship, which was a salaried office.

These absorbing cares and occupations were not

---

[1] Jowett never admitted the broad distinction that is sometimes drawn between Professorial and Tutorial teaching. All teaching that is worthy of the name appeared to him to involve close dealing with individual minds. He regretted the decay of Catechetical instruction in the University, and the substitution of lectures to large classes, for the College lectures of old times; though this was perhaps an inevitable result of the inter-collegiate system which he approved.

altogether unrelieved. He found refreshment in intercourse with his old pupils and in identifying himself with their interests. Sellar had now been married for some years, and in the summer of 1855 he and his wife visited Oxford just at the time when Jowett had revised the last sheets of the *St. Paul*. He received them with all the honours of College hospitality, and Mrs. Sellar's presence brought in an element of gaiety and brightness, to which he fully responded. He visited them at Artornish, where there was a large family gathering in the autumn. That visit was long remembered on both sides, especially one incident, which is worth preserving. Conversation had turned on Political Economy, and Jowett had declared that he never gave to beggars. Mrs. Sellar was an adept in 'Mystifications,' an accomplishment popular in Scotch society since Sir Walter Scott's time. She disguised herself as a poor Highland woman and waylaid her husband and Jowett at a cross-road, begging importunately and telling her tale of woe so piteously that Jowett at last said : 'Poor thing! She seems very miserable ; give her half a crown.' Sellar had no money with him, and before the alms were forthcoming, the secret was triumphantly unveiled. The same friends had invited him to spend Christmas at their home, Abbey Park, St. Andrews ; and their little boy Frank—better known as 'Tornie[1],' not yet three years old, had dictated a letter entreating his friend to come. To this Jowett, who had taken refuge with the Tennysons, sent the following reply :—

FARRINGFORD, I. OF WIGHT,
December 26, 1855.

MY DEAR TORNIE,

　　I was very pleased to have a letter from you. I always thought 'Pupsy was a brick.' Give my love to him. Mr. Grant

---

[1] A derivative from Artornish.

is coming to see you, and has promised to bring a ball as big
as your head.

I hope that you are a good boy and never afraid of anything.
Has Mama been dressing up like a beggar-woman lately?

I will come and play at soldiers next summer, but in the winter-
time I must do lessons.   A little monkey of an old gentleman,
who dresses himself in black and has three pokers walk before
him, has been teazing me lately, and I should be in a great row
if I had not such good friends as Mama, Papa, and Tornie.

Good-bye, Tornie dear.

Don't forget UNCLE JOWETT.

PS.—Please not to let anybody read this letter but yourself.

The friendship of Bishop Ewing was another source of
comfort which did not fail him at this time.   The Bishop
wrote as follows, shortly after Mrs. Ewing's death [1] :—

'Jowett has been of use to me, because he believes in the great
essentials—the life of the dead and the deity of Christ.   What
he says is very comforting, because he knows on what foundations our faith rests.   Others have been most kind and sympathizing; but cut-and-dry sentiments, in which everything is
taken for granted, do me no good at all.'

In spite of such alleviations, the situation was not the
less grave.   He retained his calm demeanour, keeping an
obstinate silence under all attacks, and could even make
allowance for the asperity of his assailants, taking account
of Pusey's Huguenot ancestry and S. Wilberforce's
Evangelical origin.   'Mere Christian love,' he said,
'should make one tolerant, but philosophy is also a great
help.'   What grieved him more than the attacks, was to
find that (through the action of others) he had given real
offence to simple minds, and also that he received so
little support from his old comrades.   'I thought I had
so expressed myself that religious minds could not be
offended.'   'Men join in denouncing what they admit in

[1] *Life of Alexander Ewing*, p. 253.

private conversation.' 'How hard it is to find a perfectly firm will!' With reference to one whom he had thought at least as far advanced in speculation as himself, he said, 'I have often talked to —— on these subjects; he was as free as air.' Even the attitude of Stanley, his fellow-labourer, did not altogether satisfy him :—'He has failed to make people understand what he meant.' On the other hand he was quite touched when the Bishop of Bath and Wells, whom he had formerly visited (and had aided with salutary counsel in the conduct of the Denison case), paid him the common attention of a morning call. In what Jowett felt about all this, as he himself was afterwards fully aware, there was some exaggeration of sensitiveness, an almost fond simplicity, and a want of knowledge of the world. He said in 1857, 'People go on expecting more from friendship than it can ever give.' And when a pupil, who was leaving Oxford for another sphere, on Jowett's saying, 'I am sorry for you, going amongst people whom you cannot understand,' replied cheerfully, 'I suppose I shall find them out in time,' he rejoined with sudden bitterness, 'Oh yes, you will find them out!' His letters to younger men, and his own memoranda, are full of remarks on the evils of a sensitive nature.

'Without were fightings;' but there was no sign of 'fears within.' His courage was unabated and his will only roused to more strenuous action. The Balliol Tutorship, which he could not afford to relinquish, continued to be the main centre of his operations. It was natural, after what had happened, that he should feel the limitations of the sphere. His ambition had been awakened only to be suppressed, and he sometimes hankered after the society and culture of Trinity College,

Cambridge, the natural home of distinguished Paulines. But he found much comfort in working amongst his pupils. Some hope of enlargement was afforded by the Visitor's reversal of the new Master's policy for the continued exclusion of Dissenters from the College. But he was out of sympathy with his colleagues, and had no pleasure in the proposal to rebuild the Chapel, which was carried out in 1855–7. 'They may build another Chapel,' he said, 'but never one that has the same associations.' The new Chapel was opened on October 15, 1857, and there was, of course, a gathering of old Balliol men. Jowett said to me, 'I rejoice in the prospect of seeing so many old friends; but not in the destruction of the old Chapel.'

He was still absenting himself from Hall and Common Room, and on this occasion he did not take his place at the high table. He sat amongst the undergraduates, about halfway down the room, on the left side of the long central table. His old friend Tait, by this time Bishop of London, who had officiated at the opening service, made a generous reference to him in his speech, dwelling on the excellence of his Tutorial work: 'I was his Tutor in the old days; he was much more worthy to teach me.' There was a pause after this speech; then Jowett rose from where he sat, and said with deep emotion, 'Any one who labours amongst the young men will reap his reward in an affection far beyond his deserts [1].'

[1] There is no appearance as yet of any strained relations between Jowett and Tait. He had written a line of hearty congratulation to the Bishop on his appointment, and had simply added in a postscript, 'Will you tell Mrs. Tait that "latitudinarian" is a tremendous long name to call a fellow?' (*Life of A. C. Tait*, vol. i. p. 199). Some time before this, when visiting the Taits in their affliction, at Carlisle, he writes of his host to Stanley: 'He still retains his interest in many subjects, reading Grote, &c. (most

His many occupations made him sometimes appear oblivious, and as if unconscious of his own speech or silence; and his fastidiousness about language, touched on in the last chapter, led to a sort of incapacity, real or assumed, of understanding anything that was not perfectly expressed. Instead of helping out his interlocutor, who was struggling with some half-formed conception, he would say, 'I don't think so,' or 'I don't understand,' or if some word were used which did not come into his purist vocabulary, he would say, 'What does that mean? I never heard it.' He was totally unaware of the effect this had on youths who were already more than sufficiently in awe of him. He had a command of countenance which made it difficult sometimes to know his real intention. Like Ulysses, he had a way of 'trying the spirits,' by taking an unexpected line. 'I suppose you get your parallels out of Ast's *Lexicon*,' he would say, and one had gravely to assure him that they were the result of one's own reading. In dealing with his most intimate friends, he seemed to work on general views of human nature. When persuading them to some attempt which they were really eager to make, out of affection for him, he would preface the proposal with 'One man is as good as another until he has written a book,' or 'I am thinking how much money you may make by that work' (one of critical scholarship!).

The Professorial lectures were continued, and he was full of schemes for rendering the Greek Chair more effective. There also he was exposed to detraction.

commendable in a Dean), and practising "robust Sophistries" as you and I remember him in former days. He makes many observations, prudential and otherwise, on my book. I cannot say that the observations appear to me to be of much weight, but it is much to the credit of a Dean to make them at all.'

THE OLD CHAPEL AND LIBRARY, BALLIOL COLLEGE

From the North-east End

Although his name had been more prominent in the world, there were others who, from the peculiar Oxford point of view, were regarded in the University as 'technically' better scholars [1]. Jowett had failed for the Ireland, and Pauline scholarship was not considered on a par with that of Shrewsbury, or even Rugby. John Conington, a man extraordinarily gifted and possessed of wide literary culture, had in the previous year (1854) been elected to the new Corpus Professorship of Latin. His edition of Aeschylus' *Agamemnon* had given him a great reputation for Greek scholarship, which was fully sustained by his subsequent edition of the *Choëphoroe*. This Jowett afterwards acknowledged. But in those opening years the Latin and Greek Professors were not in sympathy. Although a pupil of Arnold's, and in earlier days [2] an 'Oxford Liberal,' Conington had recently fallen under religious impressions of a different order; and to his old friends it seemed that his intellectual interests were becoming strangely narrow. He was not unnaturally distressed at the vague, rhetorical tendencies of Oxford scholarship, and sought to correct them by professing a predilection for the exact, verbal methods of the contemporary Cambridge School. And when Jowett, in his dislike of conjectural emendation [3], betrayed a sceptical doubt as to the infallibility of Porson's famous rule, Professor Conington was genuinely scandalized. Thus an *Odium Philologicum* entered into conspiracy with the *Odium Theologicum*. Yet Conington was generous enough to say, in speaking

---

[1] Among those who had been talked about were James Riddell and Basil Jones, afterwards Bishop of St. David's. Before coming to Oxford, both these men had studied Greek under Kennedy at Shrewsbury.

[2] p. 176.

[3] See this expressed in the 'Essay on Interpretation' (published 1860), *St. Paul's Epistles*, third edition, vol. ii. p. 53.

to a younger man for his good, 'Whatever one may think
of Jowett's scholarship, it must be admitted that he lives
the life of a Philosopher.'

Jowett himself took these carpings very lightly.
'I often think,' he said with a touch of irony, 'that
unworthy as I am, I have to deal with the greatest of all
literatures.' He must have found no small compensation
for the local disparagement, although he never spoke on
the subject, in the recognition of continental scholars.
Otto Jahn, in the preface to his standard edition of
Plato's *Symposium* (published in 1864) for which Jowett
had collated afresh the MS. in the Bodleian Library,
spoke of him as 'an accomplished Grecian, and a man
distinguished alike for independence and liberality of
mind.' He set himself at once to revive his classical
attainments—going regularly through Pindar, and at
one time reading a book of Homer every day. He
had a note-book filled with lectures upon Sophocles,
and Aeschylus was continually in his thoughts. But his
main designs already centred on Plato. About a year after
his appointment he was making preparations for an
edition of the *Republic*, and enlisting various old pupils [1]
and other friends for an edition of the chief Dialogues
to be prepared independently, but in a common spirit. He
had commenced his own portion of this work, in which
some of his lectures were to be embodied, when the
demand came upon him for a new edition of the *St. Paul*,
the rapid sale of which was a natural result of the recent
outcry. His first impulse had been to say, 'I will not
alter a word.' The book was the ripe fruit of intense,
unremitting study through the best years of manhood.

---

[1] J. Riddell, Sellar, Grant, Henry Smith, Lewis Campbell. E. Poste of Oriel undertook the *Philebus*, and Jowett at one time hoped that Max Müller might help him with the *Cratylus*.

In preparing it he had learned all the Epistles in the Greek by heart. When he brought it out he said, ' I hope I shall not change my opinions again.' He did not change his opinions. But reflection brought calmer thoughts, and less for his own sake than for that of the religious public, he determined to explain himself more perfectly. He had written to Stanley in 1856: ' It is a great misfortune to be even unintentionally the cause of stirring up a row in a place of education.' Indeed, he had himself grown dissatisfied with some things in the first edition;—' Six months ago I thought these Essays perfect, but now I see such gaps and rents in them !' The revision was a work of great labour ; and it was not made easier by the attacks to which he was still subject. He asked friends for suggestions, but would listen to no advice that seemed to imply a yielding to clamour.

' I fear I cannot expunge the Paley,' he writes to Stanley, ' because, however disagreeable, it is perfectly true, and it would be thought that I retracted it if I did. Notwithstanding the counsels of Johnson and Temple, it seems to me that any cowardice would be very injurious to me.'

He wrought at the new edition through constant head-aches, and, as Grant told me, was compelled to reserve for future completion an Essay on the Interpretation of Scripture, begun some years before, which he had intended to form part of the new edition. Of this more will be heard in the sequel.

The unexpected return of his parents to England from Paris in 1856 did not lessen his embarrassments. His father, always unconscious of the actual situation, was bent on bringing out his own metrical version of the Psalms; and while interested in his son's labours, was far from understanding or sympathizing with them. A note of

Mr. Jowett's dated 'The Norton, Tenby, October 9,' is curiously significant:—

'Benjamin has just spent five days with us, but he has been so taciturn that I think everything he has said might have been said perhaps in five minutes. He is certainly much occupied, but this need not prevent him from unbending a little. I had for my portion one brief question on business, and the mono-syllable "No," in answer to a question. I am happy to say that he appears to be carefully revising his work, which certainly needed it.'

Yet the old man was keenly alive to any shadow of outward success. Towards the end of 1857 an attempt was made to have Jowett elected as a representative of the Professoriate on the new Hebdomadal Council. He was not elected, but the minority was a strong one, and he was touched and moved by the expression of sympathy. When Henry Smith and others went to see him on the declaration of the result: 'My old pupils! My old pupils!' in a voice broken with emotion, was all that he was able to say.

On this subject Mr. Jowett wrote to his son Alfred in India:—

'The contest was creditable for your brother, though not successful. Macbride had sixty-four votes, Benjamin sixty-one. At one part of the day Benjamin, by the newspapers, was likely to get in [1].'

This was the year of the Indian Mutiny, and there was naturally much anxiety on Alfred's account. Though not in immediate danger, he was constantly transferred from station to station, and was liable to much harassing overwork. His death in 1858 was a blow from which the father never recovered.

[1] He was also really much interested in his son's book on St. Paul, and copied out long passages of it for Alfred's benefit.

Alexander Grant of Oriel, on going to India with his young bride, Professor Ferrier's daughter, was charged with the duty of inquiring into the circumstances of Alfred's illness and of recovering his papers. These were afterwards kept by Mrs. Jowett amongst her treasures.

Jowett's father died at Tenby in March, 1859. When in hourly expectation of his death, Jowett wrote to F. T. Palgrave : ' He has been the most innocent and blameless man possible. I don't suppose he ever did a wrong thing. Though not wanting in ability, he has been like a child through life. I am glad you saw him.'

After this his mother and sister resided at Torquay.

The second edition of the *Epistles* was published in the summer of the same year. The work was in great part re-written and was much enlarged. The Essay on the Atonement in particular was entirely re-written, and had threatened at one time to grow into a separate volume. The concluding passage of the new Essay on the Atonement may be taken as the author's one answer to his many assailants :—

' If our Saviour were to come again on earth, which of all the theories of Atonement and Sacrifice would He sanction with His authority ? Perhaps none of them, yet perhaps all may be consistent with the true service of Him. The question has no answer. But it suggests the thought that we shrink from bringing controversy into His presence. The same kind of lesson may be gathered from the consideration of theological differences in the face of death. Who as he draws near to Christ will not feel himself drawn towards his theological opponents ? At the end of life, when a man looks back calmly, he is most likely to find that he exaggerated in some things ; that he mistook party spirit for a love of truth. Perhaps he had not sufficient consideration for others, or stated the truth itself in a manner which was calculated to give offence. In the heat of the struggle, let us at least pause to imagine polemical disputes as they will appear a year, two years, three years hence; it may be, dead and gone—certainly more truly seen than in the hour of controversy. For the truths about which we are disputing cannot partake of the passing stir; they do not change even with the greater revolutions of human things. They are in eternity, and the image of them on earth is not the movement on the surface of the waters, but the depths of the silent sea. Lastly, as a measure of the value of such disputes, which above all other interests seem to have for a time the power of absorbing men's minds and rousing their passions, we may carry our thoughts onwards to the invisible world, and there behold, as in a glass, the great theological teachers of past ages, who have anathematized each other in their lives, resting together in the Communion of the same Lord.'

The *Times* was no longer 'muzzled.' Stanley was now established at Christ Church, as Professor of Ecclesiastical History[1]; and though his welcome from Pusey was a strange one[2], his canonry had not been disputed. He sent to the *Times* a review of Jowett's second edition which appeared in due course, October 15, 1859. In this article, while deprecating what seemed to him a disproportion between the constructive and destructive elements in the work, and drawing somewhat illusory parallels, as his manner was, between Jowett's position and that of Butler, or even Anselm, he fearlessly puts forth his just appreciation of the beneficial tendency of the book's main purpose and effect. The article concludes as follows:—

'We congratulate the University of Oxford and the Church of England on the completion of a work of which we may be justly proud. We gratefully acknowledge that a treatise such as this, which has been able to win for itself a place in the Theological Libraries of foreign countries, and which commands

[1] His appointment dated from December, 1856, but he became a member of the Chapter of Christ Church only in March, 1858.

[2] *Life of Dean Stanley*, vol. i. p. 508.

the respectful attention of the intelligent classes of our own, is
the best kind of support which the cause of religion can receive
in an age like ours. Professor Jowett is well known to have
acquired by his personal character, and by his unwearied devotion to the work of education, an influence over the rising
generation such as few, if any, of his academical contemporaries
have attained. Let that influence be used in the direction indicated in the foregoing extracts from his work, and we may rest
well assured that the cynical and sceptical spirit of the time will
have met with an antidote such as we shall vainly expect from
any other quarter.'

That was well and truly said, and has been too little
regarded; but it was rather strange that Stanley,
who prided himself on having an eye for resemblances
where other men saw differences, should have put so
clearly as he does in other parts of this review the
points of divergence between his own opinions and those
of his ally. Yet the fact of the contrast only makes
the bravery of the defence more honourable. His
friend's picturesqueness, on the other hand, sometimes
rather grated upon Jowett. At a luncheon party in the
room in the Fisher Building, Stanley once described
with great animation a Byzantine procession in which
the *fasces*, which had been the symbol of Imperial power
and were carried before some magistrate, had been gradually reduced to a single reed. 'And with that reed,'
said Jowett, looking archly mischievous, 'disappeared
the last vestige of the Roman empire!' 'I am glad,'
said Bunsen, speaking of the Introduction to the Thessalonians, 'that he has touched on the topographical fancifulness of some of his good friends.'

Conversing in Christ Church meadow in October,
1859, Stanley showed great curiosity as to the authorship of the review of the first edition, which had
been stifled in 1855. The author confessed, and the

printed copy was sent to Stanley, who acknowledged it as follows:—

'Many thanks for the enclosed. Had it appeared when it was intended to have appeared, the whole history of the last five, perhaps of the next fifty, years would have been different. The beginning and end will be always available for future use. I envy you the adaptation of the story of David in the last paragraph.'

Almost immediately on the publication of the second edition of *St. Paul*, after indulging himself, as Mr. W. L. Newman tells us, with Aristophanes, Jowett returned to his commentary on the *Republic* of Plato, and had finished the series of notes in a first draft before the beginning of September. These notes, however, though he continued working at them, were not to see the light for thirty-five years to come.

It was about this time that a group of his old pupils, including Sellar, Grant, Palgrave, and a few more, subscribed for a portrait of Jowett, in crayons, by G. Richmond, which was presented to Mrs. Jowett. The reproduction of this drawing is well known, and a reduced copy of the original forms the frontispiece of this volume. One who was not a 'Jowett-worshipper' remarked at the time, 'To do Jowett justice, he is not such a lady-killer as that makes him.' On the other hand, some of those who saw his face in the repose of death were involuntarily reminded of this early portrait [1].

Mr. W. L. Newman's Reminiscences (continued from p. 210).

'His gifts ensured him unbounded influence with young men of ability. His marked individuality of character, which made itself felt in everything he said or did, his kindly peremptoriness, his combination of force of character with gentle-

---

[1] See Lord Lingen's remark, p. 228.

ness, of many-sidedness with intensity, of great powers of
thought with practical ability, won enthusiastic acceptance
from clever young men. His interests were almost as
varied as his gifts. Here was a man who seemed to
stand at the parting of many ways. Religion, philosophy,
poetry, Greek literature—these were his favourite studies, but
he added to them a keen interest in human nature and in
practical business. There was nothing cramping about his influence over us. I never found that he made any effort to enforce
on me any particular set of views. His strong sense of humour
was an added charm. I think it was just after he brought out
the second edition of his book on St. Paul that he said to me,
needing no doubt some relief from the drudgery of proofs,
" Now I must read some Aristophanes."

‘ When the disappointment about the Mastership came, some
slight indications of vexation were traceable in his conversation
even with an undergraduate like me, but his work with his
pupils continued precisely as before. It was not, I think, till
some time later that he ceased to dine in Hall and to appear
after dinner in Common Room. The exact date at which this
happened I am unable to recollect. I was absent from Oxford
owing to illness from December, 1855, to October, 1857, and I
think that this change in his ways may have commenced during
my absence. I doubt whether he dined much in Hall after my
return to Oxford. We lost much by his absence, but even
without him the Balliol Common Room remained a notable
gathering. There is nothing in my Oxford life to which I look
back with more pleasure than to the evenings which I spent
there in the company of H. J. S. Smith, E. Palmer, J. Riddell,
T. H. Green, and many others who might be named, men
who were as valuable and acceptable socially as they were in
all other ways. Jowett's withdrawal did not make his relations with the rest of our body otherwise than amicable. Some
of the Fellows had been his pupils, and felt towards him as
pupils would. Achilles preferred his tent, but his tent was
a hospitable one, and I used often to breakfast and dine
with him, and we often took walks together. Smith, and
I think Green, saw still more of him. He of course saw
much of his pupils, but he also saw much of friends

from London and elsewhere of an age and position similar to his own. Our friendship for him did not interfere in any degree with friendly relations with the rest of our seniors among the Fellows. On some topics our opinions were not theirs, but we found them, and the new Head of the College, so genial and kindly, and some of them so useful as models and advisers, that we worked together with real pleasure and in complete harmony. The College prospered well, and Jowett's influence in it grew as one of his pupils after another was added to the body of Fellows. As far back as I can remember, Jowett always suggested the subject of the English Essay in Scholarship and Fellowship examinations. Many good and useful measures adopted in College meeting originated with him. One of the earliest of these was the foundation of the Domus Exhibitions (about 1858). At a still earlier time, if I do not mistake, the wholesome rule was adopted, thanks, I believe, to Theodore Walrond, that all undergraduate members of the College should go in for honours in some examination school or other. Another useful change was made when undergraduates were allowed, with the advice of their Tutor, to choose their own lectures [1]. Jowett was unwearied in maintaining or increasing the strictness of the matriculation examination. All these things did much for the College.'

[1] This was not carried out till 1867.—L. C.

CHAPTER IX

THEOLOGICAL attitude—Desultory studies—Advice to young writers and preachers—Society in Scotland and elsewhere—Preparation of *Essays and Reviews*—Publication of the volume—Letters.

THE preceding chapter does not exhaust the interest of the years from 1854-60. I proceed to make a few general observations on Jowett's mental attitude during this period.

First as to Theology: 'after toil and storm,' having mournfully realized 'that there is no elder person in whose footsteps one can tread[1],' he had by persistent efforts reached a point of view from which, while retaining all that seemed essential in the traditions of the past, he felt able to bring the spiritual principles involved in them to bear with fresh significance on the life of the present. He wrote to a young friend: 'I do not know that you care to plunge into the abyss of theology. But I shall always maintain that there is no abyss, and that, without relying on fables or fancies, any who will may find their way through this world with sufficient knowledge to light them to another.' But there were obstructions to be overcome, and these proved more serious than he had reckoned. He was all the

[1] p. 227, note.

S 2

more bent on overcoming them. No greater benefit could be conferred on any age, he thought, than to clear and purify religious ideas. The greatest of all difficulties lay in the attitude of religious men, who refused to recognize the obvious results of historical criticism, and persisted in maintaining the sacredness of propositions, against which the intellect and moral sense of mankind, at the stage of culture which the world had attained, could not but revolt. They appeared to think it possible to keep knowledge at one level in England, when it had reached another level in Germany. He had felt this even before the publication of his book, as appears from his letters to Stanley of August, 1846[1]. The great danger, in his opinion, was—not lest reason should destroy religion, but lest intellectual persons should reject the truth itself, when stated in grotesque and impossible forms. Jowett was profoundly attached to Christianity, which had penetrated to the very core of his nature; to the Bible, which he desired to see made the rule of life, not in the letter, but in the spirit; and to the Church of England, whose ministry seemed likely to be impoverished by the unrealities of popular theology, and the refusal of Ordination on the part of highly educated men. To cast off the incrustations with which historical Christianity was so heavily encumbered, and to bring into clearer light what was of eternal import, without breaking rudely with the past or ignoring present needs, was the problem which he had set himself to solve. He was thwarted in this course, but, having set his face that way, was more and more determined to continue in it. Reformations, he began to feel, were not to be made with rose-water.

Philosophy held the second place in his thoughts.

[1] pp. 150, 153; cf. p. 175.

He still acknowledged the debt which as a thinker he owed to German philosophy. The hope which Kant had raised of laying hold upon an Absolute behind the Relative, had involved the mind in difficulties, which Hegel seemed to have cleared away, by showing that the Absolute was a unity within which all relations were embraced, and that it was to be sought in the universe and not beyond it.

'The study of Hegel has given me a method,' he used to say; but he refused to be bound within the limits of any system, making fact the final test of theory.

He looked with interest, but with imperfect sympathy, upon the rise of the Positivist sect in Oxford. R. Congreve had returned to Wadham from Rugby about 1848; his pupils, Frederic Harrison, J. H. Bridges, and E. S. Beesly, graduated in 1853-4. These were amongst Comte's earliest converts in England. When he saw young men taking up a radical or extreme position, Jowett always wondered what their future would be. Speaking of G. H. Lewes's *History of Philosophy*, he said he thought it a poor thing to have studied all philosophies and to end in adopting that of Auguste Comte.

At this time he still encouraged the ablest of his pupils in the study of Hegel. He valued Plato even more for his marvellous originality and suggestiveness. 'Germs of all ideas are to be found in Plato.' And in recommending the study he used to say, 'Aristotle is dead, but Plato is alive.'

In interpreting Plato, as before in interpreting St. Paul, he sought to get behind the accretions of after ages, such as the Neo-Platonism of the fifth and fifteenth centuries, and to bring out the original meaning of his author.

Neither in religion nor in philosophy did he ever

†

seek to form a school. He rather discouraged some
too eager disciples, saying that 'to meddle in theology
required an exceptionally happy nature.' His one
thought in dealing with his pupils was, what was best
individually for them. Nothing angered him so much
as to find that a former pupil had been incurring odium
in defending him. 'We must all fight our own battles,'
were his last words at parting from one of them, and
they were said with energetic warmth. 'I was sorry
to hear that you had got a reputation for heterodoxy
with Mr. ——. Will you be careful of this? A young
man is in great danger of becoming powerless who is
shelved in this way.' The power of personal influence,
which had been conspicuous in some members of the
High Church party, he thought might have been valuable
if they had also had the power of respecting the independence of the persons whom they had influenced.
Once in passing Littlemore, he glanced at the building
where Newman had drawn together his followers in the
year before his secession. 'It was very unfair to those
young men,' he said. Nor was he readily disposed to
strengthen his own position by allying himself with
others, merely because they had also fallen under the
ecclesiastical ban. Some of F. D. Maurice's disciples
were provoked at his persistent silence with regard to
their teacher. 'I shall never join with that modern Neo-
Platonism,' was his remark to one who had hinted this:
'it is so easy to substitute one mysticism for another.'

No speculative difficulties confused his practical sense.
While exercising the utmost freedom in speculation,
his constant aim was to hold a just balance between
philosophy and actual life. He often quoted the saying
of Coleridge, 'The only common sense worth having
is that which is based on metaphysics'; and he upheld

the converse proposition, 'Metaphysics should be grounded in common sense.' Far-seeing as were his views of future possibilities for mankind, he seldom practically approved of radical change.

No part of his theological writings was more directly the outcome of his experience, than the passage in the essay on Natural Religion, in which he seeks to overcome the opposition which religious minds had been too apt to make between the Church and the World, 'the one half of human nature and the other[1].' He was fond of that sentence of Sir Thomas Browne's, 'For my conversation, it is as the sun's with all men, and with a friendly aspect towards good and bad.' Another paradox which sometimes led to misunderstanding was his determination to keep apart moral and political considerations, and at this period he was sometimes understood to insist that while moral goodness made for the happiness of its owner, intellectual power was more beneficent in its action upon the world at large. Yet in his dealings with the world he never lost sight of his religious vocation. He knew well how to blend the tenderest sympathy with unbending severity.

The widow of one of his old friends, who had observed his dealings with undergraduates about this time, says :—

'I always admired Mr. Jowett's wonderful reticence and refinement, coupled with sternness and swift, decided action,

---

[1] *The Epistles of St. Paul, &c.*, third edition, vol. ii. pp. 241–243. A remark of the Warden of Merton expresses a very general view upon this subject: 'He never affected or specially admired an "unworldly" character. Though no man was ever less actuated by the lower forms of ambition, he was always disposed to regard worldly success as a test of merit in a sense against which I rebel, and, in one of my early conversations with him, he expressed a most earnest hope that his pupils would not, like those of another great teacher, "make a mess of life" !'

when needful, in cases where moral corruption called for
drastic measures. At the same time he never seemed to
give any man up as hopeless or beyond the reach of sympathy
and help.'

He found time amidst all his pressing avocations to
write to a young friend, who was going for the first
time to a public school, a letter to which the recipient
reverted in later life, with mingled gratitude and
admiration, as having conveyed to him with equal
delicacy and frankness a horror of schoolboy vice, which
secured him from contamination.

He still found relief from his exhausting labours
in voracious reading, going back again and again to
his old favourites, Boswell's *Johnson*, Pepys' *Diary*, &c.,
and fastening upon each book of interest as it came
out. He was greatly interested in *Adam Bede*, which,
it will be remembered, was at first attributed to a clergyman. 'He has succeeded in seizing the characteristics
of all the classes of English society.'

To the few whose vocation it was to carry classical
studies into later life, he held up an ideal which differed in
several ways from the ordinary models. Although he felt
the slur which had been cast on his reputation as a scholar,
he returned with interest the disparagement of pedantic
critics. Ignorance of Greek, he thought, was more excus-
able than ignorance of the nature of language. 'I sometimes think the souls of the old grammarians must have
transmigrated into our verbal scholars.' His method was
to read the great writers over and over again; 'One
gets to know them in this way far better than in reading
about them. I have read Sophocles hundreds of times.'
When he heard of some one who had a wonderful knowledge of the commentators on Aristotle, he said, 'That
sort of learning is a great power, *if a man can only*

keep his mind above it.' His influence thus tended, at this time more than afterwards, rather to discourage extensive reading. 'It is so easy to give an impression of great learning. The power of interpretation is a different thing. Every author is best interpreted from himself.' He had already formed the fixed opinion, which he held to the last, as to the futility of conjectural emendation. He thought Bekker had deserved more of Greek Philology than Bentley.

He was always ready to read over a friend's writings and to criticize them. 'I can do no less,' he would say, 'for one who has done so much for me.' But it must be owned that his gratitude sometimes took rather a trying shape. It was difficult not to feel some contrariety between the sanguine eagerness with which he had encouraged some attempt, and the dry light of judgement which seemed apt to burn up the thing attempted. And sometimes, though not often, what he trenchantly rejected has not proved a failure. But when he disapproved of a friend's work, on grounds of taste, or even of morality, though he expressed himself with candour, it made no difference whatever in the warmth and strength of his attachment. His was a spirit which always gave more than it received.

He repeated his visits to the Sellars and other friends in Scotland, amongst whom was Thomas Erskine, of Linlathen, a friend of Bishop Ewing's. He was a thoughtful mystic, of great liberality of mind, and after retiring from the Scottish Bar, had written several theological essays, which had a powerful influence in promoting the reaction against Calvinism. He was an admirer of William Law, and F. D. Maurice acknowledged himself to have derived something from him. Jowett used to say that his defect as a religious leader was, that he had not set himself to any great practical effort for the good of mankind. Erskine's conversation, which from whatever point it started always came round to his theological ideas, had a peculiar charm. He was the sworn brother in matters spiritual of J. Macleod Campbell of Row, who had been ousted from the Church of Scotland on account of his opinions shortly after the secession of Edward Irving[1]. Campbell's book on the Atonement, in which he sought by metaphysical argument to eliminate the crudities of current theology, and justify the ways of God, appeared in 1856, a year after Jowett's *St. Paul*; and about the same time Jowett's annual visits to Linlathen began. Here he also made the acquaintance of Sir W. Stirling Maxwell of Keir.

Henry Hill Lancaster was settled in Edinburgh as an advocate, and was interested in the *North British Review*. Another Edinburgh acquaintance which he greatly valued was that with Dr. John Brown, the author of *Rab and his Friends*.

At St. Andrews he was introduced to Principal Tulloch, then in vigorous youth, and to Professor Ferrier, the metaphysician, whose daughter was married to Jowett's friend and pupil Sir Alexander Grant.

Visits to Scotland were continued annually for about thirty years; and he often expressed his admiration of the country and people, against whom he had shared Dr. Johnson's prejudice in earlier days. At the Sellars' summer home, which at this time was Harehead in Yarrow, he seems to have relaxed his studies more than elsewhere, and a photographic group with Jowett in his wide-awake, playing croquet there, was extant a year or two ago.

His life in Oxford itself was not unrelieved by rare

[1] Cf. the Duke of Argyll's Preface to his *Philosophy of Belief* (1895).

intervals of social enjoyment. The Greenhills, before
settling at Hastings, remained in Oxford for a while.
George Butler of Exeter had married, and was for a time
settled there with his young wife: their house was
a pleasant centre of reunion for the younger dons.
Mrs. Josephine Butler, in her memoir of her husband, has
given us her impression of the Oxford society of that
day, with its curious limitations and its intellectual
interests, tempered with ignorance of the world. Another
oasis in the wilderness of celibates was the home of the
Principal of Brasenose, Dr. Cradock, whose wife was sister-
in-law to Lord John Russell. Mrs. Cradock was a lady
of decided originality, and loved to bring young people
together in her drawing-room and her rose-garden.
A. P. Stanley was much at home there, and brought
Jowett with him when he could. Charles Wood (Lord
Halifax), Augustus Hare, Charles Bowen, and Lyulph
Stanley, then a junior undergraduate, were also frequent
visitors at the house. There was hymn-singing on
Sunday evenings, and little fêtes champêtres in summer,
especially on June 18—Waterloo day—which was the
genial hostess's birthday. On these occasions Jowett's
unworldly simplicity sometimes amused the younger men:
as when he gave a rose that had been plucked for him
by one young lady to another who happened to have
none! Mrs. Cradock's young friends were expected to
provide entertainment for these birthday fêtes by writing
short stories or poems. One day when the party were
driven in from the garden by rain, these compositions,
which had been thrown into a bag, were taken out at
random and read aloud. One story greatly struck Jowett's
fancy; he asked to be allowed to take it home, and had
it copied.

It was here that Jowett made some friendships which,

like all his friendships, remained through life; Lady
Stanley of Alderley, the daughters of the Dean of
Bristol[1], and others. Through Mrs. Cradock he afterwards had a meeting with Lord John Russell, which
interested him greatly, and was the first step in
an acquaintance with the Duke of Bedford's family.
which ultimately, through other circumstances, became
more intimate. Dr. Symonds, of Hill House, Clifton,
was another friend with whom he repeatedly stayed,
having made his acquaintance on young J. A. Symonds'
coming to Oxford in 1858. He had casually met
Dr. Symonds at a banquet in Magdalen College, earlier
in the same year.

Jowett used to say of Dr. Symonds, that he was the
only busy man who made an agreeable host, always
seeming at leisure for the entertainment of his guests.
He often spoke of him as the 'beloved physician.' About
the same time he became acquainted with the family
of Mr. Nightingale, of Embley, Surrey, and Lea Hurst,
Derbyshire, with whom he gradually formed a friendship
which continued to the end of his life.

Through Stanley he made the acquaintance of Mr. and
Mrs. Grote (whom he afterwards visited at their country
house, Barrow Green, in Kent), and had at least one
interview with Dean Milman.

His friendships were multiplying. Grant could already
say of him, 'He is the only man who can maintain close
friendship with about fifty people at once.'

All these threads were interwoven in his after life.

More conscious than heretofore of the limitations both
of his circumstances and of his powers, he was more
than ever determined to make his mark; and as he was

[1] The Very Rev. Gilbert Elliot.

thrown back upon Balliol he was resolved henceforth to do what in him lay to make Balliol great. He was still for some time after this in a minority amongst his colleagues, but the minority was a strong one. With Henry Smith, W. L. Newman, and Charles Bowen on his side, he felt confident that he could fight his way. And he obtained some concessions of real importance, such as the foundation of the open Exhibitions in 1858. But the contention was acute and undisguised. He said to a friend who was opposing some measure in another College, 'Your Head seems to be an astute person, who works by winning confidence; here we have a bare struggle for power.' Very rarely, however, out of College meeting, did any resentful word escape him, although he knew that he was himself the subject of perpetual obloquy. Such words had always reference to the state of the College. A case of gambling had been discovered, and it had been treated, as he thought, too lightly. 'I do not know what is to become of the College,' he said. He was also concerned about the selection of men for entrance. The 'old Master' had been used to select men from two classes; first, those who had high connexions, and, secondly, men of marked ability; and by offering rooms to those who did well for the Scholarship, the Tutors had given the preponderance to the latter. Jowett fancied that the new Master was departing from this tradition, but his fears were hardly justified in the sequel; this, however, was largely due to the attractive force of Jowett's own personality. The silence which he maintained about all that concerned himself, and his indomitable persistence in doing what he saw to be best for his pupils, and for the truth which he held sacred, did not prevent his judgement from being coloured to some extent by his

personal feeling. His remarks to **private** friends **during
these years** had often a tinge of bitterness, **but even what**
appeared like cynicism **was** the **veil of** deeper feeling.
When told of a young family **who were** beginning life
with prospects **of a roseate** hue, he said, '**Is life to be all
art and culture and music?**—poor people, poor people!'
The slight tone of contempt belied **his real sympathy.**
However **pressed with occupation, he never turned**
aside **from helping those who sought** his assistance,
reading **and criticizing** long ambitious arguments **in
MS., and often hoping more from them than the result
has justified.**

Yet **it was to the interest he took in other people's**
writings that he owed some **of those intimate friendships**
that were **his** chief solace during **the years of** gloom.
After reading **a** book in MS., which **had been introduced
to him,** I think, through Arthur Clough, he said, '**It
seemed to me as if** I had received the impress of **a new
mind.'** Philanthropic efforts also greatly interested **him,**
and he rejoiced in any opportunity that brought **them**
within his ken. A familiar passage in the Essay on Interpretation having obvious **reference to the nurses in the**
Crimea, **strongly reflects this feeling:—'And there may**
be some **tender and delicate woman among us,** who feels
that she has a Divine vocation to fulfil the most repulsive
offices towards **the dying inmates of a hospital, or the**
soldier perishing in a foreign land[1].' How he found
time for all these interests is a perplexing **thought, but**
one thing which secured **him some degree of leisure was**
his resolute avoidance of polemical disputation. 'There

[1] *St. Paul's Epistles,* **third** edition, vol. ii. p. 33. He visited Miss Carpenter's industrial school at Bristol, and keenly sympa- thized in the movement **started** in that quarter for the **relief of** destitute incurables.

is nothing to be done, but to do nothing,' was his single rule for meeting all attacks.

His judgement on persons, then and always, was wholly independent of their opinions ; but not of their conduct. Personal character counted with him for much. For R. Hussey, Canon of Christ Church, Stanley's predecessor in the Chair of Church History, who was a consistent High Churchman, he had the most unfeigned respect. He said of Canon F. C. Cook[1], an opponent of Liberalism, ' He is the only person in England, whom I have met, that could be called really learned.' He was disappointed in Thirlwall, contrasting his attitude on leaving Cambridge 'multa et praeclara minantis,' with his episcopal charges. 'A man should not be broken down with fifteen years of being a bishop.'

The time had now arrived when the opening of the Fellowships, the most important factor in University reform, was taking full effect. And one result of it, which was cheering to Jowett, was the colonizing of the rest of Oxford by Balliol men. He took intense interest in their work, especially when they became Tutors. ' You will turn those rough undergraduates into First Class men,' he used to say : ' You must treat them very much as gentlemen,' and (perhaps thinking of his own experience) ' Do not assert your authority too soon : let it come naturally and by degrees.' Also, ' Never speak of their faults to any but themselves. You are sure to lose influence if you do.'

Three Balliol men, A. G. Watson, W. H. Fremantle, and Godfrey Lushington, had been elected Fellows of All Souls under the reformed Statute. But in a year or two an attempt was made to revert to the former system, in which birth and breeding were preferred to learning and

[1] Editor of *Aids to Faith*.

ability as qualifications for election. The three juniors fought hard to vindicate the spirit of the University Act, and were successful in doing so. Jowett was keenly interested in this contest, and greatly pleased with the result, which was obtained in 1861.

To those of his pupils who became parish clergymen, he gave advice which was sometimes ironical, but always sagacious, and kindly meant. If asked how to manage one's parishioners, he would say, ' Please every one, and displease none.' He repeated the saying of the butler at Lichfield Palace, who, when asked how Master James Lonsdale was getting on, had replied, ' He offends the people by reproving them for drunkenness. 'E should 'a stuck to the doctrine, sir, that could do no 'arm ! ' Then without irony he would say, ' You can do good to the poor by visiting, and to the rich by society.'

About preaching, he had a more serious tone. ' I have long thought about the value of sermons, and I think I know it now. They idealize life for us. But there must be more in your discourse than mere morality. If you give them a moral essay, not a poor woman in the congregation but will feel that there is something wrong.'

In the same spirit he wrote to James Lonsdale, when appointed to the preachership at Lincoln's Inn :—

' There is nothing by which more good might be done than by good preaching. I mean chiefly : (1) The connexion of religion with life, (2) The assertion of a regard for truth as a sort of religious duty—the spirit of truth. I hope you will devote yourself to sermon writing ; no one can succeed better ; and don't be over simple (if I may say so) ; simplicity is the best of faults, yet there is some danger of mannerism even from simplicity.'

He spoke with respect of Renan's article on the Future of Metaphysic (*Revue des Deux Mondes*, Jan. 15, 1860).

I have referred above to an Essay on Interpretation, which had been prepared with a view to the second edition of the book on St. Paul[1]. Having this in reserve, Jowett was approached by the Rev. H. B. Wilson, the Bampton Lecturer of 1851, once his colleague in the Examinership, who desired a contribution from him to a volume, in which theological subjects should be freely handled in a becoming spirit.

Henry Bristowe Wilson was a man of great elevation of character, and of an extraordinarily keen and penetrative mind, who, after serving his College and the University for a quarter of a century, had taken a St. John's living, the Vicarage of Great Staughton, Huntingdonshire, in the year 1850. The widening of theological opinion and of Christian communion was thenceforward the main interest of his life. The concluding passage of his essay finely expresses the restrained fervour and intense spiritual thoughtfulness which characterized him. Those who read it here will think it strange that it should have been made the ground of a condemnation which, though afterwards reversed, suspended him from his office for a year:—

'The Christian Church can only tend on those who are committed to its care, to the verge of that abyss which parts this world from the world unseen. Some few of those fostered by her are now ripe for entering on a higher career; the many are but rudimentary spirits, germinal souls. What shall become of them? If we look abroad in the world and regard the neutral character of the multitude, we are at a loss to apply to them, either the promises, or the denunciations of Revelation. So, the wise heathens could anticipate a reunion

---

[1] p. 251. The first hint of such an essay occurs in a letter to Stanley in the autumn of 1847: 'I find that St. John expands, and it will perhaps have two subordinate essays, on the Critical Study of Scripture, and on the relation of Faith to Knowledge.'

with the great and good of all ages ; they could represent
to themselves, at least in a figurative manner, the punishment
and the purgatory of the wicked ; but they would not expect ·
the reappearance in another world, for any purpose, of a
Thersites, or an Hyperbolos—social and poetical justice had
been sufficiently done upon them. Yet there are such as
these, and no better than these, under the Christian name—
babblers, busy-bodies, livers to get gain, and mere eaters and
drinkers. The Roman Church has imagined a *limbus infantium* ;
we must rather entertain a hope that there shall be found,
after the great adjudication, receptacles suitable for those who
shall be infants, not as to years of terrestrial life, but as to
spiritual development—nurseries, as it were, and seed grounds,
where the undeveloped may grow up under new conditions—
the stunted may become strong, and the perverted be restored.
And when the Christian Church in all its branches shall have
fulfilled its sublunary office, and its Founder shall have sur-
rendered His kingdom to the great Father—all, both small and
great, shall find a refuge in the bosom of the Universal Parent,
to repose, or be quickened into higher life, in the ages to come,
according to His Will.'

The remaining contributors to the volume were Rowland
Williams, Vice-Principal of Lampeter College, the author
of a work on *Rational Godliness*[1], a man of genius,
somewhat dangerously blent with Celtic fire, whose
essay was on Bunsen's Biblical Researches ; Baden
Powell, the mathematician, who had written an essay on
Theism for the Burnett Prize, and now wrote on Christian
Evidences ; Mark Pattison, who described eighteenth-
century Theology, and C. W. Goodwin, the only layman
of the seven, whose subject was the Mosaic Cosmogony.

One valuable trace of the negotiations by which the
work was arranged, appears in a letter of Jowett's to
Stanley, inviting him to contribute :—

[1] It was reviewed, with Jowett and Stanley on St. Paul, in the
Quarterly Review for October, 1855 ('The Neology of the Cloister ').

'CHESTNUT HILL, KESWICK,
August 15, 1858.

'Wilson wishes me to write to you respecting a volume of Theological Essays which he has already mentioned, the object of which, however, he thinks he has not clearly set before you, trusting to my being at Oxford, &c.

'The persons who have already joined in the plan are Wilson, R. Williams of King's, Pattison, Grant[1], Temple, Müller, if he has time, and myself. The object is to say what we think freely within the limits of the Church of England. A notice will be prefixed that no one is responsible for any notions but his own. It is, however, an essential part of the plan that names shall be given, partly for the additional weight which the articles will have if the authors are known, and also from the feeling that on such subjects as theology it is better not to write anonymously. We do not wish to do anything rash or irritating to the public or the University, but we are determined not to submit to this abominable system of terrorism, which prevents the statement of the plainest facts, and makes true theology or theological education impossible. Pusey and his friends are perfectly aware of your opinions. and the Dean's, and Temple's and Müller's, but they are determined to prevent your expressing them. I do not deny that in the present state of the world the expression of them is a matter of great nicety and care, but is it possible to do any good by a system of reticence? For example, I entirely agree with you that no greater good could be accomplished for religion and morality than the abolition of all subscriptions; but how will this ever be promoted in the least degree, or how will it be possible for any one in high station ever to propose it, if we only talk it over in private? We shall talk A. D. 1868. I want to point out that the object is not to be attained by any anonymous writing.

'As it is good to look at things on all sides, I don't object

---

[1] Grant's Indian appointment prevented him from carrying out his intention of contributing.

to Mrs. Stanley or Mrs. Vaughan, if she is in Oxford, applying
the fable of the fox who has lost his tail.

'I don't write so often as I once did, but am not the less
truly your sincere and affectionate friend.'

Stanley disapproved of the policy of such an open alliance, and Jowett, in persevering with it, acted against his
friend's advice. As he told Dr. Symonds of Clifton[1], he
strongly felt the duty of continuing his efforts to clear the
minds of his countrymen from religious prejudices. He
determined, therefore, to complete his Essay and to send
it in. He also obtained the adhesion of Dr. Temple, whose
University sermon on the Education of the World lay in
the direction indicated, and when preached had given no
offence, escaping even the suspicion of heresy, except, it
is said, in the mind of Dr. Hawkins, the keen-scented
Provost of Oriel. Dr. John Muir of Edinburgh, the
Sanskrit scholar, was a zealous promoter of the scheme.

Jowett was hampered with the accumulation of many
duties: he said one day to a friend, with momentary
impatience, 'I ought not to have so much to do': but
if he could only get to the seaside for a few weeks
together, he thought he might make a good thing of this
piece of writing. He was working at it during a visit
to the Tennysons in the winter of 1859, and wrote one
passage at least, that on the Parables, at Milford Vicarage,
Hampshire[2], where he talked anxiously over this and other
schemes. At one moment he turned suddenly and asked
his hostess, 'Can the truth do harm?' On her replying,
'It can surely do no harm to tell the truth,' he said, 'That
is the verdict of the simple mind.' Not that he had
fully calculated on the storm which followed, but he was
apprehensive of some misunderstanding, and he desired

---

[1] *Life of J. A. Symonds*, vol. i. p. 188.   [2] I was then Vicar of Milford.—L. C.

to make his own position clear[1]. The book appeared in March. 1860. He wrote to me quite simply, on April 6. 'I am glad that you like the volume of *Essays*.'

Henry Smith remarked soon afterwards, with reference to the enterprise, which he appears to have watched with some misgiving, 'The stone has sunk quietly into the waters after all.'

LETTERS, 1854-1860.

To F. T. PALGRAVE.

HARROW, *April* 7, 1854.

I cannot but write to thank you for your most kind note. It is the last thing I should have imagined that you were indifferent to the event of last Tuesday. You and a few others (if you will excuse my saying so) have a ridiculous opinion of what I am and can do, but though I am aware of this, I must always feel deeply grateful for the affection you show. . . . The event of Tuesday, about which you speak so kindly, is a little hard upon me. . . . But while I can keep the regard of my pupils, I shall stay on and do the utmost I can, though I cannot but feel sadly at having lost a position that in this world seemed all I could desire.

To A. P. STANLEY.

BALLIOL, *April* 12. 1854.

I will not trouble you any more with the hateful subject of the Balliol election.

---

[1] He wrote in 1861: 'The great difficulty in writing is to adapt your thoughts to the apprehension of your readers.' Cf. *Autobiography of F. P. Cobbe*. vol. i. p. 349.

. . . On Monday we had another meeting at Macaulay's. He talked again about the Oxford Bill—said the debate was as dull as possible, that the Ministry were going to give up the certificate clauses, and declaimed against Whewell's bigotry ; gave an amusing account of what he called Lord Rutherford's conversion by being taken to Trinity College Chapel, illustrative of the effect on the minds of Dissenters of so many hundred surplices. His conversation does not give you a high idea of his intellect. He strikes one rather as a fine old fellow, very hearty and simple, but 'excellent at monologue,' with a most sincere and genuine pleasure in hearing himself talk. In power of mind he is very inferior to Gladstone, but more straightforward, with no 'ins and outs.' On the whole the Commission has prospered greatly thus far. We have agreed to leave the age for exit from Haileybury twenty-three, and only to require six months' residence there, which will open the Indian service to the Universities. Macaulay does not believe that any University men will be found to go. He would rather be a serving man himself,

> ἀνδρὶ παρ' ἀκλήρῳ . . .
> ἦ πᾶσιν νεκύεσσι καταφθιμένοισιν ἀνάσσειν[1]

i. e. be Governor General.

A large work of Pusey *v.* Vaughan[2] has appeared.

I still look forward to some happy time when you and I and Temple may be working together at Oxford. Many thanks more than I can express for your deep affection and sympathy for me.

To A. P. STANLEY.

BALLIOL, *July* 11, 1854.

. . . How many things have happened since we met, though only three months ago. I am delighted at the abolition of tests, which is a real good and rests the University on a solid national foundation, independent of Church, Ministries, &c. Notwithstanding the great number who signed the petition[3]

---

[1] 'Under a poor master ... than lord it over the people of the dead.'—Hom. *Odyss.* xi. 490.

[2] *Collegiate and Professorial*

Teaching; see *Life of E. B. Pusey*, vol. iii. pp. 386-388.

[3] Against the abolition of tests.

I believe that people are already a good deal softened, and in a few months will have shifted to a new point of view. Gladstone is a great peacemaker. At present they busy themselves with the hope that by enforcing a very strict system of chapels, &c., they will be able to exclude Dissenters from the Colleges.

If you are not likely to be in town next week, will you be at Canterbury in the middle of August? I cannot tell you how strongly the isolation in which I feel myself here makes me turn to you and Temple and the few true and warm friends of my own standing whom I have elsewhere. If I could begin life again it should not be in a College.

To A. P. STANLEY.

[October ? 1854.]

To hear from you reminds me of old times which I wish I could recall, when you and I and Temple were Tutors here together. 'Omnes composui—felices! nunc ego resto.'

There seems to be little hope of good from the new Hebdomadal Board. It is said to be the general intention to vote for as many Heads as possible, e. g. three for Professors, four for Masters, besides their own six. That is to say in other words, the worst Heads are to be elected with a view to the exclusion of the best Professors. Such a Board will throw every impediment in the way of a Commission. It seems that the admission of Dissenters, who will be excluded by every means it is possible to devise, has led to this result. This is a weary place, in which little good is effected by much pains and thought. I bury myself in my book and pupils. . . .

To A. P. STANLEY.

[January ? 1855.]

Your letters are a great pleasure and comfort to me. I shall try to follow your advice and bury all animosities towards everybody.

Yet allow me to make a philosophical reflection. What a bad school for character a College is! so narrow and artificial,

such a soil for maggots and crotchets of all sorts, fostering
a sort of weak cleverness, but greatly tending to impair
manliness, straightforwardness, and other qualities which are
met with in the great world. A man said to me the other
day, ' How very unworldly a friend of ours is,' which meant
that he was disposed to lose the best years of his life between
twenty-three and twenty-eight in reading poetry and dreaming
about philosophy. . . .

To go to another subject. It has occurred to me several
times lately that I have been inconsiderate in trying to press
upon you opinions and ways of life that, whether right or
wrong, were natural to me, but not natural to you. I remember your writing to me about this in September, 1849[1].
Afterwards I wanted you to come to Oxford and help a
scheme for poor students. I entirely see now that it was
a mistake[2]. . . .

To A. P. STANLEY.

[1855.]

I do not propose my rule of proceeding with the Puseyites
for anybody else. I only allude to the subject again to
explain that I wish them to have entire toleration, but I do not
wish to act with them because I think the union hollow and
false. They will be too much for me and I shall get nothing
out of them.

Certainly I desire also to remember that there will come
a time when all these differences will have an end, and that in
some way, we know not how, those who have any shadow
of love or truth will be transfigured into His image. But
I wish to wait for another world before joining in a closer
union with them.

I write this in a reading-room at Folkestone, where I took up
the *Record*. There were two articles in it; the first on Miss
Stanley and Miss Nightingale, explaining that the *Record*
had done the latter injustice, and that it was still willing to
do Miss Stanley injustice. Then followed an article on

[1] p. 166. Cf. *Letters of Dean Stanley*, p. 137.   [2] p. 212.

Mr. Stanley and Mr. Jowett, setting forth that the former was bad, but the latter worse, and that the former was implicated in the sins of the latter. Remember me to your sister. Though I protested above that I wished to have nothing to do with Puseyites, I was glad to see my name honoured by being on the same page with hers.

Pascal does not clear up to me. His evidences of Christianity are only for those whom he can first bring into that state of spiritual desolation in which he finds himself. It appears only during the last five years of his life that he had any deep religious feeling.

To A. P. Stanley.

[July? 1855.]

Yesterday I was at Fox How and spent the day with Mrs. Arnold, who sent her love to you. It was a great pleasure to me to see the place again in which he lived. I think the thing which interested me most was that old portrait of Arnold as a young man in the dining-room, which has a strong resemblance to Tom : also more of the fierceness of untamed youth than is traceable in his later years.

Mrs. Arnold seemed very happy and cheerful, but I was sorry to see her looking so aged ; it is ten years since I saw her last, and she has become, as she called herself, an old woman in the interval.

. . . I have brought your book with me, which I am reading with great pleasure. Two criticisms I have heard made on it by one who had a great value for it : first, that it was in places too rhetorical, and that there was too great an absence of doctrinal statements. The first criticism I agree in, and if I may venture to give a judgement in such a matter, I would be glad if you would tone down your style in the new book [1]. because it would be more effective with rather more of the 'ars celare artem.' The pleasantest picture loses its beauty when it does not seem 'to come sweetly from nature.' I am not quite a fair critic in the matter, because I feel that

[1] i. e. *Sinai and Palestine.*

my dreamy, hazy suggestions of things are not to be compared with the good, substantial, bright colours in which you present them.

To Mrs. Greenhill.

BALLIOL, *October* 21, 1855.

I have not answered your kind note because I have been overwhelmed with work during the last three weeks, and I wished to sit down and feast upon the congratulations [1] which I have received, and answer them at leisure. Congratulations is a bad word, because it is supposed to mean nothing, and I am sure the letters that were addressed to me meant something, viz. the attachment of a great many warm-hearted persons to me, for which I cannot be too grateful both to them and to Providence who has given me such friends. They make me half believe what the Dean of Wells [2] said to me the other day: 'You have the sympathy of everybody.'

I ought to except your friends, the Heads of Houses, with whom, however, I wish to be on peaceable terms. I sincerely pity them, for they are fallen on evil days. And you will observe that we have now got two trusty reformers among the Heads, in the Dean of Christ Church (Liddell), and in the Provost of Queen's (Thomson). The first is one of the most able and most honest men living, quite free from Christ Church or any other prejudices. His first act has been to abolish the Servitors, whom he intends to convert into Exhibitioners. He has been very kind to me about the Professorship: not that I asked him, but of his own accord he took great pains and trouble about it.

I wish Arnold were alive: how gladly we would have welcomed him, if he had settled amongst us !

To a Friend on a Conversion to the Roman Catholic Church.

1856.

I am indeed sorry to hear that your thoughts have been occupied by a painful subject. Think of it as it will be a year hence

---

[1] On the Greek Professorship.   [2] G. H. S. Johnson.

and as it will seem in another world when these miserable divisions will have passed away, and keep it to yourselves and God. The greatest possible allowance must be made for things done or said by persons in a half-distracted state of mind. How it is, as I have seen it, that the best persons pass into such states of mind, is a great mystery ; yet their Heaven may clear before they die, and we may be perfectly reconciled to see them such as God has pleased or allowed them to be. . . .

It is a part of the illusion that converts to a new faith do not feel the pain that they cause to others. Happy for them, I think, that it is so—or they would break down under the conflict.

The mind is so abstracted and so perfectly at rest that they cannot admit any distracting thought. Does not this seem to have been the case with the first Christians ? . . . .

To Sir Alexander Grant.

August 19, 1856.

Dear Grant,

I was sorry to observe in the *Illustrated London News* to-day a mention of the death of your father.

I am afraid this event is a great trouble to you and Lady Grant, more especially as you had seen little of him of late years. Do not let this grieve you. Family trials frequently cannot be avoided. I do not think accidents of this sort should increase sorrow. Death is an aweful thing, about which our greatest comfort must ever be that the departed are in the hands of God, to be judged not by the pedantry of divines on earth, but by the larger rules of His mercy. It seems to me wrong and foolish to dwell much on anything but this. There is nothing probably that those who are gone would less wish than that we should recall painful recollections.

To yourself I think the succession to the Baronetcy a great good. Many persons say that rank is a misfortune without wealth. This is not true. There are three kinds of goods, as our friend Aristotle would say, rank, wealth, and talent. It seems to me that a man may do well with two out of the three. With the last only, life is a painful struggle.

Your book[1] is often in my mind. I hope it has prospered during the vacation. But if not, do not be discouraged. Nothing seems to me more uncertain than composition. One month a good harvest is reaped : the next all barren. In these fits and starts, with much pain and melancholy I calculate that I accomplish somewhat less than half of what I always intend. Whether you accomplish the work six months sooner or later must depend on health and many other causes. I feel confident that you will succeed at last.

This letter is nothing, yet I send it because I do not want you, who have shown such warm sympathy and kindness for me, to suppose that I can be forgetful of you at any crisis of your life.

Ever yours affectionately,

B. JOWETT.

To JOHN NICHOL.

August 22, 1856.

. . . The subject of the Stanhope Essay is 'The Life and Place of Wycliffe as a Reformer.'

You could not have a more interesting subject. The books about it you probably know better than I do.

. . . Great reformers are generally misrepresented when the world has settled down into a calm. Mankind are afraid to acknowledge how wild and fierce they were. I expect you will find Wycliffe to have been a kind of 'Socialist,' as a man whose mind was turned loose upon Scripture might very well become, especially in an age when the division of ranks was so strongly marked. The rebellious spirits of the Middle Ages are a strange phenomenon.

To A. P. STANLEY.

DOVER, 1856.

I took up the *Record* at the reading-rooms to-day ; it points out for the edification of the Ministry that Providence whitewashed their misdoings by two large majorities immediately after the Sunday bands were put an end to. 'I had

---

[1] Edition of Aristotle's *Ethics.*

rather believe all the fables in the Talmud and Alkoran than this.' . . . I think Arnold was dangerous in the sense that every man is dangerous. Arnold's peculiar danger was not knowing the world and character—not knowing where his ideas would take other people, and ought to take himself. Yet had he been living, how we would have nestled under his wings!

To Mrs. Stanley.

December, 1856.

I write to thank you for your kind note. Shall I congratulate you? It is no great matter as a preferment for him, but I congratulate myself three times a day. Yet it is also a matter of congratulation to you that he is in the right niche—a place in which he can build up a reputation worth many bishoprics. As Professor of Ecclesiastical History, he may have an influence on the English Church which no bishop has ever exercised or can exercise. And therefore, though stripped of some of the accidents of greatness and without the sweet sound of 'my Lord,' I do not think he could be better off than he is.

Of course he will keep the Canonry at Canterbury until Dr. Barnes, who is now about eighty-six, sleeps with his fathers. I do not know whether he would care to have a permanent abode at Oxford at present; if so, he could probably have Mr. Butler's house, one of the few habitations convenient and suitable for him.

We will give him a welcome such as shall gladden you.

To F. T. Palgrave.

December 4, 1857.

Many thanks for your kind present, which was most welcome to me, both for the sake of the giver and the beauty of the work itself. It seems to me as though I had not seen you for an immense time. . . .

I have now got three works of A[lbert] D[urer]. My ambition is next to possess a little landscape of Rembrandt. All the ideas I have about art I learnt from you, though you have not much reason to be satisfied with my proficiency. A little *real* pleasure I got from it, whether to be set in the scale against a good dinner I do not know. Certainly not against an opera or oratorio of Handel.

You should have tried for the Balliol Scholarship this year. Our subject for English Essay was 'Whether a good artist must also be a good man.'

To Mrs. Greenhill.

KNELLER HALL, ISLEWORTH,
Christmas Day, [1857].

It is extremely kind of you to write and ask me to come and stay with you. Alas! I fear the visions of going to Rome have melted into thin air. I have engaged to take some undergraduates this vacation, with the view if possible of keeping them to their work.

Therefore I fear I must put off until Easter or the summer the pleasure of coming to see you. Give my love to Kate, who I hope is becoming an accomplished young lady, and tell her not to forget me until then. I wonder whether she is up to writing a letter to me yet. My little godson is, I suppose, grown and more entertaining than when I last saw him.

Oxford is at last beginning to stir itself and set its house in order. During the last part of the Term we were very busy at Balliol with a scheme of reform which has just received the consent of the Visitor, and will, as we hope, shortly become law[1]. It is charming to see the way in which the anti-reformers change their opinions, and a great satisfaction to have been a 'republican of the day before.' Everybody seems to be discovering that the founder after all is only the ghost of a founder.

To F. T. Palgrave.

October 24, 1858.

'I will be guilty of this sin no longer[2],' and only hope you will not measure the value I set on the gift by the apparent

---

[1] pp. 258, 269. The Balliol ordinance of the Executive Commission of 1854 was issued in 1857.

[2] Shakespeare, 1 *Henry IV*, ii. 4. It was a favourite phrase of Jowett's, and, as often happened in quotations, was applied by him

thanklessness of not answering your letter. The St. Paul[1] seems to me to be a very fine work, which I am extremely glad to possess. I like particularly the style in which you have mounted it; it hangs over the mantelpiece in the outer room. I hope that you will soon come and pay a visit to it.

Shall I offer a criticism on the St. Paul, a very general one? I think I would have thrown into it more of unrest and perturbation of feeling—at any rate more trace of the struggle and conquest over it. The 2 Cor. xii, xiii, 1 Cor. ix, Gal. vi. 17, 2 Tim. iv. 5-8 would express what I mean. But I am not sure whether it would be possible to make so great a departure from conventional ideas on the subject.

My book is nearly all printed, but is at present interrupted for Homer, in which I find great delight.

To A. P. STANLEY.

TENBY, *Friday, March,* 1859.

MY DEAR STANLEY,

I write to you as one of my dearest and oldest friends to tell you that my dear father has been taken from us. He died peacefully after about a fortnight's illness, and I believe without pain to himself.

He was one of the best men I ever knew, perfectly guileless and childlike, and would have been one of the happiest, if life could have been spent only in doing kindnesses to others. Though possessed of considerable ability and very great activity of mind, he was entirely ignorant of the world and of business, in some respects like a child throughout life.

There is no need of knowledge of the world or of business where he is now.

My mother and sister are better than I could have expected, and have borne up and are borne up under this great blow.

The post is just going out.

Ever yours affectionately,

B. JOWETT.

without any reference to the original meaning and connexion of the words, which through some trick of association had taken his fancy.

[1] Woolner's relief. pp. 233, 289.

To A. P. Stanley.

Tenby, March 10, 1859.

I write to thank you for your most kind letter, which was a great comfort and good to me as far as words could be.

We have experienced the greatest kindness here from very many persons. The Rector told me that it was the impression of the whole place 'that a good man had passed away.'

I make no progress with my book, for my mind seems dried up. I have written what would make above 100 pages of print for the two last essays of the second volume (all the rest is printed), but the form of it is not good, and just at present I feel incapable of putting it into a better. I will wait a day or two and try again; therefore do not expect the book for a few weeks. I return on Monday evening.

To the Tennyson Children.

February, 1860.

My dear Hallam and Lionel,

What an age it is since I saw you! Love and kisses. I must write you a few lines, for I want to hear from you.

Can you carry a message? Tell Papa that I have got a Homer for him, but not a Boswell. The Homer is in five volumes and costs five shillings.

I wish I had you after dinner to sit opposite me on two chairs and hear about 'Louisa' or the tale of Troy. Try and persuade Papa to bring you in the summer.

I think I told you that I keep a large school to which you are to come by-and-by. All the boys in my school are very big, some of them six feet high and more. They are very busy playing at soldiers at present; in fact, they can hardly be got to do anything else [1]. But they are good boys, and I like them very much.

Do you know the name of a large school where there are only old boys? It is called a University.

---

[1] The Rifle Corps movement was at its height in 1860.

Give my love to Papa and Mama. I shall add two pieces of advice to you in large letters that you may remember them :

NEVER FEAR.

NEVER CRY.

Good-bye. You may as well guess from whom this comes, therefore I shall only sign myself

Your affectionate friend,

OXONIENSIS.

Note on Woolner's St. Paul (p. 287).

Mr. F. T. Palgrave has kindly furnished us with the following account (October, 1896) :—

'Woolner's St. Paul—with three similar figures, Moses, David, and (perhaps) St. John Baptist—was modelled by him and cast in plaster; from which the four figures were carved, in some local stone, for the pulpit in Llandaff Cathedral nave. Woolner did not superintend the carving, which I have heard is rough. The series was in the R. A. Exhibition about 1858 or 1859. He never did better work.'

CHAPTER X

(Aet. 43–48)

Essays and Reviews—Panic in the religious world—*The Quarterly* and *Edinburgh Reviews*—Bishop Wilberforce—Stanley at Oxford—Dr. Pusey's attitude—Bishop Colenso—Prosecution of Williams and Wilson—The Vice-Chancellor's Court—Continued agitation for the Endowment of the Greek Chair—E. Freeman and C. Elton—Endowment of the Chair by Christ Church.

IN this chapter it will be necessary for the sake of clearness to travel beyond the strict limits of Biography, and to recall a series of incidents which had important consequences not only for the subject of this memoir, but for some public institutions. They gave to his career its final bent by binding him to Balliol; and while thus enriching that College, left Christ Church, and the Church of England also, poorer than they might otherwise have been.

In the summer of 1860[1] the meeting of the British Association was held at Oxford. The encounter on that occasion between Mr. Huxley[2] and Bishop Wilberforce, during the discussion that arose concerning Mr. Darwin's *Origin of Species*[3], was long vividly remembered and

---

[1] June 27—July 3.　　[2] The Right Hon. T. H. Huxley.
[3] Published in 1859.

has been described elsewhere[1]. But the excitement evoked by that great argument gave place in clerical circles to the outcry shortly afterwards raised about *Essays and Reviews*. Dean Church, in writing to his American correspondent, Dr. Asa Gray, early in 1861, observes with reference to Darwin's volume, 'The book I have no doubt would be the subject still of a great row, if there were not a much greater row going on about *Essays and Reviews*[2].'

It is hard for the present generation to realize the violence of this disturbance. The 'religious world' lost their heads at once, and there was a danger lest even sensible persons among the laity should be carried away. Few indeed of those who professed orthodox opinions shared the temperate and calm judgement of the distinguished clergyman whose words I have just quoted. 'There has been a great deal of unwise panic,' he adds, 'and unjust and hasty abuse; and people who have not an inkling of the difficulties which beset the questions, are for settling them in a summary way, which is perilous for every one.' The mischief was already afoot, when it was sedulously fomented at a great gathering of the Oxford M.A.'s, who had come up to vote in Convocation against the appointment of Mr. Max Müller to the Chair of Sanskrit. That distinguished Orientalist was suspected of 'Germanism,' being in fact a German, and also an acquaintance of the Chevalier Bunsen, whose name (if only on account of Dr. Arnold's friendship for him) was a bugbear to many of the orthodox at the time.

The clergy who came up on that occasion had their attention called to an article in the *Westminster and*

---

[1] See *Life of Charles Darwin*, vol. ii. pp. 321, 322.
[2] *Dean Church's Life*, p. 157.

Foreign Quarterly Review of October 1, 1860, headed
'Neo-Christianity,' and dealing with the volume in
question [1]. The tenor of that article was calculated to
excite their horror. The *Westminster* was then the
organ of the Positivist school, whose reputed aim
was to reconstruct society upon the ruins of existing
systems; and the liberalizing of Christianity plainly
did not fall in with such a project. Accordingly the
line taken by this periodical was to caricature a position
such as that of the Essayists, in which Conservative
and Progressive principles were combined, as one of
hopeless inconsistency, and, in short, to push these
writers over the precipice, on the brink of which it
represented them as standing. Instead, however, of considering the questionableness of the warning ('Quis
tulerit Gracchos de seditione querentes?'), the clergy, who
had hardly recovered from the Darwinian scare, were
in the mood to think, 'If this gives offence in such
a quarter, how bad it must be!'

The clerical 'caucus' was immediately followed by an
outburst of abuse, more or less tempered with decorum,
in the *Record, Guardian*, and other 'religious' newspapers; and the matter was seriously taken up by the
Church's representatives, assembled in both Houses of
Convocation (whose powers, long suppressed, had been
revived in 1860) [2]. The bishops, led by the Bishop of
Oxford, formally denounced the book, and every diocese,

---

[1] A letter from Jowett to
Stanley of April, 1862, shows that
the writer of this article was afterwards believed to have regretted
his vehemence, and that when he
was threatened with persecution
for his opinions, Jowett exerted
himself strenuously on his behalf.

[2] They met on March 26. In the
Upper House Thirlwall supported
Wilberforce, and Bishop Hampden
(of all persons) said, 'This was a
question between Infidelity and
Christianity, and that we ought
to prosecute.'—*Life of Bp. Wilberforce*, vol. iii. p. 213.

archdeaconry, and rural-diaconate throughout the land became a busy hive for the manufacture of memorials against the notorious 'seven.' Still heavier artillery was brought to bear. In the January number of the *Quarterly Review* for 1861, there appeared an article on *Essays and Reviews*, in which the subtle influence of Bishop Wilberforce [1] was easily detected, at once depreciating the literary merit of the volume, and emphasizing both its dangerous tendency and the invidious position of the clerical contributors. This article became a rallying point for controversialists on the orthodox side. And two imposing volumes, *Aids to Faith* and *Replies to Essays and Reviews*, both now forgotten, though produced under high auspices, helped to swell the cry of alarm which they proposed to allay. But besides the Comtist critics, and the clergy of every grade, the book had other enemies. There were laymen who claimed that 'Free Inquiry' should be the privilege of 'Free Inquirers.' To such persons Jowett's position was wholly incomprehensible. Penetrated as he was with the conviction that the religion of Christ ought to be the religion of all men, and seeing in the Church of England—could she but know 'the things belonging to her peace'—the best hope for the future of Christianity, he had overcome the difficulties of his position, difficulties which were not greater for the Christian Philosopher than for the Sacerdotalist or the Evangelical Protestant. He saw the religion of his countrymen dying, like poor Dean Swift, 'from the top'—losing touch, that is to say, with intellectual and rational life; the clergy, meanwhile,

---

[1] The writer professes to trace in Mr. Jowett's Essay 'a certain sense of disappointment and concealed bitterness.' This was shrewdly aimed.

ignoring plain facts, or industriously obscuring them,
or explaining them away, and the civilization of the
age in danger of becoming, as he himself described
humanity without religion, 'a truncated, half-educated
sort of being[1].' The average English layman 'cared for
none of these things.' His withers were unwrung.
Looking at the matter from outside, he only saw the
prima facie discrepancy between seventeenth-century
Articles, or mediaeval formularies (already at variance
with each other), and nineteenth-century enlightenment[2].
It followed that no enlightened person should become
a clergyman, and that the clergyman who became
enlightened and let men know it should be unfrocked.
It did not occur to such observers to ask the further
question, what then would happen to religion? Nor
did they stop to think that by maintaining silence,
the Essayist might have served his personal interest,
but would have sacrificed a noble end. Hence they
were ready to join in the cry of 'disloyalty.'
Mr. Carlyle, the Chelsea oracle, who often cared not
whom or what he smote, so he smote hard enough,
was at once ready with his epigram. He had himself
proclaimed the 'Exodus from Houndsditch[3],' but had
not shown a way through the Wilderness; yet the
moment some one from within the camp spoke words of
truth and soberness, he broke out with 'The sentinel who
deserts, should be shot[4].' And the organ of sceptical Con-

[1] *Epistles of St. Paul*, third edition, vol. ii. p. 96.

[2] See *Letters of Matthew Arnold*, vol. i. pp. 131, 135, 178.

[3] His quaint phrase for getting rid of *Hebrew old clothes*, that is, of Jewish tradition.

[4] Cf. the *Life of Bishop Wilber-force*, vol. iii. p. 8: 'Rode with Carlyle . . . Carlyle against the Essayists on dishonesty ground and atheistic.' Some who cling to Carlyle's authority in such a matter may bear to be reminded of the more considerate utterance of John Stuart Mill: 'I hold

servatism, not untinged with clericalism—the *Saturday Review*—in two articles, headed 'Essays and Reviews' (March 2, 1861) and 'The Storm in the Church' (March 23, 1861), while solemnly professing reluctance to meddle with the subject, indulged in unworthy sneers at the position of the writers:—

'Fair dealing, after all, is an essential part of practical religion ; and liberty of conduct may do as much harm to morality as liberty of speculation can do good to Truth. That there has been, and will be, abundance of applause, as well as of indignation, is true ; but it does not follow that those who think it politic to drive in the wedge, in their hearts respect the wedge which they drive in [1].'

Then with reference to the foolish action of the bishops in denouncing, i.e. advertising, the book :—

'Has any perpetual curate with fourteen children a volume of dull sermons which no publisher will take? Let him entirely with those clergymen who elect to remain in the national Church, so long as they are able to accept its Articles and confessions in any sense or with any interpretation consistent with common honesty, whether it be the generally received interpretation or not. If all were to desert the Church who put a large and liberal construction on its terms of communion, or who would wish to see those terms widened, the national provision for religious teaching and worship would be left utterly to those who take the narrowest, the most literal, and purely textual view of the formularies ; who, though by no means necessarily bigots, are under the great disadvantage of having the bigots for their allies, and who, however great their merits may be—and they are often very great—yet, if the Church is improvable, are not the most likely persons to improve it. . . . Almost all the illustrious reformers of religion began by being clergymen, but they did not think that their profession as clergymen was inconsistent with their being reformers. They mostly indeed ended their days outside the Churches in which they were born; but it was because the Churches, in an evil hour for themselves, cast them out.'—*Inaugural Address at St. Andrews*, February 1, 1867.

[1] *Saturday Review*, March 2, 1861.

insert into the volume a few passages sufficiently questionable
in their tendency to call down his diocesan, and his little
ones will be fed.   Is any would-be popular preacher languish-
ing under a sense of neglected talent?   Let him spice high
with heterodoxy, and he is a famous man [1].'

Such words, in looking back upon them, only provoke
a smile ; but they caused some anger at the time ; not in
Jowett himself, who attributed them to ' a fit of indiges-
tion ' on the part of the writer, but in his friend Charles
Bowen [2], who withdrew from the staff of the *Saturday
Review* in consequence of them.   Yet the writer of the
first article made an important admission : ' The book
has a conservative as well as a destructive side, which it
is not fair or wise to overlook.'   Had this conservative
purpose been carefully weighed by those ecclesiastics, who,
like Dean Church, were not unaware of the difficulties
involved, the Church might have profited by a controversy, which, as it was, had only a desolating effect [3].
I mean for the time.   For that the joint endeavour
of the seven Essayists was fruitless, it is idle to affirm [4].
To say that they formed no party is wholly to mis-

[1] *Saturday Review*, March 23, 1861.

[2] The late Lord Bowen.

[3] The *Spectator* of those days formed an honourable exception to the spirit of panic which had seized on the periodical press. In reviewing the *Essays* on April 7, 1860 ('Open Teaching in the Church of England'), it spoke of the book as a 'splendid example of sincerity, of courage and truth-fulness in action '; and the writer of an article on May 25, 1861, pleaded against legal measures as unwise: 'Open discussion is better than secret propagandism.   Free speech, indeed, is not truth ; but it is the condition of securing truth.'

[4] Cf. Lecky's *Democracy and Liberty*, vol. i. p. 425: 'The first very marked change in this respect followed, I think, the publication in 1860 of the *Essays and Reviews*; and the effect of this book in making the religious questions which it discussed familiar to the great body of educated men was probably by far the most important of its consequences.'

apprehend the situation. Professor Jowett, at least, as
I have already shown, never sought to form a party.
His object was to reconcile intellectual persons to
Christianity, and to exhort the clergy to the love of
Truth. If he was not wholly successful, he shared that
fate with others who have striven to combat the pre-
judices of their age.

Why is it that what then raised such a tempest
appears so harmless now? May not something be attributed to the contention of those days? Not that Jowett
openly took part in any contention. Again he acted
on the rule—'The only thing to do is to do nothing.'
The Bishop of London, A. C. Tait, after saying to
Dr. Stanley that he saw no matter for condemnation in
Temple, Jowett, or Pattison, gave his signature to the
Bishops' letter, which condemned the Essayists in general.
This course of his, although it shook Jowett's confidence
for the moment—'It is natural in him but it ruins
confidence'—did not interrupt his friendship towards his
former Tutor. He wrote an elaborate letter to A. C. T.,
but did not send it[1]. Dr. Stanley, who was still at
Oxford, came to the front in his own gallant fashion
with what his biographer describes as a 'fiery' article
in the *Edinburgh Review* for April, 1861[2], in which, with
provoking coolness, he claims the declared adversaries
of the volume as its real supporters[3]; and quotes many
latitudinarian precedents from Anglican divines. This
action was the more chivalrous on his part, as he had

[1] p. 346.

[2] He had previously taken part
with T. H. Green in the publication of some extracts from Prof.
Jowett's works entitled *Statements
of Christian Doctrine and Practice*,
intended to illustrate the spirit
of piety and of Christian feeling
which pervaded those writings.

[3] He begins with an effective
appeal to Bishop Thirlwall as an
historian, who had himself admirably described the effect of
religious panic.

dissuaded Jowett from allying himself with others in
this attack on the orthodox position[1]. Jowett always
maintained that Stanley's article made the whole situation different from what it might have been.

It was in January of the next year (1862) that Bishop
Wilberforce said to Stanley at Cuddesdon, with a furtive
smile, 'The Augurs have met,' so confessing the authorship of the attack in the *Quarterly*[2]. The restless
activity of the bishop had not ended there. He denounced the Essayists from the University pulpit in two
sermons which he published[3]. One of these contained
an amazing paragraph on 'the Doubter's death,' which
was much approved in certain quarters at the time.

In a series of 'Tracts for Priests and People' which
were coming out as a manifesto of the Maurician
school, a sort of middle course was taken, claiming some
latitude of interpretation and deprecating injustice, but,
with evident sincerity, professing to hold firmly by the
Creeds and Articles[4].

Even if he had chosen, the Tutor so assailed had no
opportunity of reply. He had long been excluded from
the University pulpit. In Balliol itself 'Catechetics'
had taken the place of the sermon (the successive
Lecturers being Lonsdale, Riddell, and Woollcombe), and
the terminal address before the Communion gave even
less room for controversy. Jowett's voice was occasionally heard, however, in out-of-the-way parts of London.
His old friend W. Rogers was glad to have his aid in
Bishopsgate Street from time to time. (They had
renewed their intercourse while Rogers was acting

[1] p. 276.

[2] *Dean Stanley's Letters*, p.
313.

[3] *The Revelation of God, the
Probation of Man*: two sermons

preached before the University
of Oxford, 1861.

[4] See especially F. D. Maurice's
own essay, entitled *The Mote and
the Beam*.

on the Duke of Newcastle's Commission of Inquiry into popular Education, which reported in 1861.) The Rev. Harry Jones, of St. Luke's, Berwick Street, was another clergyman who honoured himself by welcoming the heretic to his church. Miss F. P. Cobbe, who heard him there, has given a good description of his manner in preaching [1]. A sermon preached in 1864 so struck some of those who heard it that they requested him to publish it; but he would not. It was not till 1866 that Dean Stanley ventured to nominate him as a Preacher in Westminster Abbey, and in 1870 it was still an exceptional privilege to hear him, as, for example, in Mr. Haweis's pulpit, St. James's, Marylebone. Although the sermons generally contained some expression of liberal opinion, their main tenor was hortatory—'idealizing life.'

He was also afterwards silently left out of the Board of Theological Studies, whose institution he had advocated in 1848-51, and on which the Professor of Greek as well as the Professor of Hebrew had a natural right to appear.

Jowett himself did not heartily accept the appellation 'Broad Church.' What is *broad* has *limits*. He would have preferred some expression conveying more the sense of a diffusive and expansive spirit, leavening humanity. He wrote to Stanley in 1862: 'A lady said to me some time ago that we Liberals should not talk about freedom, but about truth—that was the flag under which to fight. I think that was a just criticism.' He grew very weary of the continual buzz. When eleven editions of *Essays and Reviews* had sold, he said, 'We have had enough of this volume: let us turn to something else.' He never 'started aside,' however, from supporting his companions in distress, but stood by them with unflinching loyalty.

---

[1] *Autobiography, &c.*, vol. i. p. 356: 'He looks at one as I never knew any preacher do.'

Some friendly clerics, amongst others Tait, the Bishop of London, sought to divide Jowett and Temple from the other Essayists, 'making a difference,' according to an Apostolic precept[1]. Jowett deliberately refused to second this attempt, although he hinted, in conversation with his private friends, the discomfort which attended his alliance with the perfervid Celtic spirit in such an enterprise.

But he stood manfully by Rowland Williams and by H. B. Wilson, in the well-known trial[2]. He wrote on the subject: 'I am not anxious about the event of R. W.'s case. I feel convinced that sooner or later the Church of England will find it impossible to subsist as a fabric of falsehood and fiction.'

The scandal caused by the claim for latitude on the part of the six clerical contributors to *Essays and Reviews*, was quickly followed by a fresh excitement arising from a similar claim on the part of a bishop of the Church of England, though only a Colonial bishop— Dr. Colenso, the well-known Bishop of Natal[3]. Nonconformist bodies were similarly disturbed. Dr. Samuel Davidson, the author of a learned Introduction to the Old Testament, was cast out by the Independent Synod. The last-mentioned fact recalls an incidental result of this whole controversy. Not only were the differences between the High and Low Church parties considerably softened in making common cause against the supposed enemy, but the jealousy of Dissent, only a short while since 'so rich within their souls,' gave way before the advantage of a temporary alliance with

---

[1] Jude 22.

[2] See *Ecclesiastical Judgments of the Privy Council*, by Brodrick and Fremantle (Murray, 1865), pp. 247-290.

[3] Oct. 1862; ib., pp. 293-317.

the right wing of Nonconformity. Church order for
the time seemed less important than orthodox belief.
Among the Essayists, the chief sufferer in all this was
the Rev. H. B. Wilson, who defended his own cause with
great ability and learning: and although suspended
from his office for a year, and completely broken
down in health, probably did more by his individual
efforts towards enlarging the boundaries of free inquiry
within the Church of England than any other single
man. Both with Wilson and Colenso Jowett maintained an active friendship, in which, while preserving
his own independence of action, he gave invaluable
support to others.

His first impression of Colenso's book appears in
a letter to Stanley:—

'I think the tone is a good deal mistaken. But don't be
hurt or pained by it. You work in one way, he in another,
I perhaps in a third way. All good persons should agree in
heartily sympathizing with the effort to state the facts of
Scripture exactly as they are. Then you really seem like
Athanasius against the whole Christian world, past and
present. My impression is that mankind will never seek for
anything better, until they are convinced of their true position
about Scripture.'

He wrote to me in reference to the Judgement in the
Court of Arches (in a letter dated Linlathen, July 16,
1862): 'I am satisfied and pleased with the Judgement
of Dr. Lushington on the whole. A great step has
been gained in freedom for the Church of England.'
He meant, no doubt, that although the two Essayists
had been condemned on single points, the rejection of
so many of the articles of accusation formed a precedent
of solid value.

Dr. Williams and Mr. Wilson, however, were naturally

not satisfied; and on their appeal to the Queen in
Council, Dr. Lushington's partial condemnation was
reversed by Lord Chancellor Westbury's Judgement on
February 8, 1864 [1]. Jowett had written to Stanley in
August, 1862, 'I think it well that the suit should
continue. More freedom will probably be gained.'

Meanwhile Jowett himself had become involuntarily
the centre of a local conflict which harassed him for
several years. The question of the salary had slumbered
until March, 1858, when Stanley as Professor of Ecclesiastical History succeeded to a Canonry at Christ Church,
and came into residence at Oxford. For the reasons
stated [2] in a previous chapter he found the question at
Christ Church already foreclosed. But he at once began
to exert his influence in the University, especially with
members of the Hebdomadal Council; and the motions
recorded by him in his speech of November 20, 1861 [3],
were due to his suggestion. All that had been done
before his coming had been to refer the question of
unendowed Professorships generally to a Committee of
Council, which had not reported.

The first intimation of one of these efforts of Stanley
and his friends came to Jowett when away from Oxford
after hearing of his brother Alfred's death. He wrote
to Stanley in a letter which it would be wrong to
mutilate, although the part referring to his personal
loss is not relevant in this connexion:—

'I return the papers which you sent me. I have hardly
looked at them, but enough to show me the great kindness

[1] Mr. Bowen, afterwards Lord
Bowen, wrote on the margin of his
copy of the Chancellor's deliverance—'Hell dismissed with costs.'

[2] p. 242.

[3] *A Speech delivered in the
House of Congregation on the
Endowment of the Regius Pro-
fessorship of Greek*, by Arthur
Penrhyn Stanley, &c., p. 5.

of my friends. I hope that they will not think me cold or ungrateful. I had no idea that you were going to take any step during this Term, or I should have written to ask you to do so in the way you have done.

'I cannot express to you what I feel about this matter, or about your kind sympathy respecting my dear brother's death. It does not make any great difference to the world, but it makes a great difference to me, for he was a dear good brother to me, and always to the end of his life retained the strongest sense of what I had done for his education in old times amid many troubles and difficulties, which are with the past now. But I sometimes wish that I could bring them back, if I could bring back all those who were then living, and especially if I could use the experience that I now have for their good.' (Tenby, December, 1858.)

Stanley's hands were strengthened by the return to Oxford of Dean Liddell, who resumed his place in the Council in 1859. And in Michaelmas Term, 1860, Stanley himself became a Professorial Member of Council, while Dr. Pusey was re-elected. Then both champions were in the field, and the fight began in earnest. After several proposals, including that of the Dean of Christ Church, had been successively overborne, Dr. Pusey, to the surprise of every one, took the matter in hand. He had probably begun to see that the continued withholding of the salary was likely to alienate young men from the party of which he was the head, the more so if Stanley gained his point, which he was sure to do in the end. And, although the movements of such a mind are somewhat inscrutable, there is no reason to doubt that Dr. Pusey, as an English gentleman, was acutely alive to the painfulness of his position. He sought, however, to reconcile the step with his peculiar principles, by introducing a proviso, which would have given the University authorities an effective

voice in future appointments[1]. Cumbrous as the resolution was, Stanley accepted it as a *pis aller*, and it was
proposed in Convocation[2], but not carried. A scheme
involving so many complications had little chance with
a body so ready to listen to objections. Dr. Pusey
sought to throw the burden of odium on those Liberals
who had voted against his measure[3], and remained
deaf to any further proposal.

Jowett not only possessed his soul in patience all this
while, but was ready to extend sympathy to others who
like himself were victims of the spirit of religious
intolerance which had gone abroad. I select one of
several letters which he wrote about this time to
Mr. Charles Voysey, whose theological views expressed in
sermons had brought him into trouble with ecclesiastical
superiors :—

'WHITBY, *July* 26, [1861].

'I think I told you in one of my former letters that I had
little means of assisting others. But I will certainly do what
I can to help you. I am very glad that you went to Yarmouth
and proved what you could do in parish work. Would it
be possible to stay on till Christmas and so leave with as
little of "a scene" as possible? Supposing that an attempt
were made at any future time to get you a living from the
Bishop of London or the Chancellor, it would go much against
you that you had left a curacy for what they call "heterodoxy."
This is what Sydney Smith would have called "a dreary time
for clergymen of liberal opinions." But I believe that it will
clear and that we shall live to see much truer ideas prevailing of the nature of Christianity.

[1] For Dr. Pusey's views on
the Professoriate and on Crown
appointments, see *Life of E. B.
Pusey*, vol. iii. pp. 382-391, and
his pamphlet on *Collegiate and
Professoriate Teaching*, 1854.

[2] Convocation, not Congregation, because the motion took the
form of a resolution to petition
Parliament.

[3] *With whom lies the responsibility of the approaching Conflict
as to the Greek Chair?* by Pacificus,
Nov. 1861.

'I have sent your two enclosures to Dr. Stanley, and requested him to show them to a friend of his and mine who may have it in his power to assist your views.

'Thank you for your sympathy amid all this noise. I really do not think it has occasioned me any trouble or anxiety.'

In October, 1861, Stanley again brought the matter forward in Council, and carried there a form of Statute for endowing the Greek Chair, which was accordingly submitted to Congregation[1]. The vote took place on November 26, 1861, and the measure was rejected by a majority of three (99 to 96). The majority in this case was only partly moved by theological prepossessions. Academical prejudice also had its share, and Pusey's contention that Crown appointments were dangerous—because the ecclesiastical authorities were no longer consulted, as formerly (see next page)—found an echo amongst those who thought that, on the ground of scholarship, a University Board would have made a better choice. They demurred to subsidizing the nominee of the Crown. The measure had been promulgated in a previous meeting, November 20, 1861. The discussion as reported in the *Oxford Chronicle* for November 23, 1861, contained some points which should not be passed over. One speaker said 'he did not see that the present Professor had any claim on account of his labours, which were purely voluntary.'

Mr. Osborne Gordon, Student and Censor of Christ Church, said, 'The proper quarter from which to obtain the endowment was Christ Church, which had accepted an estate from the Crown chargeable with the stipend, and had actually proposed in 1854 to endow the Professorship.'

---

[1] The Hebdomadal Council (see p. 183) had the sole initiative in University Legislation. Measures passed in Council were afterwards submitted (1) to Congregation and (2) to Convocation.

The former fact was flatly denied by Professor Pusey, who said 'that Christ Church had received no estate, but only the burden of making the payment. . . . Crown nominations were likely to be made on political grounds. Formerly such nominations were good, because the highest ecclesiastical advice was taken, but this practice had been discontinued [1]. He must oppose the endowment of the present holder on theological grounds: . . . in his opinion the second edition of the work [2] was worse than the first.' Professor Mountague Bernard disliked Jowett's theology, but 'did not think it advisable to discountenance unsound theology by means of bad morality.'

It was after this adverse vote in Congregation, which effectually stopped further proceedings for the time, that some of Jowett's private friends without his knowledge subscribed £2000, which sum was presented to him through Mr. Lingen.

He replied as follows:—

BALLIOL COLLEGE, OXFORD,
January 24, 1862.

MY DEAR LINGEN,

I hardly know how to express the feeling with which I received through you the information that the sum of £2000 had been placed at my disposal in payment of the salary of the Regius Professor of Greek, which has hitherto been withheld.

It is the greatest pleasure to obtain from my friends such a testimony of their regard. I will try to show my gratitude in the only way that I am able, by increasing energy in the work of the Professorship.

But I cannot accept their munificent present. Though I wish to see an endowment provided for the Chair, I ought not to receive money from those on whom I have no claim.

[1] The Dean of Christ Church *had* been consulted in the present case by Lord Palmerston. See p. 237.
[2] *The Epistles of St. Paul, &c.*

Could I have anticipated such generosity, I would never have allowed you and others to take so much trouble on my behalf.

Will you give my best thanks to the subscribers, and assure them that the possession of the list of their names gives me a satisfaction far greater than the pecuniary advantage which they designed for me?

In a private letter to a friend abroad, he wrote as follows on February 2 :—

'You saw in the Italian papers about the poor *indotato* Professor. What do you think has happened to him since? His friends collected a subscription of £2000 to pay his salary for the last five years: (Earl Russell, Lord Lansdowne, and various old Whigs and lovers of religious liberty were among the subscribers). It is a great pity that though he loves money, which he believes to be the source of every good, he could not make up his mind to accept it. . . . It does not do, and is not consistent with the dignity of a human being, to have received about £20 from everybody you meet at dinner. Yet he is very sensible that it is a great thing to have such friends. . . .'

Strangely enough, at this juncture Stanley seems to have imagined the possibility of Jowett's preferment to the Deanery of Exeter. Jowett refuses to believe it (unless indeed some pious Minister wished to remove his influence from Oxford), but adds that while he would not be sorry if it were offered (on public grounds), he is clear that it would be wrong to accept it, and that he ought to continue there the educational work in which he and Stanley were jointly engaged.

The troubles of this period were aggravated by his relation to his colleagues in Balliol, which, as he wrote to Palgrave in 1861, sometimes affected him more than any public attacks. His attitude in withdrawing from Hall and Common Room had no doubt tended to make the position there more strained, and though he had the support of a minority, chiefly amongst the junior Fellows, these men had not yet that experience of life and of the world which would have enabled them to enter into all his anxieties. They were sometimes neutral where he felt most need of help, and his obstinate silence on all personal matters prevented them from understanding the effect of this. In the summer of 1862, a permissive ordinance of the Commissioners for relaxing the marriage restriction in the case of a Professorial Fellow gave rise to a practical question, which was settled in favour of another Fellow of the College; and a motion of Jowett's for abolishing the restriction altogether and making Fellowships terminable except for College officials, was referred to a Committee which did not report. Whether or not Jowett would have availed himself of the privilege, had it been granted, must be left in doubt, but it is certain that he felt himself aggrieved. 'My College want to get rid of me, which is rather hard[1],' he wrote to an intimate friend at the time, and expressed himself on the subject with considerable bitterness to two others severally, of whom the late Professor Nichol was one. It is also true that when the salary of the Greek Chair was augmented in 1865, he observed to more than one friend that the benefit had come too late to be of importance to him personally, though it might have been so a few years before[2]. It has been already seen, on two previous occasions, that where Jowett was thwarted he renewed his energies. And the result of this and of other crosses in his relation to the College

---

[1] A piece of gossip repeated by Matthew Arnold in a letter of Nov. 19, 1862, probably reflects this feeling: 'There is a move to turn the latter (Jowett) out of his Fellowship for his heresies' (*Letters of Matthew Arnold*, vol. i. p. 175).

[2] See *Autobiography of Frances Power Cobbe*, vol. i. p. 353.

was that he threw himself with ever-increasing perti-
nacity into the educational work to which his life was
now irrevocably devoted. Even his younger colleagues,
however, after this perceived that he was more reserved
in his dealings with them than formerly. They were
aware of a coolness which they could not account for.

There is an entry in one of the latest of his note-books,
where in counting up the blessings of his life he says,
'There is one happiness which I have never had'; and
some years earlier, in 1880, 'The great want of life can
never be supplied, and I must do without it.' The
reasons for this are expressed in his letter to Dean Stanley
of March 10, 1865[1].

Whatever he may have thought and felt in his own case,
he was strangely persistent in advising more than one of
his friends to marry—'It is not good for man to be
alone'; 'It won't do to live without a companion[2].' And
in congratulating another friend he wrote: 'There is
nothing better under the sun than to be happily married.'

But if he ever felt a void in his life, he had rich
compensation in his many warm friendships, and in the
College which, as he said long afterwards, was to him
in the place of a family :—'I mean it seriously,' he added
after a pause. He rejoiced in the happiness of other
married lives, and the ideal light in which he had viewed
such relationships in the days of his youth never really
left him, though he talked sometimes with playful irony
about the actual state of things and persons in the world.

Prosecution in the Chancellor's Court.

Professor Jowett's opponents had been often encountered
with the taunt: 'You should not treat as a heretic one

---

[1] See p. 374.   [2] This is from a letter dated July 9, 1893.

who has not been condemned in any court.' They waited until the Dean of the Arches had pronounced judgement in the cases of Dr. Williams and Mr. Wilson. This he did in effect on June 25, 1862, although the sentence of suspension was not pronounced until September 12. Then Dr. Phillimore, the Queen's Advocate, was consulted (1) Whether Professor Jowett, in his Essay and Commentary, had so distinctly contravened the doctrines of the Church of England that a court of law would pronounce him guilty; and (2) as to the legal position of Professor Jowett.

The answers of counsel were to the effect (1) that Professor Jowett's Essay on the Atonement contradicts the Articles, while the Essay on Interpretation is at variance with the doctrine of the Church of England concerning inspiration '*according to the recent judgement of the Dean of the Arches,*' and also that it contradicts the eighth Article, concerning the Three Creeds: (2) That while the provisions of the Clergy Discipline Act could hardly be construed so as to affect proceedings against a Professor, the Vice-Chancellor would notwithstanding be bound to admit articles containing charges of heresy against any Professor resident in the University, and might be compelled by *mandamus* to hear and try such a charge.

Professor Baden Powell, 'after denying Miracles,' had, in the pious language of the Preface to the 'Case and Opinion,' been 'removed before a higher Tribunal'; and the Professor of Greek was therefore singled out as the object of the proceedings which followed [1].

---

[1] Of the remaining members of the seven, Mr. Goodwin had resigned his Fellowship at Christ's College, Cambridge, while still a layman; Mr. Pattison held a small living, which, however, as 'donative,' was not subject to episcopal institution; and Dr.

This new move made no difference in Jowett's outward bearing, but the first intimation of it caused him real anxiety both for himself and for the cause he had at heart. He wrote to Stanley:—

'February 3, 1863.

'I hear that this monition¹ is to be issued at the V.-C. Court next week. This seems to take for granted that the V.-C. will act. Will you consider the matter, and, if an opportunity offers, talk the matter over with Bowen (33 Alfred Place, Thurlow Square)? Pattison counsels submission. But submission appears to imply that the limits of the Church of England in the University are acknowledged to be narrowed, and gives up all the legal difficulties.

'Will you get two copies of the Church Discipline Act? Do you think I should put the matter in the hands of Stephen? Will you call on Murray and warn him not to

Temple as Head Master of Rugby and Queen's Chaplain was subject to other than ecclesiastical or academical discipline.

¹ The monition (a copy of which seems to have been enclosed in the above letter) purported to be issued by the Chancellor to the Yeoman Bedell of Law in the University, commanding him to cite the Rev. Benjamin Jowett, &c., 'to appear before our Vice-Chancellor or his Assessor . . . to answer to certain articles to be administered and objected to him by virtue of our office concerning the reformation and correction of his manners and excesses, but more especially for infringing the Statutes and privileges of the University by having published . . . a certain book entitled *The Epistles of St. Paul,*

&c., &c.: also in a book called *Essays and Reviews* a certain article . . . entitled "On the Interpretation of Scripture"; and by having in such book and such article . . . advisedly promulgated . . . certain erroneous and strange doctrines . . . contrary to and inconsistent with the doctrines of the Church of England....

Prayer.

'On legal proof being made of the charges, the said Professor Jowett be duly corrected and punished according to the gravity of the offence and the exigency of the Law and Statutes of the University.' The original document is in the possession of Mr. H. A. Pottinger, of Worcester College.

give any assistance in proving the publication ?—he cannot be compelled.

'I am sorry to give you trouble. But I need the help of friends and feel the value of such a friend as you. I must get you, when you return, to stir up the Dean and Jackson [1] and everybody to help. It is the isolation in which they have left me which makes the attack possible.

'I never had a better class than this Term, or so many men coming to me as pupils, I think.

'PS. Can A. C. T. be got to do anything in the matter?'

The case was opened in the Chancellor's Court on February 20, 1863, before Mountague Bernard, Esq., B.C.L., as the Vice-Chancellor's Assessor.

Parties were summoned to the Apodyterium (or 'Vestry') of the Convocation House; but the Court actually sat in what was commonly called the 'Cock-pit,' where viva voce examinations used to be held; and the place was of course crowded with undergraduates.

The prosecution relied partly on the Church Discipline Act, but chiefly on the University Statutes respecting Tutors and Professors and the powers of the Vice-Chancellor.

It was urged for the defence 'that the Court has no jurisdiction in the matter.'

Mr. Pottinger, who was Proctor for Professor Jowett, based his protest (1) upon section 23 of the Church Discipline Act of 1840 (3 & 4 Vict. c. 86), which enacted that no prosecution can be brought against a clergyman except according to that Act : (2) on the special privilege of the Regius Professors as holding of the Crown : (3) on the absence of any provision for the jurisdiction of the Court in matters spiritual : (4) on the absence of any precedent for a judgement of the Chancellor's Court in such matters.

[1] Bishop of Lincoln, Visitor of Balliol.

The Assessor refused to admit that the Court had no jurisdiction, but said :—

'If I have jurisdiction in this matter, which is doubtful, it is a jurisdiction which the Statutes do not imperatively bind me to exercise upon this citation . . . I shall reject the protest, but I shall refuse to order Professor Jowett to appear, and shall refuse to admit articles on the part of the promoters. . . . From that refusal the promoters are of course at liberty to appeal.'

Mr. Frederick W. Farrer, of the Messrs. Farrer, Lincoln's Inn Fields, who was professionally present on the occasion, writes: 'In a walk with Jowett afterwards, he was very low at the decision. I remember his saying, "You don't know Pusey; he has the tenacity of a bull-dog."' Jowett wrote to a trusted friend on March 15 :—

'I think I have escaped from my adversaries. Their only way of proceeding now is by an appeal to the Court of Queen's Bench for a *mandamus*. But lawyers seem to think that there is so little chance of their obtaining the *mandamus* that I should doubt whether they will make the attempt.'

The question was not finally determined until the second week of May.

It appears that in their anxiety to follow Dr. Phillimore's first opinion, the three prosecutors overlooked a Statute (Tit. XVII. 18) which required them to appeal, if at all, to the House of Congregation; and they consulted counsel again as to the expediency of applying for a *mandamus*. Under all the circumstances the advice of Dr. Phillimore and Mr. J. D. Coleridge was adverse to their taking that step. And the withdrawal of further proceedings was intimated to the Vice-Chancellor in a letter from C. A. Ogilvie, E. B. Pusey, and C. A. Heurtley, the Prosecutors in the case, dated Christ Church, May 8.

The Vice-Chancellor, Dr. Lightfoot of Exeter, on May 11 sent a copy of the letter to Jowett, who lost no time in forwarding it to his mother.

In March, 1863, on the evident collapse of this vexatious suit, Stanley returned to the charge about the salary, with a motion in Council, which was lost by a narrow majority. Next autumn Dr. Pusey, in his character of Pacificus, again endeavoured at once to obviate the increasing odium against his party, and to satisfy an exacting conscience, by proposing a form of Statute according to which the salary of the Greek Professor was to be made up to £400 from the University Chest, until such time as other provision should be made, *on the understanding that the University shall be held to have pronounced no judgement upon his writings, in so far as they touch the Catholic Faith.* This arrangement had been formerly suggested by Mr. Keble, and was now accepted by Stanley. Jowett himself seems to have hoped that it would succeed. Having passed Congregation by a good majority, it was submitted to Convocation on March 8, 1864. But Dr. Pusey found that it is easier to raise a storm than to allay it. Many of those in the University who had hitherto supported him saw clearly the inconsistency of the measure, and the futility of the reservation; and their appeal to the country M. A.'s proved for once more potent than his own. The stalwart Archdeacon, George Anthony Denison, stood forth manfully as the champion of the opposition, and strongly protested in Latin against the proposed Statute. A curious incident occurred, characteristic of the flurry and excitement which had seized the whole assembly.

The Senior Proctor, W. Chambers of Worcester, proclaimed, 'Majori parti placet.' Liddell ran with the false news to Jowett, who took it very quietly. But the words had barely escaped the Proctor's lips, when he discovered that he had made a mistake, 'not in time, however, to prevent a burst of cheering from the undergraduates and friends of Professor Jowett, which being continued for some few minutes, left the Proctor in a very unpleasant position.' The Vice-Chancellor after some difficulty having restored order, the Proctor announced, 'Majori parti non placet,'—the numbers being: non placet 467, placet 395; majority against, 72. The result was received with loud cheers from the opponents of the Statute, and violent hissing from the undergraduates' gallery.

This Act of Convocation[1] raised an all but unanimous outcry in the public Press, with copious correspondence in the *Times* and other newspapers, the most remarkable feature of which was an encounter between Dr. Pusey and Mr. F. D. Maurice. The wheel of public opinion had come fully round; the two Essayists who were suspended by the Court of Arches had been finally acquitted by the Judgement of the Privy Council, delivered by Lord Westbury on February 8, and it may be noted as an interesting fact, that amongst those who came at great inconvenience to vote in favour of the salary, was Dr. Stephen Lushington, now an aged man—though not so aged as when he voted afterwards for Stanley's appointment as Select Preacher.

At this juncture, Lord Chancellor Westbury initiated a new phase of the struggle by introducing in the House

[1] Jowett to Stanley, March 15, 1864: 'I see nothing to lament in the business of last Tuesday, except the noise and bustle. The move of throwing out the endowment was a false one.'

of Lords a Bill entitled, *An Act for the better endowment of the Regius Professor of Greek in the University of Oxford.* By this it was proposed that the first Canonry or Prebend in the Chancellor's gift which should become vacant after the passing of the Act should be annexed to the Regius Professorship of Greek in the University of Oxford. The Bill was thrown out in Committee on May 14, the previous question, moved by Lord Redesdale, being carried by 55 votes against 25; majority 30. The objections which appeared to have most weight with the Lords were that endowment by a Canonry would preclude the appointment of a layman in the future, and that Canonries were now designed by public opinion for purely ecclesiastical purposes. Lord Westbury's argument[1] that the University had broken faith in not endowing the Chair—so repudiating the obligation involved in the privilege granted to the University Press, and the remission of the Stamp Duties—was two-edged and provoked some opposition. The rejoinder was obvious, that if the onus lay on the University, the University should see to it; and Lord Derby (on May 23), as Chancellor of the University, somewhat feebly denied the existence of any such obligation. It appears from a letter to Stanley that Jowett himself doubted the wisdom of introducing such a measure in Parliament at all.

On October 31, 1864, the Vice-Chancellor, Dr. Lightfoot, started a fresh proposal to make up the salary to £400 out of the University Chest, in a form of Statute which still reserved judgement on the Theological opinions of the Professor. But this motion, although supported by Dr. Pusey, who had now become the defender of the

---

[1] Anticipated by Dr. Stanley and Professor Conington.

Greek Chair against George Anthony Denison, was lost in the Hebdomadal Council by a majority of one [1].

Soon afterwards a wholly new face was put upon the question by Mr. E. A. Freeman [2], then residing at his place of Somerleaze in Somersetshire, who published in pamphlet form a letter of his which had appeared in the *Daily News* [3].

He showed that in a letter addressed by the Dean and Chapter of Christ Church to Viscount Palmerston, which had been printed in the 'Correspondence respecting the proposed measures of improvement in the Universities and Colleges of Oxford and Cambridge, presented to both Houses of Parliament by command of Her Majesty, 1854,' the following statement occurs :—

'If it should be deemed desirable to make any further disposal of the College funds for Academic purposes, the Dean and Chapter would respectfully submit that it is the Regius Professor of Greek who is best entitled to benefit by it. For of the ten original Chairs founded by King Henry VIII, five at Oxford and five at Cambridge, and endowed by that monarch with stipends of £40 per annum, the Greek Chair of Oxford is the only one which never received an additional endowment;—while the Greek Professor at Cambridge, by virtue of a recent Act of Parliament, holds a stall at Ely, his brother Professor at Oxford only receives his original £40 per annum. Unless the Crown should be graciously pleased to make some other provision for the Chair at Oxford,

---

[1] Dr. Stanley was by this time Dean of Westminster, and had therefore no longer a seat in the Council.

[2] Afterwards Professor of History, Oxford.

[3] 'The Oxford Regius Professorship of Greek,' October, 1864. Mr. Freeman's attention had been called to the subject in March, 1858, when a brother Fellow of Trinity, Mr. North Pinder (now a Canon of Windsor and Rector of Greys), wrote to him that 'almost the only subject they' (the Hebdomadal Council) 'can agree about is the best means of starving a Professor with whom they do not happen to concur.'

the **Dean** and Chapter would propose that they should **be** empowered to set apart an estate of the value **of** between **£300** and £400 per annum, **of which the lease** is now running out, and that upon the next avoidance of the Greek Chair, the same estate should be made **over to the new** Professor and **his** successors.'

The **Historian proceeded** to show the reasonableness of this proposal, which he characterized as especially creditable on the part of **a** corporate body, from whom fair dealing **in** such matters was not always to be expected. King Henry's manifest intention had been that the estates of Christ Church should provide for Regius Professors and Canons in the proportion indicated by the original charge on **the estates of £40 a** year and £25 **a year** respectively.

But the Chapter had the right of **administration ; and,** as **Mr.** Freeman with characteristic bluntness adds—

'**Wherever money** stipends have to be paid to officers **of any kind, the story** is always the same . . . there is always some **class** of people receiving **a** less proportion of the corporate **income than the founder** meant them to receive. . . . The old **Bishops who** founded the elder Cathedrals, **more** wise **in** their **generation, guarded against this** evil by giving so **many** officers **separate estates.** But when a Chapter has to pay certain **payments, though after** three centuries it is very plain that **the £40** ought **to be** increased to £400, there is no particular **year in** which **it is plain** that £40 should be increased to £45 or £45 to £50. Had King **Harry, instead of** granting estates to Christ Church, granted them to **the University, the** Professor would now have his proper income.'

The **burden** thus fell on Christ Church (1) of showing why the proposal **made** in 1854 had not been carried out, **and (2)** why it should not **now** be renewed.

On the part of **Christ Church** it was explained (1) **that** '**the** Commissioners had **stated their** opinion that, since five Canonries of Christ Church were now employed in endowing Professorships (including the Margaret Professorship of Divinity), enough had been done out of the funds of the College for the service of the University.' The Commissioners preferred therefore to suppress two Canonries for the better endowment of the studentships as rearranged. 'And (2) that it had not been shown that the Chapter held lands specifically granted for the purpose of paying the Professor.' The Dean added that if this could be shown, he would 'immediately propose to the Chapter to augment the stipend now paid to the Professor according to a fair estimate of the changed value of money[1].'

This promise stimulated the investigations of another historical inquirer, Mr. Charles Elton, formerly of Balliol, then a Fellow of Queen's, who discovered the missing link by tracing the conveyance of certain lands which (1) had been granted by King Henry to the Chapter of Westminster for the support of Professors of Divinity, Hebrew, and Greek, and (2) when that Chapter declined the burden and restored the lands, had again been granted by the King to Christ Church under a corresponding obligation[2], the revenue of these lands (£120) exactly covering the three salaries of £40 each.

The authorities at Christ Church were now fairly brought to bay. But instead of at once carrying out the proposal of the Dean, they consulted counsel as to the existence of a legal obligation. None such was found to exist, because the income of the lands was not by the Instrument of Foundation apportioned in certain proportions against different objects, but given subject

---

[1] Statement by H. G. Liddell, Dean of Christ Church, November 18, 1864.

[2] See Mr. Elton's letter in the *Times* of January 16, 1865.

to the payment of certain specific sums, and because on an appeal of the Students in 1629 the King as Visitor had stated that the improved Revenues of the House wholly and properly belonged to the Dean and Chapter.

Armed with this opinion, and refusing as a body to recognize any moral obligation, the Dean and Chapter notwithstanding on the ground of expediency 'agreed to take such measures as might be necessary for increasing the yearly salary of the Regius Professor of Greek to the sum of £500.' This resolution was intimated by the Dean to the Vice-Chancellor on February 17, 1865 [1].

[1] The Dean declares (May, 1895) that even at the last moment he had great difficulty in bringing the Chapter to agree to this.

CHAPTER XI

(Aet. 43-48)

PERSONAL effects of controversy—Extracts from correspondence—Professorial and Tutorial work—Letters from W. Pater and Professor G. G. Ramsay—'Colonization'—George Rankine Luke—Society at Clifton and in Scotland—Vacation parties—Letters.

THUS ended the ten years of deprivation, by which, not to dwell here upon the personal aspect, the University had not lost, while Balliol had gained; but Christ Church, in all probability, had been a heavy loser. Had she earlier taken thought to provide an adequate endowment for the Greek Chair, she might have enlisted in her service an educational force of hitherto unsuspected potency.

It were long and tedious to repeat the ingenious arguments and more or less brilliant witticisms [1] which the conflict had evoked. In reviewing them, one cannot but be struck with the slight account that was taken of devoted educational work as a service to the University. The opinion expressed in Congregation that Professor Jowett's labours might have earned gratitude from individuals, but the University had nothing to do with that, was one in which the speaker did not by any means

---

[1] That which attracted most attention, 'The Evaluation of Πῖ,' was attributed to 'Lewis Carroll.'

stand alone. It concerns us more to collect some hints of the way in which Jowett himself regarded the whole business. He retained outwardly, all through, his serene, unruffled bearing. J. M. Wilson, Professor of Moral Philosophy, the most staunch of Oxford Liberals, said : 'If Jowett continues to take these things as he is doing, and keeps up the freshness of his interest in high subjects, he will be a great man.' But he was not really apathetic. Amongst many other expedients, it had been suggested that a new Professorship of Greek might be endowed with a Fellowship at Corpus or St. John's, and that Jowett might be appointed to it. I referred to this in walking with him in Christ Church meadow. It was one of the only two occasions on which I have known him shed tears. ' I shall never leave Balliol,' he said.

In order to give some indication of the personal feelings which at the time were hidden from the world, I will here insert some extracts from a series of his familiar letters which now lies before me.

1. *October* 27, 1860. '. . . There is to be another battle at Oxford about the endowment of the Greek Professorship. If anything good happens to me, I will write and tell you. But I do not much expect that they will succeed. For five years I have had only a nominal salary. One of my friends asks whether I don't like the idea of being a Martyr. Indeed I don't ; it is extremely inconvenient.'

2. *January* 22, 1861. 'Do you see the *Quarterly Review?* If you do, you will see no good about me. The book called *Essays and Reviews* has been making an unreasonable stir among the intolerant world. I am astonished at the carelessness about truth which there is in the Church of England. If it goes on, it will lead to utter unbelief among intellectual men. I mean to be quiet, and take no notice of attacks. I used to be grieved to find how readily my friends chimed in with the attack (though in private they agreed with me)— I suppose on the principle that there is something in the

misfortunes of one's best friends not wholly unpleasing. But after the first bite or sting, the power of feeling is almost lost : it is worth while to be attacked for the sake of being free from attacks for the rest of your life.'

3. *February* 8, 1861. (To Dean Elliot.) 'A new attempt is to be made to endow the Greek Professorship with £400 a year, which the University is to consent to give at the instigation of Dr. Pusey, on the condition of the Crown handing over the Patronage to a Board consisting of three Cabinet Ministers and the Chancellor and Vice-Chancellor of the University. Having been appointed by the Crown, I cannot say that I like the Crown giving up the nomination to an important position, and wrote to say so, that the Government might know the exact state of the case ; but having been hard-worked and starved for five years, I feel that it would be quixotic in me to oppose what the Government sees no objection to.—I think however the measure, though agreed to by the Government and the Council, is very likely to come to grief in the House of Commons[1].'

4. *March* 22, 1861. (To Mrs. Tennyson.) 'I cannot but express to you what I feel, especially in all this tumult, that it is the greatest blessing and good to me to have friends like you and Mr. Tennyson, who are so true and affectionate to me.'

5. *March* 22, 1861. (To F. T. Palgrave.) 'Many thanks to you for caring whether I am troubled about the "persecution." I think I am not deceiving myself in saying that I don't mind about it. Annoyances in College, which I sometimes receive, trouble me more.'

6. *April* 1, 1861. (To Dean Elliot.) 'I feel a great and in-creasing responsibility about this Spirit which has come (not at our call) from the vasty deep. But I have had, thank God, no pain or annoyance from the attacks on me, though the clergyman of this parish (Freshwater) does call me and others "Judas Iscariot" in his sermons.'

7. *April* 1, 1861. 'No one ever stood by a friend better than Dr. Stanley has stood by me in this tumult. While he lives

---

[1] p. 303. It was thrown out in Convocation—as Dr. Pusey averred, through some 'Liberals' having joined the Opposition.

I shall certainly not be ashamed when I speak with my enemies in the gate.'

8. *April* 16, 1861. 'I think the "tumult" has dwindled to a calm, and therefore I shall say no more about it. I can only hope that some good may spring out of all this notoriety (you should see the letter of the Bishops and the names of those whom it condemns printed on an enormous placard which was sent me the other day), and I am very grateful to friends who show me sympathy in all this row. . . .

'Attacks on the Utilitarians have their place and their use : only they were not meant for people who "revel in Scepticism¹" like me. Is it not very Irish of them to say so?'

9. *April* 27, 1861. (To Sir A. Grant.) 'I cannot tell you what good and pleasure I have in Stanley's active help and support.'

10. *May* 9, 1861. (To Stanley.) 'I won't trouble you with reflections about the event of Tuesday². I am glad that Pusey behaved well. . . . I should not altogether despair of his mind, having exhausted itself with religious experiences, taking a healthier tone.

'I hope I shall live to see a better state of feeling in Oxford, in which those who hold liberal opinions in religion or in University matters will not have the troubles that I have had.'

11. *August* 4, 1861. 'It was very good of you to tell me the kind things Mrs. Somerville said of me. Of course I don't deserve them, but I have a sort of hope that I may deserve such fine things to be said some day, if I devote myself to the truth and to the good of my pupils. Mr. Carlyle says "men put there as sentinels should be shot instantly"; so I must balance Mrs. Somerville with him.'

12. *November*, 1861. (To Miss Cobbe.) 'The vote of last Tuesday, deferring indefinitely the endowment of my Professorship, makes me feel that life is becoming a serious business to me ; not that I complain ; the amount of sympathy and support which I have received has been enough to sustain any one, if they needed it. . . . But

---

¹ *Saturday Review*, March 9, 1861, on 'Intolerance at Oxford': 'Mr. Jowett's genius is one which seems almost to revel in uncertainty and doubt.'

² p. 304.

my friends are sanguine in imagining they will succeed hereafter. Next year it is true that they will get a small majority in Congregation. This however is of no use, as the other party will always bring up the country clergy in Convocation. I have therefore requested Dr. Stanley to take no further steps in the Council on the subject ; it seems to me undignified to keep the University squabbling about my income [1].'

13. 1862. (To Stanley.) 'As to "complicity" with Baden Powell or Wilson, I do not wish to be separated from them or any other professing Christian man who cares for truth. I think this is right in the long run, though it leads to immediate misrepresentation.

'I have no personal feeling about —— any more than about —— [2] (not from Christian charity or magnanimity), but because it seems to me absurd to allow personal feelings to come into public questions.'

14. *July* 19. 1862. (To Stanley.) 'I think I had an average of between fifty and sixty at the lecture on Thucydides last Term, more at first and fewer at last : and about forty brought me exercises in Greek and English.

'It gives me pleasure to see that I am in a better position now than I was a year ago at Oxford. And I cannot feel or express too often to you and to every one, how much I owe it to your courage and generosity.

'May I not be wanting to myself.'

15. *February*, 1863. (To Mrs. Tennyson.) 'Thank God, I fight my enemies with a cheerful heart [3]. On Friday at Oxford we object to the jurisdiction of the Court, which is trying to smuggle in an ecclesiastical cause under colour of a breach of the Statutes of the University. If the Assessor refuses to hear the cause, all will be at an end ; if not, I am advised to apply to the Court of Queen's Bench for an inhibition of their proceeding. Will you give my best love to Alfred and the children ? I certainly believe that no harm will come of the matter.'

16. *March*, 1863. (To Mrs. Tennyson.) 'I think I am in

[1] This letter has been published in the *Autobiography of Frances Power Cobbe*, vol. i. p. 353.
[2] The writers in the *Saturday Review* and the *Westminster*.
[3] See pp. 311-314.

a better plight than when I wrote to you last; and have only now to fear the appeal to the Queen's Bench, which is not very likely to succeed. . . . I cannot but be greatly pleased and inspirited at the support my old friends have given me in the matter of this stupid prosecution.'

17. *December* 21, 1863. (To Mrs. Tennyson.) 'I mean to do a great deal more mischief now that they are going to give me some money[1].'

18. *December* 25, 1863. (To his mother.) 'You and Emily will be glad to hear . . . that there is a prospect of their paying me my income, with a chance of the arrears[2] hereafter. . . . I thought you would like to hear of this on your birthday, and therefore write.'

19. *March* 12, 1864. (To Mrs. Tennyson.) 'I am truly sorry that so kind a friend as you are should be disappointed. I believe the Judgement[3] was the cause of the result; if so, there is ample compensation.'

20. *July* 12, 1864. (To Sir A. Grant.) 'As for myself, I get on well except as to personal interests; and those, I really feel, are lost in higher ones. I have in the thought of my old pupils in India and elsewhere a great deal to make me happy.'

21. *February* 19, 1865. 'This is the last you will ever hear of this matter. I am greatly indebted to some of my young friends, who without my knowledge hunted this matter out and assailed the Dean and Chapter in the newspapers.'

22. *February* 27, 1865. 'I wish to thank you for your kind letter of congratulations which gave me great pleasure. I am glad that the world will cease to hear any longer about the Greek Professorship. As to being a Martyr, I am afraid that is impossible, unless you are bodily burned in the flesh; and no pious old woman can be found, "in holy simplicity," to pile faggots nowadays, though they are not indisposed to practise lesser modes of annoyance. Speaking quite seriously, I am sure that I place the support and sympathy that I have received far above the money, and therefore I consider I have

[1] p. 314.

[2] This was never realized: unless the grant of £500 in place of £400 was meant to cover the arrears.

[3] Lord Westbury's, February 8, 1864. See p. 315.

been a gainer on the whole. I am delighted that my friends are so pleased, and the money will really enable me to do work more efficiently than before.'

The best proof of his 'happy nature[1]' and firm will is the unimpeded energy with which he had been throwing himself all this while into his educational and literary labours. These went on precisely as before, only with increased assiduity. as if nothing particular were happening in the world outside.

The work both of his Tutorship and his Professorship became more and more interesting to him. Among his pupils at Balliol during these years were men of marked ability, and also men whose position in life, combined as it was with intellectual promise, made their education of exceptional importance to themselves and others. Amongst these were Lord Duncan[2], Lord Boringdon[3], Lord Kerry[4], and others whom it is superfluous to name. Jowett felt to the full the responsibilities involved in this. Already men accused him of flattering the great. Attentive readers of the letters in these volumes will perceive the hollowness of the imputation.

But they will also perceive the obligations which he laid upon himself, or which he conceived the whole position to involve. 'If I had not hampered myself with these ties,' he once said to me, 'I should be all over Europe, collating MSS.' And in writing to another friend, excusing himself from foreign travel: 'If I had gone abroad, —— would have done nothing, at the most critical moment of his life.'

In other ways also these were brilliant years for Balliol. *Atalanta in Calydon* was written about this time, and for many years to come Balliol was never without its

---

[1] p. 262.
[2] Earl of Camperdown.
[3] Earl of Morley.
[4] The Marquis of Lansdowne.

poet (or poets rather). Not that as a rule Jowett's influence lay in that direction. In speaking of some one
who had been doing well in a profession, he would say:
'At College he took to poetry and that sort of nonsense.'
But he rejoiced in any real success; and although the
genius of Swinburne, the ever-active brain of J. A.
Symonds, and the vigorous individuality of John Nichol
were largely independent of his teaching, they yet owed
to him what was more valuable still, the blessing of
a friendship which never wavered, which gave unstinted
help at critical moments both in youth and after life,
and would make any sacrifice of leisure and of ease
to serve them. In former days he had said, on its being
suggested that a poet might come forth from Balliol, 'If
a poet came here, we could never hold him.'

A few words may be added parenthetically on his
supposed worship of genius and of success. The former
imputation was more rife in earlier years, the latter
afterwards, when his own position was now assured.
Both really turned on one peculiarity: that in judging
of persons and in determining his relation to them,
he never separated their individual characteristics from
the thought of what they might effect. This was equally
his way of regarding his own life and the lives of
others. But neither in his choice of friends, nor in his
treatment of those with whom he had to do, can it be
truly said that he was ever influenced by any sordid or
self-regarding motive. If he sometimes argued as if men
of genius should not be judged according to common
rules, or that allowance should be made for irregularities
which seem inseparable from an exalted station, his
estimate of the worthiest aims and his ideal of character
and conduct remained unaltered. Nor is it a wholly
insignificant circumstance that he knew from experience

what consequences may ensue from an ineffectual, albeit blameless life.

In College meetings he still contended for the objects which he thought desirable, supported by an increasing minority, to which the powerful aid of the Hon. E. Lyulph Stanley was added in 1863.

The Professorial lectures continued as before, chiefly in connexion with his work on Plato. A pleasing testimony to his labours as Greek Professor in 1860–62 was given me by the late Mr. Walter Pater, in a letter which has since acquired a pathetic interest through the writer's too early death :—

B.N.C., *May* 6, 1894.

My dear Campbell,

You have asked me to write a few lines 'describing the impression Jowett made on out-College, i. e. non-Balliol men,' when he taught the University for nothing. Like many others I received much kindness and help from him when I was reading for my degree (1860 to 1862) and afterwards. A large number of his hours in every week of Term-time must have been spent in the private teaching of undergraduates, not of his own College, over and above his lectures, which of course were open to all. They found him a very encouraging but really critical judge of their work—essays, and the like,—listening from 7.30–10.30 to a pupil, or a pair of pupils, for half an hour in turn. Of course many availed themselves of the, I believe, unprecedented offer to receive exercises in Greek or English in this way, and on the part of one whose fame among the youth, though he was then something of a recluse, was already established. Such fame rested on his great originality as a writer and thinker. He seemed to have taken the measure not merely of all opinions, but of all possible ones, and to have put the last refinements on literary expression. The charm of that was enhanced by a certain mystery about his own philosophic and other opinions. You know at that time his writings were thought by some to be obscure. These impressions of him had been

derived from his Essays on St. Paul's Epistles, which at that
time were much read and pondered by the more intellectual
sort of undergraduates. When he lectured on Plato, it was
a fascinating thing to see those qualities as if in the act of
creation, his lectures being informal, unwritten, and seemingly
unpremeditated, but with many a long-remembered gem of
expression, or delightfully novel idea, which seemed to be
lying in wait whenever, at a loss for a moment in his somewhat hesitating discourse, he opened a book of loose notes.
They passed very soon into other note-books all over the
University; the larger part, but I think not all of them, into
his published introductions to the *Dialogues.* Ever since
I heard it, I have been longing to read a very dainty dialogue
on language, which formed one of his lectures, a sort of 'New
Cratylus.' Excuse the length to which my 'brief' remarks
have run. On this closely-written sheet there is only room
to sign myself

Very sincerely yours,
WALTER PATER.

Professor G. G. Ramsay, of Glasgow, with reference
to the same period, after a similar description of the
evenings in Jowett's study, adds :—

'An acquaintance was thus begun which was of interest
and value to us throughout our lives. His criticisms were
kindly and encouraging; but it was a severe ordeal to have
to listen to them, especially in the presence of others. You
did not feel exactly that you could resent anything that he
said: and he took you at your word when you replied "Certainly not" to his not unusual query, "You don't mind my
saying what I think about this essay?" When the criticism
came, it was often pretty cutting, always curt, simple and
fundamental; his eyes twinkled with satisfaction when you
made a point in which you agreed with him . . . not less
when he made some point himself in which he felt he could
carry you along with him. But he never struck undeservedly,
never harshly, unless he detected a flavour of impudence: he
never seemed to wound you, but only to put into your hands

a weapon for discovering that you were a fool. To most men the discovery was invaluable, and constituted the great intellectual effect of his criticisms. Some few were sceptical and resentful, and these usually would not return.'

The 'colonization' of other Colleges by Balliol men had begun to make itself distinctly felt ; and Jowett watched with keen interest the growing influence of some of his pupils, especially of Mr. George Rankine Luke, who had gained a senior Studentship at Christ Church in 1860, and held a Tutorship there until his lamented death on March 3, 1862. He was the son of an Edinburgh tradesman, and, after a distinguished career at the Edinburgh Academy [1] and Glasgow University, had come to Balliol with a Snell Exhibition in 1855. After obtaining a senior Studentship at Christ Church, he devoted himself to his Tutorial labours there with the most enthusiastic energy and extraordinary success. When told that Luke was killing himself with work, Jowett said, with a kind of fatherly pride, 'Young men don't die so easily.' Young Luke became subject to fits of giddiness, however, and was upset in his skiff upon the river. When the body was brought home, his friend Nichol, wild with grief, went straight to Jowett's rooms. With eager promptitude and resolute calmness, Jowett set himself at once to prepare an obituary notice of his friend, which appeared in the *Times* next day. Some passages in this are so expressive of his own habitual thoughts that they are inserted here :—

'During the last two years he had been quietly growing in reputation, and was exercising a great and beneficent influence in the University by devoted and unremitting attention to

---

[1] I was present once at an examination of the Academy where Luke was examined vivâ voce by A. C. Tait, then Dean of Carlisle.—L. C.

his pupils. The secret of this influence, which was exerted over his contemporaries as well as his pupils, lay in the uncommon energy and intensity of his character, which blended with a singular affectionateness. . . . Though instinctively a lover of truth, he was never led from his practical duties by vague speculation. The supposed theological difficulties of Oxford passed through his mind, but certainly left no hurtful impression on his strong and innocent nature. A few days ago he had said to a friend that he was not afraid to die at any moment. Nor was such a feeling, combined with such a life, in any degree a presumptuous one. . . . He understood perfectly the secret of success as a College Tutor. The secret is chiefly devotion to the work, and consideration for the characters of young men. No young man is really hostile to one who is labouring, evening as well as morning, wholly for his good—who troubles him only about the weightier matters—who knows how to sympathize with his better mind—who can venture to associate with him without formality or restraint. To men like Mr. Luke, the difficulties of maintaining authority in a College absolutely disappear. The feelings with which the young are capable of regarding such a man, and the true estimate they form of him, are indeed surprising. . . . No one would do more for a friend or think less about it.

'His work is left unfinished, and has to be continued by others. Those who come after him will find that their only chance of raising the great aristocratic seminary with which he was connected to its rightful position in public estimation is the performance of services like his, with the same untiring energy, the same regardlessness of self. In the fulfilment of such a duty to the University and to the nation, the lives of many good or even great men will not be spent in vain.'

The grief for Luke's death was shared by Stanley, who had witnessed his success at Christ Church. He made an affecting reference to him in the sermon on 'Great Opportunities' with which he bade farewell to Christ Church and to Oxford on November 29, 1863. This is mentioned in a letter from Caird[1] to Nichol, which reflects the feeling of the younger graduates at this time :—

'How I wish you had been up to hear Stanley's noble sermon on Sunday last, with its picture of Oxford as it is and as it might be, and above all to hear his eloquent tribute to our dear friend. . . . The University turned out to hear it better than I have ever seen them do before. I said to Jowett after, " Who will sing us battle-songs any more ? " " We must carry on the fight though," said he, looking as pertinacious and as saintly-wicked as usual.'

Jowett was eager to complete his edition of the *Republic,* 'to get rid of Plato and return to Theology,' and he actually took leave of absence for the Summer Term of 1861, with this object in view. But his literary work was being more and more crowded into vacation-time. In Term-time he could only direct his reading with a view to it, and to the preparation of his lectures. For the sake of Plato, and of a select number of his pupils, including some old friends, he resided for long spells in summer at some country place—chiefly during these years at Whitby (1861), Braemar (1862), High Force in Teesdale (1863), Askrigg in Wensleydale (1864)[2], Pitlochry, and Tummel Bridge. The Plato, which he had hoped to finish in a year or two, still remained on hand, throwing the projected works on Theology more and more into the background. In revising the notes to the *Republic,* it had occurred to him that a complete analysis of the *Dialogues* would form a suitable 'Prolegomena' to his book. The analysis, as he conceived it, was to be a sort of condensed translation, in which nothing essential should be omitted, and even the force of connecting

---

[1] Now Master of Balliol.

[2] 'Askrigg was recommended to me by an old fellow named Walter White.' From a letter of 1883. White was the author of *A Month in Yorkshire,* &c.

particles should be preserved. All was to be in perfect English, and the labour spent on such a work was naturally great. When I was with him at Askrigg, in the summer of 1864, he was struggling with the analysis of the *Parmenides* and the other dialectical dialogues. His taste in language was becoming more and more fastidious. At this time he was resolved to turn every sentence so as to exclude the colourless pronoun '*it.*' I troubled him with the remark that '*which*' was not much better, and one or other was inevitable. After this he became more tolerant of '*it,*' but still objected to it, except in the impersonal verb. Finding the commentary sometimes tedious, he used to say, 'I am longing to get at the more general treatment of the subject.'

While speaking of our Yorkshire sojourn, it may be worth while to trace the course of a day. Breakfast was not very early, and was apt to be unpunctual, partly because Jowett would take a pupil or a friend, Lord Kerry, Lord Boringdon, or Lord Duncan, for a walk and talk. Conversation after breakfast lasted some time, and it was well after ten before we settled to work. But the work continued with hardly any intermission till dinner-time, four o'clock. This also was apt to be a movable feast, as Jowett disliked stopping in the middle of a piece of writing, and sometimes had letters to finish. About six we started for a two hours' walk, returning to tea at eight, and work was resumed before nine and continued till midnight. Jowett wrote his letters at odd times, mostly, I suspect, after the day's task was done. Four pages of fresh writing and rather more of revision were his *quantum* for the day. In working with him, one was astonished at the number of ways which occurred to him for turning a particular phrase.

If, holding firmly by the Greek, I objected to an expression, another was produced, and then another and another,
until Greek and English appeared to coincide.   But
perhaps the one last hit upon would be afterwards discarded, as not harmonizing with the rhythm or colour
of the whole.   This protracted labour was almost finished,
when a casual remark of Pattison's (I think) convinced
him that the analysis could never be complete, and that
the *Republic*, at all events, must be translated in full.
As he proceeded with this in 1865, he formed the resolution of translating the whole of Plato.

But to return.   On Sundays the work was so far laid
aside as to secure attendance at morning church, and
a longer walk in the afternoon.   Lord Camperdown (then
Lord Duncan), who was with him at Braemar in 1862[1],
tells how one Sunday there was spent.   Jowett decided
to climb Loch-na-gar, and fixed on Sunday for the
expedition.   Lord Duncan expected to start early, but
Jowett insisted on going to the Kirk.   No guide being
found available on the Sabbath, they had to make their
own way, and the shades of evening were falling ere
they had descended far from the summit.   Jowett got
very tired with stumbling in and out of the peat hags,
and his companion had to support him, while feeling
apprehensive that they had lost the path.   He would
only take one sip from the spirit-flask.

At this point they heard the floundering of an animal,
which for a moment they supposed to be a deer, but
Lord Duncan went up to it and discovered that it was
a pony with the saddle turned right round.   He put the
saddle straight, but Jowett would not mount.   However,
the pony, kept moving by Lord Duncan, led them

[1] His other companion there was Mr. G. W. Kekewich, afterwards of the Education Office.

to the keeper's lodge at Callater. There, the ground being smoother, Jowett consented to mount, and they got back safely. The fact was that J. M. Wilson, of Corpus, who was at Braemar at the time, had heard of the projected expedition and had expressed himself rather doubtfully as to its success. He had started to follow them on the pony, but had given up the chase and, leaving the creature to its fate, had descended on foot. There was a good deal of talk about this escapade, for they had disturbed a great herd of deer at the summit, and the sportsmen, whose Sunday occupation was to watch the deer, had their spy-glasses directed that way.

The following letter from R. A. H. Mitchell, Assistant Master at Eton, April 15, 1894, contains some further reminiscences of Jowett's manner of spending the vacations in these years:—

'Nearly thirty years have now passed since I journeyed to Yorkshire to join the Master at a little country inn in the village of Askrigg, some twelve miles' drive from the station at Leyburn. I found there, besides the Master himself, the present Lord Lansdowne, who was about my own standing, Lord Camperdown, who had I think taken his degree, and Purves, who was, I believe, helping the Master with his work. . . . Our method of living did not altogether commend itself to the hungry undergraduate, for we had only two regular meals in the day, breakfast nominally at nine, dinner at four. I don't think the Master ever supplemented these meals, though we did, as you will not be slow to understand. The Master never thought anything about his food, and was content with the simplest diet. At that time his whole thought seemed to be engrossed in his Plato, and he was not so ready to talk as he was in his later years. He worked entirely in his own room. I have never seen him at work, but he used to begin immediately after breakfast and work on till dinner at four o'clock. He then went for a walk, and on coming in retired again and worked, I believe, till about twelve o'clock. He was not an early riser, seldom appearing before ten, but he would not allow breakfast to be ordered later than nine—not altogether a comfortable arrangement. When we subsequently moved off together to Pitlochry he proposed that any one who was five minutes late for breakfast should be fined the sum of one shilling. The first morning he appeared quite punctually, the second he was a little late, the next he said that, as he was late, he thought he would take his shilling's worth. After that, he found that ten o'clock suited him better than nine. However, at the end of the time he insisted on paying a shilling a day to the common expenses.

'His example of hard work and simplicity was of great value to us, and made hard work all the easier at a time when it was very essential for me to be kept to my books. He did not profess or attempt to coach us regularly, but he was anxious that we should ask him questions, and he took great trouble in explaining difficulties and making his answers clear. Knowing that he was working so hard himself, I think we were reluctant to burden him with too many questions, ever ready though he was to help us. What I found most valuable was his sympathy and encouragement; he led one to suppose that one could do well, provided there was hard work, and there can be no doubt that many in life "*possunt quia posse videntur.*" His encouragement caused many to persevere. I do not think that we found it very easy to converse with him: his interests and thoughts were very far removed from those of the ordinary undergraduate, or the small-talk of life; but he had a quiet sympathy for all that with one's pursuits, with a word of warning against spending too much time upon them.

'I was afterwards with him at Pitlochry, and in the following year (1866) at St. Andrews, where we were both the guests of Professor Lewis Campbell[1]. . . .'

---

[1] Mr. Mitchell adds, 'Jowett's interests did not lie, as mine did, in cricket. But I remember he once said that he was coming to see me play in a College match against Christ Church. On that occasion, the only one within my knowledge, he indulged in the evil habit of betting, for he wagered one shilling, I think, with

In 1863 he attended the meeting of the British Association at Newcastle, where he was the guest of Sir W. and Lady Armstrong.

The range of his friendships was still widening. Clifton now becomes an important centre. His widowed cousin, Mrs. Irwin, came thither to reside with her children in Canynge Square. Jowett continued his visits to Dr. Symonds and his son and daughter, at Hill House. They persuaded him, somewhat against the grain, to be photographed, October 7, 1861[1]. He also accepted an invitation to the Deanery of Bristol in 1860.

Before doing so, however, he thought it necessary to show his colours, and presented a copy of his Essay to the Dean. It was kindly received, as appears from a letter of July 29, 1860 :—

(To Dean Elliot.) ' I am glad you do not wholly disapprove of my Essay. I hardly expect any one engaged in practical work to approve of it. But I hope liberal-minded persons may indirectly find some help and service from it, though they may disagree.'

The Dean *was* liberal-minded, and willing to reason temperately with the younger clergyman on the limits of free discussion within the borders of the Church. Dean Elliot's position, as Prolocutor of the Lower House of Convocation, might have been of great importance at this crisis ; but he was compelled to travel for the health of one of his daughters, and on his return circumstances had occurred which induced him to resign.

the late Principal of B.N.C. (Dr. Cradock) that I got forty. A rash bet, but I am glad to say

he did not lose his money.'

[1] *Life of J. A. Symonds,* vol. i. pp. 184-189.

Jowett, with characteristic tenacity, endeavoured to dissuade him from this step; and not less characteristically acquiesced in it when taken, and congratulated his friend on his freedom. He still ventured, however, to remonstrate with him on his entire withdrawal from the proceedings of the Lower House:—'I am sorry to see that you no longer lend the weight of your presence to that disorderly assembly over which you used to preside.'

In 1861 he paid his first visit to Lord and Lady Stanley at Alderley. The friendship which was thus cemented with that family continued through his after life, and led in particular to his acquaintance with Lord and Lady Airlie, which he improved with annual visits to their seat of Cortachy, in Forfarshire. In 1862 he began his frequent visits to Mr. Nightingale, of Embley, Hants, and Lea Hurst in Derbyshire, and also to the Earl of Camperdown.

An annual visit to the Tennysons at Freshwater about Christmas-time became a matter of course, and besides the Christmas visit he often took a lodging near them, at Woodland Cottage, or elsewhere. He writes to Mrs. Tennyson (December, 1862): 'I sometimes think that merely being in the neighbourhood of Alfred keeps me up to a higher standard of what ought to be in writing and thinking.'

In the autumn of 1862 the death of Archbishop Sumner left the See of Canterbury vacant, and in the changes that were sure to follow, it seemed likely that a Bishopric of some kind might be offered to Stanley. Jowett urged him to accept one if offered, whether small or great. 'In some respects a small one is better than a great one, because allowing more leisure and having less routine.' Not that he could desire his friend

to be Archbishop of Dublin : 'an Irish Bishop or Archbishop I could not be, as I should feel always *judico me
cremari* [1].'—By-and-by it appeared likely that Tait might
be called to Lambeth. On this Jowett wrote still more
urgently, giving reasons why Stanley should not refuse
London if offered. The situation changed again when
Longley was translated to Canterbury and Tait was
offered the Archbishopric of York. While Tait hesitated
Jowett wrote once more to Stanley, repeating his advice.
He was equally decided in dissuading him from accepting
a Deanery. Whilst Stanley was at Canterbury, the
Deanery of Westminster had seemed to Jowett a desirable
position for his friend ; but now, in the midst of the
great battle for liberty at Oxford, he would not have him
leave it for any Deanery ; and when Stanley, on returning
from his Italian tour with his sister Mary and Canon
Hugh Pearson, in October, 1863, announced at once his engagement to be married and his acceptance of the Deanery
of Westminster, Jowett, while rejoicing in the former
announcement, regarded the latter as a disastrous step.
To him personally the loss of Stanley's help at Oxford
was in any case a severe blow, and the new position
did not seem to offer any compensating advantage
to the cause of liberal thought. That he did not
immediately recover from the change appears from his
writing in a familiar letter some years afterwards, ' I have
not yet quite forgiven *Anglicanus* for deserting me ' ; but
when he saw the step to be irrevocable he resolutely
made the best of it ; and, besides the opportunity of
preaching at Westminster which came in 1866 and the

---

[1] When the Archbishopric of
Dublin was vacant and Stanley
was talked of for the place Jowett
said, ' I hope he will not take it :
it would *cross* him.' Cf. *Dean
Stanley's Life*, vol. ii. pp. 97–99,
131, 132.

following years, Jowett gained from Stanley's new position an additional foothold in London society, where the Deanery, graced with Lady Augusta's presence, became a rallying-point for all that was most illustrious both in the Church and in the world. It is evident, however, from the letters above referred to, that in dissuading Stanley from accepting Westminster he had no thought of interfering with his friend's preferment; the truth was that he had larger views for him.

In the autumn of 1863 the Sellars went to Edinburgh, where Lancaster was now married, and had young children [1]. Jowett had god-children in both houses, and made friendships with all the young ones, becoming most intimate with those that were the liveliest, and had least of what was called intellectual promise. His own shyness made him relish talkativeness in others. Several of his old Scottish pupils were pushing their fortunes in their own country. I had succeeded Sellar at St. Andrews (1863), where our home became one of his favoured resorts; Nichol, after being rejected for the Logic Chair at St. Andrews, had been appointed to the new Chair of English Literature at Glasgow (1861). Another contest in which he took great interest was that of T. H. Green for the Chair of Moral Philosophy at St. Andrews, vacated by Ferrier's death in 1864. The Rev. Robert Flint, of Kilconquhar, was the rival candidate. The University Court, of whom Professor J. C. Shairp was one, preferred the Scotch minister to the young Oxonian, whose youth and, it must be said also, what was then regarded as the obscurity of his Essay on Aristotle, told against him.

Burdened as he was, there was no trouble which Jowett

[1] See Jowett's Preface to H. H. Lancaster's posthumous volume of *Essays and Reviews.*

would not take for a friend, travelling any distance to
a marriage or a christening, at either of which ceremonies
he was often the officiating minister. He went to
Berlin in 1864, for example, merely to christen Morier's
child. He sought to reconcile his work with travelling,
by reading and writing a great deal in railway trains.
I have seen a pencil analysis of Plato's *Laws*, which
bore evident marks of having been composed in a shaky
carriage.

Jowett never sought for Court favour, and he sometimes
felt that Stanley's real position had been rather weak-
ened by it. But he was genuinely pleased by two
instances of sympathy in high places which reached him
in 1863.

The Tennysons had been at Osborne, and Mrs.
Tennyson had written a letter which Jowett reported to
his mother. Mr. and Mrs. Tennyson had both spoken
of Jowett to the Queen, who said that 'Oxford had
used him shamefully,' on which Tennyson burst forth
again with, 'I am so glad your Majesty appreciates
Mr. Jowett.'

To Mrs. Tennyson Jowett wrote in reply :—

'I am very glad you went to see the Queen. It is a great
recollection for the children to have ; and good for her to see
people who come from the fresh air of the outer world. . . .
Best love and grateful thanks to Alfred.'

Soon afterwards the Crown Princess of Prussia went
incognita to Oxford on purpose to have an interview with
him. This also is recorded in a letter to his mother:
'I never saw a person who pleased me better. She sat
and talked about an hour about Philosophy and matters
of that sort. I thought her quite a genius. . . . This
is partly due to Dr. Stanley, partly to my old friend
Morier, who is a friend of hers.'

LETTERS, 1860–1865.

To Dean Elliot.

[Oxford,] *October* 17, 1860.

I venture to send you a short paper that I have written upon the revision of the Liturgy. I have no intention of publishing it, but think I would like to inflict upon you, and one or two other persons who are acquainted with the subject, the trouble of reading it. Would you kindly return the paper to me when you have looked at it, as I have no copy ; though if you care to keep it, I could easily get one made and send it you ?

You will perhaps consider that I am making for you, *à propos* of nothing, a very laborious amusement.

I hear that you are going to leave England for an indefinite time. I am very sorry indeed that you should be obliged to take such a step, even as a measure of precaution. The Cradocks tell me that they have begged you to come here before your departure for a day or two. Another person will be glad to welcome you also.

. . . You will smile at my Act of Parliament to revise the Liturgy. I merely wanted to show, from beginning to end, by what simple means the suggestion might be effected.

To Miss Elliot.

January 22, 1861.

I read yesterday with **great pleasure** a pamphlet on Destitute Incurables[1] (it appears to be written by some one who bears your name). I thought it extremely well done, very touching and simple, and really practical and businesslike. When you have any scheme of Philanthropy on hand (like Miss Cobbe, I hate Philanthropists), it is a very good rhetorical artifice to pretend to be hard-hearted. If you are a political economist,

---

[1] *Destitute Incurables in Workhouses*: a paper by Miss Elliot and Miss Cobbe, read at the Social Science Meeting in Glasgow, September, 1860. *Autobiography of F. P. Cobbe*, vol. i. pp. 316, 317.

you should appear before the world as a philanthropist; if you are a philanthropist, make people believe that you are a political economist; always appear to be what you are not, and use words to conceal your thoughts. What shocking advice! If you think so, it can be reversed; but is it not partly true notwithstanding?

I, who am really, and not in pretence only, very hard-hearted, read the pamphlet about the poor Incurables, not without some excitement of feeling. It was a very happy and Christian thought of the person who first took up their cause. Perhaps they will be met by a company of incurables at the gate of the celestial city coming to welcome them. For myself, I do little or nothing for the poor, but I have always a very strong feeling that they are not as they ought to be in the richest country that the world has ever known. In theory I have a great love for them, and some day, if I live, hope I may be able to write something about them.

To Dean Elliot, at Cannes.

Balliol College, Oxford,
February 8, 1861.

Dear Mr. Dean,

It is a formidable thing to commence a correspondence uninvited (especially with a dignitary of the Church) when you are secretly conscious that you have nothing worth telling to say. Nevertheless I venture to trouble you with a few lines, lest I should wholly fall out of acquaintance.

I was glad to hear that you have found the experiment of going abroad so completely successful. The columns of the *Times* will show you that this winter has been very ungentle to invalids. Surely the desire of life must be very slight, or the spirit of indolence strong, to make weak chests and throats stay out such a season in England.

As I really feel a difficulty in 'breaking the ice,' I shall hope you will receive all I say—wise, foolish, amusing or otherwise—with the same kindness you showed me at the Deanery last summer. Now I shall imagine myself at home and begin to talk. I should be glad if you would repent of the 'Nolo Episcopari'; but as you refuse, I can only wish you the best of Deaneries and many peaceful days in it. Do you know that Convocation, at the instigation of Dr. Jelf, are going to consider and perhaps censure the book called *Essays and Reviews*? How injurious to Convocation, to what is termed orthodoxy, to every one except the writers of the book and their friends! I am glad you are not likely to be there. I should not wish to draw upon friends (if I may call you so) to drag us out of the ditch. At present the book is a sort of bugbear among the Bishops and Clergy, showing, I venture to think, that some inquiries of the sort were needed, if the evidences of religion are to have anything but a conventional value. In a few years there will be no religion in Oxford among intellectual young men, unless religion is shown to be consistent with criticism.

I wish the Bishops were alive to the great and increasing evil of the want of ability among young clergymen. The two great literary professions of the Bar and the Church seem to be fast degenerating. In the Church I am convinced that one of the principal—I think the greatest—cause is 'Subscription.' To-day I was walking with a grandson of the Bishop of Exeter, who was expressing his strong desire to go into Orders and his inability to do so.

The political horizon seems unusually dark, by which I don't mean that I myself have no chance of obtaining preferment, or that the country is going to ruin, but that 'our friends' the Whigs appear to me unlikely to retain their places and to have by no means a good store of political capital with which to commence opposition. I wonder they have not felt that Reform was needed, not only for the good of the country, but to enable them to retain office; without it the Conservatives gain on them every year, and would have been in office long ago if they had been trusted in their foreign policy. I suppose that Lord Palmerston has cast his spell over the party, and is satisfied if the present strange combination last his time.

I hope you will go to Rome and see the last of the Pope. What is to be the future of the Church of Rome? I suppose we may reckon that it will not die for centuries, but go on in a perpetual state of relaxation and nationalization. The Ultramontane element however, which is said to be so strong among the Clergy (the less the power, the greater the assumption), makes a difficulty : it will neither learn nor unlearn anything. I expect L. Napoleon and Cavour will give it a knock on the head when the time comes. Marrying the Clergy in the present state of Catholic feeling is impossible, perhaps ; but educating them in the light of day and not in Catholic Seminaries is feasible ; and something of this kind we shall perhaps see attempted. Do you ever see the *Revue des Deux Mondes* ? You will be interested with an article of E. Renan's on the subject. . . .

To A. P. STANLEY.

[*February*, 1861,] *Friday*.

I have just written out my letter[1] in fair calligraphic hand (beautiful writing, and the term which you added about the Formularies of the Church of England quite admirable). But I have determined not to send it. My reasons are :—

1. The enclosed letter from Wilson[2], which is very amusing (the description of the old squire is charming). I should do more harm by seeming to detach myself from them, with whom I don't (nevertheless) wholly agree, than any advantage I should gain, if the letter were successful, from a sharp hit at the Bishop of London.

2. I should irritate the Bishop of London, who perhaps has more reason for his conduct than we know (though I cannot conceive of what kind): at any rate he would have to cast about in his mind for a defence, which would end in an attack on me or some one.

3. The contest will be a long one ; I am afraid in my case as long as life ; and there will be other opportunities of showing that I am not cowed by this apparition of the twenty-five Bishops ; in the meantime it is of great importance to speak evil of no one and to irritate no one.

Whether this plan is successful or not, depends partly on

[1] To the Bishop of London, A. C. Tait. See p. 297.
[2] The Rev. H. B. Wilson.

the manner in which it is carried out, and this on health and other matters over which I have no control. When I look at the matter seriously and not comically, as I do sometimes with you and Mrs. Vaughan—who is positively deserting me in my misfortunes, no doubt for good and wise reasons, (when I am burnt in the Churchyard at Doncaster, the Vicar[1] preaching a sermon on the occasion, I expect her to give me breakfast)—I believe the motto should be, 'in quietness and confidence shall be your strength.' Therefore I shall cease to trouble you and Mrs. Stanley[2] any more on the subject.

To F. T. Palgrave.

March 22, 1861.

It is almost too late to answer your first note about the joint authorship of the *Essays*, except to say that Grant's statement goes beyond the truth, which is, that the authors knew one another slightly, for the most part, and took the subjects which suited them, without concert and without seeing one another's writing, except in the case of Wilson, who edited and superintended, but without, as far as I was concerned, making any alteration.

I do not know anything about the address to Temple, unless it be one set on foot by Spottiswoode. My own impression is that addresses are no good, unless they are intended to avert some libel or danger of ejectment, which in Temple's case is not likely.

I hope that you are not taking life too sadly. 'Be cheerful, sir[3].'

To Dean Elliot, at Genoa.

BALLIOL COLLEGE, OXFORD,
April 1, 1861.

You kindly ask whether there is anything which you can do. I believe not (I mean as far as I am concerned). The worse the behaviour of Convocation, the better for those

---

[1] Dr. C. J. Vaughan, now Dean of Llandaff.

[2] Dr. Stanley's mother.

[3] Shakespeare, *Tempest*, iv. 1.

who are attacked by it, though not, perhaps, the better for the Church of England. I made up my mind at the commencement of the clamour that the best course was also the easiest—to do nothing. With my College and University work I have not had time hitherto to write answers, hardly to write letters, if I had had the inclination.

I am sorry that the Clergy are so determinedly set against all the intellectual tendencies of the age. They are trying to pledge the Church of England to the same course in which the Church of Rome has already failed. The real facts and truths of Christianity are quite a sufficient basis for a national Church, but they want to maintain a conventional Christianity into which no one is to inquire, which is always being patched and plastered with evidences and apologies. I wish I could persuade you that it was right to alter the Church of England from within, for I think that it will never be altered from without, unless it is destroyed.

I had not forgotten your words to me at Bristol about freethinkers entering the ministry. But unless you admit some freedom of thought, men of ability will be absolutely excluded, and the Church of England will become more and more the instrument of bigotry and intolerance. Moreover I cannot see that freethinkers about Scripture, &c., who were not contemplated by the Articles, are more nearly touched by them than the High Churchmen who were, or than the Evangelicals are by the Baptismal Service. Though I dislike 'Subscription,' I am inclined to think that if we are all dishonest together that proves us to be all honest together [1].

Do you think of writing anything on the present position of the Church of England—'A letter to Convocation from the Prolocutor of the Lower House'? There will hardly occur such an opportunity again of saying useful truths with equal effect. And yet, perhaps, by the time the letter was ready the tempest may have lulled ; and it seems a kind of profana-

---

[1] An application of W. G. Ward's saying as recorded by Jowett in *W. G. Ward and the Oxford Movement*, p. 438, 'At one time he used to say that in sub- scribing to them (the Articles) we were not all dishonest together, but all honest together.' Cf. the letter to B. C. Brodie of February, 1845 (p. 94).

tion to contaminate the lakes and cities of the North of
Italy with controversy. I hope you will write, however,
some day.

To Miss Elliot.

BALLIOL COLLEGE, OXFORD,
April 1, 1861.

Let me only thank you for your great kindness and consideration in troubling yourself about me in this storm. Such
letters as yours and the Dean's outweigh many times the
attacks of the *Guardian* and *Record*.

The truth is we have nothing to complain of and are in
no danger. It is obvious that any one who runs against the
religious prejudices of the time must expect to be a mark
for attacks. There seems to me to be very little malignity,
except perhaps in the subtle genius of the *Saturday Review*,
who no doubt supposes himself (whoever he is) to be writing
in the most honourable and conscientious spirit. I think
it should be understood that in controversy, as in love, everything is fair. I think people may be allowed to tell lies,
for they really can't help it.

To Dean Elliot, at Florence.

FRESHWATER, *April* 16, 1861.

. . . I think matters are calming down. I am very glad
that you were not in Convocation, as it would have been
impossible to have stemmed the first strength of the torrent,
and it would probably have been a waste of power to have
attempted it.

Looking at the subject (not with reference to our personal
interests or feelings, but) with reference to the questions
at stake and the interest of the Church in the long run,
which cannot really be separated from the interests of truth,
I think the course of events has been favourable. Many
persons have admitted into their minds inquiries which they
would have resisted but for the manner in which the subject
has been forced upon them by the Bishops. It is the beginning of a long controversy which has now for the first

time taken hold of the Church of England. And I believe it may tend not merely to a negative and critical theology, but to the making of religion more natural and effectual. The false position of educated persons with reference to their practice is quite as striking as their false position in speculation.

This will probably reach you at Genoa or Florence, or an Italian lake, some beautiful spot which should make one forget that there is such a thing as controversy in the world.

To Sir Alexander Grant, in India.

FRESHWATER, *April* 27, 1861.

Perhaps I shall be as well employed in writing to an absent friend this Sunday morning as in going to hear Mr. Isaacson preach, who calls me Judas Iscariot. Let me thank you, once more, for the great pains you took about my brother's[1] affairs, which are now quite settled, and assure you what great pleasure your last letter gave me and others who read it.

Lady Grant[2] is here, quite well and satisfied, as she tells me, that you should be useful in a distant land. We all look forward, however, to your coming home to a changed world and to a changed Oxford perhaps, (for it really is changing more rapidly than could have been expected,) but not to changed friends.

I am living here at a lodging about half a mile from Tennyson's, who talks of you with great regard and affection. The other evening, going upstairs we stopped to look at Maurice and you, as you hang beside one another. Tennyson said, 'That man (Maurice) I never allow anything to be said against, and that Mannie (Grant) there *is* nothing to be said against.' Mrs. Tennyson wants you to be governor, not of the island of Barataria, but of Madras or Bombay. And *I* wish for you that you should leave behind you in India a sort of reputation like Bishop Heber's for kindness and friendship to the natives.

[1] Alfred Jowett: see p. 253.
[2] The Dowager Lady Grant, Sir A. Grant's mother.

I believe that you are in a far better position for doing them good than you would be as a missionary or Bishop. Is not the late change in the admission to writerships favourable to education? Men who owe their admission to the service to education will surely believe more in its value than the old civil servants. I hope you will not depend only on the College[1], but write and try to get political connexions. We students and pedagogues lose influence often by not doing our part sufficiently in the world and in society.

There has been a great tumult about *Essays and Reviews*, which is now dwindling to a calm. The folly of the Bishops has led to the book selling about 20,000 copies. I have been a great deal more pleased by the kindness and support which the book has called forth than hurt by the attacks of enemies, which, like the attacks of mosquitoes, seem to produce little impression after the first day or two.

At present I am busy with Plato, which is my reason for staying away from Oxford, and have hope of finishing by the end of the year.

Please to reconsider what you say about the *Ethics*[2]. It must be out of print and may be set aside by some interloper. Would you like me to do anything or get anything done in the course of the next year?

. . . I am very desirous that you should write about India, not hastily, but when you have had time to collect facts and review impressions. Probably no one at present in India could do so as well, and it would at once give you a position above the ordinary civil servants.

So you have got a son[3]. He has my best wishes. Some day you will send him over to Eton or Rugby, and perhaps to Balliol, if I am living:—I get more and more determined to cast in my lot for life at Oxford.

Pray let me hear from you about India. I am always interested.

[1] Grant was now Principal of Elphinstone College, Bombay.

[2] The first volume of Grant's edition of the *Nicomachean Ethics of Aristotle* was published in 1857.

[3] The child died in infancy. In writing to the mother, Jowett said, ' One can say of infants, more truly than of any one else, they fall asleep in Jesus.'

To Miss Elliot.

Torquay, *June* 9, 1861.

I hope you will enjoy Switzerland. Don't relinquish Venice (if Rome has become impossible), nor Verona, which is almost equally beautiful, and the Lago di Garda. Let me tell you also what I thought the most beautiful thing in the Alps—the Val d'Anzasca ; you go to it from Vogogna, and, if you are very brave, might contrive to get over the Monte Moro to Saas and Zermatt. I see you don't like to trust yourself with an English summer.

The *Essays and Reviews* have long ceased to be talked of in good society. They are permeating, as people say, the lower strata : 'Gents' in railways talk about them to their sweet-hearts : God help them !—The last I heard of them was that they had been condemned by a Synod of Quakers (who have a certain affinity with the Bishops), which, my Quaker in-formant adds, has greatly stimulated the appetite of young Quakers. Though I try to make fun of them to you, you must not suppose that I regard the whole affair altogether as a joke.

Lord John Russell is said to have produced a great effect by a speech on Foreign Politics about ten days ago. There seems to be a general feeling that he has entirely succeeded as Foreign Minister. No one has gained so much in this session.

To A. P. Stanley.

1 Royal Crescent, Whitby, [1861].

Will you kindly read the enclosed and show them to Fremantle if you have an opportunity? This[1] is a man whom we ought not to desert, I think. Can you find him a curacy under some Rector or Bishop by whom he will not be molested? He appears to me to be just the man for a Bethnal Green church, or something of that sort.

I received this morning a copy of the articles against Rowland Williams. They appear to be concocted in the most

[1] The Rev. Charles Voysey.

monstrous spirit. . . . The Bishop of London, and still more Thirlwall, have not a leg to stand upon in the Church of England if the articles against Rowland Williams are affirmed. Pseudo-orthodox as the Bishops are, I believe that there is not one of them who might not be dethroned by a similar process of inferential and constructive treason.

To Miss Elliot.

WHITBY, *August* 4, 1861.

On my way here, I went to see the Arch-heretic Dr. Williams, who, for 'his soul's health' (that is the form), has been put into the Ecclesiastical Court by the Bishop of Sarum. Dr. Williams is a learned and good man, and a gentleman—but a Welshman, which (as is the case with all Welshmen) it is absolutely necessary to bear in mind, if you would judge them fairly. The articles against him are monstrous. If they are admitted, I think it will be impossible for any Clergyman who preaches or writes or says anything, to escape the charge of heresy. All Bishops (also Deans) have certainly been guilty. The only possibility of avoiding such a charge will be to read the homilies instead of composing anything of your own. The case comes on after the Long Vacation : I do not think it will succeed on any article, especially as the prosecution of it is against the wish of Canterbury and London, and against an implied understanding of the Bishops when they signed the letter to Mr. Fremantle[1].

Three acquaintances whom I have made this vacation deserve to be noticed. One was Mr. Macleod Campbell, author of the book on the Atonement, a more than ordinarily good, and truthful, and spiritual man : (there are a small class of such persons who lift themselves and others out of common life). He was deposed in the Church of Scotland about thirty years ago, Dr. Chalmers, who partly agreed with him, refusing to raise a finger in his defence. My next new acquaintance (I am afraid that this cannot possibly interest you) was Mr. A. J. Scott, of Owens College (did you ever hear of him ?), a most excellent

---

[1] The Vicar of Islip, to whose published letter the denunciation of the twenty-five Bishops was the reply.

talker, one of the very few persons who satisfies you in conversation. He is also a deposed minister, and what the poor
call a very fine man, of handsome presence and full of thoughts
and words. My third acquaintance was Dr. John Brown,
a physician at Edinburgh, best known to the world as the
author of *Rab and his Friends*, and also of a most admirable
memoir of his own father. He is certainly a writer of real
genius and feeling, and a most excellent man. He had
a charming wife, I am told; but his life has been utterly
spoiled and darkened by her going hopelessly out of her mind.
Do you agree with Mr. Mill in the last number of *Fraser*, that
if persons manage properly they can be sure of getting considerable portions of happiness out of life?

Dr. Williams's cause has as yet made no progress. He has
got Mr. Stephen [1], brother of Miss Stephen at Clifton, for one
of his counsel. A law court is better for justice than Convocation, but a law court easily gets inspired in these questions
by public opinion. None of the ordinary rules of law are
applicable: the judge does what he likes and the world calls
this common sense. Still, I hope that a Protestant judge will
pause before he determines that the evidences, prophecies,
&c., are a fiction (for that is what the decision would involve)
to be maintained not by weapons of reason and argument, but
by the authority of the Court.

Do you ever hear anything of Mazzini? He seems to be
more abused than any other man in this world. I think
he must be a great man, though a visionary and perhaps
dangerous. The present state of Italy is greatly due to him.
His defence of Rome raised the Italian character. I don't
suppose that you hear the truth about him in the North of
Italy. Some friends of mine, who know him, assure me
that he has the greatest fascination of manner they have
ever met with.

I am sorry to see Mr. —— resigning his living. No
doubt one ought to say, ' God bless him,' to every man who
makes a sacrifice for what he believes to be the truth. But

[1] Sir J. Fitzjames Stephen. The Miss Stephen referred to was
really his cousin.

if men drop off in this way, they will at best only get into the
position of Nonjurors or Unitarians. If the present condition
of religion in England is ever to be improved, I am convinced
it must be through the Church of England. . . .

To Dean Elliot, at Florence.

BALLIOL COLLEGE, OXFORD,
October 10, 1861.

I hear that you are thinking of giving up the Prolocutorship
on the ground 'that Convocation is so unjust.'

Perhaps your mind is made up. But indeed, I am truly
sorry if it is, and hope you will not think me impertinent for
telling you the reason why :—

1. It seems to me that you would be doing what all High
Churchmen and enemies of inquiry most desire. They would
be extremely pleased to enthrone Canon Wordsworth in your
place. I hope that you will not give them this pleasure.

2. I think it is an error (and one which is almost sure to
cause pain in the retrospect) to retire from any position in
which you have attained success and honour. Never resign,
especially in the Church, where such a magic power attends the
words of any person in authority. It is true that you cannot
say as much, but what you say has tenfold weight and power.
In any matter affecting Convocation you would have a claim,
as Prolocutor, to be listened to by the Ministry, which you
would not have as a mere Dean. Though, as Chairman, you do
not take part in the discussion, there are doubtless ways in
which you may prevent evil and do good.

3. Let me suppose that you resign : in doing so, you would
either hold your peace or publicly give reasons. If the first,
your High Church friends would get exactly what they want,
and would repay your kindness to them by a warmly-expressed
vote of thanks for your services. The latter course would
certainly produce a great effect, but hardly a lasting one. In
this *impressible* country no statement, however ably written,
holds out against a powerful party more than a few days. My
own impression is that, in case of resignation, it would be better
to give reasons. Still this would make you the mark for

violent attacks, and would lead to the attempt to push you out of the stream of religious feeling in England. I do not think that any good could be done by a statement of reasons so great as might be done by remaining.

4. As to the injustice, it is quite right that Convocation should be reproached with it, for the sake of the Church of England. But as far as the authors of heretical books are concerned, it does them no harm, and is indeed absolutely unmeaning. The proceedings of Convocation ought never to give them a moment's pain or uneasiness. I don't think you need mind Convocation thundering against opinions with which in some measure you agree. Those who hold such opinions would wish, not that you should sacrifice yourself out of a sense of the wrong to them (if any), but that you should use all the weight which high station assists in giving, to bring Convocation and the Church of England to more tolerant and also more natural views of religion. . . .

To Mrs. Tennyson.

BALLIOL, *November* 13, 1861.

I was very glad to see your handwriting again. I am afraid the last year has been an anxious and troubled one to you. Still a long journey, notwithstanding its cares and illnesses, is a good patch in life to look back upon. I have always found pleasure in travelling—after it is over.

If I am not troubling you I should like to hear again how Mr. Tennyson is; perhaps, one of the children could write and tell me. I am very sorry that he should be suffering. Indeed a poet deserves to have some of the good and enjoyment that he gives to others. But it seems often to be otherwise. My doings have been so very monotonous, that they are not worth narrating to you. I have gone on with Plato, slowly, but I hope steadily, and shall finish in the course of the next Long Vacation. The interminable battle about the endowment of the Greek Professorship still goes on. When I am old and the endowment is of no value to me, it will probably be carried. Dr. Stanley is the best of friends to me; I am afraid in some degree to the injury of his own interests.

To A. P. STANLEY.

FRESHWATER, ISLE OF WIGHT,
[*January*, 1862].

I am so glad that you are going with the Prince of Wales.

I have received from Lingen a document[1] that fills me with astonishment. It is most kind, generous, thoughtful to take so much trouble about me. It will be one of the happiest recollections of my life that I have received such a testimonial. But, my dear friend, I cannot accept it.

1. No one ought to take money from others who is not in absolute need of it, or without a definite public object.

2. I am far from wishing to feast upon a grievance or go in for being a martyr (don't suppose this), but I am afraid of lowering the position in which you and others have placed me, far beyond my deserts.

3. I should not feel on equal terms with my great friends and should feel pained at my poor friends if they gave me money.

Yet I really feel the greatest contentment and satisfaction in the matter. I shall never complain again, but work on cheerfully. If anything is done for me, well; and if nothing is done, well too. Taking the whole of my life I am sure that I should do wrong in accepting a sum of money: it is not worth while. I should never feel disinterested and could never be equally thought so again. . . .

To A. P. STANLEY.

March 9, 1862.

MY DEAREST FRIEND,

The greatest trial that you could ever have in this world has come at last[2]. I wish I could be with you ; it grieves me to think of what you must suffer when you receive this packet. May you have strength to bear it.

---

[1] p. 306.

[2] For Stanley's answer to this letter, see *Life of Dean Stanley*, vol. ii. p. 75. Most of the letter has been published in the volume of *Dean Stanley's Letters*. p. 325.

I have no faith in words being able to do anything to alleviate such a blow. But the remembrance of the strong inextinguishable affection of many friends may be of some value even in this great trouble. Let me assure you how many care for you as though you were a relative, and what a sense there is (as a person said to me) of the noble and useful life you have been leading—how increasing this has been since your return to Oxford. Indeed, though the blank and the chasm is great, other ties are beginning to weave themselves for your support. Don't let yourself wither in sorrow like one without hope, but embrace the ever increasing field of duties that is opening before you.

I know that she was father, mother, brothers, and friends to you all in one. Considering her extraordinary ability and intense affection it was most natural. And now perhaps there is only one thing that she would have cared for on earth, or does care for if the spirits of the departed retain the memories of such things :—that the end of your life should answer to the beginning of it and be consecrated, not without the thought of her, to the service of God and of mankind. I can hardly conceal from myself that life must be for years painful to you ; but things may be done in it far beyond, and of another sort from the dreams of youthful ambition.

Please write to me, if you are able, to tell me whether there is anything you would like me to do for you. I called in Grosvenor Crescent on Friday and saw your sisters : they were quite well and took their great sorrow quite naturally : they were full of kindness and thought about others. You need have no anxiety about them : they are sure to do exactly what you would wish. All that I heard from them and from Lady Stanley would have given you comfort if accidents could give comfort in such an overwhelming trouble.

Write to me for another reason, which is, perhaps, a selfish one, that life is very dark with me at present. I can't bear to think that I shall never more see that dear kind smile which used to greet me at Christ Church : that I have lost a friend who will never be replaced, who always greatly over-estimated me for your sake. Alas, too, we have both of us lost poor

Luke —there was no life in Oxford more valuable. And on Monday I sent away poor Simcox, the young undergraduate that I pointed out to you as a genius—as I fear in consumption. He was as innocent as a girl of fourteen, and had a great intelligence. It grieves me that the life should be crushed out of so rare and tender a flower.

I trust you will have strength to continue your journey and fulfil the great trust which you have undertaken. Don't allow yourself to think of any other alternative ; indeed, it would be wrong. It was her last request, and I hope you will not think me hard for saying that you ought to show yourself able to fulfil such a request and worthy of such a mother. They told me that she never for a moment regretted your absence,—she was glad of it and said that 'she had thought much of its being better as it is.' What should you come back for ? To leave a duty and do nothing, for nothing can be done. All her arrangements, as I heard of them from Lady Stanley, were as good and wise as possible, and such as might have been expected from her.

Rest assured, my dear friend, that there is a divine love as well as a human love which encompasses us, the dead and the living together, which leads us through deserts and solitudes for a time to make us extend the sphere of our affections beyond living relatives to other men, to Himself and to the unseen world. I am most afraid of your being stunned by the first news ; not at all of your failing in the duty which you have undertaken, if you would reflect for a moment.

Let me remind you that your sermon at Oxford was one of the last. if not the very last sermon that she could have heard—with what happiness and pride ! Will you think that I make a singular request if I ask you to read over the last chapters of St. John when you receive this news ?

Ever affectionately yours,
B. JOWETT.

I shall often talk to you about her when you come home, if the subject is not too sad a one.

To Mrs. Tennyson.

BALLIOL, *March* 31, 1862.

Will you be very much surprised if I propose a short visit about Friday week? I think of spending a few days with you and then going into lodgings with two of my friends and pupils, either at your house or at Mrs. Dawes' for a fortnight.

I can't make up my mind to leave Oxford next Term. Plato, you will be glad to hear, has been making good progress, but this Term has been sad to me, owing to the loss of two friends, Mrs. Stanley, and Mr. Luke of Christ Church, and I fear I must add a third (one of the most promising undergraduates who ever came up to Oxford), who appears to be in a consumption.

I hope Alfred is well, and the boys. Give my love to them. I trust the poem is prospering.

To Miss Elliot, at Paris.

OXFORD, *June* 4, 1862.

. . . You greatly undervalue Plato, who is a most faithful friend to me—too faithful, for indeed I can't get rid of him, and he is even now inviting me to come and see him at Paris where he resides—Bibliothèque Impériale [1],—and I would go if I could get away. I wish you would write a book, and then you would be at once absolved from all the duties of life.

A friend of mine says that his heart always sinks within him when he sees the Dover cliffs. Do you experience this patriotic sensation? I hope not. The good people of Bristol will be mighty glad to see you, and especially the poor people.

Your friend Johnny Symonds was examined to-day, viva voce, in the Schools; I am told that he did capitally, and believe there is no doubt of his getting a first class. Every one must be glad of any good or happiness or honour coming to

[1] The chief MS. of Plato's *Republic*, Paris A., can only be consulted in this library, now Bibliothèque Nationale.

Dr. Symonds. I don't wonder at the respect felt for him. I never knew any one who had such a genius for kindness.

I hope you are a Northern and not a Southern. . . . I am provoked with English people for siding with the South because they fancy the North are 'snobs.' We were very eager to teach the North good manners five months ago ; now that they are winning, we seem to grow more respectful towards them.

Your letter is written from the most beautiful place in the world [1]. The place to which I direct this is, I fear, losing upon the whole rather than gaining in interest and beauty. I am told that you can no longer stand on the Pont Henri Quatre, and look on one side at the Old, and on the other at the New, for that all is new.

To Hallam Tennyson.

October 31, 1862.

My dear Hallam,

It is a long time since I have heard of you or Lionel or Papa and Mama. Suppose you write and tell me the news. . . .

I have been in Scotland most part of the summer. Such a beautiful country, with mountains and streams and woods and huge deer forests. (You must know that these forests have no trees in them ; they are only huge bare hills many miles in extent.) And one day I went out deer-stalking : I wish you had been there. First we went on ponies to the top of a mountain with dogs and men and guns—and a great way off in a valley and on the opposite hill we saw two herds of red deer, and they did not see us, and the wind did not carry the scent of us to them, as it was blowing the other way. Then the people who were with the guns and dogs went all round the head of the valley on the other side, out of sight of the deer, several miles, and we sat at the top watching them. At last they crawled down the bed of a torrent (we could only just see them with a glass); and then we heard two shots fired and down came two stags, and

[1] Venice.

away all the rest bounded with leaps that would make you wonder. I ought to tell you that the stags were not like those you see in a park, but red deer, much larger and stronger. Give my love to Lionel and to Papa and Mama. I am writing this at Torquay and go back to Oxford to-morrow.

I hope you improve in chess, and learn to look a few moves forward. Think of the consequences in chess and in some other things too.

Ever yours affectionately,

B. JOWETT.

Are you a Northerner or a Southerner?

To DEAN ELLIOT.

BALLIOL COLLEGE, OXFORD,
March 4, 1863.

. . . I begin to believe that the ice of the Church of England is breaking up, and that the mass of the educated laity, if not of the clergy, are learning to look on these subjects in a more natural manner. I cannot help anticipating that increased freedom of opinion may lead to a real amendment of life. Hitherto, religion seems to have become more and more powerless among the educated classes. Do we not want a Gospel for the educated—not because it is more blessed to preach to the educated than to the poor, but because the faith of the educated is permanent, and ultimately affects the faith of the poor?

To MRS. TENNYSON.

HIGH FORCE INN, MIDDLETON IN TEESDALE,
July 14, 1863.

It is so long since I have written to you, that I am almost afraid of falling out of acquaintance with you; therefore I write, *à propos* of nothing, from a wish to have some tidings in return about yourself and Alfred and the boys. I am staying with Lord Boringdon, a pupil of mine, at a country inn amid the moors in Durham, busy with Plato, which is an everlasting thing on my hands. We are as far out of the world as we can well be, having no railroad within fourteen miles, and no gentleman's house within five or six. I think this, and a very fine country, and a warm welcome, and a curious geological formation, might be an inducement to Alfred, if he comes northward, to come and see us.

I have been reading Renan's *Vie de Jésus* during the last few days. If you have not read it, shall I give you Mr. Punch's advice to young gentlemen disposed to marry—don't? Yet I hardly know, as I incline to think that an intelligent and educated person ought to be willing to read anything and find a higher faith, not in denying but in being above everything that can be said. The book is extremely interesting, and will no doubt have a great effect. The Christ with which Renan presents us appears to me to be essentially a 'French' Christ with some traits taken from Renan's own character. The miracles are for the most part explained as a sort of unintentional impostures, forced upon Him by the credulity of the multitude. The book, though very far from presenting the ultimate truth in which the world will rest, is very significant of the change which is coming over the Christian Faith. May we be prepared to meet it!

I should like to hear about the boys. I hope you will find a good school and send them to it without delay, as they are getting too old for the matriarchal form of government.

TO LADY STANLEY OF ALDERLEY.

BALLIOL COLLEGE,
November 9, 1863.

This note will reach you in a house of mourning. I was sorry to hear of the death of the venerable lady[1]. I am glad to have seen her, and talked with her of 'the times before the flood.'

Will you and Lord Stanley kindly consider Arthur's interest about the Deanery of Westminster? There is but one opinion on the subject here. That cannot be better expressed than in the words of one of the opposite party : 'Lord Palmerston has

[1] Maria Josepha, Lady Stanley Dowager of Alderley (*née* Holroyd), d. 1863, aged 92. See the record of her *Girlhood*, Longmans, 1896.

done very wisely in removing him from a position in which he was doing great mischief to one in which he will be comparatively innocuous.' I am grieved beyond measure that such a joyful occasion as his marriage should be spoilt and undone by such a fatal error.

He has had a great and signal success at Oxford. If his ambition were only preferment, I should be well content to let him follow 'limping' after the Archbishop of York. But his ambition is of another sort than this. At present he has one of the first positions in the country, touching both ends of society—the Queen at one end, and the poor students of Oxford at the other. He is not regarded as a courtier, but as the independent friend of the Queen and the Prince. If he goes to Westminster, all this will be changed. Besides, he is excellently fitted for Oxford, and is an admirable link between College life and the world. But for London, except perhaps for society, he is not equally well fitted. The clergy are not capable of being influenced in the way that he supposes, and his most eloquent sermons are ill-suited to an average London audience. He can never expect to have any influence at Oxford again ; the people here will regard him as having deserted them, and will say (though untruly) that he has degenerated into a courtier. My impression is that he had better turn his mind at once to the antiquities of Westminster Abbey. The High Churchmen will say, 'We always welcome him in this field.' You see that I, and others, feel pained at his leaving us without a cause. Since I wrote to him on Sunday evening, I have seen several persons who all speak as I do ; the Dean of Christ Church even more strongly. I am sure that a person needs counsel when all his friends think that he is going to make a fatal mistake. This makes me write to you. I will not trouble you with any other reasons.

To Lady Stanley of Alderley.

[1863.]

I write a line to thank you very much for your note. If the time at which any change can properly be made has passed, I shall do all I can to soothe and help Arthur.

To Lady Stanley of Alderley.

December 6, 1863.

Arthur's sermon [1] was exceedingly interesting, and gave me great hopes that my sinister auguries about the Deanery of Westminster will not be verified. I thought he had a 'poke' at me in one passage which he has not printed, in retaliation for various offences, such as writing to you. I most entirely desire his happiness and success.

To Mrs. Tennyson.

Rectory, Devonshire Square, Bishopsgate,
December 21, 1863.

We all go to-morrow to see Dr. Stanley married at the Abbey. I was very glad to hear that you had succeeded in finding a tutor.

I am afraid that I have not thanked you for the verses [2], which I like extremely. The Homer is excellent (except 'honey-hearted'). I think the alcaics a very noble imitation, and I doubt whether people will be found for the future to write barbarous hexameters, of which I am glad.

Will you give my best love to Alfred and the boys? I always think with pride and pleasure of your friendship for me.

To Dean Stanley.

Alderley, *January,* 1864.

Here am I in your old haunts, enjoying the kindness and hospitality of Alderley. I suppose you have been rejoicing in that unclouded happiness which is only granted to human beings once in the course of a lifetime.

Since I saw you I have been to Berlin, and had a good deal of conversation with 'our friend' the Princess. . . . Nothing could be kinder than she was to me. I think she left a some-

---

[1] Dean Stanley's farewell sermon on leaving Oxford, 'Great Opportunities.'

[2] Translation from *Il.* viii, and 'Experiments.'

what different impression from what I got at Oxford, but not
a worse one. . . . She was very much interested about your
marriage, and both the Prince and she talked about you and
Lady Augusta and sent kind messages. Will you give my
most kind regards to Lady Augusta? I scarcely know her, but
cannot regard her as a stranger, as she has become yours.

I went to-day to see your dear mother's monument. The
inscription is excellently descriptive of her.

To Lady Stanley of Alderley.

March, 1864.

I was greatly pleased at your most kind letter. I often
think myself truly fortunate in having such friends. I
certainly would not exchange them for the best of positions
or preferments.

I shall try to avoid being 'snuffed out.' But I suppose that
life (which through a combination of unfortunate accidents
has been rather against me) must be a battle, and no battle
can be won without a battle. I believe the Judgement was the
cause of the defeat [1]. I wonder what the end of all this will be.
It sometimes seems as if no educated man, woman, or child
would have any more belief, if religion is to be identified with
the union of Dr. Pusey with the *Record.*

I have been reading a very clever little book (with a bad
title) by Miss Cobbe, called *Broken Lights.* It is an extremely good statement of the present condition of things in
the Church.

To Mrs. Tennyson.

Balliol, *April* 12, 1864.

I write a line to thank you for the photograph of
Hallam, which gave me great pleasure. I sometimes pull
him out and look at his honest intelligent face. I hope
that I shall live to be of some use to both the boys, remembering the long and faithful friendship which their father and
mother have shown me.

[1] See p. 315.

I hope that Alfred is not troubled at my small criticisms on his poems. I consider myself to be a ' foolometer ' and nothing more. I should make the ' Sermon ' more intelligible for the benefit of stupid people, and leave out the ' Sea Dreams ' and ' The Ringlet ' and (perhaps) ' The Lincolnshire Farmer,' as tending to dislocate the volume—although a first-rate thing of its kind. I have no doubt of the general success of the volume[1]. But it should have the character of a new book as much as possible.

So you have had Garibaldi with you. What did he say and do ? Will Hallam or Lionel write and tell me ? I think he must be intensely bored by fêtes, and must wish himself back in some scene of real danger and interest. I perceive that the common people recognize that he is *their* friend and one of them, and that the higher classes fall in with the general admiration.

I am always anxious that Alfred should be employed about some great poetical work which should express what this age is longing to have expressed. When old things are beginning to pass away and new things to appear, I think the poet's function is very plain and clear. He fancies that his thoughts have been killed by the *Quarterly.* My impression is that he could do the work now, but could hardly have done it five-and-twenty years ago. I know that I bore him about this. But I shall hardly let him rest until he makes the attempt.

I saw Mr. Dakyns in passing through Clifton ; he is very prosperous and much liked at the College.

Love to Alfred and the boys.

To Dean Stanley.

Askrigg, *July* 17, 1864.

. . . I have some thoughts, if there is anything left of me from the Plato, of coming to town for eight or ten Sundays next year and preaching and publishing the sermons in a small volume. I don't mention this to any one but you, because so many accidents of health, &c., may prevent.

[1] *Enoch Arden,* &c.

. . . I was sorry to see Tait's speech in the House of Lords [1], cautious in a certain way, yet so utterly unconscious of the real state of matters. What is Truth against an *esprit de corps?* The Bishops think that they are fighting a few clergymen who must be put down. They are really fighting against Science, against Criticism, against the Law or at least the spirit of the Law, against the Conscience and moral perceptions of mankind ; things which I believe to be invincible even when arrayed against that figment of theologians, the Catholic Church. The Bishop of Oxford certainly puts clergymen in an awkward position by bringing them back to the letter of their obligation. Does he consider in what a much more awkward position he puts himself and the Church by wholly, without a rag to cover him, giving up the very pretence of truth of fact ?

This is a village at the head of Wensleydale up in the hills, far out of the world and the atmosphere of Convocation. . . . I heard of your chivalrous speech in Convocation [2]. I think the Bishop of London is encumbering himself and the world a good deal by proclaiming the necessity of consulting Convocation on all occasions : especially at this time when they are acting with so much violence. The natural sense of truth or fair play seems to be quite ridiculous in these Church questions, and no Bishop can be expected to utter them.

. . . The Ministry and the foreign policy appears to me utterly contemptible, and a positive discredit to have shouted for place and office while the Danes were bleeding.

To ———

SCOTLAND, *September*, 1864.

I don't know whether one colours objects with one's own vision, but I sometimes think that the state of religion in England gets worse and worse. The very idea of the truth is becoming ridiculous, and, more and more, religious teaching is losing its moral character. The two great parties which really could say ' Rise up and walk ' in the last generation, hardly

[1] Powers of Convocation to pass judgement on Books: Hansard, clxxvi, 1553.

[2] Synodical condemnation of *Essays and Reviews* : June 22 and 24, 1864.

have any moral purpose at all. The effervescence of their
spirituality has passed away, and cunning, and activity, and
political tactics, have filled up the vacuum. Build churches,
fill them with Low Church ministers, or set up the authority of
the Church—that is the great end. One healing word of the
evils of mankind, one voice in behalf of truth among the so-
called orthodox clergy, I cannot hear. I am rather afraid that
the Established Church, which has many advantages, rather
increases the evil—you have not the chances of Dissent.

I often feel that I should like, if I could, to write about
this. What seems to be wanted is a restoration of natural
religion, not in the narrow abstract sense, but as based on the
past history of man, and as witnessed to by conscience and
faith, and supported by our first notions of a divine Being.
Natural religion should so leaven and penetrate Christianity
(without the word 'natural religion' ever appearing) that the
doubtful points and doctrines of Christianity should drop off
of themselves. Utilitarianism and German theology have both
of them, in different ways, a zeal for criticism and for truth
which is very commendable. But neither of them have ever
found a substitute for that which they were displacing. They
have never got hold of the heart of the world. The attempt
to show the true character of the Pentateuch and the Gospel
History is very important negatively. But it does nothing
towards reconstructing the religious life of the people.

To ———

SCOTLAND, *September*, 1864.

This is a farm-house in which I am writing: it is full of
religious books of the worst and most unmeaning kind ; *The
Arminian Skeleton*, &c. The people's ways seem to be honest
enough, so I suppose that they are not much affected by them.
Still a great opportunity seems to be utterly lost in the
education of the common people. Half the books that are
published are religious books. And what trash this religious
literature is ! Either formalisms or sentimentalisms about the
Atonement, or denunciations of rational religion, or prophecies

VOL. I.   B b

of the end of the world, explanations of the Man of Sin, the little Horn, and the number of the Beast—even these last are no inconsiderable part of English literature.

People sometimes say to me, 'Ah, you don't mind raising a blister occasionally, but you won't tell us what you think.' If you won't think me very egotistical I will tell you why I have as yet been able to do so little on these subjects. First of all because I know that it is very doubtful whether I could in any degree succeed in working them out, and I certainly could not succeed without entire health and rest, and a good deal of reading and thought. But then at present I have the translation and edition of Plato on hand, and besides this, my pupils;—this last is a perfectly unlimited field, and when I see men passing through College or in the University, to whose course I might have given a twist in the right way, if I had only had time or energy, I feel very much the responsibility of this. And the result is that I cannot possibly add a third object to the two which I have already. But when Plato is completed, if I live, I shall try schemes of another sort.

To ———

BALLIOL, *October*, 1864.

I send you a book of *Polish Travels* which is written by a pupil of mine[1]. I want you to look at the poem of Krasinski, at the end. That touches a chord far deeper than ordinary poetry.

I sometimes wonder that a poet does not understand that he ought to be a prophet. But no English poets seem to have felt this. They have art and sentiment and imagination, but no moral force. Our dear friend Clough had a touch of something that might have been great had he been in other circumstances. There is no one whom I oftener wish for back again.

I hope you cultivate peace of mind. I am sure no one has more right to do so. No one can overcome physical pain; beyond this I don't see why there should be one anxious

---

[1] W. H. Bullock, Esq., now Mr. W. H. Hall.

moment or one mental pain in our lives :—at least when we have determined to give everything to God. Then I think we have fairly won and ought to enjoy rest. The thought that should fill our minds is His all-pervading truth and love. The result is with Him. Why should we vex ourselves over the details of our work? or seem to deny at each step the general principle on which our minds really repose?

To ——————

INGLEWOOD. TORQUAY,
January, 1865.

I see that you think I am hungering after the fleshpots of Egypt. But indeed that is not the case. I have long been aware that this head is so oddly constructed that, if mitres were to rain from heaven as thick as hail, not one of them would fit it: also I agree with Lord Melbourne. 'My dear fellow, would you wear such a dress as that for £10,000 a year?' Deaneries have more to be said for them. But not having quite forgiven 'Anglicanus'[1] for deserting me, I am not going to give up the young life of Oxford (so full of hope) for the dead men's bones of a Cathedral town. Still I have difficulties; the greatest of them all is perhaps Balliol College, which is to me 'the War Office,' in which I am only an inferior clerk, having to force along the inefficiency of others, and this will probably continue all my life. Also, though I am aware of the great opportunity which has been given me at Oxford, and truly thankful to have such an opportunity, I feel often very uncertain whether I can use this, owing to my being tired in mind. Though I have the will, and am really not afraid, yet I believe that I never had the intellectual power which was needed for the task. But I am not going to trouble you with any more such reflections. You know Carlyle's saying, 'Consume your own smoke,' which perhaps has the advantage of increasing the internal heat.

I entirely agree with you about the *Théodicée*[2]. Instead of

---

[1] Dean Stanley wrote in the newspapers under this *nom de guerre.*
[2] p. 384.

this sham religion, which is true neither to the facts of history nor to human nature, people must begin again and gather first from conscience, secondly from experience, [more] of the nature of God, and of His manner of working in the world. There is a good deal of difficulty in reconciling these —not the old metaphysical difficulty but a practical one. For though conscience tells us that God is just and true, and though experience tells us that man has an indefinite power of turning evil into good, both in himself and in the world— this hardly seems true for the mass of mankind ; the stream of improvement is so narrow in the whole of the world and the whole of history, and such a mere rivulet, even in the improving countries, that instead of casting your eyes far and wide over the world, you have rather to look forward to some ideal future. And so far as religion has any dwelling-place on earth, I suppose we should rather, like the Jewish prophets, get the habit of looking onwards to the future and not backwards to the past. This would be a new kind of Millenarianism founded on fact and not on the interpretation of prophecy. All countries and all individuals hang to the past, but they seem hardly to think of the future ; and the tendency of the popular religion is to make us imagine that it will be at least as bad, if not worse than the present, and to be cured by the same fictitious remedies. The world are always being told that they are to make no progress in religion, and therefore they never do make any progress.

The danger in this *Théodicée* is the danger of being too abstract. There seem to be wanting intermediate ideas and associations to take the place of the systems of doctrine in the human mind. 'God is just ; God is true.' These are great 'types,' as Plato would have said, in which to cast our ideas of God ; but where are they to be found in nature, and how are they to be engraven in the human heart ? The best chance seems to me to be through the old forms of religion, showing that this, more really and persistently than anything else, was what they meant, though often, as for example in their ideas of the divine justice, led from entertaining such an idea into a per-version of all justice in the popular doctrine of the Atonement. 'Whom ye ignorantly worship, Him declare I unto you.' The whole world and all things in it, instead of being secular and external to revelation, needs to be brought back within the sphere of revelation.

I have been staying with Tennyson, who is in great want of a subject for a poem. Can you think of one? It is worth while, if you can. I have given him one—the 'Grandmother,' which has answered, and have been urging *Galileo* upon him, but he is not inclined to this. He has been amusing himself with translating passages of Homer.

To Mrs. Tennyson.

BALLIOL., *February* 27, 1865.

You will have seen that Christ Church have agreed to endow the Greek Professorship—at last, after having done and undone the same thing ten years ago. But Dr. Pusey, who first raised the opposition, has got his party into a scrape, and therefore to get them out again has made Christ Church fulfil their obligation (not a legal one, but I think a moral one, as they had estates given them for the support of the Professorship). I am neither grateful nor ungrateful. You must not look a gift horse in the mouth. I was rather glad that you did not write to congratulate. Having more money I hope to get more done for the undergraduates.

I hope Alfred is well and at work. I always maintain that he should look forward with hope to the remaining age of life, as he may do greater, more human, more divine things than he has done yet. Life ought to harmonize man and become stronger and also gentler as we get older. . . . I sometimes think that poets have not done enough for the good and elevation and inspiration of the world. I believe that the world, however bad, would put a crown upon the head of any one who would really instruct them.

To Dean Stanley.

INGLEWOOD, TORQUAY,
March 10, 1865.

Many thanks indeed for your kind letter. We thought that my mother was dying on Saturday, but since then she has revived and the disease seems to have left her—she is however so very weak that we are quite uncertain about her recovery, which can only be a very slow one. All last week she must have been very near death. I am glad that you saw her. I cannot thank you enough for your kind letter.

So you wish me to marry. I don't wonder at this when I see and rejoice to see how happy and successful the experiment has been in your case. But I have come to the conclusion that I am better as I am now. I could not marry without giving up Balliol, on which my life has been spent, and probably signing the XXXIX Articles over again, or having to make a statement of opinions to a Bishop, if I took a living or could get a Deanery or Canonry : and I am obliged always to deduct about £400 a year from my income (this is a matter which I never mention and do not you mention ; it has continued nearly twenty-five years—I never like to speak or to think of it). The position at Balliol is a painful one, but I get more used to it, and I think the influence and usefulness, if I may say so, are greater or, certainly, not less. My chief desire is to make the most of the years that remain. I am glad of this additional £460 a year because it will enable me to do a great deal more than I do at present in the Professorship in the way of composition and additional lectures, and also leave more leisure for permanent work.

Life has had a good deal of painfulness to me (not this matter of the Professorship, or the attacks of people in the newspapers). But I always feel that I have had a wonderful compensation in the devotion and attachment of friends and pupils. 'No one has better friends' (don't you think so ?), and among them I reckon you and Lady Augusta.

CHAPTER XII

(Aet. 48–53)

IMPROVED circumstances—Reforms in Balliol and the University — Effects of experience — Characteristics — Speculation and action—Health impaired—Mr. Robert Lowe—The poet Browning—Meeting with Mr. Gladstone—Death of his mother—Second series of *Essays and Reviews*—Why never completed—Scott made Dean of Rochester—The Mastership in view.

'PROSPERITY is the blessing of the Old Testament, adversity of the New. Still that Old Testament blessing would do a great deal of good to some of us.' So Jowett had written to Mrs. Tennyson in November, 1861. A portion of 'that Old Testament blessing' was now his. And as good fortune, like bad, sometimes comes 'not single,' the grant of the salary was shortly followed by his becoming the owner of the small estate in the West Riding of Yorkshire which derived to him from his grandmother's family[1]. To a friend meeting him in the north of England about this time he said, 'I am going to look after my estate; you did not know that I was a landed proprietor!' Years passed, however, before the settlement of certain legal complications enabled him to enter fully into his inheritance, and, by realizing, to shake off that burden. The estate (at Birstwith and Telliscliffe, in the forest of Knaresborough) was finally sold for about £5,500.

[1] See p. 9.

It was now that he began those liberal gifts to younger men, which were so often repeated in later years. His manner in doing such things was always felt to enhance the benefit[1], and it should be added that while his generosity had no limit, the claims of kindred obtained the foremost place.

In November, 1865, Mr. Ilbert[2], who had been elected to a Fellowship in 1864, completed his year of probation, and his vote turned the scale in favour of the promotion of liberal measures in College meetings. This put an end to what had sometimes troubled Jowett more than the 'persecution'—the weary striving against the dead weight of a majority in his efforts to make Balliol what he saw that it ought to be. Some plans which he had long meditated now took practical shape. The ground was laid for a revision of the College Statutes; Balliol Hall was established; College lectures, instead of being imposed compulsorily, were left open to the free choice of the undergraduates, if only they attended a certain number; the Divinity teaching was remodelled, Jowett himself undertaking part of it; and the first step was made towards an inter-collegiate system, by having one Lecture-list for Balliol and New College combined. All this was effected in the years between 1865 and 1868. In January, 1869, Jowett was appointed preacher for the College[3]. By the summer of 1868

[1] The following paragraph, signed W. Y. A., appeared in the New York *Nation*, in 1893, after the Master's death :—

'Meeting a young graduate who was making a living by private tuition, he asked him how he was getting on; the Tutor replied that he had few pupils that Term, and had been obliged to give up his hope of going to Germany in the vacation. A few days later the Tutor was sent for, and received an envelope with the words, "I hope you will go to Germany: good-bye!"'

[2] Sir Courtenay Peregrine Ilbert, K.C.S.I., C.I.E.

[3] Resolutions of the majority (1) for abolishing Catechetics,

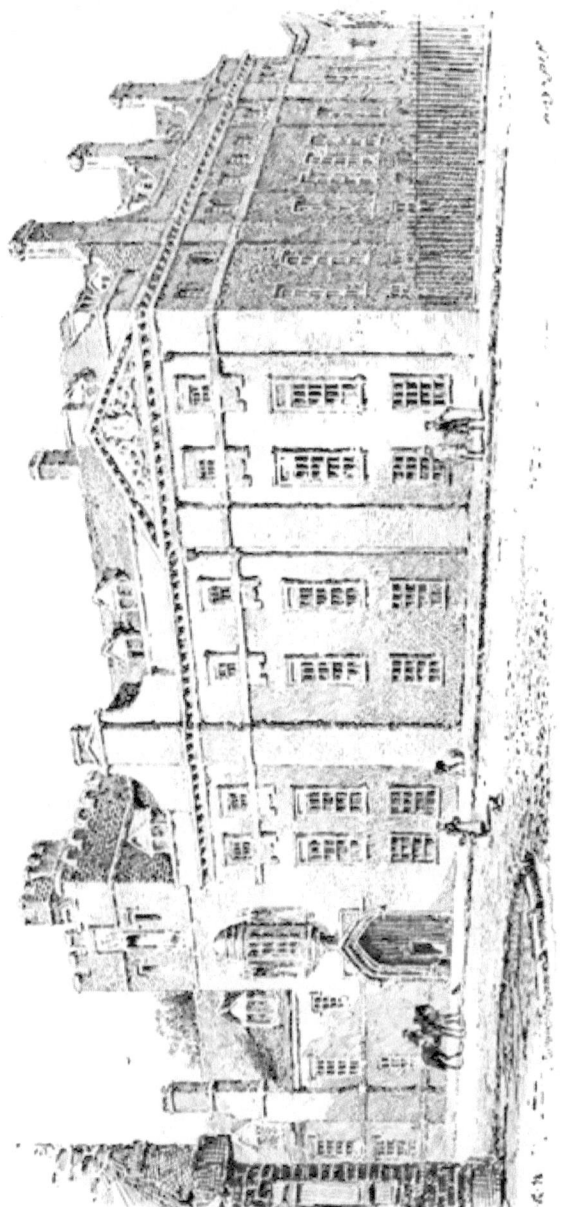

BALLIOL COLLEGE, BEFORE THE REBUILDING IN 1868

the front quadrangle had been rebuilt by Waterhouse:
Jowett, as usual, showing a keen interest in matters
architectural; and some of his old pupils were invited
by him to lecture in the new Lecture Room. An opportunity was thus given to the young Scotch Professors
who were Balliol men (and having no summer duties,
were able to give their courses in the Easter Term)
to make their voices heard in Oxford. In lecturing
on Sophocles, I suppose that I was his deputy, as
Professor of Greek. Nichol also lectured on English
Literature in the Hall of New College, and E. Caird
on Moral Philosophy.

The question of extending the benefits of the University to poorer students had greatly occupied him for
several years. A scheme which he had proposed was
thus explained by him in a letter to a friend on October 19,
1866 :—

'I found that my scheme of University Extension was very
favourably received. I want men (1) to live in lodgings which
we are to build and furnish, and let at a rent of £10 a year:
(2) to be allowed to attend the College lectures free: (3) to
have small Exhibitions of £25 a year given away by examination among the successful candidates of the middle-class
examinations [1] and others. I reckon that paying £10 a year
for rent, and having nothing to pay for instruction, they could
live for the academical year of twenty-four weeks on £50
a year, or, deducting the Exhibition, for £25 a year: (4)
I would allow the ordinary Scholars and Exhibitioners to live
in the same way, and their expenses would be completely
covered. The College would take the responsibility of the
management and instruction of all these lodgers out.

'At present not a tenth or a twentieth part of the ability of

(2) for restricting the number of
Clerical Fellowships, were quashed
by the Visitor on appeal.

[1] These, since called the Local
Examinations, had been established in 1861.

the country comes to the University. This scheme is intended to draw from a new class, and with this object I should propose that the subjects of examination be not confined to Latin and Greek, but embrace physical science, mathematics, &c. The great difficulty in working it out is the present state of the Grammar schools.

'I think that this College in five or six years' time would be able to give £600 a year towards such a scheme. But a large outlay would be required for the building and the Exhibitions. I should hope to raise this by subscription.'

This scheme was carried in College meeting without a division, and it was agreed also to petition the Hebdomadal Council to pass a Statute giving the necessary permission to lodge out [1]. Meanwhile, in pursuance of the main object, the long since thought of plan of a Balliol Hall was carried into effect: suitable premises were rented in St. Giles', and the young institution was placed under the charge of Mr. T. H. Green, a lay Fellow of Balliol already much respected in Oxford as a philosophical teacher and thinker. He had friends amongst the Nonconformists, and had done excellent public service as a member of the Schools Inquiry Commission of 1862. Jowett wrote to H. H. Lancaster:

'At this College we are going to try a small scheme of University Extension: e. g. men to lodge out and pay no College fees, receiving education gratuitously; and we hope also to supplement this by Exhibitions.'

The Hall was still maintained, and proved a valuable aid, although in 1868 it became less essential, through the success of a larger scheme. For plans of University Reform were again rife in Parliament and in Oxford. The relation of the Colleges to the University was much dis-

[1] From a leaflet entitled *The Hebdomadal Council and the Lodging Statute, Dec.* 6, 1867, it appears that the proposed Statute had 'originated in a request addressed to the Hebdomadal Council by Balliol College at the end of October, 1866.' Cf. vol. ii. p. 126.

cussed. In 1867 two Statutes were promulgated at Oxford,
and then several measures introduced in the House of
Commons. That which found most favour was Mr. Ewart's
Bill, 'To open the benefits of Education in the Universities
to students without obliging them to be members of
a College.' Jowett made it known that Balliol, at all
events, was ready to give teaching gratis to members
of the College not living within its walls. And on the
second reading, June 5, 1867, Mr. Lowe remarked that
'to their great honour the Tutors of Balliol had resolved
that, if poor students were allowed to become members
of the College without being obliged to live within the
walls, they would give to all such students the benefit of
their tuition—the best in the University of Oxford—
making no charge whatever for it[1].' The Bill was referred
to a Select Committee, and Jowett was examined on July
15 and 16. He not only accepted the principle of 'un-
attached students,' but suggested methods for applying
it successfully, such as the appointment of a Delegacy for
the purpose, and special arrangements for their tuition
and discipline. He further observed that to render the
scheme effectual, a good share of the emoluments, in the
shape of 'University Scholarships,' should be thrown open
to them. Against those who, with Mr. Mark Pattison,
were clamouring for the 'endowment of research'
and the absorption of College Revenues for the promotion of learning, he steadily maintained that learning
should not be dissevered from teaching, and that no
Professorship should be endowed without the prospect of
a class[2]. In the following year (1868) a Statute was passed
at Oxford by which the requirement of twelve terms'
residence in College, which had remained for four

[1] Hansard, vol. lxxxvii. p. 1613.
[2] Reports from Committees, 1867, xiii. 132 ff.

centuries, was finally done away [1]. This measure on the part of the University may have been hastened not only by the petition above referred to, but by the action of Balliol College. No time was lost by Jowett in taking advantage of the Statute. He gave notice of two important motions to be proposed in College meeting in October, 1868: (1) for a remission of the terminal charges to out-College students, and (2) for the foundation of £40 Exhibitions (six to be awarded in each year): the candidates to be elected after an examination in general subjects as well as in Latin and Greek. This involved a very serious sacrifice of time and money on the part of the Tutorial staff, as the Exhibitioners paid no Tutorial fees.

An important factor which came in aid of these improvements, was the munificence of Miss Brackenbury, who gave a large benefaction for the new buildings, and founded scholarships, which were applied to the support of students in law, in history and physical science. On October 20, 1868, Jowett wrote to his mother:

'Oxford, or rather Balliol, is much pleasanter than formerly [1]. I have no longer any trouble in carrying out my views, from the Fellows; and I believe that we shall succeed in making it a really great place of education. One thing gives me great pleasure; that our new building is really beautiful—the best thing that has been done in Oxford in this way. An old lady has given us about £15,000 towards the completion of it. You will be glad to hear also that I carried a plan for poor students.'

He said to a friend who remarked on the prosperity of Balliol: 'Yes, I think we have repaired the old house pretty well.'

There were other features in the life of Oxford at this

[1] The enactment that every Scholar or Scholar's servant should dwell in a Hall governed by a responsible Principal dates from 1420. See Lyte, *Hist. of Univ.* p. 200.

period which were less pleasing to him, but he does not seem to have regarded them with very deep anxiety.

Sacerdotalism was reviving, in the shape of Ritualism, a phenomenon not unconnected with the then nascent phase of Aestheticism. There was also a movement in the Catholic world to take advantage of the admission of Dissenters by bringing Newman back to Oxford, and establishing a Roman Catholic College in the University. Jowett witnessed this without alarm; he was more concerned about the new fashion of ritualism which seemed to be spreading amongst the weaker undergraduates; some of whom got up the semblance of a chapel in their rooms, with vestments and incense. The silliness of this 'playing at church,' even more than the superstition, annoyed him [1]. A similar feeling had been expressed in a letter of December 24, 1865 :—

'If you were to walk abroad you would be very much surprised to see the changes in our London churches. There is a sort of aesthetico-catholic revival among them. I wonder how many more spurious forms of Christianity are to appear in these latter days. Muscular Christianity, which was upon the whole a better form, is gone out. A sagacious High Churchman whom I know thinks that there will be an Evangelical Revival, which impresses me chiefly because he says it. How strange these "toys in the blood" are! I find myself often wishing that the Established Church were either demolished or greatly enlarged. Certainly the tyranny is very great on education and opinion.'

It is needless to say that the project of a Roman

[1] After describing this to a friend he adds, 'Is not this very funny?' But he had given one of his undergraduate pupils a *mauvais quart d'heure* on the subject. Once he had said, 'I almost think sometimes I could compound for this Bibliolatry by accepting the Sacrifice of the Mass. There is an *idea* in that.' Now, Bibliolatry seemed to be giving place to a more paltry form of superstition.

Catholic College was over-ruled, and Cardinal Newman, though he afterwards visited Oxford, remained at the head of the Oratory at Birmingham.

From this point onwards Jowett's energies were more than ever concentrated upon Balliol and Oxford; and the intensity with which he now threw himself into practical life created an impression, which prevailed even among those who worked with or under him, that his mind was relaxing its former speculative bent, and that the self-imposed task of translating the Classics was lessening his interest in Theology. That this idea represented only a partial truth appears from the tenor of the correspondence appended to this chapter, and will be still more evident when the contents of some of his note-books are made public [1]. Reason has been shown above why he may have been less communicative than formerly in his intercourse with some of those amongst whom his life was cast, and whom he was bent on directing towards definite ends.

His intellectual activities were to a great extent absorbed in the work on Plato, which appeared interminable. But his contemplative faculties were not idle, although the expression of his thoughts on the greatest things, except what could be made relevant to the Platonic *Dialogues*, seems to have been reserved for intimate friends away from Oxford. The problem of which he had written to Stanley many years earlier, 'Truth idealized and yet in action [2],' was still that which he persistently set himself to solve. Nor had he by any means relinquished his theological designs, which grew from year to year. A Commentary on the Gospels was to follow hard on the translation of Plato. On this there gradually supervened the vision, which never left him,

[1] See vol. ii. p. 85, &c.   [2] p. 92.

of a Life of Christ, and also the conception, which
sometimes competed with this, of a short treatise upon
moral ideas. These far-reaching plans remained inevit-
ably in abeyance while Plato was unfinished. And there
was another reason why the prosecution of such schemes
should be delayed:—to have given the world a new
speculative shock before his practical efforts had taken
a firm hold, might have checked the rising prosperity
of Balliol.

Meanwhile it occurred to him that by means of preaching he might give form and substance to those positive
views of religious truth which he regarded as essential
and permanent. The expedient of making sermons the
vehicle of his theological views had been suggested to
him by Mrs. Vaughan in 1857, in the hope that he
might entertain it instead of republishing his work
on the Epistles. He then wrote to A. P. Stanley:
'I have two doubts about the proposal: (1) Whether
it is possible; (2) Whether it is expedient; because it
seems cowardly to delay publishing a second edition—
which I find it almost impossible to get time to
complete.' But the reception of his sermons in London,
about 1864, led him to think more favourably of the
notion, and, with this object, in the summer of 1865 he
wrote a whole volume of theological notes. And the
idea was further encouraged by the opportunity of
preaching in Westminster Abbey [1], which came in 1866
and was repeated annually till 1893.

---

[1] How little he had sought for this appears from a letter to Dean Stanley, of April 24, 1865: 'I shall not expect you to appoint me to preach at the Abbey either in this or in future years. I really don't care, and I think this is better.' He adds, 'I wish I were a Bishop. Then the national clergy might find a place in which they could dwell securely. A great effort will be made to prevent this. That is a reason for desiring it.'

The more ambitious plans, however, though post-
poned, were not relinquished, but often occupied his
thoughts, especially in vacation time.

A valued friend—the same, if I mistake not, whose
MS., when submitted to him by Arthur Clough, had
'given him the impress of a new mind [1]'—had projected
a work on the Moral Government of God, frequently
referred to in his letters as the *Théodicée*. His remarks
on this and other high subjects show that his speculative thought was still awake [2]. Nor does he abate one
jot of heart or hope, although his hope is less firmly
anchored than formerly upon the Church of England.
For his thoughts about the religion of the future had
taken a wider range, and seemed to draw him at
different times in different directions. That decay of
religion against which he had so long striven, appeared
to him at times inevitable—and yet most lament-
able, since no other form of idealism could reach the
poor. But again, the position of an English clergyman, being independent of his congregation and of
clerical synods, was favourable to freedom. And yet
once more the actual constitution of the Church was
seen to foster prejudice and subserviency. 'The Church
is in a bad way in the nineteenth century,' he wrote
to Mrs. Lewis Campbell, 'but not worse than it has
always been. I suppose that while using its services
we ought not to set our hearts either upon the Church
of the present or the Church of the future, but to fix
our minds upon God and upon our own lives.'

---

[1] See p. 270.

[2] A speculation on the Labour
question appears as early as
June, 1865:—'I sometimes think
that the time will come when
workmen will refuse to work
except as their own employers.
I cannot help hoping that England, the old country, may raise
the condition of the working
classes as much as America, the
new one.'

But the old hopes were ever ready to revive. 'Our younger clergy,' he would say, 'are preaching more about the Christian life, and less on points of doubtful disputation.' He was ever scanning the horizon to discern the rise of any new spirit or mode of life, and to estimate it. All claimed his observation that entered into the genius of the time. His strong conservative instincts remained averse to 'new moralities [1],' and to aesthetic or sentimental fancies, but he looked calmly and steadily at all. To one set of so-called phenomena indeed he deliberately closed his eyes. In one of his earlier Essays he had spoken by way of illustration of 'Clairvoyance, if there be such a thing.' But in the end he refused to listen to the whisperings of occult doctrine which from time to time prevailed. He loved the open day. 'I do not mean to say that I can account for everything; and I feel that there is something in me to which such things appeal. But they are so inextricably mixed up with charlatanism and lies that it is mere waste of time and intellect to inquire into them [2].'

Above all, at this period, as at each critical stage in his career, he was busy in reviewing his own life and bent on beginning anew from within. To one who asked, 'Can a man improve himself after forty?' he replied, 'I am long past forty, and I mean to improve myself pretty considerably, I can tell you!' The result of this was often apparent in his advice to younger men. His power of generalizing and of detaching his thought, or rather the expression of it, from all personal content, often veiled what was really the outcome of intimate experience: his seemingly abstract observations were really autobiographical. The trials to

[1] Cf. Sir T. Browne, *Christian Morals*, i. 12.   [2] Cf. vol. ii. p. 76.

which he had been subjected, and the effort involved in acting as if they were not, had given to his mental constitution the touch of iron. *To be independent of all persons,* never to worry, to listen more to what his enemies said of him than to his friends [1], to find a *modus vivendi* with everybody, and above all 'never quarrel [2],' were among the rules which he laid down for himself. He perceived that he had resented some things too keenly, and that his opinions of persons and their acts had been too much influenced by his own feelings; also that he had been too free and open in criticizing persons to one another [3].

In looking round on his acquaintance he had been amazed to think of the amount of promise and capability which they had shown in youth, compared with the inadequacy of their performances, whether the failure arose from mistaking their career or from the fatal indul-

[1] What did his enemies say? I may be permitted here to quote an *advocatus diaboli* who shall be nameless: 'With a singleness of mind which is more than merely Christian, he has an element of bitterness, which nothing but his solitary character can have prevented him from struggling against and which makes it notoriously difficult for most of his *equals in age* to get on with him. With all his goodness he is a tyrant and careless of giving pain, or rather can't help giving it.'

[2] This was a piece of advice which Jeune, when Master of Pembroke, had been in the habit of giving to undergraduates. A young relative who had been pushing his fortunes abroad was entertained by Jowett on his return. In giving an account of his proceedings he happened to say, 'When a man insults me, I always ask him to dinner.' Jowett burst into loud laughter and, rubbing his hands, exclaimed, 'You'll do, my dear boy, you will do!'

[3] The motive of this 'defect of his quality' appears in an early letter to Stanley: 'Here I am at my old trade, *Detraction!* I think the greatest evil of the present day insincerity, half moral, half intellectual.' His later feeling was, 'I want to know people as they are, but to have expressed my thoughts about them sometimes makes me helpless in dealing with them.'

gence of some foible (as Hamlet says, 'the o'ergrowth
of some complexion'); and he was resolved, within his
sphere of influence, to obviate or check such waste to
the utmost of his power. Though often foiled he would
return to the charge again and again. Even amidst
playful sallies (as in his letters to Morier) this serious
aim is not lost sight of. But his criticism, while it
became more searching, was more and more softened
with gentleness and courtesy, and at rare moments he felt
and expressed compunction for having 'made the heart
of the righteous sad' by pressing friends with counsel
which he afterwards saw to have been unsuited to their
case. In these unwearied attempts at guiding others,
he found—as Socrates had found—men of poetic temperament his chief difficulty. The poet seemed to him a
kind of prophet; and he thought with St. Paul, that
'the spirit of the prophets' ought to be 'subject to the
prophets': but their genius was too wilful, too uncon-
trollable. Any impression made on them was sure to be
washed out by the next tide. Yet he persevered.

It was sometimes thought that in urging people
against the grain he had misread their characters, and
it may be that in individual cases he miscalculated.
He was sanguine in his view of possibilities, and apt to
credit others with a power of self-conquest equal to his
own[1]. But if his advice could have been followed it
would often have been for good.

He found that his own studies had been too restricted;
and he set himself tasks apart from Plato, such as

---

[1] Much of his own work was done *invita Minerva*. He was impatient of detail, yet he laboured out four long commen- taries, each a task sufficient for a lifetime. In 1853 he wrote to Stanley, 'I should be slow to un- dertake again a work requiring so much minute labour as a com- mentary on Scripture. It dims the eyes of the mind.'

reading through the Bible, Polybius, Lucian, Plutarch,
&c. Also he began to see, in looking backward, that his
life had been too predominantly intellectual, and that
for deeper and more lasting influence some fusion of
intellect and feeling was indispensable. Emotion as well
as will and intellect there had always been, but the
critical faculty had taken head, and he now realized
anew the force of Aristotle's words, ‘pure thought alone
is ineffectual.’ What Jowett says of Greek literature
became more and more applicable to himself: ‘Under
the marble exterior was concealed a soul thrilling with
spiritual emotion [1].’ While more than ever convinced
that nothing in the world—not even the Christ of
the Gospels—should be exempt from criticism, and that
no fact of history—not even the miracle of the Resurrection—should be accepted without sufficient evidence,
he was also more and more persuaded that mere intellect, however keen, was barren apart from the full and
just development of feeling, imagination, and, above all,
volition.

Reaction against his former self is one source of
continual growth in Jowett's life-career, which must be
recognized in appreciating any part of it. And yet
the combination of criticism with will and sympathy,
though, as has just been said, it only now came
fully into consciousness, must always be regarded as
one of his most pervading and permanent characteristics. A friendship, once established, meant for him
that his friend should have no rest while any fault
remained unreproved, any defect unremedied. And if
that friend's position in life were such as to give opportunities for influence or distinction, Jowett was never

[1] Introduction to the *Phaedrus*, sub fin. (vol. i. p. 423 of third edition).

weary of inciting to fresh exertions, nor would desist
from the attempt because of advancing age, although
he was well aware that 'miracles are only wrought
upon the young.' Perhaps never was an equal friendship more complete than that between him and Stanley,
from 1844 to 1849, and at no moment was that friendship more perfectly attuned than when Jowett wrote
the letter from Beaumaris in 1846[1], in which he dwelt
on his friend's deficiencies, and urged him to overcome them. Again and again throughout their intercourse the same persistent effort reappears. At one
moment indeed, in 1849, 'the inexorable Jowett' has
been somewhat too insistent, and his comrade begins
to find it irksome to have his genius thus subdued.
The irrepressible Mentor retires for a space; but again,
years afterwards, he sees a crushing blow impending
over his friend far from home, when in the midst of a
responsible task; and he writes to him that letter of
thoughtful sympathy in which he seeks to obviate a
possible shrinking from the course of duty[2]. And only
a twelvemonth before Stanley died came that strange
exhortation to 'fix his mind exclusively on higher things,'
to 'plan out a course of study and writing,'—and in short
to commence a ten years' labour that should crown his
life[3]. That is the way in which Jowett dealt with
other persons also, too numerous to think of. And it
was the presence of a firm, persistent will, in combination
whether with the criticism or the sympathy, which made
it so effectual. Hence it resulted that a letter of consolation from him, as a friend remarks, 'was not only the
greatest comfort, but seemed to have the effect of making
one pull oneself together.' There was a depth of reality

[1] See p. 152.   [2] p. 359.
[3] Vol. ii. p. 177.   *Dean Stanley's Letters*, p. 442.

in all his intercourse that is difficult to describe : inexhaustible hopefulness went along with unaffected disappointment even at small defects. And when he saw that some fault, such as egotism or eccentricity, was all but ineradicable, he still laboured at overcoming it.

But his advice even when distasteful was always carefully weighed, and if it were sometimes aimed too high, this was in accordance with his rejection of the practical fatalism 'that men can only be what they are,' and his resolute clinging to the ideal which he saw so clearly. Still in some cases it might be rejoined that his counsel resolved itself into, 'Do as I mean to do,' or 'Do not as I did formerly.'

He tried to meet every man, woman, and child on their own ground, yet in such a way as to impress on each of them something that was all his own. It cannot be denied that in general society, especially in Oxford, the scene of so many responsibilities, this persistent effort was apt to create about him an atmosphere of restraint. His presence was felt to dominate all that surrounded him, giving an almost painful thrill, and, unconsciously to himself, tending to damp the initiative of other men. When a topic had been raised that interested him, he at once put the question that went directly to the heart of the matter ; and there he left it.

His ideas were gaining at once in speculative range and comprehensiveness and in directness of aim. He reasoned more and more in the concrete, striving at every step to take in the many-sidedness of things and persons, and to look steadily at the whole of everything. Plato in the *Phaedrus* has imagined a dialectic in which the various complexity both of outward things and of personalities is to be comprised. Jowett's mind seemed always to be approaching some such goal, and in conversation he sought to present that aspect of a complex subject which he conceived best suited to his respondent, and to the purpose in view. In this sense he might be said to argue *ad hominem*: to the believer he appeared a sceptic, to the sceptic a believer, to the Humanitarian an Economist, to the Conservative politician a Socialist, and so forth. If told that some liberal-minded friend was growing conservative, he would say, ' Is he? the rascal! I must prick him.' In his fearless outlook on the future he kept clear possession of the present with all its conditions ; and if these were altered in a manner contrary to his previous ideas, he adapted himself to the altered state with unfailing readiness of resource. Thus practical and speculative thoughts were never wholly sundered, yet they were resolutely kept apart.

One thing is very noticeable throughout, as to his estimate of character: his judgement of those with whom he had to do invariably softened when they were dead. This may seem a commonplace ; but it is true of Jowett in a special degree. It then appeared how deeply he had appreciated what was best in them, and that the temporary difference which had veiled this appreciation even from himself had been magnified by the earnestness with which he had sought to perfect what he thought defective, and to draw those round him on towards some goal of perfection. In this effort, as he was ready to acknowledge, he was sometimes mistaken, and failed to take sufficient account of individual peculiarities.

Two sayings of Erasmus might well be applied to him in every period of his career: first, what he said of Colet: ' Conversation is his chief pleasure, and he will keep it up till midnight, if he finds a companion '; and, secondly, what he said of Sir Thomas More: ' When he can give nothing else, he gives advice. He is patron general to all poor devils.'

The energy with which he threw himself into each fresh avocation led to a forgetting of 'the things behind,' that was sometimes a little provoking to those who worked with him. In resuming a piece of work which had been laid aside, instead of taking it up again where it was left, he seemed to regard it as a *res integra* to be considered over again from the beginning. This was one of many causes of apparent procrastination.

The period now under review was in many ways a time of new departures. For example, he was gradually becoming aware of impending changes in Political Economy. 'I used to know the old science,' he says; 'the new applications rather puzzle me, but I shall have to make them for myself.'

Two public questions mainly occupied him during these years : (1) the Condition of the Poor, and (2) Education.

(1) His attention had been recalled to the former subject through the sympathy with philanthropic efforts, which began at Clifton, in connexion with the Destitute Incurables[1]. He now becomes more deeply concerned about the state of the lower classes generally and the best methods of dealing with it.

In 1865 he wrote elaborate papers on the subject, in which he took up the question of equalizing rates on property, and the best means of using the money when obtained ; and also made a number of suggestions as to (*a*) Sick ; (*b*) Aged ; (*c*) Incurables ; (*d*) Mad persons ; (*e*) Destitute children. It was in this connexion that he became finally convinced of the importance of Sanitary Reform. Although he had long held generally that moral improvement could not be effected without

[1] p. 343.

material changes, a certain fastidiousness, and perhaps some prejudice from early association[1], had kept his mind from dwelling on the subject. But when once persuaded, he held firmly to the importance of these things. 'That is a good gospel that you preach,' he said to a friend who was zealous about such matters.

(2) With the Education question his mind had long been busy, and it was stimulated into fresh activity on the subject through his increasing intimacy with Mr. Robert Lowe. He had always thought that a great opportunity for educational purposes was lost for the country by statesmen taking no advantage for this end of the high tide of prosperity which followed the abolition of the Corn Laws. He now pressed his views very earnestly upon Mr. Lowe, whose name, after the enactment of the Revised Code, was more identified with popular education than that of any other public man. Two letters on the subject attest his eager interest and his characteristic way of going to work :—

[1867?]

'I had a very pleasant stay with Gorgias[2], who is the best of friends with me. I can hardly tell whether he will be induced to take up the subject of Education. We had a sort of consultation about it at which L. assisted, and he said that he would see what could be done if opportunity offered. L. and he both thought that it was useless for any one to bring forward the subject who was not in the Ministry. They agreed that the first step was to have educational districts, on which the inspectors could report, and that this would involve divesting the inspectors of their denominational character. Gorgias thought strongly that a general permissive Bill for rating should be introduced, and was quite willing to support this. But he was against introducing any compulsion on parents.'

[1] See the letter to F. T. Palgrave, p. 414.
[2] i.e. Mr. Lowe.

[1868.]

'I went and took luncheon with Lowe, who appears to be profoundly in earnest about Education, and talked extremely well about it. I ventured to give him a sort of lecture about being more conciliatory, and the necessity of uniting persons and classes if he means to do anything with Education. He quite agreed, and thought that he would draw up a short Bill. I am more hopeful about him than I ever was before, notwithstanding his desertion of the classics[1].'

He visited Mr. and Mrs. Lowe at their country house near Caterham, Surrey, and on one occasion entertained the company there by reading long passages from his translation of the *Phaedrus*.

The edition of the *Republic*, which he had hoped to finish in a year or two, was now thrown aside for the translation of the whole of Plato, that is to say, of the genuine *Dialogues*, to which some doubtful ones were afterwards added. It is not wonderful that the end of this labour seemed to fade before him as he advanced in it. For his design enlarged; he revised again and again, and he never turned aside from other calls upon him, which grew and multiplied. Also, he was at last forced to limit his hours of labour.

For the long strain of the preceding years had told. 'All things come to those that wait;' but sometimes they come when the power of using them is partly spent. He had never had a severe illness, but his health from time to time had been unequal[2], though

[1] In lecturing at Edinburgh (Nov. 1867), and in a speech to the Liverpool Philomathic Society (Jan. 1868), Mr. Lowe was understood to disparage classical education. Jowett told me that when taxed with this Lowe had said, 'I could not recommend the wearing of broadcloth to people who had not a shirt to their backs.'

[2] In the summer of 1858, when struggling with his second edition of *St. Paul*, he made a short expedition in the Lake country. 'Even then,' says the Warden of Merton, 'he felt that he could

his great recuperative powers enabled him to rally from
brief intervals of exhaustion and depression. But in
the years 1866 and 1867 he became gradually convinced
of the necessity of husbanding his physical powers in
order to make the most of life. He tried certain experiments in diet, and for a time even attempted total
abstinence[1]. As early as 1861 he had complained to
Dr. Symonds, of Clifton, of 'headache, powerlessness of
brain, want of sustained thought, and imperfect memory[2].'
A throat affection to which he was liable, especially in
springtime, now threatened to become chronic. He had
overworked his eyesight: the pince-nez, so familiar in
the recollection of many friends, became a necessity, and
this, with the use of the steel pen, which he reluctantly
adopted, tended to alter his handwriting. His advice
to friends in sickness, which often both consoled and
strengthened them, was 'to keep the mind above the
body.' 'Little time is lost through ill-health, though much
is lost through idleness,' he would say in encouraging
a delicate pupil[3]; and he had a profound belief in
the possibility of dominating infirmities by an effort of
will; but he now found that there were limits to this.

A friend who had shared many of his thoughts, now
not trust his heart for mountain climbing: and in walking from Langdale to Lodore he paused so often and advanced so slowly up the steep ascent of Rossett Gill as to make it impossible to reach our destination before dark.' Cf. *Life of J. A. Symonds*, vol. i. p. 187: 'Toiling up Constitution Hill from the cathedral (at Bristol), he said, "Our young legs don't mind this, do they?" puffing all the time.'

[1] His motive in this was to help one of his dependents by his example.

[2] *Life of J. A. Symonds*, vol. i. p. 188. His power of memory often seemed dependent on conditions of health. But it is also true that the very vividness of his thoughts tended to swallow up details in general views, and that the intensity of each new phase of mind obliterated past impressions for the time.

[3] *Benjamin Jowett*, by Lionel Tollemache, p. 1.

pressed upon him the expediency of remitting somewhat
the intensity of his continuous labour. 'I perceive,' he
wrote, 'that you will keep me living and thinking to
the utmost of my power. And I am very glad to have
a friend who can help me to do this. Twenty years
of life probably remain to both of us, and how much
might be done in that time, with the experience that we
already have and the increasing influence that time gives.'
He yielded to his friend's advice in promising to cease
from study always at midnight; and when this did
not prove sufficient, he cut down his work for a time
to three hours a day. Writing from Alderley Edge in
March, 1867, he says :—

'I am not going to work hard, but only three hours a day,
and never more than an hour at a time, or after eleven o'clock
at night. I think that you are partly right and have done me
a great service.'

'But I mean to do more in three hours than I used to
do in six,' he said to me. He had given similar advice
to pupils who suffered from overwork, as early as 1853.
'I owe him,' says one, 'what I consider the most valuable
piece of practical advice which I ever received: to limit
my reading to five hours a day, including lectures, but
always to read with concentrated attention [1].'

This change in his habits was on the whole maintained,
although the late hours were after a while replaced by
an hour or more every morning before breakfast. In
the course of 1867 he hit upon another plan for easing
his labours. His College servant, Knight, had a son,
Matthew [2], now aged fourteen, to whose education Jowett
had given attention personally: making him repeat the
Latin Grammar and lines of Virgil at odd times (for
example, while his dinner, brought from the kitchen half

---

[1] Cf. p. 203.   [2] See vol. ii. p. 3, &c.

an hour before, was lying still untouched within the fender). Under Jowett's supervision Matthew had learned to write a beautiful hand, and had, as Jowett once said to me before the boy, 'a good sprag memory[1].' He now employed him regularly in transcribing the notes to the *Republic*[2], and in other ways as an amanuensis. The use he made of Matthew may serve to exemplify Jowett's method of composition. A page which had been written would be scribbled over with corrections almost innumerable, and given to Knight to copy. The copy was again corrected till it was almost illegible, and then had to be copied over again, and so on. His amanuensis became, as a matter of course, a favoured pupil.

'He would occasionally ask me to write essays for him,' says Mr. Knight, 'but he taught me most *more Socratico*, by conversation. We talked of everything under the sun, and he endeavoured to arouse my interest in the most varied topics. This educational process was the more effective because he expected me to understand all of which he spoke, and so compelled me to use my mind to the utmost of my power. Finding that I had a taste for Architecture, he gave me a copy of Fergusson's *Architecture*, and used to discuss the various buildings in Oxford with me, and to speak of the Cathedrals which he had visited.'

If the completion of his literary labours was frequently delayed, the work of teaching and educating was uninterrupted. The cry of heresy did not succeed in warning off men of high standing in the country from sending their sons to Balliol. It is needless to enumerate well-known names, but one connexion with a noble house deserves to be mentioned, as it was the commencement

---

[1] Shakespeare, *Merry Wives*, iv. 1.

[2] A great part of the commentary had been previously transcribed for him by the kindness of Mr. Jackson of Worcester, a former pupil.

of one of Jowett's deepest and most lasting friendships. The Honourable Francis Charteris, son of Lord Elcho[1], came to Balliol in 1865.

Other pupils belonging to this period who were destined to after distinction were: William Addis, William R. Anson, Ernest H. Coleridge, Henry Craik, John Arthur Godley, C. B. Heberden, F. H. Jeune, Andrew Lang, Kenneth Muir Mackenzie, Ernest J. Myers, Richard Lewis Nettleship, William Wallace, John Cook Wilson. Also of exceptional promise, though foiled by ill health or early death, were Alfred Barratt and Edwin Harrison. The latter was one of Jowett's chiefest friends.

From 1867 onwards Jowett held the College in his hand, and he was practically Master. Still his ends could not be effected without a certain amount of friction. His views were steadily opposed by a small but compact minority; nor were his followers in Balliol the sort of persons who could be absolutely reckoned on to vote mechanically in his favour. They were men of active intellects and independent minds, who shared his liberal principles, but did not therefore accept his *fiat* on every practical question. The continual need of persuasion and management, and of over-ruling opposition, grew more and more distasteful to him; it was the one crook in his lot; and it may be that the painfulness of the position in part accounted for what seemed to his younger colleagues the undue vehemence with which he sometimes pressed his advantages. Long pent-up forces are impetuous when they find an outlet, and impetuosity, although mostly held under firm control, and often unsuspected, was one of his native characteristics.

The annual progress amongst his friends in Scotland, preceding and following his summer sojourn at Pitlochry,

---

[1] Now the Earl of Wemyss.

Tummel Bridge, or Grantown, had now become an
established custom with him.   His visits to Lord Airlie
at Cortachy and the Tulchan, and to Linlathen and
Camperdown, as well as to St. Andrews, Edinburgh, and
Glasgow, were amongst his rare pleasures.   A visit to
Cortachy, in which he met Lord Kimberley and others, is
referred to in a letter to his mother.

The competition for vacant Scotch Professorships, on
the part of old Balliol men, continued, and became
painfully interesting.   John Nichol's rejection for the
Logic Chair at Glasgow in 1864 had been a keen
disappointment to Jowett; and when, in 1866, the Chair
of Moral Philosophy in the same University fell vacant,
he was disposed to press Nichol's claim.   Edward Caird
was unwilling to stand against Nichol.   But there were
other strong candidates; and when it became known
that a majority of the electors would in any case not
vote for Nichol, Jowett, with Nichol's full concurrence,
urged Caird to declare his candidature.   In the successful
result of this policy, no one rejoiced more heartily
than Nichol himself.   Jowett was much pleased with
the way in which Nichol took his friend's election and
his own failure.

Jowett made a special visit to Edinburgh in the winter
of 1866, having agreed to give two lectures at the Philosophical Institution on Socrates[1].   He stayed with the
Sellars.   On this or some similar occasion, in the Sellars'
drawing-room, Professor Blackie sang, unasked, a song of
his own making on 'The Burning of the Heretic': then
stepped across to Jowett and said, 'I hope you in Oxford
don't think we hate you.'   'We don't think about you,'
was the impassive reply.

Again, in the spring of 1869, soon after his friend

[1] The first of these will be published in *Lectures and Addresses*.

Sir A. Grant's election to the Principalship of Edinburgh University, he delivered before the same audience two lectures on Education, (1) in Youth and (2) in After Life, which were much appreciated [1]. He also preached for Dean Ramsay in St. John's Episcopal Church, taking for his subject the Divisions of Christendom [2].

On his southward journeys he was a frequent guest at Lea Hurst, in Derbyshire, the seat of Mr. Nightingale.

A new acquaintance of great interest comes now to be mentioned. Mr. Robert Browning had returned to England from Florence in 1865, after the death of Mrs. Browning, and was engaged in composing *The Ring and the Book*, which appeared in 1868. He was anxious to have his son educated at Oxford, and made Jowett's acquaintance. A warm friendship was quickly formed between the two men; not the less sincere on Jowett's part because he was not, as yet, an admirer of Mr. Browning's poetry. 'Ought one to admire one's friend's poetry?' was one of the few questions of casuistry which I have heard him raise. But he was keenly interested in the story which Browning had told him as forming the subject of the new poem. Jowett's first impressions of his new acquaintance were thus communicated in a letter to a friend:—

'*June* 12, 1865.

'I thought I was getting too old to make new friends. But I believe that I have made one—Mr. Browning, the poet, who has been staying with me during the last few days. It is impossible to speak without enthusiasm of his open, generous nature and his great ability and knowledge. I had no idea that there was a perfectly sensible poet in the world, entirely free from vanity, jealousy, or any other littleness, and thinking no more of himself than if he were an ordinary man. His

---

[1] These will also appear in the volume mentioned above.
[2] The text was 1 Cor. xii. 13.

great energy is very remarkable, and his determination to make
the most of the remainder of life. Of personal objects he
seems to have none except the education of his son, in which
I hope in some degree to help him[1].'

Another friendship, maintained by many pleasant
visits, was that for Sir Henry Taylor and his family.
This he probably owed to Mrs. Cameron.

In the summer of 1867, being now more in funds than
formerly, he sought to return some of the hospitality
which he had received. He thus describes the occasion
to a friend who could not be present: 'What do you
think that I have been doing for the last two days?
Entertaining a large party of folks, Mr. Browning, Lady
Airlie, Mr. Matthew Arnold[2], Mr. Munro of Cambridge,
Mr. Lecky, the Lingens, &c. Mr. Lecky is an extremely
tall and very thin man, with a free expression and a great
deal of genius. I like him and Mr. Munro of Cambridge
(who is a great scholar) very much.' It appears from
his letter to Mrs. Tennyson of July 29, 1867, that he
had indulged a vain hope of persuading the Laureate
to be of the party, and so to effect a meeting between
Tennyson and Browning.

These festivities, repeated in May, 1869, were a characteristic anticipation of many similar hospitalities
during his Mastership, which was not yet in view. He
felt the interruption to his work, but threw himself into
the unaccustomed business with hearty enjoyment; overcoming, as well as he could, his habitual shyness. While
expecting his guests, he said to me, quoting Abraham
Slender, 'I had rather than forty shillings I had my

---

[1] The last words I heard Browning utter were spoken to myself
shortly after his visit to the
Master, in the summer of 1889.
He grasped my hand at parting
and said, 'Jowett knows how I
love him.'

[2] See Matthew Arnold's account
of the dinner in Hall, *Letters of
Matthew Arnold*, vol. i. p. 365.

book of songs and sonnets here[1].' When they had all departed, he said, 'It is sad dissipation; but it is worth doing, though one can do nothing else for the time.' It may be mentioned, in passing, that his rooms in the Salvin Building had been decorated with a collection of works of art: etchings of Rembrandt, casts from Michael Angelo, &c., which he had gathered from time to time with the advice and assistance of his friend, Mr. F. T. Palgrave[2].

In the following year (1868) he took Browning's poems with him into the country, and, when staying with Mr. Evelyn Abbott on his way north, at Filey, in Yorkshire, he read one night a passage from *Luria*[3] 'very beautifully.' He thought that Browning's poetry showed great learning, but that the world had succeeded better in assimilating Tennyson. 'Browning deserves a shady First,' he said, as reported by Mr. Tollemache. To me somewhat earlier he had said, 'Browning has more knowledge, wit, and force of mind than Tennyson, and I can imagine him at any moment rising to the first rank in poetry. At present he is hardly a poet.'

Two matters of grave importance claimed his attention in 1869-1870, the Voysey trial and the project for a second series of *Essays and Reviews*. The prosecution of the Rev. Charles Voysey for heretical doctrine became imminent in the course of 1869. In spite of many wise cautions from Jowett[4], Mr. Voysey had found it

---

[1] Shakespeare, *Merry Wives*, i. 1.

[2] See p. 285.

[3] Act v. The speech of Luria beginning 'My own East!'

[4] e.g. 'Shall I state to you my conviction that it is impossible for a clergyman holding liberal opinions to be too cautious in his mode of stating them? Such caution is not timorousness or self-interest, but the condition of any real usefulness.' (Feb. 8, 1861.)

impossible to avoid this entanglement. **Far** from re-
proaching him, Jowett continued to advise and help
him : attending meetings of counsel, suggesting the line
of defence, &c.   **But** the case in its earlier stage had
gone adversely, and the constitution of the Committee
of Privy Council at this juncture made it improbable
that they would reverse the judgement of the court
below.   Jowett saw that to proceed further would
endanger freedom, not for himself, but for others in the
Church of England.   The following letters to Mr. Voysey
will show what course he took :—

OXFORD, *February*, [1870].

I do not think that there would be any giving up of the
truth or of the cause of freedom by your resignation.   **That**
appears to me to be the right course, if your counsel and
lawyers are of opinion that there is no hope of a favourable
issue on the principal points.

Your reason for resigning would be generally appreciated,
viz. that you fear lest by trying the question under **unpropitious**
circumstances you may curtail the liberty of others.   **Your**
sermons and the articles of accusation against you contain
most of the distinctive tenets of the Anglican Church, and
it would appear ridiculous and impolitic to settle these at
one swoop by the authority of Phillimore, Chelmsford, and
others, and would probably overthrow the tribunal itself.
That is my view, and is in general that of H. B. Wilson,
with whom I had the opportunity of conversing about the
matter last week.   I should like you to hear his opinion ;
for he has experience and is very acute in these matters.
I should like also to talk the matter over with Bowen,
whom I shall see this day week.

There is no hurry, I suppose, about the resignation, as
the cause cannot come on until November, and perhaps
not then.   I shall not mention your possible intention
of resignation to Bowen or to any one, and I would advise
you not to speak of it yourself.   It will require some

consideration if you determine to resign : What is the best time and manner of doing it ? I shall be glad to help in any way that I can.

> With sincere regard and respect,
>> Believe me, yours most truly,
>>> B. Jowett.

TUMMEL BRIDGE, PITLOCHRY, N.B.,
August 14, [1870].

I have nothing to say in answer to your note except to assure you that I have never considered you as under the slightest personal obligation to me. In giving my name to your defence fund I acted on public grounds.

As to the main question, I still think with Dean Stanley, Mr. Westlake, Lord Justice James, and others, that it is very undesirable to pursue this trial further ; that nothing can be gained and that something will probably be lost in the way of liberty ; that though to myself personally these decisions are not important, they affect very hardly a great many Liberal clergymen ; and also that the discussion of the limits of the Articles and Liturgy leads to casuistical questions (like No. 90) about the meaning of the words, which the public ill understand, and which do not tend to the cause of truth.

I saw Messrs. Shaen's letters some time ago. But I do not think that the decision of the York Court does bind the Church ; and that I find to be the opinion of others.

Although his own special work in Theology had been relegated to the future, he now consented to undertake a more immediate task, which was nothing less than to contribute two long essays to a second series of *Essays and Reviews*. Mr. H. B. Wilson had been pressing for this for some time past ; and Dr. John Muir, of Edinburgh, the Sanskrit scholar, was eager in promoting the idea. Other possible contributors are mentioned in the letter to Professor Caird appended to this chapter.

Jowett had applied to Grant, who declined, on the ground that his share in such a volume might cripple his usefulness in Edinburgh [1]. Mr. Wilson himself undertook two essays, (1) on the Principles of the Reformation, and (2) on the Sacramentarian Theory, and Jowett finally chose for his subjects the Religions of the World and the Reign of Law. For the former he read largely and wrote many notes, but neither essay was completed. The volume came to nothing, chiefly, I believe, in consequence of the illness of Mr. Wilson, whose health, already broken, was shattered by a stroke of paralysis shortly after this. But Jowett himself may well have hesitated, after his appointment to the Mastership, to risk another storm while his honours, in which Balliol was involved, were 'in their newest gloss.' The only portion of the projected work which saw the light, so far as I am aware, was my own essay on the Revision of the English New Testament, which was published in the *Contemporary Review*, in May, June, and August, 1876.

The subject recalls another consideration. The Committee of Revisers began to sit in 1870. It is perhaps one of the most regrettable consequences of the theological *odium* which surrounded Jowett's name, that he was passed over, not only for the Oxford Theological Board of Studies (which he had recommended in 1848), but for this more important committee, which included, as a matter of course, the name of Dr. Kennedy, as Professor of Greek in the University of Cambridge [2]. A remark of Jowett's on the work of the committee when it appeared is perhaps worth recording here.

[1] He had accepted a share in the former volume (see above, p. 275), but the Madras appointment had come in the way.

[2] The selection rested with the Convocation of the English Clergy.

'They seem to have forgotten that, in a certain sense, the Authorised Version is more inspired than the original.'

Early in the October of 1869, Jowett met Mr. Gladstone at Camperdown House, Dundee, where both were guests of the Earl of Camperdown. It was not the first occasion of their meeting[1]; but a country house gives opportunities which are not to be had in London, and for the few days which Jowett spent at Camperdown the politician and the thinker were much together. He had looked forward with great eagerness to this visit, and his host reports that he had never seen him so absorbed in any one. They talked incessantly for hours in the library and about the grounds. Jowett was very much provoked one morning when Gladstone had insisted on rising early and going to hear an Episcopal preacher at Perth. Mr. Gladstone at this time was considering the outline of his first Land Bill of 1870, and Ireland was one chief topic of their conversations. Mr. Gladstone tried to impress on Jowett's mind that no one hitherto had understood the Irish, or had rightly sympathized with them. Jowett came straight from Camperdown to St. Andrews, and told me of the great interest he had felt in this meeting. 'It was the first time,' he said, 'that any one of such great simplicity had been in so exalted a position.' It would be curious and interesting to mark the sequel; but it seemed to him to be full of peril, because the great statesman was 'so powerful and so unsound.' He observed that Mr. Gladstone failed to recognize the truth, that the moral excuses for political crime ought not to make a statesman less firm in repressing it.

On the Sunday after his return to Balliol in October,

[1] They had breakfasted together in London.

he was summoned to Torquay, where his mother was
dying. She died on October 16. Her death moved him
deeply, and called up many old memories. The following
passage from a sermon which he preached a few years
afterwards may be, to some extent, as the Rev. W. H.
Langhorne has suggested, a picture drawn from recollections of his own family :—

'The thought of our childhood touches us when we remember
that we were once as they are now—surrounded by brothers
and sisters who have gone different ways in life : some to
distant lands, where they rest and will no more return to us ;
and others, like ourselves, have been fighting the battle of life
here for twenty or thirty years or more, to rest like them
before long.

'The history of any family recalls many recollections known
to themselves only : of little acts of kindness done to one
another, and inseparable companionships, and old servants and
their rare devotedness and self-surrender : of some mistakes
and misunderstandings, too, which may have arisen out of
differences of character. We can see now how they might
have been avoided, but we could not place ourselves above
them at the time.

'The old family life, the house in which we dwelt, the
circle which met round the fire or the dinner-table, the very
books and furniture we used, are still present in the mind's eye,
and the memory of these is sweet to us. They are a sort of
Kingdom of Heaven in the past, and to some of us there seem
to be none who can look on us as others have.'

After this he spent what time he could at Torquay,
haunted by his mother's image, ruminating on old
memories, and finding the quiet of the bereaved household conducive to uninterrupted labour. 'I like this
place, at which I always do more and with less exertion
than anywhere else.'

His work proceeded as before, without check or
intermission. Returning from Torquay to Oxford on

November 18, he was once more 'immersed in juvenile English Essays,' and 'feeling that a new place puts the sorrow in a new light.' He found satisfaction in the election to a Fellowship of Mr. Lewis Nettleship, 'a University scholar, and a man of some genius as well, with a slight trace of Clough in him.' Clough's sister was at this time looking for some post in which she might promote the higher education of women, and Jowett conferred often with his friend William Rogers, of Bishopsgate, about a scheme for a new girls' school of which they hoped that she would be the head. The arrangement was not concluded, for shortly after this Miss Clough saw her way to starting Merton Hall at Cambridge, the germ of Newnham College, over which she presided so long with eminent success. But the fact is noticeable, as marking Jowett's first contact with a movement which sprang into vigorous life soon after this; but from which at first he seemed to hold back, with his habitual tendency to resist practical novelties.

It is pathetic to recall the fact that Mrs. Jowett did not live to see the dawn of a new hope about the Mastership, which had been the object of her son's frustrated ambition sixteen years before. The first trace of this in his correspondence appears in a letter of December 26, 1869 (the day after his mother's birthday), written from Torquay, with reference to a visit to Caterham in the previous week:—

'I had a delightful visit to Mr. Lowe, who is a devoted friend to me. It is impossible to see him at home and not to be charmed with him. . . . He said that he had been told by Gladstone to ask whether he could do anything for me. I told him that I did not intend to leave Oxford, and therefore that the only thing that could be done for me would be to make Scott a Dean or a Bishop. Mr. Lowe thought that this would

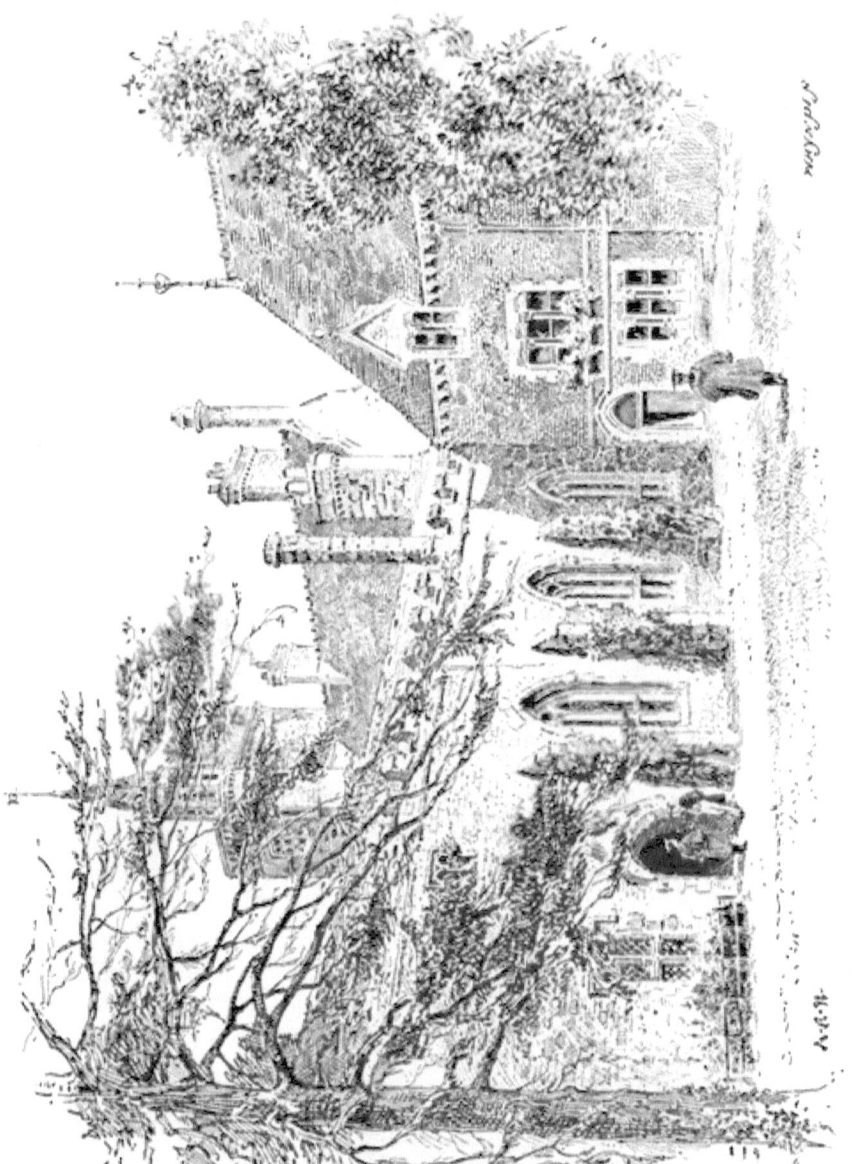

THE OLD HALL AND MASTER'S LIBRARY, BALLIOL COLLEGE.

be done, and set about the matter with great zeal.   But I do not expect this, nor much care[1].'

Dr. Scott was appointed to the Deanery of Rochester in June, 1870, and Jowett's election as his successor in the Mastership was a foregone conclusion.   The news came to him when staying at a country house, the home of a friend.   'He leant his head against the mantel-piece and *prayed aloud*, "O spare me a little, that I may recover strength, before I go hence, and be no more seen."'   He wrote to his sister :—

'You will have seen that Scott is to be the new Dean of Rochester, which will make me Master of Balliol.   This is Lowe's doing.   I find great good will in Oxford about the proposal.   I consider this is the second piece of good luck which I have had in life—the election to the Fellowship thirty-two years ago was the first.

'I wish that our dear mother had been alive to hear this news.'

LETTERS, 1865-1870.

To R. B. D. Morier.

Address OXFORD, *March* 7, [1865].

MY DEAR SIR JOHN[2],

I knew that you would have died for me (at least after the fashion in which your renowned ancestor died on the field of battle); but I had no idea that you would write to me

---

[1] It appears, however, from a previous letter, written early in October, that he had already been counting on the possibility of pre-ferment coming to Scott.   Even now this was a hope deferred, for the vacant bishopric of Man-chester was given to Jowett's old acquaintance, Fraser of Oriel.

[2] He jestingly compared his 'fat friend' to Falstaff; see Shakespeare, 1 *Henry IV*, v. 4.

of your own accord. I did not believe such a thing to be within the compass of nature.

I am delighted to hear of the commissionership[1]. That is a real opportunity for doing something. . . .

You are very good in rejoicing at my endowment. Christ Church are getting great credit for this, which they did and undid ten years ago, and which Dr. Pusey has now carried because he knew that he must be beaten in the University. But I shan't look a gift horse in the mouth. I was always very fond of money, for money is a means of doing mischief, and I have always been a great lover of mischief. I am not insensible to the value of £125 a quarter, though on the other hand I do not know how to get on without the character of a 'martyr.' To be a martyr is a delightful position and just suits me; it consists in doing nothing, and that I understand. As an un-feeling but sagacious friend once said to me, 'Next to having a good place, there is nothing like a good grievance.' How much more truly might *you* be called a martyr—to the gout! Like your great ancestor, again, you have found that there was something mysteriously wrong—in the great toe. Yet don't suppose, my dear fellow, that I am not sorry you should have been in bed for six weeks. . . .

When do you go to Vienna? and will you be in England next summer? I wonder whether your wife, who is worth ten of you for any practical purpose, would write and tell me.

To ———

OXFORD, *March* 16, 1865.

Prayer, as at present conducted, is an absurdity, if it means praying for fine weather, &c. (faith must snap in the face of universal obvious facts); or an ambiguity of the worst kind, if the Theologian refuses to say, in reference to an action of everyday life, whether it is supposed to have this effect or not.

There is nothing that more requires to be stated than that prayer is a mental, moral, spiritual process, a communion or

---

[1] Morier was British member of the Mixed Commission at Vienna to inquire into the Austrian tariff (March, 1865).

conversation with God, or an aspiration after Him and resignation to Him, an anticipation of heaven, an identification of
self with the highest law, the truest idea, the blending of true
thought and true feeling, of the will and the understanding,
containing also the recognition that we ask for nothing but to
be better, stronger, truer, deeper than we are. I am afraid
that the anthropomorphism of much of what is called revealed
religion has obscured the natural religion of men on this subject.
On the old theory, all answers to prayer were necessarily
miraculous, and therefore the belief in them could not be
otherwise than unreal.

I think that 'the human race is inspired.' But how short
the moments of inspiration have been—a little stream in Greece
and Judaea—dammed up after a century or two in the original
fountain :—all other progress, or nearly all, is but the dilution
of this water of life. Great men like Luther and Bacon have
been inspired, but how muddy the inspiration has been with
the previous elements! Even Spinoza is a schoolman warring
against scholasticism : I mean in such things as his notion
of substance and the importance that he attaches to mere logical
demonstration.

To ———

May 28, 1865.

I send you some books, one very good book among them, the
works of a Saint, and one very bad book, *Fable of the Bees*—
one of those books which are condemned equally by the world
and the Church ; by the world because it is partly true, and
by the Church because it is partly false, or vice versa—one
of those books which delight in turning out the seamy side
of society to the light. (Don't read it if you object to the coarse-
ness of parts.) Dr. Johnson says, 'Mandeville, sir, never did
me any harm, but he opened my views into life very much.'
Nor do I think it a bad thing to read the book with patience
and ask how much is true of ourselves.

Also I send you some of my translations[1] of Plato. I have
done the whole of Plato in that way. If you look at any-

---

[1] This refers to the *Analysis*, which was now nearly complete. The *Republic* was still the only dialogue fully *translated*.

thing, read the *Crito*, and the end of the *Phaedo* and the *Apology*.

Plato has been a great labour. Yet I like being in such good company always. There is nothing better in style and manners, not even 'in the first circles.' I more and more wonder at the things which he saw and prophesied. Hardly anything important about law or natural religion which has ever been said may not be found in Plato.

To ———

PITLOCHRY, *August* 31, 1865.

I certainly mean when my Plato is finished to devote two or three years to preaching, giving up my whole mind to this and publishing the sermons. (I try to collect 'stock' for myself ; that is the term cooks give to their materials for soup.) I have not told this design to any one but you, and I mean to go about it as quietly as I can, putting off the more heterodox aspect of things until I have gained, if I can, some hold.

There are a great many other things that might be done, e.g. a Commentary on the New Testament, at once true and practical. This should be the joint labour of many persons. Also tracts of another sort from those which are commonly circulated among the poor.

Any religious movement should be also, like that of the Jesuits, an educational movement. And this, I think, is to a considerable extent going on at the schools ; e. g. Harrow, Rugby, Marlborough, and even Winchester. And there is a great change in education at the Universities, especially at Oxford. When I was an undergraduate we were fed upon Bishop Butler and Aristotle's *Ethics*, and almost all teaching leaned to the support of doctrines of authority. Now there are new subjects, Modern History and Physical Science, and more important than these, perhaps, is the real study of metaphysics in the Literae Humaniores school—every man for the last ten years who goes in for honours has read Bacon, and probably Locke, Mill's *Logic*, Plato, Aristotle, and the history of ancient philosophy. See how impossible this makes a return to the old doctrines of authority.

The 'Hebrew Conservative¹' has just found this out, which he ought to have found out long ago, and is going to try to upset all this by appointing what he calls a Board of Studies, who would be nominated by himself and his friends. But I think that we can hinder him, as the Tutors are almost all on our side.

I was going to say when I made this digression, that I think something needs to be done for the educated, similar to what J. Wesley did for the poor. A real religious movement among the educated would be more permanent than any revival. What is wanted just now is not preaching for the poor, but teaching in schools, better and more of it, and preaching to the clergy and educated classes.

To Sir Alexander Grant.

August 27, 1865.

I have been working at Plato steadily for the last two months, and make some impression, although the work is very long. I believe you will see the four volumes in India in the course of next year.

I have been reading Grote with very great interest, but with a good deal of disagreement. The mode of handling critical questions is very defective: his arguments about the Canon of Plato are like the arguments of divines about the Canon of Scripture, and I think also without fancy that there is far more in Plato than he supposes. I object to a kind of modern rule by which he judges him, and I don't believe Socrates to have been a mere professor of negation, as he supposes.

I hope we shall live to see more of one another before life is over. Meanwhile take care of your health, save your money and come home as fast as you can, and keep the notion of collecting materials and thoughts for some work in view which you may execute when you come home. I may possibly live twenty or twenty-five years longer, and I can assure you that I mean to make the utmost of the years that remain, more than I have done, and I hope you will do the same. . . .

¹ Dr. Pusey.

This is really written in Scotland, Tummel Bridge Inn, Pitlochry, which has been the best, I think, of my summer residences.

To F. T. PALGRAVE.

OXFORD, *September* 26, 1865.

I most entirely agree with your remark about the [Cambridge] Apostles. We must try and avoid that at Oxford. To teach men how they may learn to grow independently and for themselves, is perhaps the greatest service that one man can do for another, and how to grow, if possible, in after life. I hate to meet a man whom I have known ten years ago, and find that he is at precisely the same point, neither moderated, nor quickened, nor experienced, but simply stiffened; he ought to be beaten. He had the charm of youth once; now, like many a pretty girl, he has the plainness of middle life.

Is it too late to alter 'Sanatory'? The word has a bad smell, and reminds me of a story that some one told me of Mr. Chadwick's children, 'playing at drains.' Poor innocents! 'gracious,' 'ennobling,' 'elevating.' . . . I mean to make the utmost use of my money and my time for the future, and I am a good deal strengthened in this by the affection that you and many of my pupils have so abundantly shown me—it seems to me like the only return that I can make. And perhaps my free way of life is as good for this purpose as any position could be.

To R. B. D. MORIER, C.B.

OXFORD, *January* 10, 1866.

MY DEAR OLD FELLOW,

Let me tell you what real and honest pleasure your success gives me. You have, indeed, accomplished a great work. And I think this is only the beginning and not the end[1].

I am sure that you are right about these international questions becoming of great importance. Europe will be much more one nation in fifty or even in twenty-five years (if only some of the limbs could be reset by L. N.[2] or any

[1] See p. 436.   [2] Louis Napoleon.

other operator'. The force of the international commercial principle will be much greater on the continent than in England, because there is no insularity.

I should like to see two rough calculations made : (1) the present cost of the standing armies of Europe, (2) the loss (incalculable really) that the nations of Europe incur from Protection. (1) would probably be much above 100 millions sterling per annum ; (2) would probably be much above 1000 millions sterling per annum. Subtract (1), add (2). When we think of these things and think of the evils of caste, priest-hood, petty princes, oppressed nationalities, &c., does not Europe seem to be at the beginning and not at the end of her politics ?

I am fond of dreaming of a millennium, not in the super-stitious sense, but of one which we may make, and which you may help to make—when you have reached the higher diplomatic position many opportunities will occur.

I am delighted at the C.B. I never thought you would be the 'fat knight'; that is the only thing wanting to complete the parallel.

You kindly ask me to write to you about myself, but that subject will soon come to an end. For I have had no adven-tures ; only carrying on pupils and the everlasting book which has now got into four or perhaps five volumes, including a complete translation of Plato. I keep on hand also notes for sermons, which I mean to work up when Plato is finished ; in one respect I am glad to have held my tongue about Theology, for I begin, as I fancy, to see my way clearer.

Five hundred a year additional is certainly a great comfort. Thou wilt come to me yet to borrow a thousand pounds—and thy love, Jack, is worth a thousand pounds[1].

I have made two new friends during the last year—one, Mr. Browning, whom I like extremely ; he is a man of great genius and power without the faults of genius—the other, R. Lowe, whom I also like ; he is a very honest man and very clear and able ; it is only in politics that he is a cynic, for in his natural character he is a kindly, genial man, having a great

[1] Shakespeare, 2 *Henry IV*, i. 2.

interest in Plato and the classics, which is a bond between us. Also he has administrative imagination, but is devoid of all power of political construction ; his measures contradict his own first principles.

I see that I am getting to gossip with you as we used to do at Berlin. Are you coming to England this summer? If not, I shall certainly go to Darmstadt ; I shall like making friends with your little girl, being always a lover of children, who are delightful creatures. . . .

Will you give my kindest regards and love to your wife and child? Two things I wonder at : (1) Why you retain your old undergraduate affection for me. (2) Why your wife is not jealous. I can only wish you in return the accomplishment of some really great work, not this year or next, but as the result of life. That is a reward fitting the most faithful of friends.

I believe that your wife thinks me an ambitious dreamer who suggests impossibilities to you. I should like to make all my old pupils ambitious, if I could, of living like men and doing silently a real work. I think that this sort of idealism increases upon me as I get older. But I should be more disposed also to leave the way and manner to themselves, and to allow for differences of individual character.

To ———

April 6, 1866.

Surely while life can be of any use the prayer should be not only, 'Thy will be done,' but, 'Let me live to do Thy will, O Lord.'

Thank you for wishing me a long life. I think that I do desire that, sans teeth, sans eyes, sans ears, sans everything, except mind. It seems to me that I have made so many mistakes, and started so late in life, that I would, if I can, still have my life before me. I think that I had hardly any idea of what sort of a place the world was until about fifteen years ago. I see the same fault in the rising generation of young men—they ought to be in character and judgement at twenty-three where they don't arrive until thirty-three. And they take so long fermenting.

To ——

[THE DEANERY, WESTMINSTER.] *June*, 1866.

I shall not answer your letter, but I shall do what you ask. Part of my work cannot be given up for three weeks or a month. But I shall reduce the Plato to about one-half for the next two months, and that will leave the work very light during the first part of the vacation. And I will never work after twelve for the future.

I am quite well in health, but I am aware that my mind is tired. It seems wrong to give up any man who is dependent on me, and it seems wrong to give up the Plato. And the end of that has been that every meal is utilized, and every hour taken up in seeing the men, or in lecturing, or both. But I will manage better another Term.

Lowe's speech [1] was one of the most able speeches ever made against all reform in all ages. There was a sort of philosophical appeal to history and experience, which in the House of Commons neither Gladstone nor any one else seems able to answer. I suspect that L. has supplied a good many political ideas to London society this season.

My friends here talk to me a great deal about Carlyle, whom they saw in the winter. I can't say that I altogether like him : a man of genius, and in some respects the first man living, an independent man, a tender-hearted man—the most graphic of all painters, though in an irregular, magic-lantern way. Yet, on the other hand, a man totally regardless of truth, totally without admiration of any active goodness—a self-contradictory man, who investigates facts with the most extraordinary care in order to prove his own preconceived notions. He has stirred up the minds of young men (those impressionable beings), but not really elevated them. I know that he can say things with a tenderness and power in conversation that no one else attains. But this does not atone at all to me for his utter recklessness and his habit of expressing his own personal fancies in the likeness of intellectual truths. If I were engaged in any work more than usually

[1] On the Reform Bill of 1866.

good (which I never shall be), I know that he would be the
first person to utter a powerful sneer, and if I were seeking
to know the truth, he would ridicule the very notion of
an 'homunculus' discovering the truth. I don't think that
he has any real insight, but only a great power of painting
and embossing and crystallizing scenes real or imaginary.
Nor is he a great doer, nor even a great artist.

The spirit of the twenty-third Psalm and the spirit of the
ninetieth Psalm should be united in our lives.

To ——

August 12, 1866.

I don't think that the war[1] was right, or the *coup d'état*
right, or that Germany may not very likely become an odious
military aristocracy. But I think that we must accept *faits
accomplis*, or in politics we become hopeless and isolated, anti-
pathetic to all things, sympathetic with nothing. This is a
state of great weakness, when all our ideas are dominated by
antagonism to L. N. The L. N. *régime* has fallen very hard
on the press and literary men ; it was bad in its beginning and
is immoral in its private ways. Still it has some elements
of real greatness which are wanting in other Governments of
Europe.

I am really taking care of my health, for I never work more
than six hours a day, and before going back to Oxford I mean
to have an entire rest. You see that I am obliged to go
through this long mechanical labour of translating Plato,
about 2100 pages ; this will be finished next March. Then
I have about half-finished a sketch of the history of the Early
Greek Philosophy, and of Plato. I fancy this to be important
because the history of Greek ideas is the history of the ideas
of the civilized world, and to most persons the very notion
that ideas have a history is a new one. I want to throw
my whole mind into this when the translation is done. Then
I have also an edition of the *Republic* with notes, which
is likely to be used by students in the Schools, in which I try

---

[1] The 'Seven Weeks' War' between Prussia and Austria.

to give, in a condensed form, modern views of the questions treated of, as well as explanations of the Greek. So that, you see, I have my hands full, and am not idle, though people naturally think I am gone to sleep or am dead.

(I told my mother to send you one of my sermons. The other[1] is, I fear, still in the pocket of Dr. Stanley's cassock. The sermon on Prayer has too much negation and too little positive. A lady told me that it would be a good excuse to my pupils for not going to church.)

To Professor Lewis Campbell.

Tummel Bridge, Pitlochry, N.B., [1866].

I am at one of my old haunts with Lord Donoughmore and E. Myers, who is good enough to be his tutor, preparing the *Republic* for the press; also some Divinity lectures for next Term. I shall hope to come to St. Andrews about September 8 for a month, and then, as iron sharpeneth iron, I shall be sharpened by you. At present I am going on in a very plodding, mechanical manner.

To Professor John Nichol.

[1866.]

I imagine that when this reaches you the matter of the Professorship will have been settled. . . . But I cannot help writing to assure you that nothing which happens to you is indifferent to me. I think that I would do anything to promote your interests, and you must promote them yourself. You and I are in the same difficulty; we can look for no external help, but must fashion our lives for ourselves, and that ought to unite us: if opportunities don't come, we must look at life calmly and make them; it is no use complaining of having public opinion against us. We have challenged that, although perhaps undesignedly, and now we must fight it out and make a place for ourselves. You know as well as I do that to have written a good book is worth a great deal more both in real useful-

---

[1] i.e. the first which he preached at Westminster.

ness and distinction than to have gained many professorships.
. . . I hope that you will contrive to do something in the way
of writing this vacation. Don't fall into the mistake that
I have made during the last ten years, of being too much of
a drudge, and getting nothing done. 'Mais nous changerons
tout cela[1].'

To Henry H. Lancaster.

October 18, 1866.

Whately was a very narrow, clear intellect—logical, shallow,
with a genius for illustration—very conceited and egotistical,
but also very noble and disinterested, quite princely in his use
of money, and utterly careless of popular favour. He was
certainly a man of great force of character—in a narrow sense
a great man ; much more distinguished than any other Bishop
and much more honest. Considering the pranks he played as
Archbishop, putting his head under water at a dinner-party,
crowing like a cock to the clergy, sitting swinging on a chain
in College Green while his house was building, throwing a
boomerang on Sunday, &c., he must have been a very remarkable man to be respected at all, for he trampled underfoot all
respectabilities and conventionality. He was narrow and bigoted
in theology—v. his charges.

To ———

Alderley Edge, *January* 1, 1867.

I must tell you again and again not to despair—to keep some
sort of life and light in your mind, and not to lose sight of the
consolations of the future. Most persons of deep feeling have
alternations of light and dark, and we should let the sun shine
sometimes. Even in London it does this.

January, 1867.

What do you think that I am doing? Nothing. For during
the last week I felt an extreme idleness and stupidity, and
satisfied myself with the sophistical theory that you suggested
to me, that the brain needed to go to sleep, and put off beginning

---

[1] This letter has been quoted in Knight's *Life of Nichol.*

again till January 15, and feel as unwilling to work as any negro.

Now I am putting your doctrines into practice, you must occasionally enforce them by your own example, or I shall relapse. I am changing my views of life and begin to think that rest and recreation are really required if I am to last for twenty years longer. And I mean to get younger as I get older, even sans hair, sans teeth, and, what is worse, sans memory, and sans everything. And I am hoping that ten years hence, according to your advice, I shall succeed in making myself disagreeable to somebody. Will you adopt my view? . . .

The worst of planning anything for Gorgias is that the execution, even if he could be got to take it up, requires not more ability, but more policy, more reticence and management of mankind, than he seems to be capable of. He is the quickest, the clearest, the ablest, and one of the most public-spirited men (really) whom I have ever known, but he wants to do everything by force. He is the only man that I see who would fearlessly attempt great administrative reforms. But when he came to have a whole profession, the Army, Church, arrayed against him, and he came to be deserted by his colleagues, he would be likely to sink under the load of unpopularity.

I trust that you never allow yourself to doubt that you can still complete your life (lives, like pictures, lose more than half their value by being unfinished), and that in the greatest suffering you are in the hands of God, who has thus far made you His instrument.

To Dr. Greenhill, at Hastings.

BALLIOL COLLEGE, *April* 3, [1867].

My dear Greenhill,

It may be, as you say, that in what remains of life we shall not see much of one another. For our work has to be done in different places, and probably we have got to look at many things in very different ways. But I shall always remember with pleasure and gratitude that old kindness of thirty years ago. I have since found the blessing and the good of giving away money to others, and I think that you first showed me the way to do this.

I cannot say that I shall pray for your boy at his confirmation (though he has my best wishes). But, if he comes to Oxford, I will try to help him as far as I can, in his College course, for your sake.

With very kind regards to Mrs. Greenhill,

Believe me, yours truly and affectionately,

B. Jowett.

To ———

Oxford, *May* 31, 1867.

I want you to admit the possibility of better and happier days coming; and I believe that they will come, not exactly in the sense which youthful holiday-making, love-making follies expect them, but days in which you will see your work more fully carried out, and bless God for the retrospect of the past with all its great trials.

What do you think that I have been doing during the last month? Translating the *Politics* of Aristotle. You will say that I am mad about translating. But I am not. It was necessary to read the book carefully for my work upon Plato, and the translation is much wanted, and is now half finished.

To ———

Oxford, *June*, 1867.

At what a rate the chariot of democracy is driving! It almost takes away one's breath. Last week the democratic movement might have been stopped, the Ministry driven from office, and a Bill something like that of last session introduced. But all that is now impossible. Household suffrage, lodger franchise, one year's residence, are fairly given and cannot be withheld. And if the Conservatives are, as appears, really willing to give up principles which they held sacred a month ago, the Bill is certain to pass. For their opponents cannot, if they would, oppose them, and the Lords dare not.

Think of the effects on the Church of England (that of

Ireland is gone anyhow) and on the whole country.   Then
of the exultation of the Jew, who has revenged all his
personal wrongs, triumphed over the virtue of Gladstone,
made himself an historical name, and really done a great
service (not taking into account the means).   He has got
his pound of flesh out of these Tory magnates, who have
scoffed at him.   People have often said that he would be
the leader of the Radicals, but they never guessed that he
would accomplish it by making the Tories Radicals.   There
is something that is not quite intelligible in his colleagues
neither actively supporting nor opposing him.   Think of all
this also in connexion with the Conservative reaction of six
years ago. . . .

That you may not think me mad in translating the *Politics*,
I transcribe a short passage for you.

'Now we ought to be careful of the health of the inhabitants ;
and this will depend, first, on the situation and aspect of the
place ; secondly, on the use of good water, the care of which
ought to be made a first object.   For those things which we
use most and oftenest have the greatest influence on health ;
and water and air are of this nature,' &c. —Ar. *Pol.* vii. 2. 4.

And I could find similar passages in Plato's *Laws*.

To ———

OXFORD, *June*, 1867.

When you think that you have done nothing, that may
be in some degree true, as a fact, amid the difficulties and
hindrances of human things.   But is not the greater part
a certain state of nerves or a certain attitude of character,
like the way which good people have of declaring that they
are miserable sinners ?

I like to hear my friend Mr. Browning say, 'I have just
finished a poem (I am ashamed to tell you the length—about
20,000 lines) : I am sure that it is by far the best thing
which I have yet done, and when I have done that I shall
try to do something better still, and so on as long as I
live.'   And I like to think of myself as beginning and not
ending.

My boy[1], who is extremely clever, has been reading St. Theresa's life in the English. 'Don't you think, sir, that she was religiously mad?' 'Well, not a very bad kind of madness.' 'Are not all persons mad who take sincerely to a monastic life?' He is only fourteen, and he seems to me to be always reading and thinking about what he reads.

To ——

OXFORD, *July* 18, 1867.

I went before the Committee[2] on Monday, and was examined for an hour, and then cross-examined for more than three hours on Tuesday. Lowe, who was present, was quite satisfied, and very much pleased, but I don't trust his judgement of my performance, because he is partial to me. (And yet how often in the last four years have I been encouraged by good words, which I did not believe notwithstanding?) To return to our Committee, I really believe that we shall succeed in getting free Education at Oxford independent of the Colleges, which will make an enormous difference. You have no idea how much greater liberality there is at Oxford than at Cambridge about University matters. I read the Cambridge evidence; it was quite miserable to see the adhesion, even of liberal men among them, to the old routine.

I sometimes think that the work of Christ lasted only three years, and we have (probably) five, six, and seven times three years to live—though I remember that you object to having life parcelled out to you twenty years at a time. But why not look at this another way? God has given you a work to do, of which about one-third or about one-half is completed: why should you not look forward to saying 'It is finished'? If there have been mistakes, let us watch and observe them for the future, and let us try to get the intensity without the drawbacks. If we don't, are we not as stupid as the people who refuse to clear out drains, which as you, and I who have been taught by you, know is the lowest depth of human stupidity?

[1] Matthew Knight.   [2] See p. 379.

To Mrs. Tennyson.

July 29, 1867.

I daresay that you have received a book of Persian poems (Omar Khayyam) with a French translation. When Alfred has read them, will you send them to Mr. Fitzgerald? I heard that they were being published under the superintendence of M. Jules Mohl, and begged a copy of them for him, as he certainly has a right to the first copy which arrives in England. I hope that he will be stimulated to make some more of his admirable translations.

M. Mohl is only responsible for the printing of the Persian. He disapproves of the translation and the notes, which, he says, are written under a 'pernicious Sufi influence.' I am on my way to Scotland, where I hope to be settled in a day or two at the old work. However, I feel that I am printing, which is the beginning of the end.

The party was very pleasant. Mr. Browning was very sorry to miss you and Alfred. I shan't give up all hope of seeing you next year.

Will you do me a little favour? There is an old lady whose courage and clear-headedness have done (or rather may have done) me a very considerable service. She is very desirous of having Alfred's autograph. Will you send me, without troubling him, a few lines? I hope Hallam is well. Tell him to write to me : I always like to hear from the boys. . . .

I am very glad to hear of your Surrey purchase.

To Professor Lewis Campbell.

Strathpeffer, nr. Dingwall,
August 3. [1867].

I made acquaintance with 'Ecce Homo' the other day. He is a very modest, good sort of man. His book has the advantage of considering the subject in some way, whereas most persons are contented with words and formulas. But it is wholly uncritical in not examining the documents—and unspiritual in regarding Christ as the founder of a Church rather than as a sacred individual—and unphilosophical in imagining that moral defects are reached by the Church in the same way that legal offences are reached by the law.

I should have liked very much to have seen and talked with Rothe [1], who is an excellent man. In criticism all the German divines seem to me unsatisfactory, with the exception of the Tübingen (barring some degree of fancifulness and hypercriticism in them), and in a religious point of view these are unsatisfactory too.

To ———

STRATHPEFFER, DINGWALL,
August 4, 1867.

I read *St. Theresa* yesterday (the book which the boy [2] says that I am always reading). I know that the visions are all imaginations. Still the book has a great interest for me. I think that this is in some degree due to the style, for as a literary work it has very great merit: but much more the attraction is the intensity of feeling, so far beyond anything that is now to be found in the world. Some day I should like to draw out at length in a sermon how feeling and intellect ought to be combined. The secret seems to be lost in modern times.

To THE MARQUIS OF LANSDOWNE.

ST. ANDREWS, *September* 14, 1867.

I think that you deserve your holiday after eight weeks' work. Still I hope that you will not give up the resolution of finishing the *Ethics* before you return to Oxford. One owes it to oneself as a matter of honour and conscience to carry out resolutions. I am always sensible when I say these sort of things to you that if I had been placed in your circumstances in early life I should never have read at all. The great importance of the matter makes me dwell on these 'personal' subjects.

The object of reading for the Schools is not chiefly to attain

---

[1] Author of the *Theologische Ethik*. I had seen him at Heidelberg.—L. C.   [2] Matthew Knight.

a First Class, but to elevate and strengthen the character for life. If you ask how this is to be effected, I would say the means was, first, hard work; secondly, a real regard for the truth, and independence of mind and opinion; thirdly, a consciousness that we are put here in different positions of life to carry out the will of God, although this is rather to be felt than expressed in words. I think you would find an advantage also in getting more hold on politics and literature, and getting to know all manner of persons who are worthy of being known.

To R. B. D. MORIER, C.B.

[1867.]

MY DEAR SIR JOHN [1],

I was just thinking of sending another letter in search of the last, when your first letter came. I rejoice at your victory over the man in buckram, but I am sorry to hear that, like your great namesake, you are still troubled with the gout. . . .

How is it, my dear Sir John, that you make so many enemies? I have quoted the place to you before, but I must quote it again, because it contains such excellent advice: 'Use them well, Davy, use them well' (that is to say, all the genteel rogues, sneaks, and men in buckram that you come across), 'for they are arrant knaves and will backbite.' Also, as I am taking upon me to give advice to a great diplomatist, hear another wise saying: 'I forgave him, not from any magnanimity of soul and still less from Christian charity, but simply because it was convenient to me.' The moral of which is that you should make friends with the Right Honourable H—— at the earliest opportunity. If you 'imitate the honourable Romans,' I commend to you as a diplomatist the example of that great Ancient (not that I believe he ever lived) to whom it was only necessary to do an injury in order to make him your friend.

I am getting on well with my Oxford plans. By the dog of Egypt—if I may be allowed to swear after the manner of Socrates—it is not difficult to manage a College when you have a large majority. Formerly all my schemes used to fail, but now they succeed.

---

[1] See pp. 409, 436.

To Alfred Tennyson.

March 8, 1868.

My dear Tennyson,

Will you look at the enclosed letter which, though long, is not unamusing, and will you see whether you can write a few lines addressed to Sellar or Professor Fraser (who is an excellent man) which might be of service? I would not ask you to do such a thing for any one but Grant, and there is no reason why you should do it at all if you think that you can't or would rather not, as I have not spoken to them. But I am sure that a 'pithy' word from you would have effect, and if you don't mind it had better be addressed to Professor Fraser, as he is not supposed to be a friend of Grant's [1].

I hope that you are well and have 'thoughts which voluntary move harmonious numbers': I heard of you in London, where you were reported to be looking 'quite youthful.'

Don't write any more in Magazines if you can help: indeed it is a good-natured mistake and will do you harm. The Magazine-writers say, ' Art thou become as one of us?' &c.

With most kind regards to Mrs. Tennyson and the boys,

Believe me, dear Tennyson,

Ever yours,

B. Jowett.

To ———

December 16, 1868.

My voluntary Divinity lectures have come to an end: I think prosperously, judging by the examination. I must invent some more general subjects for next Term. I think that I shall endeavour to preach once a month as long as I live. . . . There is nothing I believe in less than the effect of a great deal of routine or mechanical work.

To ———

December 28, 1868.

I have been looking through Janet's book on Materialism; interesting but not very good, and written with a party spirit

---

[1] Sir Alexander Grant was standing for the Principalship of Edinburgh University against Sir James Simpson.

against Materialists. I think that a philosopher may very well ask himself whether he is writing for his own generation or for the ages to come. All flatter themselves that they are doing the last when they are really doing the first; and the beginning of philosophy is to be aware of the illusion. As Hegel, Kant, Sir W. Hamilton, Cousin have passed away, so also Comte and Mill will pass away. And what next? Anything that is to be permanent must recognize all facts and all our highest moral ideas, and leave no sort of knowledge outside which may undermine the fabric. And it must begin again, like Bacon, by purging away indirect notions, such as matter and mind, cause and effect, which to many seem to be the foundation of the faith. And it must avoid sentiment and sentimentalism, and must be aware how all classes, poets, prophets, metaphysicians, physicists, have their narrow and limiting points of view.

To ———

January 17. 1869.

All persons' thoughts seem to be turning towards the poor of London, and your thoughts should be in that direction too. The question is: How is this perpetual flocking into the towns and accumulation of masses of pauperism there to be prevented? Is it practicable to say that food shall under no circumstances be given without a previous labour test? First, the Poor Law requires to be recognized in London; secondly, all private charity must be required to conform to certain regulations. I do not see why there should not be a rate in aid, say, over the whole of London, when the poor's rate is less than 2s. in the pound: (1) for Education, (2) Emigration, (3) Sanatory Improvements.

I am appointed College Preacher. I begin my preaching on Sunday, January 31. I see that I have undertaken a difficult enterprise, and if I do not succeed greatly, I shall fail greatly. What shall I begin preaching about? 'The Truth makes free,' or 'The Nature of God,' or 'In understanding be ye men'? I want to keep before myself that the work which I have to do in Oxford, both in the way of religion and education, is much greater than it has been hitherto, now I have got a standing ground in the College. The preliminaries are all well enough now, but a long time has been taken in attaining them. And I do not know whether life or power remains for all that I have to do. Where I am now I ought to have been ten years ago.

To ———

January 31, 1869.

I send you my sermon written (rather hastily) but never preached, through a ridiculous *contretemps*. The Catechetical Lecturer[1] had forgotten that I was to preach on the last Sunday in every month, and started to his legs before I could stop him. As the sermon is rather patchy and ill expressed I am not very sorry. The fault of all my sermons is that they have many crude ideas and jump from one to another, instead of a single one well developed. I wish that I had more time.

I tried the subject which you suggested, but got into a muddle about it and gave it up. I seem to have so little to say about this when I have once said that God works by fixed laws and that we have the power of co-operating with them.

I think that biographical sermons would be good, reading the lesson of individual lives. This is suited to mixed congregations and is new: Wesley, St. Bernard, &c.

I have been reading some of Newman's sermons over again. I am rather surprised at their great reputation. For they are not really good, except here and there, as literary works. I think that South's are the best sermons in English. In general the Puritan divines have a great deal more life in them than the Anglican. Robertson is far better than Newman.

To ———

March 16, 1869.

Now the hour of midnight is striking, so, in accordance with our compact (having read Polybius), I will leave off. And some day I will make another compact with you, not to speak

---

[1] Edwin Palmer. Jowett had a habit of making a long pause before rising to preach.

evil of any one, which I am always doing, and which I always feel to be a great weakness, and can often trace in myself to a personal motive. I think it is well to know people as they really are, but that it would be nobler and better to hold one's tongue about them.

I was glad to see Mr. Mundella exhorting the trades unions to take up education. I am inclined strongly to think that the spirit of education and improvement of the dwellings of the poor may come from some inspiration of their own.

To ———

May 19, 1869.

I don't mind real prophetic denunciations of bad people, and I wish to keep my head clear about political people and their motives. But I think if you ever mean to act in the world you should exercise great reticence in speaking of them.

This is my theory, but has not been my practice hitherto.

I think that things are said against people chiefly from a want of self-control. And when you come to act with them or talk with them, your influence over them seems to be taken away by the consciousness that you have not always spoken well of them (perhaps deservedly). I think that the world requires infinitely more courage and infinitely more caution than it possesses at present.

I had a very nice party here on Saturday.

To ———

May 28, 1869.

We have three compacts: First, that you are to give an hour a day to writing or some unprofessional occupation (and not to overwork), in return for which I will observe hours and days. All this is to be strictly observed. Secondly, we have a minor compact, not to be observed so strictly, not to speak evil of others—even against Simon Magus not to 'bring a railing accusation'; this, however, may be occasionally broken when human nature can endure no longer. N.B.—It does not rest on any religious ground, but merely on expediency.—Thirdly, we will have a great compact that every year is to be calmer, happier, and more efficient and productive of results than the one which has preceded.

I lecture on Political Economy. I really knew the old Political Economy, but I have to invent the new, which is not a satisfactory process.

To ———

June 28, 1869.

Please not to suppose that I am thinking about the Mastership when I said that I ought to have been where I am ten years ago[1]. That used to trouble me in days before I knew you, and when I was uncertain of the future of the College. But I have sometimes thought that I ought not to have spent so much time in lecturing and so little in writing. To lecture is a great strain and the effect is comparatively slight. However, if the mistake has been made, I shall not continue to make it. I intend not to give more than four lectures a week after this Term.

To Mrs. Jowett.

July 4, 1869.

I was intending to come and see you this week. But I found that I must stay at Oxford and get a portion of Plato completed. The first volume, pp. 620, is now completed. There will be five or six of them.

I think the sermons[2] have been fairly successful. I will send you one or two of them when I get them back, as I have lent them.

On Saturday I go to Mr. Nightingale's at Lea Hurst, when I hope to meet Miss Nightingale, who has not been there for nine or ten years. (Did you see her paper in *Good Words* called ' Una and the Lions[3] '?) Thence I am going to see the Vaughans and Mr. Wilson, and to Scotland to work.

You will be glad to hear that I am prospering in College, and in every way I am in a better position than formerly. They have been making great changes in the University, which will, I think, be for the advantage of Balliol College.   Students

---

[1] p. 430.   [2] Preached in Balliol Chapel.
[3] *Good Words* for June 1, 1869.

are now to be allowed to lodge out, which will enable them to come to Balliol instead of going to other Colleges. If we had a little more money we could absorb the University.

To ———

[DONCASTER, with the Vaughans],
July, [1869].

The first condition of working for a few years longer is absolute calmness: the great effort must be a quieter one, more free from anxiety and personality. As we get older we ought to know ourselves, and to know the world, better, and to direct the blow better, and to be indifferent about the result, knowing that no single thing is of so much importance as appears at the time, if we only go on to the end. The secret of rest is to live and act on a higher stage of life.

To ———

TUMMEL BRIDGE, *July* 15, [1869].

I will promise you not to work after eleven o'clock at night. I enjoy being here, and work with pleasure. Here is a good air, good food, perfect retirement, and a pleasant stream, which is always murmuring night and day—much better than the best society.

To ———

July 29, [1869].

I get more and more struck, I think, with the practical infidelity of the present age, including the Bishops and the newspapers. The spirit of a part of the age is expressed in C. Buller's witticism: 'Destroy the Church of England, sir? why you must be mad! It is the only thing which stands between us and real religion.'

Is the Church of England like an old house which will stand for ever unless it is pulled down ; or like the figure of the Etruscan king suddenly exposed to the air? Figures of speech may be found for all things. But I think there will be changes :—Because ideas have sustained a rude shock by the easy victory over the Irish Church; because Bibliolatry can only support itself by priestcraft, and that the English people will not stand.

To the Marquis of Lansdowne.

Tummel Bridge, Pitlochry,
August 8, 1869.

I was very much pleased to hear of your approaching marriage, and wish you and both of you every good and happiness in life. A marriage brightens up a family and does good in all sorts of ways. And the greatest good of all is the effect on a man's own character of having some one for whom he deeply cares and who deeply cares for him.

There is a considerable touch of poetry in being in love, and there ought to be also a touch of poetry in life. I mean by 'a touch of poetry' some romantic desire to do good, some ideal higher than the opinions of the world. There is nothing that your future wife will care about half so much as your being honoured and distinguished.

No one ever had blessings more richly showered upon them than you have, including this last and greatest blessing. And, to speak plainly, I want you to consider how you can use this great wealth and rank for the highest purposes.

You have two almost inexhaustible interests, the management of your estates and political life. You will probably hold your estates for fifty years, in which time almost anything may be accomplished for the agriculture, for the houses, and, above all, for the people. I wish that you would sometimes think what you would desire to have done twenty-five years hence. This seems to be very important in the management of landed property. There is another thing which occurs to me to say to you. It is of great importance if you have a large property to know all about it with the least possible trouble. And with this view I would train all the people whom I employed to make returns of the state of the farms, houses, schools, and sums spent upon them. I should begin by getting an accountant to put the accounts into the very best form. But I daresay that you have already much greater experience of business than I have, and therefore my hints may appear superfluous.

Great success in politics depends on working, and the power which you have of taking an interest in them. It is easy to foresee the coming questions. The Irish Land. National Education, Pauperism. Do you possess the art of picking other people's brains? I mean, besides reading and study of questions, getting hold of the person who knows most about them viva voce, and learning his opinions. This is a great shortening of labour and saves many mistakes.

I look back with great pleasure to the time which we spent together at this place. We might have succeeded better, but I don't care much about the Second Class, as I see that you are not going to be a second-class man for life. I feel very strongly your regard for me, and I wish that I could have done more for you than I did. I shall be delighted to see you again, and hope that you will bring your bride to visit me at Oxford.

[PS.] I heard of the engagement from you first.

To ———

TUMMEL BRIDGE, *August* 9, 1869.

I agree with you very much about the Prayer Book, and have never thought that the relaxation of subscription is any great assistance to us. The making people repeat the Creed, prayer for fine weather, and other relief from temporal calamities; also, in another way, the reading of parts of the Old Testament, is thoroughly demoralizing. And do but think of the hymns they sing. A good essay might be written on the Ideal of Public Worship.

You require (1) some common feeling concentrated in special acts or words; (2) the greatest latitude for individual thought or prayer; (3) every word should be true; (4) every word should be elevating. You would have to select out of ancient liturgies and mediaeval prayers. For no one can write a prayer now any more than he can compose an epic poem: and in some ways antiquity has such a curious religious power, stronger perhaps than the belief in a future life.

To ———

[*September* 1, 1869, at Cortachy.]

I enclose a letter from my beloved 'Jack'[1]. 'Jack' has got two commissions from the Government, or rather, three : (1) to report upon the land laws of Prussia (this is for the Cobden Club) ; (2) to report upon the Poor Law in Prussia (I helped to get him this) ; (3) the Ecumenical Council.

To ——— (AFTER THE DEATH OF MRS. JOWETT).

Torquay, *October* 23, 1869.

I have her face following me as she looked when she was alive. It was the pleasantest face, when she was laid to rest, and the youngest for her age that I ever saw.

More and more for myself I see two or three things which this late trouble rather tends to impress on me. First, that I must be absorbed in my work and use all means towards this (not neglecting health), and shut out all trivial thoughts and personal feelings of all sorts. Secondly, that I must aim at perfect calmness. As you get on in life this is the only way in which strength can be husbanded and made effectual. Thirdly, that I must try to act more simply and on a larger scale, not tiring myself with mere drudgery, or shrinking into a coterie, or caring only for the affection of admiring friends. Few persons have worked harder, and yet I have wasted a great deal of time and have not managed well.

Torquay, *October* 31, 1869.

I went to see my dear mother's resting-place to-day. Her appearance seems to follow me about. I was pleased to see that some friend had put flowers on the grave.

To R. B. D. MORIER, C.B.

Inglewood, Torquay,
November 3, 1869.

I should like very much to hear from you. I am staying here (for the next fortnight) in consequence of the death of my

[1] Mr. Morier, who, from being very fat, 'his waist being great,' as well as other points of resem- blance, was always called 'Jack' with his familiars.

dear mother. She was taken from us a few days ago, quite painlessly (for she was thought to be asleep). As you may suppose, this has made a great blank to us.

I hope you are well and vigorous and have made progress in your three schemes. To be at Darmstadt is very dull, but in some respects it is advantageous, because it gives you time to read and write and make a name for yourself, which you may never have again. I like being here because I never go out and have absolute undivided time for work. In this way I get on far better, for I have generally been at a great disadvantage, having two lives to lead instead of one.

I hope you will not disappoint us in your reports; if you send me any of them I shall read them carefully.

To R. B. D. MORIER, C.B.

INGLEWOOD, TORQUAY,
November 12, 1869.

Many thanks for your kind letter, which gives me great pleasure. My mother's death makes me think of many things. I seem to see her constantly, and I hope the memory of her will follow me about through life. Her loss makes me feel that the time is shorter for myself, and I am determined to make the utmost use of the years which remain.

I am glad that you are so well; now that you are well do not let yourself get ill again or you will spoil all. I believe that anybody may keep well, (1) who takes great care about diet and exercise, (2) who lives in fresh air, and who, (3) being determined to do his work, never allows an anxious thought to intrude: (4) Shall I add, who does not make a chimney of himself?

I am rather sorry that you are going so much into the historical and antiquarian view of the question [1], because I do not see how this can be made a basis of legislation for the present, and people like Lord Granville or Lord Clarendon (as you know better than I do) will not read further than Charlemagne

---

[1] Of the Prussian Land Laws: see p. 436.

in your essay, if you go back to such topics. Do not be oppressed with your work, but limit it, and if you get perplexed, stop for a day or two and begin again. My plan in writing now is to read over and over again every day twenty or thirty pages of what I have written, after reading something on the subject. I generally find that without trouble to myself new thoughts occur to me. You will be an eminent writer some day. But no one reaches that without immense labour.

To ———

TORQUAY, *November* 12, 1869.

The weeks pass well with me here, for I do neither more nor less than I intended, and am none the worse. My dear mother's face follows me about, and though I can hardly believe that she is gone, never to return, I feel a sort of companionship in that.

To ———

INGLEWOOD, TORQUAY,
December 31, 1869.

There was a time ten or twelve years ago when I was out of health and overworked and had only lukewarm help from friends. Then life did seem dark and miserable. But that has long passed away.

I do not anticipate much from Mr. Lowe's zeal and kindness. For Gladstone will surely say (if he has no mind to appoint Scott) that he cannot make a man a Bishop for the sake of doing me a favour, for which too he will never get any credit. I am quite happy to be as I am. Though I acknowledge that I should be glad to carry on the College without this perpetual strife.

To MRS. TENNYSON.

INGLEWOOD, TORQUAY,
December 31, 1869.

DEAR MRS. TENNYSON,

I am at the old place, and at the old work, though indeed I feel that this is not the old place, since my dear mother was taken from us.

I am very much pleased with the new volume[1]. I think that Alfred must feel a great satisfaction in having worked out, though in another way, his old thought of King Arthur. He has done enough and more than enough for a lifetime. But still I hope that he means to go on, and that he may find new ideas and feelings suggested by the successive periods of life.

I have come here to work at my book, of which I hope that a few months will now see the completion. At the end of the vacation, about the last week in January, I shall hope to come and spend a day or two with you, if you will have me. I often think with gratitude how many happy days during the last fourteen years I have spent with you, and hope that this much-prized friendship may last as long as I live.

With most kind regards to Alfred and the boys,

Believe me, dear Mrs. Tennyson,

Ever yours affectionately,

B. JOWETT.

To ⸺

INGLEWOOD. TORQUAY,

January 12, 1870.

. . . The Bishopric[2] with which I amused you and myself is all a flare, as I suspected. Mr. Lowe says : 'Try again, better luck next time.'

But I can tell you a better thing. I finished Vol. iii to-day, and shall send the few remaining sheets to the printer to-morrow.

I do not care about the matter at all. I have long seen that my main chance either of usefulness or distinction is writing. . . .

I stay here to Sunday week and shall then take a few days' holiday. I work hard, but I find myself quite well. . . .

To ⸺

TORQUAY, *January* 14, 1870.

How very good of you to write me a scrap of a note because you thought I should be grieved about the Bishopric of Manchester.

[1] *The Holy Grail:* published early in 1870. Jowett had seen an 'advanced' copy.

[2] For R. Scott : see p. 408.

Fraser is a contemporary and acquaintance of mine—an honest, free-spoken man—a good speaker and preacher—not much speculative intelligence, and what there is will probably disappear in the episcopal swaddling.

There is a good deal both of comfort and of serious meaning in that saying of Lord Melbourne's, 'My dear fellow, would you wear such a dress as that for £10,000 a year?'

This is the best place in which I ever was for work, the only place in which I do any work. And as yet I do not feel the worse, and expect to survive until the 1st of June.

To R. B. D. Morier, C.B.

[*January*, 1870.]

. . . I spent two days in a Scotch house[1] with Gladstone, who talks (I thought) rashly about the Land Question. I imagine that he and Bright are the only members of the Cabinet who are likely to be in favour of extreme measures.

Have you read any books about the Irish Question? I am told that the right books are : (1) The Report of Lord Devon's Commission ; (2) Lord Dufferin's book ; (3) Mr. Maguire's book. The great difficulty is the small holder. When it is said, as Gladstone says, that land is a question of life and death to the Irish peasant, I think it should be remembered that he has the Poor Law and employment as a farm labourer and emigration. G. had a ridiculous notion (he had a great many) that the reason why the Irishman in America hung about the great cities was that he had such melancholy recollections of agriculture in his own country!

I am hoping to finish Plato if I am industrious and don't go visiting this spring. If I am alive I shall come and see you at the beginning of the summer, and bring the four volumes with me. It would have been a gain for me if Scott had been made a Bishop, but I don't complain, for I have the College better in hand than formerly. I shall go on as I have done with the College, and try to find more time for writing. Though I am not yet old, I feel that the years are getting

[1] Viz. Camperdown, near Dundee. See p. 406.

on. I think in the next ten or fifteen years I must do what I have to do.

. . . I am very anxious that you should take care of your health, and should make the reports[1] a success. Would you like me to look at any of them? I am sure that you may become a first-rate writer: the great art is to combine weighty words with perfect consecutiveness. You have plenty of imagination and expression—a severer logic is the thing to be aimed at.

If you come over to England for a day or two, let me know and I will try to meet you. We must both of us do our utmost in life, and a good talk is sometimes a great help in this.

To Professor Edward Caird.

January 28, [1870].

I feel very guilty in not having answered either of your kind letters. I did not answer the first because I hoped to come to you, and I did not answer the second because I had something of importance to say which I was not able finally to determine. These are the excuses that bad correspondents make. I do not defend myself, and can only hope that you have attributed my silence to the true cause—carelessness, and the pressure of other matters during the last few months.

What I am going to speak about I will request you to keep strictly private. Wilson and I have determined to have a second volume of *Essays and Reviews*, to appear on or about January 1, 1871. We mean to take every possible pains that this volume should be adequate to the subjects of which it treats, and should be written in a religious spirit. Wilson proposes to write on the progressive principle of Protestantism, showing the element of progress in the Reformation, and the element of fixedness. I am intending to write (perhaps) two essays. The first, on the Reign of Law, showing (1) the relation of the laws of Nature to Morality, and (2) the impossibility of

---

[1] Morier's report on *The Agrarian Legislation of Prussia during the Present Century* was published by the Cobden Club in their series of Essays on Systems of Land Tenure in Various Countries.

basing religion on miracles. The second essay would be on the present and future position of the Church of England, discussing its present state and possibilities of establishment and disestablishment. Campbell has promised to write on the mis-translations and mis-readings of the English New Testament. We think also of applying to Stanley, to Müller, to Deutsch, Pattison, and Dean Elliot. I think that we shall go on even if several or all of these refuse.

You will anticipate that this explanation is a preface to a request that you would join us. We are going to propose to you to write on Morality, Religion, Theology, though any other subject which agreed with the general design of the book we should gladly accept. What do you think ? (Excuse bad writing in a railway.) Of course no one can write on these subjects without incurring a certain amount of odium, and the adversaries will probably be bitter, because they think that they have extinguished us, and will find that they have not. The old name is likely both to command attention and bring odium. The position which we are likely to take up is the most hateful to them, that of religious men who care about the truth. On the other hand I care nothing at all for abuse— I have nothing to fear or expect—and I think it a duty to do what I can to meet the low superstition and the low materialism of the day. In another ten years half the English clergy will be given up to a fetish priest-worship of the Sacrament. What course religion will take in Scotland it is difficult to say. But it is plainly our duty to see what we can do towards meeting this. The English bishops will do nothing—nor, I fear, Dr. Temple. . . . Our principles are not worth much if they are not intended to elevate human life and are only matter of academical discussion.

I think you are much in the same independent position as myself, and that is a reason why I ask you. We propose to be careful not to get entangled with the law. I have great confidence in Wilson's ability and high principle. Poor Williams, whose warmth of temper might have been troublesome to us, has been taken just as we were about to apply to him. I think that we shall probably insert in the preface a short notice of Baden Powell and of him. If you join us

I shall hope that we may have suggestions from you about the form of the book, and about the persons to be engaged. We feel that it is a very serious undertaking and great responsibility, but are determined σὺν θεῷ[1] to go on. The volume would be 500 or 550 pages, and your essay might be of any length up to sixty or eighty pages. In June I get rid of Plato, and shall devote the last six months to this.

To ———

OXFORD, *January* 30, 1870.

. . . I am glad that you liked my sermon. They none of them seem to me at all good. I want boundless leisure to write really good sermons, if I could at all, and these are struck off rather at a heat and scamped towards the end. . . .

Here I commence the old routine for the thirtieth time at least. I have a better chance now than formerly, having the whole entirely under my control. And I hope to take a particular and individual interest in every man in College. That is my aim. The College re-elected me preacher yesterday.

To ———

February 19, 1870.

I go on happily here. I see nearly every undergraduate once a week, and I find that has a good effect on me, and I hope on them.

To PROFESSOR EDWARD CAIRD.

BALLIOL COLLEGE, *February* 24, [1870].

I am very glad to hear that you are able and willing to join us. The Plato will be off my hands by July 1, and then I shall devote my time to constructing two essays— one on the Reign of Law and another on the Life of Christ as the Centre of the Christian world—for the book.

Since I wrote to you I have spoken to Bowen and to Max Müller. Max Müller hesitates. He is giving some lectures in London on the Science of Religion, and he says that he

---

[1] 'God helping us.'

wishes to see the effect of them first. Bowen will help us if he can possibly find time, and is to let me know in April. He will take for his subject the position of the Church of England, (1) if established, (2) if disestablished; and the future modes of proceeding in either alternative. He is an excellent writer and will be a most valuable aid.

Wilson is also writing to Dr. Davidson, and will ask him to write an essay on the important mis-translations of the Old Testament parallel to Campbell's on important mis-translations of the New Testament. I put before Campbell the considerations of which you speak, but he does not seem to be moved by them, and if our book is what I hope we shall make it, and he is careful with his own essay, I do not think he will be injured by his association with us.

I quite agree with you in what you say about the importance of having an eminent scientific man among the contributors. The difficulty is to find a suitable person. I think that I will talk over the matter in confidence with Henry Smith and will write to you again about this in a few days.

I hope that we may be able to spend a few days together in the summer and talk over our respective portions of the work. I sometimes think that the world is getting demoralized by the utter disregard of truth. People have no fixed principles and no education in the higher sense, and all sorts of Ritualisms and Spiritualisms and Aestheticisms take their place (just at this moment the Aesthetic seems to have got a curious hold at Oxford). The spirit in which we want to write is the simple love of truth, the reassertion of the truism that there is such a thing as truth, and that the alarms and vague fears of scepticism—foundations of society undermined, &c., &c.—are simply tiresome, and unmeaning to a reasonable man.

I think that an interesting mode of treating your subject would be to point out historically how Religion comes first in the growth of Human Nature—then Morality parts company with it and in some degree reacts upon it: and how they must be reunited and perfectly identified before the work is completed. The true conception of Theology would seem to be the perfect intellectual expression of this.

The more we can avoid Hegelianism, Germanism, or direct assaults upon received opinions, the better.

There is a striking expression of Diderot's that 'all revealed or national religions are only perversions of the Religion of Nature.' This is true if the words 'Religion of Nature' be taken in the highest sense. And perhaps the truth would be better expressed by calling them tendencies toward a Religion of Nature.

Excuse my writing to you by the hand of another, which, having a great deal to do, I find to be a great assistance.

I am very sorry to hear of the death of Lord Barcaple[1]. Did you know him at all? He was one of the best people in Scotland.

To Lady Stanley of Alderley.

OXFORD, *June* 11, 1870.

Thank you very much for your kind note. I believe that it is to be as you suppose. There is certainly a great pleasure and pride in being the Head of Balliol College, and I hope that I may be able to do something worth doing.

Lyulph's letter is extremely interesting. I wish that he were still a Fellow[2].

To Dean Stanley.

OXFORD, *June* 13, 1870.

MY DEAR STANLEY,

Thank you for your most kind note, which gave me great pleasure. I am delighted at the prospect of having the Mastership, because it offers such great opportunities, and also because I want more rest and leisure to think, and I have been overworked for many years past. It doubles the pleasure to me that you and many others rejoice with me.

I have two schemes in which I want your help: I will tell you about them when we meet on Saturday.

Thank you for reminding me that your mother would have been pleased.

[1] Edward Francis Maitland, a Scottish Judge.

[2] The Hon. E. L. Stanley, to Jowett's great regret, had resigned his Fellowship in 1869.

To Mrs. Tennyson.

June, 1870.

My dear Mrs. Tennyson,

A thousand thanks for your kind note: it rejoices my heart that my friends rejoice. I must now endeavour to see very seriously 'what can be made of a College.'

May I have the pleasure of coming to see you for a few days on Wednesday next?

Plato is nearly finished, and I hope to bring him out on the same day, September 7, on which I am formally elected to the Mastership.

With love to Alfred (in haste).

Ever yours,

B. Jowett.

END OF VOL. I.

www.ingramcontent.com/pod-product-compliance
Lightning Source LLC
Chambersburg PA
CBHW022008110726
47901CB00006B/1442